C000005040

Richard Barnes studied medicine at Cambridge and University College Hospital and pursued a career in research at Cambridge for many years. He is passionate about theatre, education, and equality of opportunity. He now writes murder mysteries which draw on his experience in both university and secondary education. He is married with four grown up children who are out there saving the world.

To Helen, Adrian, Ruth, and Alice, who got me started writing, and to Patti who has supported me throughout the writing of this novel and the lifetime that has led up to it.

Richard Barnes

AN IDEAL DAUGHTER

AUSTIN MACAULEY PUBLISHERS™

LONDON * CAMBRIDGE * NEW YORK * SHARJAH

Copyright © Richard Barnes 2022

The right of Richard Barnes to be identified as author of this work has been asserted by the author in accordance with sections 77 and 78 of the Copyright, Designs and Patents Act 1988.

All rights reserved. No part of this publication may be reproduced, stored in a retrieval system, or transmitted in any form or by any means, electronic, mechanical, photocopying, recording, or otherwise, without the prior permission of the publishers.

Any person who commits any unauthorised act in relation to this publication may be liable to criminal prosecution and civil claims for damages.

This is a work of fiction. Names, characters, businesses, places, events, locales, and incidents are either the products of the author's imagination or used in a fictitious manner. Any resemblance to actual persons, living or dead, or actual events is purely coincidental.

A CIP catalogue record for this title is available from the British Library.

ISBN 9781398456402 (Paperback)
ISBN 9781398456419 (Hardback)
ISBN 9781398456433 (ePub e-book)
ISBN 9781398456426 (Audiobook)

www.austinmacauley.com

First Published 2022
Austin Macauley Publishers Ltd®
1 Canada Square
Canary Wharf
London
E14 5AA

Prologue

George Grover hated Zoom board meetings. Chairing them was a strain, not so much the managing of the agenda, making it run smoothly, making it produce effective outcomes, it was more the fact that everyone can see everyone else's face. George did not tolerate fools gladly, his face betrayed his annoyance, his face was centre screen and full on. There is only so much time you can spend with the video turned off and, when you are chairing, it is always difficult to keep muting and unmuting the microphone. On this occasion, it was that anally retentive computer nerd, Roger, who was continuing to annoy George. George cut him short.

"OK, there are some reasons why we might need to be careful, but could we ask the Exec to look at it again and find a way to make it work? Does anyone object to the new policy in principle?"

There was a brief pause. George looked at all the tiny panels, but drinking coffee, scratching noses and adjusting hair seemed to be the sum-total of the activity going on. There was no objection from the Board.

"Can I call DI Gregory in now?"

The detective had been sitting patiently in the virtual waiting room. He had been asked to attend the Board meeting of the Trust to update on the changes to criminal activity happening, particularly with the youth in the district, during this state of lockdown. Before lockdown, they had seen DI Gregory regularly in the Academy, helping with local intelligence about the teenage gangs and crime pattern in the district, part of the City initiative to inform and enlist the help of the academies in nipping youth crime in the bud.

Jeremy Harold Gregory, known to all in the force as Jerry, was a tall man, handsome in a rather dissolute sort of way; started life as a railway man but moved to the police force when his parents, and the family home, relocated to London. He had trained with the Met at Hendon Police College, Peel College as it is now formally known, but simply "Hendon" to those in the force. He had spent some years with the Met, working his way into the CID, and had moved to the City, with his wife and kids, when the oldest boy went off to Cambridge University. His experience with the London drug scene, and the people trafficking and underage prostitution, had given him an insight into the local issues plaguing some of the Midland towns and cities.

He was known as someone who was a bit eccentric, unusual in his methods, but very effective, stood for no nonsense from anyone, but was also known as a fair and open-minded, innocent until proved guilty sort of guy. It was just that he was always determined to prove that the guilty were guilty and he had a good track record of clearing the streets of the worst elements of society. The recent pandemic had, unfortunately, created a new climate that was much more difficult to police.

Masks, fragmentation of peer groups, idle hands looking for mischief, the explosion of social media even beyond that of the previous decade, all these made intelligence gathering and routine police observation more difficult. It was not just the usual suspects who joined the County Lines. Middle class kids were becoming entrapped, and even very young children, deprived of other social interaction, responded all too readily to the overtures of the drug lords and pimps carefully grooming them. Mum and Dad working from home wanted nothing more than that the children should 'shut up and keep out of my way, I'm working and I do not want to be disturbed'. And some seeds fell upon stony ground and withered, but others fell upon fertile ground and took root and flourished there.

"Good afternoon, Inspector. I think you know almost everyone here, apart from Mohammed Iqbar. Mohammed has joined us as a representative of the local mosque and is very heavily involved in our outreach towards the community. You know Francis Calder-Warren, of course, our Trustee responsible for child protection. Like the rest of us, I am sure he is going to be very interested in what you have to say about the local crime scene, particularly as it applies to our school age pupils."

DI Gregory began:

"Thank you, Sir George, I am delighted to have been asked to come and brief you. I rather miss seeing you all in person but there has been so much development during this period that we really cannot afford to wait for the restrictions to be lifted before I warn you about how things stand now. The situation is getting very serious so let's go."

The litany of issues that DI Gregory then recounted was truly shocking.

It seemed that since the start of lockdown in March, the number of County Lines gangs, those that were known about, had increased from 32 to 104. It probably meant that at least 500 young people from this area, some in the primary schools, were running drugs.

DI Gregory continued:

"Some kids are making a lot of money. What that is going to do for your education programmes is anyone's guess, but if you can make a few hundred pounds a week as a child, without an education, and you see the lack of employment opportunities around here, you are going to wonder which is the better prospect for the future. I can tell you that we are changing the policy on stop and search and we are going to target any youngster with connections to the gangs, no matter how tenuous the links. We expect the city Middle Class to give us a hard time, but we might then just make some progress in our campaign."

The DI went on to describe recent police activity, including stop and search.

"So far, stop and search has yielded a very poor return in terms of drug seizures but has shown a worrying trend. An increased number of teenagers are carrying weapons, a knife or a sharpened screwdriver, ostensibly for protection. Both sexes are arming themselves. So far this has not resulted in a significant increase in teenage stabbings, but as lockdown continues and mental health deteriorates, we fear that it is only a matter of time before personal violence erupts across the city.

"One thing that is puzzling us is that there have been no gang fights yet over drugs and each group seems to be sticking to its own territory quite strictly when it comes to the dealing and pimping."

The DI reminded the Board that only twelve months ago the police had successfully arrested and prosecuted the main gang responsible for drug dealing and sex trafficking in the city, but he went on to say:

"The recent lack of gang fights, and apparent cohesion of the distribution and supply chain, suggest to us that a new group of Mr or Mrs Bigs has moved in. There is someone, or some group of people, of whom the gangs are more afraid than they are of each other. Somewhere out there is someone, or a group of people, keeping the lid on things because it would be bad for business. We've not yet been able to link the gangs together, either in terms of supply or collection of proceeds, but we are working on it as hard as we can. The new overlords must be particularly frightening because, in the six months or so when we have become aware of them, not a word has been said by any of our usual sources. The dealers and pimps are very afraid."

DI Gregory paused and thought hard about what he was going to say next. A few people on the call blanked their screens and he assumed they were taking a quick drink or rushing somewhere for a comfort break. After the brief pause, he began again:

"We miss the information and early warnings that you and your staff were able to give us. Now that you no longer see the children, we have no way of detecting those early signs like withdrawal, moodiness, inattention in class, disruptive behaviour, all those things your teachers used to pick up on. And the friend who tells you that they think another child is in danger is no longer able to do so in the safety of the school environment."

DI Gregory paused again.

"I am sorry to be such a doom and gloom merchant but that is the reality of where we are in this City and some other districts are in an even worse state than this one."

There was a very uncomfortable silence after this. There is not much you can say in the face of such a gloomy report. The Board had spent a great deal of time and effort on eliminating gang culture from the Academies and, indeed, there was no gang culture within the grounds of any of the Academies in the Trust, but none of us ever truly know what goes on outside the Academy gates and in the privacy of pupils' homes. What we usually see is pupils on, if not quite their best behaviour, at least some semblance of respect and discipline. We see their work; we make deductions about their level of academic commitment.

We may know a bit about their extracurricular activities. They may be good sportspersons or musicians. They may belong to a youth club, a church, a mosque, a synagogue, a temple, a band, a youth movement like the scouts or guides. Knowing this gives us a very superficial understanding of what they are truly like. Where do they go to in their heads? Who are they really, beneath that façade? How much of what we believe them to be is our construct, and not their reality. Do we ever truly get a look at the person behind the classroom façade?

Chapter 1

After the meeting, Jerry turned off the computer and turned back towards his desk. He lit his next cigarette; he was in his own private home office. He hadn't told them the half of what had been going on. The drug squad was pretty sure that it was quite a small group of men behind both the increase in the drug activity and the rise in underage prostitution and exploitation, but they had no handle on exactly who it might be. Sure, they could see the middlemen, the dealers, and the pimps, out there on the street, but there was, to date, no lead to identify, or even start to identify, the top of the chain.

It was hard to watch young girls being groomed and pimped, it was hard to watch young kids spending too much money, earned through drug running or pimping out their bodies to older men. The directive had come down from the Commissioner, have a big presence on the street, to try to reduce the level of perpetration, but hold off major arrests until we can get a line on the organisation. No point in chopping off the tail, this poisonous beast can always grow a new one. You need to chop off the head.

Jerry had one man, or rather one woman, on the inside. Moira was an addict, a heroin addict, who had tried hard to break the habit and was on one of the local hospital's weaning off regimes. She had helped run one of the small gangs of dealers working from the leisure centre in Dudley Road and had told Jerry about the way they worked the delivery of drugs and collection of money, using the lad who worked there part-time as a courier. There was a new lad there now because the old one had left some time around September.

Moira had been sad about that because she had often chatted to him, outside his working hours, and he seemed a nice enough lad, although clearly sadly hooked on the drug running scene. He had always asked after Moira and her baby, he had just been a decent sort of kid, she thought of him as a kid, even though she, herself, was barely older than him. Moira did not know why he had left because he must have been making good money with the leisure centre job and the extra from the courier work, but he had gone and she had not seen him for a long time. He hadn't talked about his family, or his other life, or his plans.

Mostly, they had just talked about *Game of Thrones* and other TV shows that they both watched. She thought he might have been a pupil at Manor Academy, because he was sometimes met after work by a younger boy in a school blazer, but perhaps he had now gone off to Uni, or got himself a fulltime job. She had not seen him for several months, not even around the neighbourhood. On occasion she had seen him met from the Centre by an attractive young woman, who was clearly his girlfriend, because they held hands and walked off together towards Manor Road. When the lad first started, they met like that most Saturdays but, just over a year ago, the girl stopped coming and the boy headed home by himself.

Moira had a good reason to want to come off the hard stuff, she had given birth to a baby daughter and had decided that she wanted to be a good mother, something that is hard to do when your whole life is spent thinking about where your next fix is coming from. Like many addict mothers, Moira was young, only nineteen, and the local medical team were very optimistic about getting her clean. The baby was the catalyst for hope.

As part of the deal with Moira, Jerry gave her a small retainer from police funds. Stirred into action as a result of the Board meeting he had just attended, Jerry called the burner mobile that he had given Moira at their last meeting, arranged a meet at the usual place, put a fresh burner phone in his pocket and headed down town to the rendezvous.

They met in a decommissioned Church Hall that had belonged, once, to a small Christian sect called Children of the Light; a sect that had been founded by a single eccentric and wealthy leader and had died with him, and the growth of secularism. It was a red brick structure, with a very steep roof and an arched entrance way. It was padlocked, but both Moira and Jerry knew that there was access through the rear of the building, reached from a courtyard that had previously been the car park for the small congregation.

The two of them approached the courtyard from different directions to ensure that they were not seen together. It was not lit and there was plenty of tree cover to prevent those in surrounding buildings seeing their comings and goings. Both Jerry and Moira had keys to the back door. Jerry had had the locks changed when he decided to set this place up as a meeting point for any informers he might recruit. It had been done discreetly as part of the decommissioning and the developer who had bought the site from the estate of the sect leader had shown no interest in maintaining the building or applying it to alternative use. Jerry thought he was probably deliberately letting it fall into disrepair, with a view to demolishing it and developing the site as part of a grander scheme at a future date. Now was not the ideal time to be seeking planning permission in the centre of this City.

Jerry arrived first and let himself in. There was still some of the furniture that was left from its previous existence, quite a few decent wooden chairs, and a table or two. Jerry picked up and sat down on one of the chairs which was still lying face down and untouched since Jerry's last meeting with Moira. There was a thick layer of dust on everything. The very effective blackout curtains were still drawn, they had been fitted by the previous owner to allow him to run slide shows and film screenings in the daytime. Jerry thought it would be safe to light another cigarette while he waited. He managed about two puffs before Moira, looking somewhat agitated, came through the door, pulled up her chair and sat down.

"What the Hell do you want now?" said Moira. "Give us a fag."

Jerry passed one over and offered her a light. She took a deep draw on the cigarette, held it in for quite a while and breathed out slowly. It was unusual for Moira to be so agitated and Jerry was anxious to find out what exactly was troubling her.

"You know, Moira," said Jerry, "I just called you on the off chance because I had been talking to one of the Academy Boards and it got me thinking about a few matters. I've said before that I reckon there are a few very big fish around here keeping you lot in line. That is the only way I can see that there would not have been an almighty bust up between the different gangs. They must be scared stiff of something."

"I've told you before, you may be right, but you'll get nothing from me on that. I like life too much and if I even hinted about it, I reckon they would find me and Millie and do me and the baby in."

"Yep," said Jerry. "I reckon you are right, but we both know they are there and I am not going to stop until I get them and bang them up for a long time."

He let her sit and finish most of her cigarette. They were careful to drop the ash into a container that Jerry always brought with him. No point in leaving evidence of use, the meeting place was too useful to have it compromised. They were going to tilt the chairs over again before they left so that the dust free seats would not be noticeable. The floors had carpet tiles so there were no footprints.

Jerry offered Moira another cigarette, took one himself and then asked her to tell him what was bothering her.

"It is the big four," she said, and then wished she had not been quite so specific. *In for a penny, in for a pound*, she thought. *He won't be able to get anything from this so I should be safe. Might as well tell him what happened.*

"I'd bin to Dudley Road to collect my goods and I was just walking down Glover Road, just near that passage that goes to the back of the Church, and two blokes in those nylon face masks jump me, grab me, shove me in the back of the van, shove a hood over my head and take me off to some warehouse, like what I have no idea where I am. They take the hood off and start to have a go at me.

"One of them, the short fat one, slaps me about a bit. Nothing too rough but it stings, I've had worse from a client when I was on the game. 'Have you recently come into any money?' says the fat one. 'No, I fucking haven't,' I tell him. 'Know anyone who has?' says the fat one. 'No, I fucking don't," I say. 'Know of anyone leaving the area lately, anyone you didn't expect to leave?' says Fatso.

"I was scared. I reckoned they were looking for someone who had done a runner with some drugs or some money and I reckoned whoever it was was going to get done in. And it wasn't going to be me. So, I racked my brains a bit and I tried to think of someone who I could put them on to who wouldn't get hurt because they clearly weren't the one. And I thought of that kid who had gone a few months ago and who used to be the courier for the Dudley Road leisure centre drop I told you about.

"So, I mentioned that I hadn't seen him around for over six months and he was the only one I knew of who'd left. So, they stuck the hood on my head again and took me back and dropped me, shoved me out of the car so I laddered my bloody tights. Do you know how much tights cost? I reckon they've been really stung and they're looking really hard for whoever did it, whatever it was."

Moira paused and took another drag on her cigarette. Jerry stubbed his out and started to ask questions.

"What was the other guy like? Any clues about him?"

Moira paused before answering. She decided to risk it.

"He was small, he was bandy legged, he had stinking breath, he smelt of curry."

14

Not much to go on but it was better than nothing. It didn't ring a bell with Jerry, nor did the fat guy, in the context of narcotics or prostitution in the city. Not much but it was something, and more than he had had up until now.

"Thanks, Moira," said Jerry. "You take care of yourself and that baby of yours."

Moira's face lit up at the mention of Millie and she and Jerry chatted a little about how the rehab was going and about how Moira, who had been a bright little thing in school, top streams at the Manor Academy, was going to get a proper job and get back to study at the Regional College for some more GCSEs. It seemed that her Mum and Dad, who had washed their hands of her when she went off the rails, had been reconciled because of the baby and were willing to help her out and baby sit while she did her night time online courses.

Jerry handed over the retainer, they tidied up the scene, removing all traces of having been there, and went their separate ways.

"Well," thought Jerry, "The pot is stirring. I wonder if this will bring the big boys out in the open?"

Chapter 2

Freddie, Frank, George and Jason sat around in the warehouse they used as their headquarters.

"What do you reckon, you guys. The only lead we have is that kid from Dudley Road who left about six months ago, but the £500K only went missing last month. We've done the third degree on all the lead couriers and the only hint of anything we have is that Moira woman fingered the kid. I reckon it might be him. And he was our courier to the Boxing Club so he would know about the money? What was the kid's name? Shall we go and have a word with Muldoon at the club?"

"As I recall," said Freddie, "the kid's name was Liam O'Connor. I think he said he was going to University, which is why we recruited that other kid, Shaun. I think it was Loughborough University he said he was going to."

A visit to the club confirmed all this.

A week later, Bruno and Jason Miller were on the train to Loughborough, as Fat Freddie said, "We only want to talk to him."

****

At 42 Manor Road, Annie was in a family bubble with her mother, Sarah, and her little brother, Simon. Annie was 17 years old, nearly 18. She was petite, maybe just under 160cm tall, and delicate, oh so delicate, in appearance. A little heart-shaped elfin face with large round dark eyes, a small slightly button nose, even white teeth, and smile that could lift the spirits of anyone who was lucky enough to see it. Dad had left when Annie was 11 and Simon just 9 years old. They rarely saw him. He and Sarah had divorced. It was a little acrimonious, not the worst, but not good either.

He had moved to London with a new partner and had a second family there with his new wife. He had shown little interest in either of his children from the first marriage, although he never missed a birthday and, secretly, he telephoned Annie from time to time to ask how she and Simon were getting on. Both Annie and her dad secretly hoped that they might resurrect the relationship, when Annie was a little older and independent of her mother, and the acrimony of the divorce had dwindled. Annie and Simon had soon grown used to his taking less interest in them, not that it didn't sometimes, in quiet moments, hurt a little. He had been, indeed he still was, a stock-broker and had made a lot of money, so Sarah and the children had been given a house, as part of the settlement, and he was required still to provide an allowance for the children.

There were no real money worries for the family and when COVID came and made a bit of a dent in their relatively comfortable standard of living, even then, there was enough money to go around. Sarah was a ward sister at the local hospital, Simon had a paper round, which gave him some pocket money; Annie worked Saturday and Sunday in a local newsagent's, the same one where Simon had the paper round. The shop was still open, it doubled as a local grocers and greengrocers. It was a community shop, open all hours. Everyone in the neighbourhood knew it and used it as a backup to the weekly shop when they ran out of something, or as a place to buy their cigarettes and the occasional packet of sweets, magazine, or bar of chocolate.

The Tesco home delivery was due on this Friday evening, so Annie had stayed in instead of going for her usual evening walk, to help unload. Sarah was on a late shift, so it was just Annie and Simon left in the house and Simon, at 15, was not usually particularly helpful around the home; although he had been better lately and had taken to cooking for all of them whenever he was given the chance. Annie was there in charge of all domestic matters. Simon was glued to his computer, they both had small laptops, ostensibly for schoolwork but, more often, especially in Simon's case, for recreation and relaxation.

Annie was a very good violinist and pianist and so would probably practise one, or both, instruments for an hour or two each day. She was hoping to continue her music at University, although not for a degree. She had not ruled out a career as a musician but felt she needed more time to discover whether she was good enough or determined enough to become a professional. It would always be an important social activity, and, if performance was always going to be part of her repertoire, she needed to keep up her proficiency. Walks, friends, brains, music and such a beautiful smile.

As someone once said of something, "What's not to like?"

Annie had been for an interview at Cambridge for mathematics with physics last December and she had an offer, conditional on her "A" level and STEP grades. She really wanted to make it. STEP 2 and STEP 3 were looming large in her mind.

Before COVID, Annie would have hung around after school with her classmates and, especially in the spring and summer, would rarely have been home before 6 pm. Simon would have had swimming club or soccer after school, or would, probably, have gone around to a friend's house, or had one of his friends come in and play computer games, or just talk with him. Supper, with all of them sitting down together, was usually at about 7 pm so that Sarah could get back comfortably in time and the youngsters could complete some of their homework, do their various practices and still be together as a family for the meal.

The doorbell rang and, expecting the Tesco van, Annie answered it. It was not the Tesco van, it was Liam.

Chapter 3

Annie stood there in some surprise. Why, for the first time in more than a year and after a very clear message from her that the relationship was over, was Liam standing on her doorstep?

Liam was a year older than Annie. The relationship had, before it ended, been passionate and intense. They had met in the very first year that Annie moved to the Academy from Manor Grove Primary. At the age of eleven, it is probably a bit of a hyperbole to talk about love at first sight, but they, and anyone who saw them, knew at once that they rather liked each other. They became almost inseparable in their spare time. They were apart for sport and music and general family activities and Liam was there to comfort Annie through the difficult first year when her father walked out on them.

It may have been then that Sarah took her eye off the ball, just for a moment, as far as Annie was concerned. She may have been a little too wrapped up in her own feelings and in helping Simon, who did not have a Liam to support him. Whatever the reason for it, Liam and Annie were thrown together rather effectively and, as the hormones kicked in, what had been a friendship became rather more than that.

At first it was tentative kisses, on closed lips, with hugs and cuddles that could be best described as chaste in the extreme. At school they never talked to their friends about what they did together. All those little hormonal schoolboy inuendoes were not part of Liam's conversation with his mates. He had too much respect for Annie and he valued so much more his relationship with her than he valued achieving a reputation as a stud among his slightly less mature classmates. Annie too had no desire to score points as one of the first in her year to gain sexual experience, she was totally confident in her own persona and did not need the adulation of classmates to make her feel good.

The relationship between them only deepened over the early years in secondary school. They shared so much. Annie supported Liam at almost all his sports events and Liam attended every concert in which Annie took part, whether she was playing the violin or singing (she had a beautiful alto voice).

They had lost their virginity together when she was 15 and he 16. It had not been at all sordid. It had been rather sweet really. It had been a beautiful summer evening, one of those long, warm, evenings in early August, when the light is reluctant to fade and the heat of the day has left the heady scent of roses and orange blossom and honeysuckle in the early evening air. The dew was beginning to condense on the grass and they were wandering by the canal, hand in hand. Liam and Annie made a handsome couple, as older folk would say.

Liam was quite tall, not an ounce of fat on his frame. He was athletic, captain of his age group football team, a member of every team sport going. The girls all had a "thing" about Liam. And, just the same, the boys all had a "thing" about Annie. Liam moved powerfully, he exuded confidence and strength, even as a relatively young man.

Annie moved with the grace of a ballerina, with poise and attitude, secure in the knowledge that she was something special. You might ask what is meant by attitude? If you have ever seen Marianela Nunez dance as Kitri in Don Quixote, you will know what it means. Her movement seemed to involve every part of her body, it would convey meaning, it would make her clothes dance and that dance would challenge you with its sheer vitality.

On the evening they lost their virginity, they had both been drinking, not much, just enough to take the edge off their inhibitions. When they talked afterwards about how it happened they both agreed that the seduction began with the decision to remove their shoes and walk barefoot across the grass to the row of willow trees on the bank of the river next to the canal. It was a seduction by nature, by the earth and the summer and the warmth of the evening. It was a seduction by affection and knowledge and shared feelings. It was not lust. It was not just a physical attraction. It was an overwhelming need for each other, an overwhelming need to define their feelings and take the relationship to a new level, a need to become one with the joyous evening around them.

They reached the shelter of the row of trees, moved slowly across the tow path to the gently sloping riverbank. The grass was still warm beneath their feet; warm and moist and incredibly sensual. It demanded more, it was insistent, it took control.

They made love.

20

They lay there for quite a while after, but, as the coolness of the evening began to turn to more of a chill, still holding hands, they walked back towards Manor Road. They hardly spoke, the immensity of what had just happened left little room for conversation, nor was there any real need.

The next morning in school they greeted each other with a new intensity and everyone around them could feel that the relationship had changed, had gone to a new depth, and most people drew their own conclusions.

****

One might have hoped that the "Poster Boy and Girl" would have gone from strength to strength in their relationship. They discussed the foolishness of their unprotected sex and both felt a degree of shame and remorse at having behaved so irresponsibly. Annie went to the chemist and obtained a morning after pill and, whether that helped, or whether they had just been fortunate, no pregnancy resulted from that evening. Neither one of them took the blame, for they both knew that it had been a seduction by circumstance, but Annie decided to go on the pill in order to give them the freedom to make love again, if the time and circumstance were right. She claimed that she was having severe period pains, a complete fabrication, but she had heard that was a common reason for teenage girls to be given the pill and so she obtained her contraception by deceit.

The next year for both Liam and Annie was secure and comfortable. Just ordinary teenage growing. They remained apparently devoted to each other. They worked hard at school and obtained outstanding grades in all subjects and thought about future careers and University options. Annie was cleverer than Liam and had "definite Oxbridge potential". Her music was going well and she had grade 8 with distinction in both her instruments by the time she went into the sixth form, along with a string of ten Grade 9 GCSEs. She was thinking of studying music or mathematics at University.

Liam, an academic year ahead of Annie, had a mixture of 7s, 8s and 9s and was thinking of a Sports Science degree at one of the better institutions, like Loughborough. They remained very close until Liam entered year 13 and Annie began her "A" levels in year 12.

From that point, they began to drift apart. Most people, including Sarah and Liam's mum Tara, supposed it was partly the demands of sixth form study, his heavy commitment to sport and her heavy commitment to music, that gave them less time together. They supposed it was no longer being in the same groups for lessons in school. They supposed it was that the small, but significant, difference in their academic potential, began to become noticeable and to cause their interests to separate. They were sad, for each family had become fond of the other and the mothers, of different race, different colour, different religion, had enjoyed sharing the ups and downs of teenage offspring and had looked to each other for support in the absence of both fathers. Perhaps these changes had been a trigger for the growing apart but what the two women did not know, and, maybe, did not care to know, was that a far more fundamental change had occurred to drive a wedge between these two lovers.

It started at a party to celebrate the GCSE results of those in Annie's year. Quite out of the blue, having had little contact with them for years, their father had invited Annie and Simon to spend the summer holidays with him and his new family at his small house in Brittany and, after some soul searching about leaving Sarah alone, the children had accepted. The Manor Academy results that year were exceptional. Only three years out of 'Special Measures', the GCSE results were 10% better than the National Average and, given the demographic, the value-added scores were even more impressive. This was an Academy on the upward path.

Annie and her close friends, all with academic and social ambition, persuaded the Academy to let them organise a prom, for the graduating year 11s and their chosen partners, in the refectory and the gym. Annie invited Liam, whom she had not seen for over six weeks, and he accepted her invitation. The prom was fixed for the night before school started again.

He called for her on the evening of the prom. She looked stunning, in an Alice Blue Gown that set off to perfection her beautifully tanned skin and her dark, dark, hair. She looked radiant and full of life. He looked tired; Annie assumed he had been working hard at his holiday job throughout the vacation. He had been working as a general helper at the local leisure centre, doing everything from cleaning to life guarding and acting as a personal trainer. His shoes were a bit scuffed; his shirt was a bit creased and there was a hole in one of his socks.

He did not look quite right, but Annie was so pleased to see him after all this time and she had so much to tell him, that she ignored this and put it all down to the long hours and hard physical slog at the day job. She took his hand eagerly and talking nineteen to the dozen, she towed him along in the direction of the dance. Liam hardly spoke, but since Annie had more than enough to say for them both and some left over, Annie did not really notice.

The school catering staff were drafted in to provide refreshment. Of course, on school premises, there was no alcohol provided, but the music was organised by the pupils and they were all quite capable of sneaking in alcopops and stronger, in undetectable ways. What set this school dance apart, as anyone raised in the sixties could have told you, was the funny tobacco and other illegal substances that made their appearance, in the cloakrooms and the school grounds and were accessed by many on the pretence of going out for cooling air.

It was somewhat ironic that this early September evening began with the same scent of roses and orange blossom and honeysuckle as on the night when Annie and Liam had first made love. It was somewhat ironic that the warm lingering light and the slight breeze and the dew on the grass, mimicked that other evening, two years earlier. They both felt it and both yearned to walk barefoot again across the grass, and so they did, but this time, the magic was not there.

It might have been the contamination of the air with the smoke of marijuana, it might have been that, already, the relationship had become a little too comfortable, a little too familiar and stale, it might have been that Annie, in particular, was looking forward and not back, it might have been that six weeks away from each other had brought a new perspective, but it also might just have been related to what happened next.

Liam assumed he was going to have sex with Annie. Annie sensed that some of the gentleness had left him and Annie did not immediately understand why, or where, or how it had disappeared. They sat on the mound to the side of the cricket field, hidden from the view of the main school building and Liam took out and lit a cigarette.

"When did you start smoking, Liam?" said Annie. Then she noticed the smell. It was not an ordinary cigarette, it was weed, or whatever the local patois was for marijuana.

"It's only marijuana," said Liam. "I borrowed it from my Mum's boyfriend. Do you want a drag?"

"No."

He reached into his pocket and took out a small packet of white powder.

"How about something stronger?"

There was a long and uncomfortable silence. Any hint of magic, any sense of flashback, had gone up in the smoke of that stolen reefer and this last indignity, that he had no real idea of how she might react, proved, for her, the last straw. He did not seem to realise how she might not be able to accept that he had deceived her by secretly obtaining and, presumably, using drugs, and, that a drug, might matter more to him as a provider of happiness and wellbeing than she did. For her it had always been enough to be with him but clearly, for him, this was not the case.

Annie felt hurt and betrayed and she hoped that she was making too much of it, but, deep inside, she knew that she was not. She had been betrayed and he had moved on in his life to somewhere that she did not want to go. Sad, disappointed, confused, lost, it was too much for her to cope with, that this person that she had loved throughout her adolescence could now, for whatever reason, need something more than their relationship, their shared hopes and dreams, their love making, to give him pleasure. Annie snatched her hand away from his. She stood up. She walked back towards the dance. He called to her, but she ignored him. They never spoke to each other again during their time together in the school.

How she got through the rest of the evening she could never remember. The shock of her realisation that the boy who had been a part of her life for so long was no longer the person that she had known, and the sense of desolation that it brought, were excruciatingly painful. She walked home alone, went to bed and cried herself to sleep.

The next day was Sunday and Annie stayed in her room, in bed, for most of the day. She practised a little on the violin, working on Tchaikovsky's 1812 Overture this term's main Academy Orchestra piece. She hardly ate and Sarah put that down to her tiredness from the prom the night before. Annie told her nothing.

Monday was the first day of school and Annie noticed Liam in the grounds of the Academy. Her rose tinted spectacles had gone and she noticed, as perhaps she would have noticed sooner, had she been around more, that his posture was more slouched, the clear skin was blotchy and had a slightly ashen tinge, the eyes were a little blood-shot. He caught her looking at him and averted his gaze. He shuffled away towards his classes and Annie walked thoughtfully towards her first Maths class.

It was hard to concentrate, but the step from GCSE to "A" level is a big one and Annie, studying Maths, Further Maths, Physics and Music, had a particularly heavy load of classes. She had resolved not to waste time, to put love and relationships on hold while she made sure of getting good grades. Her whole focus had shifted to obtaining a place at Cambridge.

It was not that Annie became a recluse, far from it. She was still the beautiful young woman with poise and grace. She was still someone who almost every member of the sixth form wanted to know and be friends with. There were lots of invitations to parties and coffee and the theatre and the cinema. There were still concerts and dances and visits to the pub. She dated lots of boys, went shopping with friends, but she never got close to any boy and she kept her counsel with her female friends. On her 17th birthday, her dad sent her a present of driving lessons and she took them and passed her test first time. From then on, her mum let her borrow the car; her dad covered the increase in the insurance costs.

Kim, what modern youth now calls her BFF, best friend forever, asked her what had happened with Liam. It was impossible not to notice that Annie and Liam never spoke to each other now and that they avoided each other as much as possible. Liam had taken to hanging around with quite a different set of classmates, the less committed, the less academic, the more troubled kids, many of whom had experienced more than one temporary exclusion and who had a reputation for low grade disruption and misbehaviour in the classroom.

Annie made a conscious decision not to tell the truth about why she and Liam had split up. Instead, she said that she had met someone on holiday in France and that she was now corresponding with him and that was why she had dumped Liam. It was quite a good lie and Kim, to whom you would tell a secret only if you wanted it known to the whole school, spread it and embellished it. It became almost a game for Annie to develop the story, following the guidelines of every good liar in history, that the closer to the truth you can stick the better the lie is likely to convince. There was plenty about the village they had stayed in, Annie had an eye for detail and the patisserie and everyone who went in there, the local supermarket, the boulangerie, the café, the bar, they all kept Kim and everyone else in the school from knowing why the two had really split up.

Everyone assumed that Liam's fall from grace had been the consequence of his rejection by Annie and not the cause of it. For some of the girls especially, that led to a cooling of their feelings towards Annie and some former friends withdrew their friendship. Not that Annie really noticed, there were plenty who remained faithful to her and there was always the work and the music to fill any potentially lonely moment.

The awkwardness between them lasted throughout Annie's year 12. Liam applied to Loughborough and got an offer and Annie heard about it on the grapevine, but it held little interest for her. Her attention was now on other matters, the little matter of getting a place at Cambridge and the additional matter of supporting Simon and stopping him from going the same way as Liam.

Sarah had asked Annie why Liam was no longer part of her life but Sarah currently had a relationship developing, with a recently widowed consultant in A and E, and so was easily fobbed off with a story about diverging interests and the need to focus on school work. She was proud of her daughter's intellectual ability and was very keen on the idea of Cambridge. Sarah knew that the Cambridge offer required additional mathematical study for the STEP papers and that the Academy was not able to help much, it was all down to Annie, so she simply let the change in circumstance pass her by.

Simon was resentful at first. He had always worshipped Liam as a surrogate big brother. He looked up to him for his sporting skills and was glad to bask in the reflected glory of being the brother of the girl who had captured the prize alpha male in the year above her. The story of the new friend in France just did not wash with Simon, for he had been there too and knew it all to be a fabrication. He was angry with Annie for removing one of the props in his life and he resolved to continue to be friends with Liam, much to the great concern of Annie, who was afraid where that might lead.

Annie was as watchful as she could be with Simon. She watched for the signs that Simon might have got into drugs in any way. She went ballistic and shopped Simon when he started smoking and Sarah grounded Simon for a fortnight. It did not lead to good relationships, but at least Annie felt that she was keeping Simon out of serious trouble. Simon was easily led.

He had almost been caught shoplifting on one occasion when three of the other boys, who were part of the Manor Street Gang, took him with them to steal goods from the local department store. They had been caught on camera, but Simon had lifted his target just at the exact moment when a very large lady had walked in front of the CCTV camera, so he had not been detected. He had owned up to Annie afterwards and she had promised not to tell Sarah, on condition that he never did anything like that again. The other boys received an official police caution. They did not blame Simon, nor did they take it out on him, in fact they thought it rather cool that he had gotten away with it. They offered him the chance to join their gang and he accepted the offer.

Shortly after that, Simon was asked to deliver a package to a garage on the route of his paper round, about a mile away, he got a fiver for doing it. From that time and for a short while, his paper round money became a very small fraction of his earnings and his courier business became quite mainstream. Annie never suspected and Simon opened a bank account at a building society and was careful not to flash his money around. Liam became the contact for the delivery service and Annie could only watch in frustration as her young brother became closer and closer to her former boyfriend.

She breathed a huge sigh of relief when Liam finally departed for Loughborough and thought that the danger to Simon had, for now, passed. With Liam out of the way, Annie and Simon began to rebuild their relationship. Annie helped Simon with his GCSE work and Simon helped a bit more around the house with the chores that had previously all fallen to Annie. It didn't take long for them to get back on good terms.

Chapter 4

And now, here was Liam standing at the door of number 42.

He looked a shadow of his former self. His face was thin and drawn, his eyes were sunken in their sockets and his shoulders were stooped. He wore a dirty denim jacket and tattered jeans, not fashionably tattered but dirty and ragged and worn. His sneakers were old and festering. He almost seemed to cringe before her gaze.

"Help me," he said. "Please help me."

Annie saw the Tesco van pulling into the lay-by. She made a quick decision.

"Go up to my room. Stay there. Don't make a sound. I'll be up as soon as I've unpacked this delivery and got supper sorted then you can tell me what is going on."

Gratefully and as silently as he could, he brushed past her and climbed the narrow staircase to Annie's bedroom. He was limping badly and clung to the bannisters as he went up. He almost stumbled at the landing and Annie was afraid he might have made too much noise. Simon opened the dining room door and came out into the hallway, but Liam had closed the bedroom door just in time.

"Hullo Miss," said the delivery guy, through his black Tesco logo mask. "Now just you step away from that doorframe and I will put the crates on the step and get back again. Two metres, my lovely. Two metres."

Simon and Annie stepped back and the trays were duly deposited. They unpacked swiftly; that early in the crisis Tesco were still delivering in plastic bags so the weekly shop for three people did not take long to unload.

"See you next week, darling," said the guy jovially and Annie smiled, said thank you and watched him take the crates away.

It took a little longer for Annie and Simon to put the groceries and the household goods into the relevant refrigerator, freezer, or store cupboard; but Annie was conscious to take it steady and not indicate, by any unusual haste, that something might be different this week. Simon helped himself to a bag of crisps and sat down in the kitchen to nibble them while he read his emails and chatted on Instagram with some of his friends.

Annie got on with preparing supper, it was a prawn, mushroom and asparagus risotto and she deliberately made a slightly larger portion than usual. Sarah would be back in about half an hour and the three of them would sit and eat together, but there was always some left over and on this occasion that some would be enough for a fourth person hiding out in her bedroom.

"Simon. Be an angel and make a green salad, would you please?" said Annie. Since Liam had left, Simon had been much more like the old Simon, much less likely to be in trouble and much more obliging and younger brother like, much less sullen and resentful.

Simon put down his half-eaten packet of crisps and duly got on with the task of preparing a green salad. Fresh leaves from the delivery, fresh cucumber, a green apple for sweetness, some green pepper and some celery and a dressing made with olive oil, white wine vinegar, a spring onion, salt and a few dried herbs. Not as academic as his sister Simon enjoyed cooking and was seriously thinking about trying to become a chef and go for an apprenticeship or go to catering college.

A few minutes later Sarah came breezily through the door. Annie thought she noticed her mother sniffing a little suspiciously in the hall way, Liam certainly stank when he came in, but the aroma of cooking soon masked all other smells and Sarah was hungry enough from her long late shift to be ready to sit and eat straight away.

Sometimes, on Friday evening, and this was a Friday evening, Sarah would open a bottle of inexpensive but usually gently fruity, white wine, Riesling, or a Gewurztraminer, depending on which had been on offer. Simon, although not quite yet 16, would have half a glass and Sarah and Annie would share the rest of half a bottle, saving the other half for some time over the weekend. Annie, although you could not tell it from her demeanour, was internally like a cat on hot bricks. She forced herself to chat happily to her mother, asked about the day, asked about the new boyfriend, included Simon in every conversation and generally played the part that she knew so well, the ideal daughter.

It was a torment waiting for bedtime. Eventually, Sarah let Annie off the hook.

"Sweetheart, you look tired. Why don't you get an early night? You've got to be up early to help open the shop otherwise Simon will not have any papers to deliver." All said with a gentle smile and a bit tongue in cheek. Annie was grateful for this chance to go and find out what trouble Liam was in.

"OK Mum, I am a bit weary. You sure you will be alright down here with just Simple Simon?"

"I heard that," said Simon, looked up with a grin and went back to his YouTube video.

They all knew that Simon was little or no company in the evening. Not long out of the grunt stage of teenage communication, compounded by that frightening interlude when he was clearly, if, let us be charitable, perhaps unknowingly, mixed up in delivering drugs. Even though he was better now, he tended to watch his own programmes on Sky Go or You-tube videos on his laptop. Neither of the two women really wanted to watch superheroes or cooking programmes 24/7.

They exchanged a few more pleasantries and Annie said she would make a hot drink and take it up with her and she would just clear up the dishes before she went up. She went into the kitchen and made two drinks of hot chocolate. She put the remains of the risotto into a container which she put into her school bag. She put the dirty pots and pans into the dishwasher. She put a fork and spoon in her bag along with a packet of breakfast biscuits, some crisps, an apple and some grapes. She picked up her bag and walked back through the sitting room where Sarah was quietly watching an episode of *Vera*.

"Oh Mum, how many times have you seen that one?"

There was a grin.

"None of your business, young lady, now get your backside up those stairs and get some beauty sleep!"

"Night Mum. Night Simon."

The grunt king returned a grunt and went back to watching his small screen.

****

In her bedroom, Annie found Liam crashed out on the bed. He did not even hear her come in. Looking at him like that, sleeping peacefully and without that haunted look she had seen earlier on the doorstep, she felt some of her old feeling for him return. She had loved him and she knew that he had loved her. She was in a bit of a quandary. Should she wake him now, or should she let him sleep?

Recalling the hunched, shattered, figure on the doorstep she decided on the latter course of action.

It meant a problem for her, of course—where was she going to sleep? She had no desire to rekindle the sexual nature of their relationship. She normally slept naked in the summer and wearing only a thin T-shirt and her panties in cooler times (she had a really warm winter duvet) but she felt that either of those options would be an invitation to trouble, she was not sure she could trust him and she was not even sure that she could trust herself, it had been so long since she had had sex.

She settled for safety, put on her old school tracksuit and decided to snuggle on the bed under the summer weight duvet with Liam. Surprisingly, perhaps because of all the tension of the past few hours, perhaps because her old memories sneaked in upon her, she fell asleep almost immediately and slept soundly the whole night through.

In the morning Annie woke just before her alarm would have gone off. It was 6 am. On a Saturday she had to be at the newsagent's at 6:30 to set out the papers for the paper rounds and to be ready to open the shop at 7 am for the early morning trade. It didn't pay that well, she got £5.00 an hour, a few pence above the national minimum wage for a 17-year-old. What made it worthwhile was that it was a short walk from home, she worked two ten-hour shifts at the weekend and Mr Stops, the proprietor, gave her six weeks holiday pay a year and had promised to let her work there every vacation while she was at Uni. You do the sums; it was a hundred quid a week in a safe environment (Sarah was happy about that).

Annie reckoned that old Stops rather fancied her, but he never made any improper suggestions, nor did he ever try to touch her up and he didn't leer at her either as some men did. He was gentlemanly in his conduct, even if his eyes betrayed him a bit. There was something about Annie that stopped unwanted advances from the opposite, or, for that matter, the same sex. Maybe, although she was stunningly physically attractive, the strength of her personality and the aura of goodness and purity that she exuded, stopped people wanting to spoil her opinion of them and encouraged them to leave her alone.

When she woke, Liam was sitting on a chair in the corner just looking at her. He had found the food she had left out, and the drink, which would have been well cold by the time that he drank it. It seemed that he had crept out in the middle of the night to the bathroom for a pee and a crap and had, of course, not flushed the loo. He told Annie that and Annie rushed to the loo, had a pee and then flushed the toilet. She was determined not to let anyone know Liam was there until she knew why he was there, and, maybe, not even then. She cleaned her teeth and brushed her hair before going back to her room. Time was going to be a bit short this morning.

"What is it, Liam?" said Annie.

"I am really sorry, Annie," said Liam. "I want to tell you the whole story, but it is a long story and I know you are not going to like it. I am going to cut to the chase, the drug dealers I got caught up with just before you dumped me, and I don't blame you, are looking to kill me. They are looking for me. I could not go home, 'cos the bastards know where I live and it would bring my Mum and sisters into danger. I had nowhere else to go. I am desperate."

Annie remained stone-faced through this revelation. She started to get dressed. Liam stopped talking and, almost like a whipped puppy, stared imploringly at Annie's face, looking for some sort of sign that it would be alright.

"Say something, Annie, say something." Liam began to sob quietly into his hands.

"So, you don't want to drag your family into it, but you are quite happy to drag mine? You bastard."

That was not quite what Liam wanted to hear.

"I have so fucked up my life," he said. "Fucked it up so badly. I had us and a future, I had sport and work and people. I was fit and healthy. Now look at me. I look like an old man. I do not even have a family because I would destroy them if I went near them. I am so alone Annie. If you ever loved me as I loved you, please help me? I need to tell you the full story, but you are clever and I know you will be able to find a way out for me. Please?"

Annie thought for a moment and then she said:

"You can't stay here all day. Mum comes in and cleans my room after breakfast and she would find you. You stink and that is going to be a problem. You need to get out for the day. You can come back tonight and we can then see what might be done, but for the moment you need to find somewhere to hide for the day. I can hear Simon getting up. He mustn't see you because he just will not be able to keep the secret that you are here. Do you remember how to get into my bedroom from the street without Sarah knowing?"

There was a flash of a smile, a reminder of better times and clandestine love making, when there was, still, love to be shared.

"I think so, I did it often enough."

Again, a slight grin, a slight sign that the soul was still intact, buried there somewhere beneath the grime.

"Right. When I have gone you open all the windows wide, get out and down the trellis. I think it will still stand your weight, especially now that you are so thin, and you go and hide somewhere until lunch time. If you want to meet me at lunch time and begin to tell me what is happening, I have 12:30 to 1:30 break. I work from 6:30 to 5:30 with an hour for lunch. You can meet me at the back of Stops' shop in the Cooper Close alleyway. Have you got any money with you?"

Liam shook his head.

"Can you get some clean clothes that don't stink and especially another pair of shoes and is there somewhere you can get a bath or a shower?"

"I can break into the school and get a shower there," said Liam. "I'll find a way to get some clean clothes."

Annie gave him some money and a face mask, one of the big cloth ones that she and Sarah had made from a pattern sent out by the local church. Ironically it had been made from one of Liam's old T-shirts that had been left behind when the two of them had broken up.

"Wear the mask anywhere you think you might be recognised. In fact, wear it the whole time you are outside this room. Nobody will be suspicious because everyone is wearing masks these days. I am going to give you enough cash to get a pair of clean jeans, a pair of cheap trainers and some underwear and a shirt. Use the supermarket. Go there first and then go and get your shower. And buy some fucking shower gel, you really do stink. Thank goodness Roger Stops pays me in cash."

Annie looked at her watch.

"I must run. I am never late and I don't intend to be late now. I will look for you in my lunch break and if I don't see you, I'm telling you I really shan't cry!"

There was bitterness and some anger in that last statement. Annie's new found comfortable existence was being threatened and she absolutely did not like it. She was also up to her neck in work because, unlike A levels and GCSEs, the STEP papers, on which her entry to Cambridge depended, were still taking place. She left without a backward glance, sped down the stairs, grabbed an apple and banana from the fruit bowl and, with a shout to Simon not to be late for his round, sped out of the door. The last thing she heard was Simon saying, "don't be late, you're a fine one to talk."

Annie ran all the way to Stops' Shop! She put the kettle on when she got there and started to unpack the bundles of Saturday papers. There were quite a few magazines on Saturday too. The shop paper rounds served about 1,000 houses with a dozen boys and girls doing a paper round of between 70 and 100 deliveries each. Old Stops had been smart. He started with one small shop on the outskirts of the town right next to a housing estate being built in the early seventies. He was 16 at the time, a dropout from school, just married with a baby on the way. He borrowed money from the bank with a business plan that was both smart and practical. He never looked back.

Every new housing estate in the town had a Stops' Newsagents, always on the prime commuter route, always just off the main arterial road into or out of the city, picking up passing trade and serving the local much less mobile community. Annie's job was to put out the papers in piles in the large store room at the back of the shop and put the pieces of paper, with the list by house of the papers required, on separate piles by each of the bags that the paper boys and girls used on their rounds. The kids came in and made up their own bags, writing the address on the first paper in each house order and packing the papers, in order, into their bags.

Annie's task was not difficult, but she was also required to oversee the boys and girls as they picked their papers from the pile, and make sure there were no errors and no fights. The area served by this particular shop covered three different gang areas, so occasional small spats did occur, but the kids knew that any big spat would mean their losing their round and most of them, unlike Simon, came from homes where this money was needed, not for the kid him or herself, but for the family to eat and be warm and clothed. This was a real low-income job for most of the kids and their families. Annie tried to keep an eye open for them, to stop them getting into trouble, but it was not always easy to detect when a child was being exploited by a drugs gang. It had been hard enough for her to spot when Simon was heading down the wrong trail.

With coffee mug in hand, Annie supervised the emergence from chaos of the fleet of delivery kids.

Chapter 5

It seemed a very long time until her lunch break. The return of Liam into her life nearly two years after she had kicked him out of it and almost a year since he had moved out of the city, had been very unsettling and she was still not really any nearer knowing why he was in such a state of panic. Of course, he had said it was related to drugs and she would probably have guessed anyway that trouble for Liam would have involved drugs, but she had hoped that his move away to Loughborough might have given him a new start.

She had always hoped that it was just mainly marijuana and maybe a tiny bit of coke he had been mixed up with but, from the back of her mind she suddenly dredged up a picture of Liam lying on the bed and she remembered the feel of his arm as she folded it under the duvet as she covered him last night. There had been needle tracks and there had been completely sclerosed veins, not many, just one that she had felt, but that one and the tracks, had told a tale. Liam had been shooting up, not just taking drugs orally. He was a long way down the addiction trail.

Lunchtime eventually came and Annie took her banana and apple and a coffee she had made in the shop out to the parking lot at the back of the row of newsagents. It was a fairly warm spring day so it was not unusual for her to go out and get some fresh air during the brief interval that she had to eat her food and relax, only, on this occasion, there was going to be no chance of relaxing. Liam was waiting for her, just like he had in the old days, before the break-up, but it was not like that at all.

He was shaking like a leaf, grimacing in pain and clutching his stomach and looking as strained as he had the night before. She noticed right away that he had not bought any clothes and could only assume that he had not gone to get any food or shower gel either. She would have been right. He had done none of those things and the money she had given him was still in his pocket.

"Liam, what are you playing at?" said Annie. "I gave you money to get yourself sorted out a bit. You cannot come back to my place later if you still stink and are wearing those clothes. A dolphin with a head cold could smell you the minute you came through the window, because, believe me, it is through the window that you are coming if you come back at all."

"What is going on?"

Liam began to talk, he started and he did not stop until he had told Annie the whole sorry story.

"I started to take drugs when I was in year 11. I wanted to get stronger and faster so, as you remember, I started going to the Brook Street Gym. It was also a boxing and martial arts club and I always quite liked those things, so I started to do kick boxing, taekwondo and all sorts of combat type things. I just wasn't as strong as some of the other kids and that sort of shook me because I've always been one of the strongest, so I asked Olly what the hell was going on and he told me. The other kids were taking steroids, anabolic steroids.

"Olly said he knew where I could get some if I wanted and I said no at first, but once I started competing, I started losing all the time and I didn't like that. So, I said yes. It wasn't the best of times. Do you remember how bad my acne got? Well I reckon that was the testosterone. I got irritable too and I remember we started to have a few rows, which we never had before. I was sure you were going to work out what was happening, but I guess it is so far out of your experience that you never did.

"Anyway, the drugs were quite cheap at first and then the price started to go up. I couldn't really afford it with my job at the leisure centre so these guys approached me and said I could have all the drugs I wanted if I would recruit people from the leisure centre to buy drugs from them. So, I did. And what I didn't know was that they recorded me chatting up a customer and persuading him to take nandrolone and they told me they had done it and that from now on I was part of the gang and I would carry and sell and deliver and fetch whatever drugs and money they told me to, or they would send the video to the police and the press. I guess I liked the money, I guess I liked the strength the anabolic steroids gave me. I guess I was scared stiff that they would turn me in and my life would be over.

"At first it was just anabolics and a little hash. They would tell people they could buy it from me at the leisure centre and I would leave it for them in the locker room and they would leave the money in my locker there. It was a combination lock system and the gang knew my combination and gave it to customers. Everyone knew that this gang were a nasty bunch and nobody crossed them. The thing went like clockwork. I even got a bonus from the leisure centre because loads of people joined and when asked who had recommended them, they said it was me, so the management just loved me. I admit I thought to begin with that a bit of marijuana never hurt anyone and the anabolic steroids were not really all that bad, just a slight bit of cheating.

"Then it started to get serious towards the middle of year 12. The gang decided to use me to dish out cocaine and heroin to their dealers and to help them launder the money. The same system as for the steroids and marijuana but about ten dealers and that covered most of the city, joined the centre and would come weekly for a "gym session". The money got bigger and bigger and the drug drops also got bigger and bigger. There were some weeks I would be taking thousands of pounds back to the gang leader.

"Once a week, they would leave a very big rucksack for me at the leisure centre and I had to pick it up and take it to the Boxing Club for my evening session. I had an identical rucksack I put my kit in so nobody would get suspicious. I walked into the centre with a rucksack and I walked out of the centre with an identical rucksack. I had to give the rucksack to the coach there, Bryan Muldoon. It was always on a Friday.

"I suppose it could have been alright, even then, but, by the end of year 12, the schoolwork was going less well and I was beginning to lose it. I was irritable at home, I was anxious all the time, really on edge and I even lost it and hit one of my sisters in a row over a bottle of fizzy water. You were away on that fucking French holiday at the time, so I guess you didn't know about that.

"I mentioned it to one of the people I dealt with, the unfit fat one and he said he could help me. He had something which could calm you down and he asked me if I would like to try it. How stupid can you get? He was quite well spoken and very smooth, so I went with it. Deep down I knew that the only things he had that might calm me down might also get me hooked and into the drug scene even more, but I guess, having lost it and hit my sister and with you away, I wasn't thinking straight and I no longer knew who I really was, so I said yes.

"That first shot of heroin, that's what it was, hit me like a steam train. I was invincible, I was a demi-god, I could walk on water and see through walls. From that moment I was hooked. That was the stage at which you found out I was doing stuff and dumped me. I had a fix that evening before I came and picked you up for the dance. The gang needed me as a front man at the Centre and as a drugs and money mule so, all through my final year at the Academy, they kept me well supplied with H and, if I wanted it, coke.

"I remember walking along to the dance with you chatting away and I knew it was over. I knew I had blown it and there was no way back. I really did care more about H and coke than I did about you or anyone or anything else. I think offering you some coke was my way to try to get you to join me on this rotten journey, but you, you have more sense. You are the most amazing person I have ever met. I am surprised you didn't tell me to my face, there and then, to fuck off."

There was a pause and Liam doubled up in anguish for a moment, sweating profusely, salivating and shivering. Then he took up the tale again.

"I thought it couldn't get any worse. I became, as I thought, a respected member of the gang. They kept me in drugs and they even gave me some money over and above my wages from the Centre. Yes, I really missed you, but I kept thinking that it would all come right when I went to Uni. I could stop taking the drugs and, when I was well again, I would come back and sweep you off your feet with my personality and good looks.

"Fat chance, but drug dreams are damn stupid. The four big members of the gang were the overweight guy, I think he was called Freddie, someone named George, who was a nasty little man with a scar on his left cheek, then there was a short guy, with terrible teeth and bandy legs, who owned a chain of takeaways, which, incidentally, were also drop off and pick up points for drugs, I think he was called Jason something, and a rather smooth, very muscular, probably ex-military, muscle man who they used as an enforcer and who was known as Bruno, although I have no idea if that was really his name or just their idea of a joke.

"I think I might have heard him called Frank at some point, but I was probably absolutely stoned at the time, so who knows. I found out about them because one day I was asked to go and deliver a package to this big house on the outskirts in Summerland and there were the four of them there, sitting in the garden drinking Pimm's, or something, and I heard them talking. I don't know why, but Freddie, the guy who had given me my first heroin, introduced me to the others, I think they had all probably had a bit to drink. They sort of ignored me after that, I gave them the package and they sent me away with a twenty-pound note. They told me to forget about the visit and there would be real trouble for me if I told anyone I had seen them. The George guy was a bit frightening, so I did as I was told.

"Just when you thought it couldn't get worse, I got my A-level results. By some miracle, they were enough to get me into Loughborough. I told the guys at the leisure centre I would be leaving in September and I also got the message back to the drug guys. I don't know quite what I expected. Did I think they were going to jump up and down with joy and shake my hand and tell me well done boy? If I did, I must have been absolutely fucking bonkers.

"George, the one with the scar, came to see me off! He warned me that if I ever said anything about the drugs scene or any of the people I had met or worked with I would end up dead, and so would my family, and the way he said it, I believed him. He said something like 'You can fuck off to Loughborough sunshine, but remember we still have that tape and we also have a video of you putting drugs into the locker and taking the money out and putting it into your bag so, even though you are fuck all use to us anymore, you will keep your mouth shut or not only will we turn those tapes over to the police, we will also arrange for someone to go around to your place and do something nasty to your mum and your three pretty little teeny sisters. We have a number of friends who like little girls.'

"And that was that. My source of easy drugs dried up, my source of extra money dried up and I knew I had to keep quiet or my family would be badly hurt, perhaps even killed."

Another bout of stomach cramp curled Liam into a ball and then he began again. Annie was thinking to herself, *What the hell more can there be?* but the next bit of Liam's story told her exactly why he was so shit scared.

"I guess that was all bad enough but then I did something really stupid, as if what I have told you so far isn't stupid enough. I found a place in Loughborough, near to the hall of residence, where I could get anabolics and it was not hard to find a heroin dealer from there. So, for a while, I carried on with my habit, I kept reasonably on top of the work. I wasn't good enough to be on any teams or the drug testing would have found me out, the Uni is squeaky clean. I pretended to be sociable. I played some sport, but the drugs were blunting my edge and my will to win seemed to have gone.

"In truth, all I really cared about was getting my next fix. Once they knew they had me hooked, my dealers started to put up their prices and I began to run out of money. So, I had a clever idea, so clever it is probably going to kill me and quite a few other people. I decided to come back here and rob those fuckers who had shafted me. I knew where they kept the money that they collected prior to laundering it. The money was always passed to the mule on the last Friday of a month and it was always kept in the same locker at the Boxing Club at the Brook Street gym. For over a year I was the first mule in the chain. I handed the money in the rucksack to Bryan Muldoon, the boxing coach, and he put it in the locker. Just like my locker at the leisure centre this locker had a 60-digit combination lock.

"I suppose the whole idea of this arrangement is that the gang of four, their mule, the laundering team's mule, they never meet, are never seen together, the chain has a link that is almost invisible. Anyway, it had clearly been working for years so I guessed they were not about to change it. My only problem was to be sure the money had been put in there and that I had time to get in there, nick it and disappear before the second mule arrived. I knew they kept their timings tight, but they still wanted the clear time gap, so I ought to be able to find a way. I knew the combination.

"Funnily enough, I knew it because I had seen the boxing coach using that locker when I was first beginning my martial arts crap and he had once asked me to go to the locker and get some stuff for him. I remember I had asked him why he chose those three numbers, 26 left, 19 right and 53 left? He said it was the date of Queen Elizabeth's coronation. I came back here by train and made sure no one saw me. I saw you and Kim walking back from the Academy, but I made pretty sure you did not see me.

"About 5:30 in the evening the first mule arrived with a big 40-litre rucksack containing the money, it was Shaun, the kid who replaced me, and he went into the gym. I sneaked into the club building by the back door and found my way to the locker room. They hadn't changed the combination on the members' locker room door, so that problem was easily overcome. It was dead simple to enter the locker room, unlock the locker, take out the rucksack, which was heavy, at least 30 kilos and get out without anyone seeing me. I was on the train back to Loughborough half an hour later. That was about a month ago.

"I opened the bag when I got back to my digs. It was full of fifty-pound notes in tight little bundles. I never counted them, I still haven't, but I reckon it was well over half a million pounds, maybe even closer to a million. I was scared witless and I was going to bury it and forget about it and maybe just dip into it now and again. I knew I couldn't give it back and I knew I couldn't spend it. Not just like that anyway.

"I guess that might have been that, and it was, until about a week ago, when I was heading back to the hall of residence and I saw Bruno hanging around outside the entrance. I was lucky, I saw him before he saw me, so I managed to divert and avoid him. I climbed into the Halls through an open lavatory window. I went to my room and I got hold of the bag, which still had almost all of the money in it, I picked up my small stash of H, I grabbed my wallet and phone charger and I climbed back out and ran.

"I knew I couldn't go to the station because I was sure they would have that covered and I also thought it might be stupid to go to a hotel locally because I was sure they would search the Hotels and Guest houses when they knew I had not gone back to the Halls. So, I started to walk, it is about fifty miles, so I reckoned on taking three or so days to get back here. I slept rough. The bag was bloody heavy. It was, fortunately, a good waterproof rucksack and the money was packed in plastic bags as well.

"I ran out of drugs and had my last fix just before I got here. I got wet one night, slept in a hedge row and stepped in all sorts of shit and muck, I slept in a cow shed another night and a stable on the third night and I got back here yesterday morning. And the rest you know. I think they want their money back. I think they have worked out I took it and I think they will kill me if they find me. It doesn't help either that I have seen them. I am not sure that many of the people in the drug scene have seen any of the top four."

There was a silence. Liam doubled up again with the cramps, the shaking and sweating got worse.

"You stupid idiot," said Annie. Her food was untouched. She was in shock. She realised that Liam was, as they say in the trade, a dead man walking.

It took a minute or two for all that he had said to sink in and then the razor-sharp mind clicked into action.

"Go and get some damn clothes like I told you. Go and get some food. Keep out of sight. Put your mask back on. Meet me tonight around 9pm in my room and NOT before," she shouted at him.

"I have to go back in and finish my day. I'm lost with all this. Whatever possessed you? You were a kid, for Christ's sake. Those guys are professionals. They could eat you for dinner. I don't see a way back now. You must have known they would work it out. I bet that coach said you were the only kid he had ever given the locker combination to and then they would have been off to Loughborough like a shot. You told them you were going there. You dumbo. You've got me so angry. Now just go, get out of my sight before I change my mind and turn you in."

Chapter 6

Some of Annie's anger was directed against Liam. How could she not be furious that someone who had so much in his life could have thrown it all away in such a pathetically weak way. "I wasn't strong enough!". It wasn't just the physical dimension that resonated with Annie, it was the mental weakness that worried her even more. A plan to get him out of the deep hole he was in was forming in her mind, but she did not know if he had the strength in him to carry it off.

Well, only time would tell and there was nothing to be gained by dwelling on it at this moment. It might have been different if it had only been a few thousand pounds and she rather suspected that Liam had expected that sort of sum, but over half a million. People kill for that sort of sum and the guys running drug cartels are the sort of people who do kill for that sort of sum.

Annie went back into the shop, once again without a backward glance, finished the last sips of her now cold coffee and put the mug in the sink in the rest area at the back of the shop. She scoffed down the banana, threw the skin in the bin and walked through to the counter area. For the rest of the afternoon, she served papers and sweets and chocolate and occasional items of grocery, to mask-wearing local folk, many of whom she knew, either as regular customers, or simply because they were her neighbours. There were a few complete strangers and she had to confess to herself that she was on the lookout for Fat Freddie, Bruno, the guy with a scar on his left cheek and a bandy-legged short guy with yellowed teeth. To her great relief, she did not see any of them.

The minute hand went slowly around the clock; a big, immediately post second world war, analogue clock, sporting an advert for Player's cigarettes, the hour hand hardly seemed to move at all. Time dragged, not because she was eager to see Liam again, a bit of Annie hoped she never would, but rather because she was feeling that the weight of the world was bearing down on her tiny shoulders. Deep inside she knew that this was not just about Liam, what he had done had endangered his family, and, by coming to see her, he had put at risk not only his family, but Annie and her family too.

Eventually, the end of Annie's shift came and she headed for home. She still had not eaten her apple and she was, by now, very hungry. As soon as she entered number 42, she parked the problem of Liam in a deep recess in her mind and went through to the kitchen and almost burst into tears. Simon, bless him, had baked a cake and was in the process of cooking their supper. A Saturday evening, a day for the second glass of wine of the weekend and something a little bit special gastronomically. She loved this little beggar so much and was so glad that he had stepped back from the dark space into which he had been moving.

Chicken, leek and mushroom pie and he had made his own puff pastry for it. He really should become a chef. What had he done to make that pie special? There were porcini mushrooms with the button ones, there was a hint of thyme, there was cream in the white sauce; and all this after finishing his paper round, doing the house cleaning chores, which were his lot on a Saturday, and, even, doing his homework. But first the cake, Annie's favourite, lemon drizzle. Light as a feather, sweet and sour, slightly crunchy on the top with little crystals of sugar on the brown surface. And the second warm cup of tea of the day.

Annie walked over to him and gave him the biggest hug she could manage and she teared up as he said: "Love you, Sis. Will you play some music for me?"

She went and got her violin and began to play that lovely lyrical theme from the third movement of Berlioz's Symphonie Fantastique. It became a moment of calm, an oasis of peace for Annie amidst all her worries and concerns. Simon brought another piece of cake and a cup of fresh-made tea over to her and they sat and chatted, about school, and work, and inconsequential matters like that. He told her about his plans to become a chef. He had researched the possible routes and he wanted to obtain an apprenticeship with a famous name chef, or possibly to study abroad at a catering institute, perhaps in Paris.

It was still all fairly nebulous, a so-called pipe dream, but Annie admired his determination and she knew that this passion was driving his new found commitment to study, for he would need good GCSE grades to back up this risky career choice and to allow him to approach the very best European institutions.

Refreshed and renewed, Annie went upstairs to complete her music practice and some of the Maths and Physics homework she needed to up-load on Monday. She also did a couple of STEP questions, the exam was now only a few weeks away and, while A* grades in her "A" levels were very likely, the STEP was a much tougher hurdle. In a slightly miraculous way, the interlude with Simon had refreshed her and the study and the practice went well. The tricky fingering for the 'Pathetique' suddenly seemed to become easy and the mysteries of partial derivatives began to reveal themselves.

Sarah came home from the weekend shift at about 7:00 as usual and Simon served up his feast. The Gewurztraminer had kept well in the fridge and both Sarah and Annie enjoyed the sweetness of it, not swamped by the flavours of the pie. Annie kept the darkness in its place, in the deeper recesses of her mind. and enjoyed the company and the animated chatter, about inconsequential things, with the two people she loved and cared for most in the world.

But then came bedtime and she went up the stairs to the landing, completed her toilet and went to her room. Liam was waiting there.

****

She could hardly believe what she saw. He had managed to clean himself up, but he was not wearing new jeans, shirt, jumper socks and sneakers. Nothing he had on fitted him, nothing matched. He looked like a scarecrow and, had he wanted to draw attention to himself, he could hardly have dressed more appropriately. He was no longer shaking and cramping and she knew at once that he had found himself a fix from somewhere. It was all she could do to stop herself from screaming at him, but she knew that to do so would unravel the whole scheme of things and drag Sarah and Simon into the maelstrom that was dragging both Liam and her into the depths.

Liam looked so stupidly pleased with himself. It was pathetic. Where had he got the drugs? Did he not realise that the people who were looking for him would now know he was around, because whoever he had got the drugs from would be bound to talk and the gang of four would know to start closing off the exits from the City and start closing in on Liam and his location within it.

Annie sat on the bed and put her head in her hands. Then she glared at Liam and he began to wilt under her gaze. When she thought she had sobered him enough she began to talk quietly and firmly to him.

"I cannot believe that you have been so stupid. Where did you get the clothes from?"

"I nicked them from the lockers at the leisure centre. People are always leaving clothes in unlocked lockers and I reckoned, what with the centre being closed for now, that I could get in there and nick stuff and have a shower. I never gave my key back when I left."

"What the Hell were you doing at the leisure centre? Do you want to get killed?"

Liam put his head in his hands.

"I didn't think. I needed a fix so I rang this woman Moira, who I used to know a bit and I asked her to get me some heroin and meet me at the centre and I would buy it from her. I used the money you gave me for that, and some food. She's nice and she had what I needed. She told me the gang are looking for me and she said they seem to be very angry. She doesn't think just giving the money back is good enough. She reckons, from what they said to her, they want to make an example of me and kill me."

"You dumb idiot. Now you have put her at risk too. I think you are going to have to face up to something that you will not like. The only way you are going to stay alive, is if you give up drugs for good. Every time you make a buy, you touch the drug scene; that's where those guys have influence. If you hadn't stolen their money we might have been able to get you into a rehab programme with the Hospital, but the minute you go there you are dead and it means the only thing you can do is go cold turkey and that might kill you, but I am sorry, it is a chance you are going to have to take. You were young, fit and healthy once, so maybe you can get through it, but you just cannot risk getting any more drugs, ever!"

The reality of his situation began to dawn on Liam in a way that it had never done before. Uni was over for him now, getting off heroin was his only chance and he had endangered everyone he knew and had once loved, perhaps, deep down, still did love.

He looked rather pathetically at Annie, mouthed the word sorry and lay down on the floor.

Annie kicked him.

"That's it, is it?" she said with some feeling. She kicked him again, harder and with intent to hurt him.

"Get up and listen to me and don't speak until I say you can." All the anger and frustration of the past twenty-four hours was boiling over in her head and she looked at Liam with a mixture of pity and contempt that distorted her features in a way that frightened him. She began to tell him what was going to happen next.

"Tomorrow morning, Sunday, the supermarket opens at 10am. I will go and buy for you some camping gear, including a sleeping bag, a small stove, a billy can, a can opener, that sort of stuff. I will get you some more underwear, some socks and some extra blankets. You are going to feel very cold and ill. I have no idea what medications people use to deal with the withdrawal, do you? If you do, let me know and I will try and pick up some of them, but my guess is you do not know either, so I think this is just going to be you deciding whether or not you want to live. You can't stay here any longer.

"I am going to take you to Uncle Willy's allotment where he has a big polytunnel that he uses for growing tomatoes and peppers. Uncle Willy and his family are shielding because my Aunt June has cancer. You are lucky. After what you told me at lunchtime, I rang my Uncle Willy and we agreed that I would look after his allotment while he is shielding. My Mum says the prognosis is good for Aunt June, but for the moment Aunt June is immuno-suppressed, so shielding it is.

"That means the polytunnel is not going to be used, so I can put you in there, it will be warmer than sleeping outside and from what I can tell from reading about coming off heroin, you are going to need a bit of shelter from the elements. There is a tap for water at the back of Willy's plot and there is a lavatory on site, right next to the plot, so you can sneak in there after dark, or you can simply bury your crap in the compost heap. You are going to hate this and I am hardly going to think about you or anything to do with you for about ten days, by which time the worst should be over. You might be dead. I don't want to think about it. I will try to get there a couple of times a day just to top up your water supply and I will try to bring you some food, but I am not staying with you and for this you are effectively on your own.

"I will tell you what you are going to do next once you are safe and off the drugs. Where is the money?"

Liam looked stunned. It was beginning to dawn on him that what was about to happen to him was probably the worst thing he might, short of death, ever experience.

"You know the old pill-box down by the bridge over the canal? I hid it under the stone slab at the entrance. I pulled up the slab, dug a big hole, buried the rucksack and put the stone back and flattened it. I threw the spare dirt in the canal. I took about ten thousand out before I buried it. That's in my pocket in fifty quid notes. Fifties are hard to shift, people are suspicious of them and they always get tested to see if they are forgeries. I only ever use them in supermarkets. You tell the checkout lady you just got paid and you buy something small and then they break it down for you and then you have money you can spend in other places.

"Most towns have three or four supermarkets in the centre so you can break down a couple of hundred quid in a day if you want. You can also spend them on phones and things, you just say your granny sent you this money. Trouble is that at that rate it would take you a couple of lifetimes to be able to spend all the money in that rucksack." He was gabbling, just chatting on nervously, then he stopped and said:

"OK. I guess we can give it a try. I am dead anyway if I don't do it. I know it wouldn't be any good just giving the money back, Moira said that. She said she had been threatened by them and they were prepared to kill her and her baby to get what they wanted. Moira didn't know, but I know that I have seen them, and they won't want a loose end like me hanging around."

"Right," said Annie, "give me that money you put in your pockets, I will keep it safe for you. You are going to need it for the next part of my plan but I am not going to tell you what that is because I cannot trust you not to mess it up until I know you are off the drugs and I think we only have one chance at it anyway. And, if you have money, I cannot trust you not to go and buy more drugs. Turn out your pockets and hand it over. And strip to your underwear. I don't want you hiding money anywhere. Now try and get some sleep." There was a pause.

Liam handed over the money, it was considerably more than he had said, probably around £25K. Annie hid it in a cupboard.

"On the floor, you need to get used to it," she said, somewhat harshly.

Liam lay down on the rug in the bedroom, shut his eyes and tried to sleep.

Annie turned on her laptop and opened her VPN. She would have to tell Liam to subscribe to a VPN if he was going to use the internet because she really did not want his location being tracked by anyone. She couldn't trust him not to look for drugs and any shopping he did online would be unsafe if it were unencrypted. Annie was using the VPN to look up the consequences of going cold turkey from heroin, to give herself some idea of the likely time-course and the problems that Liam might face.

Despite her hostile attitude towards him this evening, Annie was trying to help him and she did hope that he would succeed in reconstructing a life, even though she was certain that it was going to be a life that did not include her. She felt she owed him something for those great years they had had, first as friends and then as lovers, although it was sometimes difficult to think back to the good times when the bad times were as bad as they had now become.

The received wisdom was that the worst of the physical withdrawal would be over in 4 or 5 days and then the psychological battle would begin. He might get very dehydrated, he might get very bad diarrhoea, he might even have seizures and, she hoped it would not happen, he might even have a heart attack. She was determined that she was not going to be there to see it. Her intention was to have minimal contact with Liam from the time she shoved him into her uncle's polytunnel and the time that he, under his own steam, sneaked back to the house and told her he was ready for the next stage.

From what she had heard, the people on the allotment were all using it as a recreational outlet during the lockdown, so the place was about as busy as Clapham Junction. She might have to arrange to go down there and, under the pretext of watering things, refill his water containers and drop off more food, but she was not going to spend time with him. Little contact meant less chance for a slip up. And, with that thought, Annie too shut down her computer for the night, turned out the light and drifted off to sleep.

Chapter 7

Meanwhile, Moira was worried. The more she thought about the contact with Liam and selling him the last of her own stash of heroin the more certain she became that he had indeed been the one who stole the money from the Boxing Club. She had asked him, casually, if he had ever been a member of the club and he said he had. She had asked him why he had come back to the City and he had told her about Frank at the University and how he was scared witless.

She, in turn, had told him that the two guys who had snatched her from the street and questioned her had said they were going to find the little rat and kill him. The boy had turned an even greyer shade of pale. Moira had told him that she had no more H, that she herself was in rehab and that she was trying to keep out of trouble and that he must not contact her again and he had promised her that he would leave her alone. He had said something to her about going away to hide and that he was, at this moment, in a safe place with a friend, but he was no more specific than that and she really did not want to know.

Moira's own fear came from the realisation that the gang would almost certainly find out that Liam had been seen at the leisure centre and they might put two and two together and think that she had supplied him and that she knew where he was. She did not sleep a wink that night for worrying about it and what might happen to her and Millie if the gang knew she had seen the boy.

Chapter 8

Annie's haptic alarm went off at 5am on the Sunday morning. This was a good hour earlier than she was used to, but, before going off to the Newsagent's she had things to do. The Sunday shift started at 7:30, a whole hour later than the Saturday one, but she knew she was still going to be short of time. She shoved Liam with her foot and, when he didn't wake up, she pinched his ear. Liam woke with a start and was about to swear rather loudly when, fortunately, he realised where he was and choked off the cry before it came out.

"Get dressed fast and get outside the house as quickly as you can. Put the mask on as soon as you get outside and head for the Wolfson Road Allotments. There's a load of garages in Wolfson Road. Wait there for me," said Annie, quietly, but in a tone that brooked no argument.

Liam did as he was told, dressed and climbed out of the window and off towards the allotments. Fifteen minutes later Annie joined him with two cups of instant coffee in reusable travel mugs, a couple of slightly stale croissants in a paper bag, left over from the Friday delivery, and a big bottle of mineral water. She also carried a blanket in her rucksack, which she gave to Liam to carry, along with his coffee.

"Come on," she said, "it's a good ten-minute walk to Uncle Willy's allotment from here and we need to be there before people start moving around too much. Besides which I need to get back, get back into bed and pretend I have never left. Mum always brings me a coffee on a Sunday morning at about quarter to seven."

They were well into summer so the morning was very light already and Annie could feel the sun getting warm even at this early hour.

They almost ran to the allotment. Annie unlocked the gate to the site with the combination that Uncle Willy had given her. He gave it to her so that the family could collect fresh salad and veg from the allotment at times when Willy had a glut, which was almost all the time. Willy liked growing things and, with just himself and June now at home, he really had not adjusted his planting and his harvest to a smaller customer base!

There were quite a few people there already, mostly watering early so that the water could soak into the ground before the sun came out to evaporate it.

"Right, you," said Annie, the anxiety and hostility it engendered was never far beneath the surface. "This is your home for the next ten days, at least." She opened the door to the polytunnel and they stepped in.

The late autumn had been very wet and from December to mid-February had been freezing. Not quite the winter of 1963, that those of her grandfather's generation had talked about, but, nevertheless, an incentive not to go and work on an allotment, which was exposed to the winds and had little shelter at the best of times. When the cold stopped the rain began and so things like the polytunnel had been a bit neglected. Just as Uncle Willy might have started back at the allotment, the COVID restrictions came in and he ended up shielding. The inside of the polytunnel remained quite a mess.

The floor was covered entirely in that black cloth ground cover that is porous to the rain but keeps out the light to suppress weeds. It was a bit uneven, but at least it was mud free. All around the sides of the structure were last year's growbags, still with the dead stems of the peppers and tomatoes that had flourished there through last summer and early autumn. In the centre of the tunnel was some cheap staging with various pots, bags of vermiculite, tomato fertiliser and other greenhouse essentials. There were also some packets of seeds in a plastic box.

They cleared the staging and the gardening items to one side, the side away from the allotment store and toilet. By piling these things up against the wall of the polytunnel they were creating a silhouette which would mask the presence of someone sitting or lying on the floor. The large water butts in the polytunnel, there were two of them, would also add to the silhouette. Annie thought this would leave plenty of room on the floor for Liam to lie down and, also, some space for him to move around.

Willy's plot was a corner plot, just inside the entrance gates and was bounded by hedge at the back and the allotment store on the other edge, so that light did not easily shine through and reveal, in outline, the contents of the tunnel. It also helped that this was one of those cheap green tunnels, which are much less translucent than the proper polytunnels, so, with the artificially constructed "skyline" it was unlikely that a casual observer would see Liam if he were to stand and move about, but Annie warned him to try to keep low to the ground during the day time.

The water butts usually stood on a plinth so that watering cans could be filled from the tap at the bottom of the butt. There was no water in the butts at the moment so Annie lifted one of the butts off its plinth and the plinth offered Liam a makeshift seat so that he could sit and eat his croissant, drink his coffee and try to relax a little. It was obvious that boredom, once the agony of the cold turkey had eased, would be an issue. Annie put her mind to thinking about how that problem too might be mitigated.

"I'm going now. Don't leave the tunnel. If you need a crap or a pee, there is a bucket there and you can empty it after dark onto the compost heap. You can use Willy's kitchen roll to wipe yourself if you need to. Don't make a sound. I will not be back until six tonight because I am going to have to get your stuff in my lunch hour and I won't have time to get back here. I'm off." Annie stepped outside, turned and shut the door.

It was a close-run thing, the run home. In fact, when she climbed in through the window, coming through the door would have been far too risky, she could hear her mother moving around in the kitchen and she had only just managed to take off her jacket and blouse, she hadn't bothered with a bra', slip her nightie over her head, kick off her shoes and jump, fully clothed from the waist down, under the duvet, before Sarah came in with a cup of coffee.

Annie sat up in bed and stretched and gave a yawn.

"Here you are, sleepyhead," said Sarah. "You need to wake up if you are going to get to work on time."

"Thanks Mum. I'll be alright. Don't start until 7:30 on Sunday and old Stops has done most of the papers by then. Anyway, most of the kids, except Simon, of course, are late on Sunday so we always have a bit more time to make up the rounds."

The inconsequential chit-chat lifted Annie's mood a bit. It was good to know that life, ordinary life, was still going on in parallel with all this other stuff she was having to deal with. She just hoped that, when this was all over and she had got Liam to a place of safety, she could also get back to normal and pursue the career she had always hoped for.

On a Sunday, Simon and Annie would usually walk to the shop together since both had the same start time but, on this occasion, Annie wheeled her bike. She explained to Simon that she needed to get a few things from the supermarket in the lunch hour and, as she had so little time, she would need her bike. Simon offered to get the things for her, but she explained that they were personal things and she would be much too embarrassed to give him a shopping list. So off they went.

Chapter 9

The Sunday morning was much as usual, although Annie had a moment of panic when a rather fat gentleman, whom she did not know, came into the shop, ' could it be Fat Freddie?', but what was clearly his wife followed him in a couple of minutes later and called him Harold, so the panic subsided.

The lunch hour was a nightmare. She pedalled as fast as she could to the supermarket. It was one of those megastore supermarkets that you find every now and again, selling everything from clothing and food items to leisure items, games equipment, electronics, kitchen appliances and, thank goodness, camping gear. Annie went to the outdoor section and bought a sleeping bag, a winter quality one, a small gas camping stove and a spare gas cartridge, some matches, an old fashioned billy can set, a knife fork and spoon set, a camping knife, which included a can opener, and an enamel mug and plate; she also bought him an inflatable pillow and one of those roll out mattresses that separate you and your aching bones from the worst lumps and bumps in the ground.

She went to the men's clothing section and got a packet of underpants, in what she estimated to be Liam's size. She went to the bedroom section and bought a spare blanket and she somehow crammed it all into her basket and panniers and got back to the shop in plenty of time to grab a coffee and a Kit-Kat. Annie was a bit worried that she might see Simon on the way back to the shop with all those items, he was sharp enough to know that they were not 'personal things' and she did not have a ready explanation for her purchases, but fortunately he was slumped in front of his computer watching MasterChef re-runs on catch-up.

Meanwhile at the allotment, Liam was, indeed, bored out of his mind and the beginnings of a need for a further fix were making it hard for him to rest. The space he was in was only three metres by five metres and, if he paced up and down anymore, he was going to wear a hole in the floor cover. He thought about clearing the growbags, to pass the time away, but Annie had impressed upon him the need to disturb as little as possible so not to draw attention now and not to give indication afterward that he had been there. He drank most of the water and was getting desperately thirsty by the time Annie returned.

Annie's shift on a Sunday also finished an hour later than on the Saturday so it was not until 6:30pm that she went back out to her bike. It was, of course, still light, this being late spring, and the clocks having gone forward to British Summertime. The takeaway at the end of the road was open so she picked up a 2-litre bottle of Coca-Cola and a portion of chips and headed back to the allotment.

"Hello Annie." It was one of the allotment holders, a friend of Uncle Willy, whose name she had never really bothered to remember, who recognised her as she approached Willy's tunnel.

"Haven't seen you for ages. How are you keeping? You come down to sort Willy's scruffy mess out for him?"

The banter was friendly enough, but she could have done without it. She had things to do and she needed to get home as quickly as she could too. She explained to the guy that Willy and June were shielding because of June's treatment and that she was just coming down to check that all was well with the plot. He seemed quite happy with the explanation and he got back on with his own tidying chores, leaving Annie to go about her business.

She parked her bike against the wall of the allotment store and began to take the items, one by one, into the polytunnel through the entrance at the rear.

It was obvious that the issues of withdrawal were beginning to creep in. Liam looked very agitated and began to talk animatedly and semi-coherently to her. He was full of questions and almost beginning to ramble. He devoured the chips, gulped down some of the Coca-Cola and then doubled up in pain. The stomach cramps were beginning to come back. The speed with which the symptoms were appearing suggested to Annie that Liam's habit was even worse than she had thought and she began to toy with the idea of making him approach the Hospital for rehab help, but the conversation that she had had last night, about Moira and the death threats, told her that to do so would be, for Liam, a death sentence. She was sure they would get him, one way or another.

There was no point in lingering, the others on the site would become suspicious if she stayed too long and they might even come and look in. Allotment holders tend to be friendly and helpful and like chatting to each other and friendly, helpful and chatty were at the bottom of Annie's wish list for the moment.

Annie went and filled the water bottle from the allotment tap. It was clean water coming straight from the mains. She also filled Liam's cup and the travel mug with fresh clean water and she left him a couple of extra Kit-Kats she had bought earlier during her shift. It was the best she could do.

"Liam, listen carefully and if you want to stay alive, just do it. I will have a bit more chance to get here tomorrow because I only have on-line lessons and not many of them. I am not going to stay at any stage, but I will come and top up your water, so you stay in this tunnel and you do not go out at all. I wish I could lock you in, but I can't. There's a bed roll mattress thing, there's a sleeping bag and if you want a hot drink you can use the stove but be careful when you light the match that you don't do it when it's dark because it might be seen through the wall.

"I can't pretend this is going to be easy, but you don't have a choice. If you want to live you have to do it. I am sorry. I have to go now."

Annie looked back this time as she shut the door and she began to feel pity. It was not just pity for Liam, sitting there, clutching his stomach and looking so very lost, it was for every poor kid who had lost their way and gone down this route, for every adult who had lost a child to these fucking shits who dealt in drugs. It was a turning point in Annie's thinking. It was the point at which she became totally committed to making this work. It was no longer just about Liam; it was about Annie too. She needed to prove to herself that human decency could support the frail and vulnerable against those who would exploit them.

Chapter 10

DI Gregory was sitting at home quietly in his front room late that Sunday evening when the telephone rang. It was the one he used to receive the pre-programmed calls from his various informers throughout the City. On this occasion, it was Moira who wanted to talk.

"Jerry," she said, "we need to talk. Can we meet as soon as possible? I have some stuff to tell you about that boy I told you about and I think it might help you."

Jerry was a bit reluctant to go out at this late hour, when he had only just come home and put his feet up, and he did not detect any urgency in her tone, so he asked her outright how urgently they needed to meet.

"I suppose it will keep until tomorrow," she said. "Can we meet tomorrow night after it gets dark. Around 9 o'clock?"

Jerry agreed.

"OK. See you then," said Moira and she ended the call.

A few minutes later, Moira's landline rang and she recognised the number as being the one that the drug cartel used to contact her. It is an understatement to say that she was scared, but she answered anyway.

"Moira," said the voice, "we need to talk. We think you are holding out on us. I'm a bit disappointed in you. You remember that lad you told us about? A little bird told us that you met someone recently and sold him some drugs. We would like to hear all about it. How about you meet us tomorrow evening. Remember where we picked you up before? Be there, 7:30, and don't tell anyone. We might have something for you, if you play nicely and tell us what we need to know."

The voice didn't bother to wait for an answer, he obviously knew that she would do as requested because she knew what might happen if she didn't.

Moira went and sat down in the front room. She picked up the phone and called her Mum, it was so nice to be back on terms with Mum and Dad, especially after all the grief she had given them.

"Mum," said Moira, "I've got a couple of errands to run tomorrow night after work and I was wondering if you or Dad could come and babysit Millie for me? I shouldn't be late. No later than ten anyway."

Moira's Mum jumped at the chance. Moira was their only daughter and they had given up any hope of grandchildren when Moira had so completely gone off the rails and they were now totally besotted with little Millie. It didn't matter that the father was unknown and could have been any one of the useless layabouts that Moira had gone out with, well, any one of the useless white layabouts, because Millie was pale-skinned and blue-eyed, like Moira herself. Millie was Moira's child and, therefore, she belonged to them absolutely. She was too young for them to spoil her, but they loved her, both for herself and for the fact that she seemed to have given Moira a new purpose in life and a real chance of turning her life back around.

Moira wasn't comfortable about meeting these people, not after the threats from the last time they met, but she knew she had no choice.

Chapter 11

Back at number 42, the evening passed pleasantly enough. Annie had been late getting home but she had covered her hands in grease and claimed that her chain had kept coming off and it had delayed her. Simon snorted about it and teased her quite a bit, about being a girl and useless mechanically, but it was good natured and they both knew she was much better at mechanical and electrical things than he was.

Quite a few times during the evening, Annie wondered how Liam was getting on. She knew it was going to get worse and worse for him, but she had no idea how bad it was going to be. She would only find that out later.

She went to bed alone in her bedroom for the first time in a couple of days and, strangely, found that she missed the sound of another human being breathing quietly in the same room. But it was only a passing thing and she soon fell asleep, tired after a very long and demanding day. She set the alarm very early again, because she wanted to make sure she had delivered anything that Liam needed before too many early risers went down to their plots to water, dig, or weed, or harvest the early crops, such as spinach, for their breakfasts.

The next morning Annie headed off to the allotments, having climbed down the trellis, to check on Liam. He was in a bad state. He was crouched in a corner, sweating and clutching his stomach and quietly rocking backwards and forwards. There was quite a smell in the poly-tunnel and Annie realised that there were some piles of diarrhoea, that had not been cleaned up, on the floor.

It hardly seemed to register with him that she was there, but she noticed that all the water had gone, as had the rest of the Coca-Cola, so she took all the containers, plus another water bottle she had brought from home, rinsed them and refilled them at the tap. Her reading about cold turkey had led her to anticipate some of this, but not really to appreciate how bad it would become, and this was only the start. She had decided that any food with fibre or spice would only go straight through and add to the problems with the diarrhoea and she had read somewhere that rich tea biscuits are good for women with morning sickness, so she had brought a packet of plain biscuits with her, just in case he wanted something to eat, and some other stuff like yoghurt and plain white bread. She had also brought a few cans of food with her in anticipation of the later stages when he might be through the worst and, according to what she had read, might become very hungry.

He showed no signs of being interested in anything at all, except the pain and anguish that the withdrawal was causing him. She wasn't even sure that he was aware of her presence, he was so out of it. She spoke to him, but he ignored her and carried on crouching in the corner. There seemed to be nothing to be done and the most important thing now was to keep his presence there secret, so Annie left as quickly as she had come and got home in time to begin her normal day, having climbed back into her room and, for the second time that morning, having got up and gone about her business.

The day passed uneventfully, with schoolwork and music practice as per her normal Monday schedule. Simon, in year 11, was not back in school, so Annie kept a bit of an eye on him while Sarah worked a normal day shift, 7 until 5. On the day shift during the home-schooling period Sarah always tried to get out of the house without waking the youngsters. She relied on Annie to get Simon up and moving before his online classes, which usually began at 9 am.

Both Annie and Simon finished their work by early afternoon and Simon wanted to go for a walk, so he and Annie put on their light rain jackets, it was June and warm, even if it was raining, and they headed out into the damp afternoon. They chatted away and Simon talked more about his plans for a career and waxed lyrical about some of the dishes he had seen prepared on the Professional version of MasterChef. Annie, meanwhile, kept wondering about Liam.

That evening, they ate a light sort of supper of bread and cheese and celery and salad and Annie announced that she was going for her evening walk. Sometimes Simon would go with her and sometimes Sarah, but fortunately, on this occasion, Sarah was tired from her shift, the weather was a bit damp, and Simon had "done his walk" for the day.

The site was quite deserted when Annie's walk took her past the allotment and she had no hesitation about going straight up to the tunnel and opening the door. The smell of faeces sweat and, this time, vomit was appalling. She almost gagged as she entered the space. Liam was almost unconscious, lying in the corner with some of his own faeces and vomit on his clothes and oblivious to the world around him. She noted that he had drunk some of the water, probably during one of his temporary lucid spells, but the biscuits were untouched and none of the other food had been touched either.

She refilled the water containers and washed out and refilled the travel mug which, somehow, had managed to be contaminated by some of the diarrhoea. Annie could hardly believe that this shrivelled being, huddled up in the corner, lying in its own excrement, was the human being she knew as Liam. But Annie knew that she could not afford, if he were to stay alive, to take him and clean him up at this stage, that would have to come later. For the moment concealment was the only thing that mattered. She did take, out of the packet, one of the pairs of underpants she had bought him, soaked it in water from the cold tap in the allotment lavatory and tried to wipe his face and hands, but that was the best she could do for now.

It was heart-breaking to see, but she hardened herself to it and reminded herself that there would be at least another two days, possibly more, of this awful ordeal for Liam. Neither she, nor he, could afford to weaken now. It was something of a blessing that he seemed to be so fatigued and unaware of everything going on. There might be more danger when he became more aware of his surroundings and the position in which he found himself. It didn't really help that this was summer and the polytunnel got hot.

Annie left the tunnel and closed the door carefully. The smell seemed to follow her and she suddenly realised that she had knelt in some of his faeces and her tights were covered in it. *It is so easy to slip up*, she thought, *I just never realised that being this deceitful would be so hard.*

She nipped behind a hedge and removed her tights and put them carefully in her anorak pocket, making sure that the faeces did not soil the anorak. It would be no problem to rinse the tights in the sink in her bedroom and load the tights and the rest of her clothes in the washing machine when she got home.

Chapter 12

At about the same time as Annie was walking away from the allotments, Moira was making her way down Fendon Road and, just as last time, the Fat guy and the other one stepped out of the bushes and grabbed her, hooded her and bundled her into the back of the car. This time she noted the car and she even noted the number plate before they dropped the hood over her eyes. She was determined to let Jerry know who had kidnapped her and she was confident that he and the rest of the force, would be able to round them up before they could harm her and, especially, before they could harm Millie.

After this lot let her go, she had the meeting fixed up with Jerry and she was going to tell him everything she knew. She needed to tell him that the boy was back in town and that the gang were looking for him, but she could now give him something much more to go on in his hunt for the gang leaders.

This time they did not drive to the warehouse but instead drove to a construction site near the canal. Moira recognised it as one of the places where a lot of junkies hung out. They could sleep under a roof, although it was a roof without walls, and keep dry, even if they were still sleeping rough.

The two kidnappers dragged Moira out of the car and pushed her into the works lift, the open caged lift, for people and goods, that you find on every construction site, once the cranes have gone. Moira was still hooded and she tripped over some bricks that were lying on the floor of the lift, landed hard and cut her knees and her hands, as she put her hands out to protect herself. She had no idea what was happening, except that as the lift began to move, she heard the whirr of the electric engine and felt the upward acceleration.

The lift stopped and she was dragged, knees and hands bleeding and stinging, roughly out onto the roof of the building. Freddie removed the hood. Freddie and Jason Miller, for it was those two again who had seized her, were not wearing masks. Moira, streetwise Moira, knew what this meant. She had seen their faces and that meant she was disposable.

Moira knew she was going to die but she was determined not to go without taking these bastards down with her. She sat down and looked around. The rain had stopped and the sun was going down in a slightly red and orange sky. *Millie will have a beautiful day tomorrow*, she thought, and that thought began to give her peace. She knew Mum and Dad would take Millie as their own and bring her up properly and they were young enough, only in their mid-forties, to be OK parents for a young child.

And having settled in her mind the important matters of her legacy, she began to concentrate on how she could get these bastards, even after they got her. She put her hands in her pocket, ostensibly to take out a handkerchief but what she did was press call twice, she knew that would dial the last number that had called her. She hoped it would be answered and the person would listen, or it would go through to voice mail and record the first few minutes of what she had to say.

She blew her nose and stood up and said very loudly, "Why did you bring me here in the grey Merc of yours. Is that a personalised number plate FOS 69?"

Freddie hit her, hard.

"You just shut up and listen. If you tell us what we need to know we will take you back home and you can forget all about us. If you don't then we are going to take out not just you, it will be that baby of yours and your Mum and Dad. Got it?"

"Where did you meet that boy?"

She told them.

"How did he get in touch with you?"

"He called me on a landline from a phone box. He always had my number from when he used to work for you," she lied.

"I don't believe you, darling. He called you on a mobile, didn't he? Hand over your mobile, NOW!" Freddie raised his voice and was clearly very determined.

Moira thought quickly; if she gave Freddie her real mobile, they would know what she had done and take steps to deal with it. There was no way she was going to do that. What if she gave them the disposable one that she used to contact Jerry? What was the worst that could happen? They could dial Jerry and that wouldn't be good for them. She just had to hope they wouldn't work out that it had no directory and only one call on it before they did whatever they were going to do to her. Perhaps, with luck, they would never find the real phone.

64

Moira reached into her coat pocket and pulled out the mobile and handed it over.

"Thank you, darling," said Freddie. "Now, where is he? What arrangements have you made to keep him supplied? Come on, when are you meeting him again?"

For Moira, this bit was easy because it was all truth.

"After I left him at the leisure centre I called him and I told him you were after him and he needed to disappear. He didn't tell me he had nicked your money, but it was obvious he had. I told him that I had given him the last of my personal stash and that there was no more where that came from and I told him never to contact me again and that's the truth."

"In what direction did he go when he left you?"

"He let himself into the leisure centre at the back. Told me he was off to steal some clothes 'cos he was going into hiding. I think he knows you guys are after him. He did say he had seen someone he called Bruno at his Uni and it had spooked him and he had run. I don't have any idea where he is now."

Freddie looked at Jason Miller.

"I reckon she is telling the truth, don't you, Jason?"

"Yea!" said Jason.

"But you have seen our faces, darling. We can do this easy or hard," said Freddie. "Either way you are going to end up dead. Would you like one last trip? Roll up your sleeve. Well, look Jason, little darling has almost gotten clean. Lovely veins."

Tears began to form in Moira's eyes as she realised that this was going to be the end. All those dreams for her and little Millie, the return to study, all the effort it had taken to get clean, it was all going to come to nothing.

She felt the needle going in, she felt the familiar rush as the drug hit her nervous system and then, all too soon, she blacked out.

Freddie and Jason had not overdone the dose, they knew that addicts off heroin had lost their tolerance and they needed much lower doses than at the height of their addiction. They wanted this to look like a genuine mistake.

They didn't wait for her to die, as soon as Moira was unconscious, they picked her up, dragged her to the edge and threw her off the roof. They left the needle and the tourniquet and all the other drug paraphernalia on the edge of the roof and they walked back to the lift and took it down to the ground floor.

Back in the car, Freddie and Jason agreed that this had been a waste of effort. They were no nearer finding the kid. The only thing they had done was to confirm that it was the kid who had taken their money, and their resolve to find and kill him became even stronger. They both regretted having let Moira see their faces. The death had been unnecessary and it was certainly going to bring some heat down on them, unless the police bought the idea of the overdose and the accident. The pair of them thought that highly unlikely.

Jerry Gregory went to the rendezvous. He sat and waited and nothing happened. Jerry dialled the number of the disposable mobile he had given to Moira and a male voice, with a local accent, answered. Jerry hung up. He began to worry for Moira's safety. Who was it that had answered? Why had someone else got Moira's phone. Jerry went out carefully as usual, back to the car parked in the bus lay-by on the London Road.

He started the car and began to drive around, looking in all the usual places that he might have found Moira, in the days when she was still on drugs. She was nowhere to be seen. He drove to Moira's house. He rang the bell. Moira's mother answered, holding baby Millie on one arm. It was just after 10 o'clock.

"Mrs MacDonald," said Jerry, "have you seen Moira? She was supposed to meet me about an hour ago and she never turned up and she isn't in any of the usual places she used to hang around in."

"Oh!" said Moira's mum. "She went out at about 7:30. Told us she would be back around 10, she said she had a couple of errands to run so I suppose you were one of them. Perhaps she got a bit delayed?"

"I don't want to worry you unnecessarily," said Jerry. "But I don't think she would have missed her meeting with me, she was the one who set it up. Any idea where she might be? I rang her number and a man answered, does she have a boyfriend?"

"No idea where she is and she doesn't have a boyfriend. She has only ever thought about the baby since about three months before the baby was born; no drugs, no drink, clean living, I think. The doctor said she must have been off the drugs for a good while before Millie was born, because Millie showed no signs of drug withdrawal and, from what he said, the babies of heroin users come out addicted and get into all sorts of trouble in the first few weeks."

What Mrs MacDonald was saying fitted in perfectly with Jerry's understanding of Moira's situation. He knew she was still dealing, in a minor way, but he also knew that she had stopped using the stuff herself and he was

66

fairly confident that she would stay off it as long as she had Millie and the family support to keep her focussed.

"OK, thanks. I'll leave you in peace then and would you mind giving me a call when she comes home? Millie knows the number but, just in case, it's a local number, 786993. Goodnight and," smiling at the baby, "goodnight, Millie."

And with that, DI Gregory left them, still worried, but knowing that, for the moment, there was nothing he himself could do. He radioed the station from the car and asked them to put out a call to all mobile units and all beat coppers, to watch out for Moira MacDonald and let him know at once if they found her. Then he drove home. He parked up in the drive, opened the front door, walked through to the lounge, poured himself a large scotch and settled down to watch a bit of television while he unwound.

Chapter 13

At number 42, they were also unwinding. No scotch for Annie, the whole family were very modest drinkers, but a large Horlicks, a small chocolate biscuit and an attempt at the Monday Guardian cryptic, which was usually the easiest Guardian Cryptic of the week. And as usual, it soon brought on sleep, much needed after the continuing tensions of the day.

The next morning at 6 am, Annie again climbed out of the window and headed off to see Liam. It did not seem possible, given what she had seen yesterday, but, if anything, he was in a worse state. How could there be any more excrement? He must have emptied his guts completely by now and he had not been eating. But more excrement there was and he was even more mired in it.

He was still almost completely out of it, but he did seem briefly to recover his awareness of the surroundings enough to recognise her, even if only for a moment and then he went back to the disturbing rocking motion crouched on the makeshift seat they had created when he first got there. Liam seemed to have drunk a bit more water overnight and he might even have had a couple of the rich tea biscuits, but the rest of the available food had had no interest for him.

At least he is still alive, thought Annie and she did her usual water run, got a bucket of warm water from the allotment lavatory, with the gas water heater over the basin, rinsed out the underpants she was using as a face cloth and cleaned him up as best she could. This time she was extra careful not to kneel in any faeces; changing tights or washing items of clothing every morning was a nuisance, and not something she normally did, and it might just attract attention at home.

Back home, into bed, get up again and start the day. Annie had no idea how many days she might be doing this but, with no option if she wanted to help keep Liam alive, do it she would.

******

DI Jerry Gregory left for the office at about 6:30am. On his way in, he was a bit surprised to see a petite young lady coming out of the allotment site on Wolfson Road. He guessed she had been running an errand for Grandpa or something like that. She waited for his car to go past, it was an unmarked car; there was no particular reason why she would have noticed Jerry and she jogged off gently in the direction of Manor Road.

At the station, Jerry's day began with the paperwork. Every policeman hates the paperwork, but it must be done. The police, just like the medical profession, need to document activities to a highly professional standard. Medical and criminal cases have in common that everyone needs to be able to follow the thread of detection. Both policemen and doctors take histories and that forms the bedrock of their analysis. Both policemen and doctors explore the case, patient or crime scene for physical evidence and subject those physical findings to scientific analysis. Both policemen and doctors rely on experience, their own and that of others, to consider most likely solutions in their quest for a diagnosis.

In both these professions the written record allows both the investigators themselves and others whom they may consult, to try to come to a logical and, hopefully, correct conclusion. Although hating the paperwork Jerry had no desire to skimp it and he was just putting some notes, about Sunday's conversation with Moira, into the meticulous file he kept on her, when the phone on his desk rang.

"DI Gregory," he said.

"Jerry, that request we got from you to look out for Moira MacDonald. Well, we found her. She seems to have taken an overdose and fallen off the top of the hotel they're building down by the Canal. The Crime Scene guys are down there now. You want to come and have a look?"

Jerry jumped to his feet and went out into the corridor to meet his Detective Sergeant. DS Steve Bronowski had been seconded to the Serious Crimes Squad, under Jerry Gregory, at Jerry's request. Steve was a good detective, thorough and professionally sound but also, and this mattered to Jerry, intuitive. He seemed to know where to look, for clues or crooks, without having to have it spelt out for him.

"You bet I want to come and look. I was due to meet her last night and she didn't turn up and, when I rang the phone we use to communicate with each other, a man answered. I don't believe she took an overdose. She has been clean for more than nine months now. She was dealing a bit, just to make money until she got a proper job, at least that's what she said, but she wasn't using. She told me that herself and her mum confirmed it again last night. She's got this new baby, Millie, and she absolutely adores the kid and she had plans. No, this is not an overdose. Let's go."

They blue-lighted it to the hotel site and when they arrived there were other police cars and ambulances already attending. Jerry walked over to the body; it lay, crumpled and badly smashed up, on the rubble and rough surfaces of the site. He looked up. It seemed a long way down and no wonder there was all this blood and brains everywhere. It seemed that Moira had landed headfirst and her skull had split open dramatically. The drop must have been about 40 metres and she would have hit the ground at about 60 miles an hour and all the kinetic energy of her body was focussed on the sharp edge of the brick where her head had first hit. Poor, poor, Moira.

"Let's go up and see where she fell from," said Jerry. So, the site foreman took them over to the electric hoist and up they went.

"There some blood on the floor of this lift," said Jerry. "Do you swab the lift's down after work every day?"

The foreman confirmed that the lift floor was cleaned out every night.

"Let's see if this is Moira's blood," said Jerry. "If it is then the circumstances are even more suspicious."

He was thinking that if it did match it would be more evidence that Moira had been hurt before going up to the roof and therefore further evidence that this was murder.

The rooftop scene was just as the two thugs had left it. The rubber tubing used as a tourniquet, the syringe and needle lying next to it, right near the edge of the roof. It would have been easy to draw the conclusions that Freddie and Jason wanted them to, if it hadn't been for the circumstances that Jerry knew so much about and the blood on the floor of the lift. He started to look for other signs that this might be a murder scene rather than a suicide or accidental overdose.

The angle of the morning light on the roof helped because it showed scuff marks, presumably where Freddie and Jason had dragged the body to the edge before throwing it over. The rain overnight had washed away any chance of finding footprints outside on the roof and there was no access from the building to the roof other than the electric hoist and several people had been in and out of that hoist already.

The crime scene guys came and bagged up the syringe and the other bits and pieces. They also took samples of blood from the lift floor.

There was nothing else to be gained by staying there so Jerry and his Sergeant went back down.

"I'm sure the tox report will show she has an overdose of heroin," said Jerry. "I am also sure that she didn't give it to herself. It wouldn't surprise me if we found traces of roofing material on the heels of her shoes, where they dragged her, and it wouldn't surprise me if we found no fingerprints at all on the syringe or the tourniquet, and then you can tell me what junkie suicide injects themselves and then wipes clean the syringe and tourniquet.

"I know this was not an accident, it was murder and I don't know why she was killed. I need to look at my notes and talk to her family and see if there is anything we can dredge up. The fact she was killed with an overdose suggests it might be those elusive bastards behind the drug scene in this city. Maybe, if we solve this murder, we can get to them?"

The two detectives went back to the office. The post-mortem was fixed for noon that day. The pathologist on the scene had said that the likely time of death was about ten to twelve hours before the body was found, although the timing was tricky to determine, because the night had been unseasonably cold and there had been a lot of rain, which would tend to cool the body rather more quickly than normal.

Jerry knew she was alive at 7:30, because that was when she had handed Millie over to her parents. He just had to assume that she had gone out to meet someone, planning to come along at 9:00 to their rendezvous. It was odds on that the person, or persons, she met at the earlier time had had something to do with the murder.

DI Gregory read his way through the morning reports on his desk. One observation report, in particular, caught Jerry's attention and that was the one from the leisure centre in Carson Road.

The report on the leisure centre said that a couple of days ago, on the Saturday, Moira had gone to the centre and, shortly afterwards, a lad who used to work at the centre had met her there. The lad was scruffy, dirty shoes, torn jeans, dirty jacket, when he arrived, but he went into the centre by the back door, he seemed to have a key and he came out, about twenty minutes later, wearing an odd assortment of clothes, almost as if he had borrowed them from a scarecrow. He was shaking and sweating when he went in.

By the time he came out twenty minutes later, all that had changed. The observers thought it obvious that he had scored. Moira had handed something over to the youth and then gone off in the direction of her home. The report was significant because this was the first time that anyone had seen the lad for about nine months, since he had stopped working there. Nobody had seen him anywhere in the city, he seemed to have vanished off the face of the earth. And here he was. He had met with Moira and the next thing you know Moira is dead. Jerry thought that to be too much of a coincidence. He needed to find out who the boy was, where he had been for nine months, and what his business with Moira had been.

The constables left at the scene had tried to identify other addicts who might have seen something but it appeared that, for once, no one had been at the construction site. A local businessman, a guy who ran a chain of takeaways, had been handing out free dinners in the market square, and all the homeless had been there from 7pm until after dark. Help from that direction was not going to happen.

Several more reports, several cups of coffee, and half a packet of cigarettes later Jerry put down his pen, switched off the computer and headed down to the morgue. Moira's belongings were laid out on the table just inside the door. There was a purse containing some money, a fifty-pound note, a fiver and some change. It also contained her credit card, a debit card, a Tesco Club Card, a card with the address of her GP and an appointment card for her next clinic appointment with Millie. Nothing much else of note.

There was a set of keys, presumably to her house. Her handbag also contained some lipstick, some sticking plasters and a pair of nail scissors, two small bottles of hand sanitiser and a spare cloth face mask, a small pack of tissues and some wet wipes, a couple of tampons and an applicator, a packet of tic-tac mints, some safety pins, a pen with the end well chewed, a roll-on deodorant and a tiny bottle of hand cream. There was no sign of any drug paraphernalia and Jerry thought this would be what any young mother might carry in her handbag. It was not an expensive bag, but it looked neat enough and quite functional.

There was also a mobile phone. It was completely discharged, the battery dead.

"Get that phone charged up quickly," said Jerry. "We need to see who she has been in touch with and we need the number and we need her phone records, so get onto it, fast."

Post-mortems are not the easiest of things to attend and Jerry felt desperately sad for Moira. Over the eighteen months or so he had worked with her she had been a reliable source of information, that was one thing, but he had also seen a young woman who was on the verge of completely destroying her life turn things around. He had seen her go into rehab at the St Katherine's Clinic, he had seen her make it through and get clean and he had seen her love for her baby and the incentive it had given her to plan for the future. She did not deserve this and he was going to solve the murder and bring her killers to justice if it killed him in the process.

A thought came to him as he watched the pathologist take the circular saw and remove what was left of the top of the cranium to look carefully at the brain and the damage it had sustained.

"Steve," he called the Sergeant over, "nip down to the leisure centre and get the name and address of that boy who used to work there and see if you can find out where he has been for the past few months and why he has come back now? Someone must know what he has been up to and I guess his family, if we can find it, is as good a place as any to start."

The post-mortem continued but it did not really hold any surprises. All the evidence pointed to Moira being alive when she had been thrown off the roof, although she almost certainly was unconscious. The internal bleeding was extensive, too extensive to be simply post-mortem bleeding, she would have bled out into her abdomen and onto the ground after the impact with the ground. The toxicology levels would have to wait for the lab analysis.

Despite three or four years of hard drug use in her past, the basic condition of Moira's organs systems had remained surprisingly good. She was still breastfeeding at the time of her death and prior to her murder, her body was well hydrated and well nourished.

"Any more accuracy about time of death?" asked Jerry.

"I am pretty sure it was before 9 pm," said the pathologist.

"OK. Thanks. If you get anything else, contact me right away and please let me have all the lab work-ups as soon as you can."

And Jerry went back up to the main building to think and await any further information. He was quite sure that something about that boy held the answer to this mystery, not that he thought the boy had murdered Moira, but he was certainly involved.

Freddie and the gang were well ahead of the police in identifying Liam. They had, after all, employed him as a courier for about a year and they knew his name and where he lived and they had tried to find him in Loughborough less than a week ago.

"Get yourself around there, Bruno, and just have a look for the moment. The family isn't going anywhere and we need to work out how to get where he is now out of them."

Freddie was going to be a little patient, the boy couldn't have spent all that cash yet, if it was he who had taken it, it was only nicked a month ago and Freddie reckoned that the boy would have no idea about how to launder it and make it useful. It took inside knowledge and contacts to shift that sort of money and Freddie was certain that the boy had neither the knowledge nor the contacts. It had taken the gang long enough to set up the chain which meant that, when they all eventually retired, they could head off to the Costa Del Crooks and live out their days in absolute luxury. It was a serious amount of money but the drugs and prostitution rackets were still raking in the cash and no one outside the top circle, now that the woman was dead, knew how much was missing, or that the enterprise had been hijacked.

Bruno left, in Freddie's grey Merc and drove around to the middleclass suburb in which Liam lived. The houses in the part of Manor Road where number 42 was situated were large interwar houses, much modernised and with large front gardens and even bigger back gardens. Bruno drove past number 42, with its clematis and wisteria clad trellis work and had no reason to even realise how close he was to unlocking the mystery of the boy's disappearance. He turned left into Grange Road, the houses were now all detached and rather expensive real estate. He stopped on the opposite side to number 23, the O'Connor house, and watched.

It was early afternoon, a little after 1:30 pm and as he watched he saw three girls, neat, well dressed, happy, lively, aged about 11 to, probably, about 16, leave the front gate and head off towards the recreation ground. They were chatting animatedly and not wearing masks. Bruno reckoned they were going to the Park to exercise, but he decided to follow them, just in case there was any chance they were going to meet their brother.

He parked up in the small parking lot by the tennis courts, got out of his car, put on his mask, no point in taking any risks of being recognised later and there was CCTV focussed on the pavilion, club house and car park. He wandered nonchalantly around for a bit, but, when it became obvious that nothing was going to transpire, he returned to the car and drove off.

Back at Freddie's office, the gang had a conversation. They concluded that any threat to these children at this stage might be counter-productive and would only bring the police down on their heads, so they decided on a more subtle approach. Bruno had seen the youngest girl, Helen, patting a dog and talking to the owner, who was clearly a stranger to the three girls. Bruno had a dog, a rather nice-looking border collie, and they decided to use the dog, Fly, as an icebreaker and get into conversation and try that strategy to get the information they wanted. Bruno's lunch hour tomorrow was planned!

Chapter 14

Annie, meanwhile, was worried about Liam. Despite her resolve to leave him to his own devices, she was aware that the state he was currently in was desperate and she found herself needing to check on him, just for her own peace of mind. She had noticed that Uncle Willy had left some beds unprepared and she would certainly go and do some digging there. That could be an excuse for visiting the site in the early afternoon. With any luck, the nice neighbours would be home having lunch and an afternoon siesta, but, at least, she had an excuse if pressed. She put on a pair of heavy shoes, not quite walking boots, but thick-soled and with a high ankle and got out her bike.

"Where are you going?" said Simon, who had emerged from his bedroom, where he was supposed to have been doing his schoolwork, but, really, had been watching video game play-throughs on You-tube.

"I was just going out for a bike ride," said Annie.

"Can I come with you?"

"Sure."

There was no option, of course. Annie could hardly say to Simon that she was off to see Liam; so far Simon had no idea that Liam had come back to the City, let alone into Annie's life. Annie needed to keep it that way. They went for a bike ride together, up to the national bike trail that ran past the allotments and on down towards the railway station. They spent a good couple of hours out there and the weather was kind to them. The cycle back was a little hard work, the wind, from the south west, was warm but quite strong and they were both quite tired and yet energised when they reached home at about 4:00.

"Teatime," said Simon. "I'll make some scones if you like, but we are out of strawberry jam and cream, so why don't I make the scones and you go and get the jam and some of that nice clotted cream from the shop? You could get Mum's late edition of the Herald if you like, save her going out again later. Mind you, I think she has a date tonight with that consultant bloke, what's his name, Daniel? Did she say Daniel?"

Internally, Annie gasped. She had forgotten about Daniel and the Tuesday date. No way could she have managed to get to see Liam once Sarah was home. She would have to stay in with Simon, that was the deal. Sarah did trust Simon to be in the house alone but was much more comfortable leaving the two of them there together. *She's going to have to get used to it when I go off to University*, thought Annie, but for the moment the status quo was the status quo.

"You know, that is a great idea," said Annie. "I love your scones and I seem to have worked up quite an appetite. I'll just hop on my bike. How long will the scones take?"

"About 15-20 minutes," said Simon, "But I'm a bit sweaty so do you mind if I have a shower first? Shall we say tea will be served at 4:45, madam?" And Simon grinned at her.

"That is a great idea," said Annie. "I can wait until this evening for my shower. I just glow; you sweat like a pig!"

They both laughed, Simon gave Annie a big hug, she kissed him on the forehead, pretended to wipe off the non-existent sweat, put her coat back on and went out.

Annie pedalled furiously to the allotment, nobody was on any site near Uncle Willy's but she noticed footprints on some of the dug ground around the entrance to the polytunnel and she surmised that Liam had been out of the tunnel at some point, probably during the day because, Annie felt sure, she would have noticed any footprints when she sorted out the water this morning, She just hoped he had not been seen.

The smell inside was intensifying. It did not help that the weather had been quite warm because the maximum and minimum thermometer inside the greenhouse was registering 44 degrees. Just for the sake of it she quickly pressed the button to reset and the temperature went straight back to 42.

Liam was a bit more with it. He looked utterly drained, sunken cheeked and hollow eyed. His skin had that dried up look, as if he had had too much sun. His lips were cracked and Annie resolved to bring some lip balm tomorrow, she could get it at the shop on the way home.

"Why did you go out?" she asked.

"Oh Annie!" said Liam. "I was so thirsty. I remembered not to be seen. I looked through the vent panels, to check there was nobody around and when it was clear, I just had to go and fill up the bottles. I am so thirsty. My head hurts, my stomach hurts and I've still got diarrhoea. Look at me, I'm covered in my own crap. Oh my God. I almost want to die, except I don't. I want to see you and Mum and my sisters. I am dying for a fix, but I keep remembering that you told me that, if I try to get drugs, I am signing my own death warrant."

Liam began to cry. He began to sob uncontrollably. His sides heaved and he was taking deep gasps between the bursts of crying. It was heart-breaking.

"Stop it!" ordered Annie. "There is no time for snivelling self-pity now. I'm going to get you some more water, you might try to eat something. You must keep hydrated. This is probably the worst it's going to get for you physically. I reckon you have a couple of more days of this and then it is all going to be about your mindset. How much do you want your life back? That is what it's going to be about."

Annie filled his water containers and added some more, which she had found in Willy's shed when she went to get a fork to dig over the ground lightly and cover up the footprints. It seems that Willy collected old litre drinks bottles to use as mini cloches, to protect young growing plants, or to cut off the bottom and sink them, neck first, in the ground to use as a water funnel to get water to the roots of growing tomato plants. There was a whole bag of these bottles in the shed and Annie washed and filled some of them at the tap.

"I'm leaving you again now," said Annie. "Don't leave the tunnel. The weather is getting better and there are more people down here in the daytime. You got lucky today, but you made a lot of footprints and people are very observant around here, and, if they see footprints coming out of this polytunnel, they are going to be looking out for their neighbours and they are going to come and investigate and you will have had it. No ifs, no buts, just do it. Oh, I've brought you some things to read. I don't suppose you will feel like it, but just in case and in case it helps take your mind off things, here they are." Annie dropped a small pile of detective novels on the floor, said goodbye and left.

She hurried back to the shop. She put on her mask. She purchased the lip-balm, the clotted cream, the extra-fruit strawberry jam and the paper. She threw them in her basket, snatched off her mask and dashed home. The speed she was cycling these days she could probably have entered the Women's Tour De France. As it was, she managed to get there just as Simon was taking the scones out of the oven.

"What kept you?" said Simon. "Did you get another chain slip?"

"No. I bumped into Kim and her mum and we just chatted for a few minutes. I miss people, don't you?"

Annie was aware that there were becoming more and more incongruities, more and more slightly off moments, as she tried to juggle protecting Liam and her normal, comfortable, everyday full existence. It had not occurred to her before how busy her normal life was, how she and Simon and Sarah had managed to, what was it that Kipling said? *Fill the unforgiving minute, with sixty seconds' worth of distance run.*

Simon said something, she didn't quite catch it. She turned and looked at him. His mouth was hanging open and his eyes stared in shock.

"I said, what is Liam's photograph doing on the front page of the Herald?"

The colour drained from Annie's cheeks. She stared at the headline Simon was holding up to her.

"Have you seen this youth?" Immediately below the headline was a picture of Liam and, slightly smaller, a picture of Moira. The sub-heading read, *Wanted in connection with the murder of Moira MacDonald.*

Chapter 15

It had been about 2pm when Steve got back from the leisure centre with the name of the boy, Liam O'Connor. They knew he had been a pupil at Manor Academy and they knew he had gone to Loughborough University. Steve had gone around to the family home, close to the leisure centre and had spoken to Liam's three sisters. They said they had not seen Liam for about six months, he had come home for a few days at Christmas but had mainly sat in his room watching videos and generally being rather moody.

They gave Steve Liam's mobile number and his email addresses, both the University one and the Gmail address he had created for himself when he first got into email, liamoc3103@gmail.com. Steve got the impression that Liam was almost completely estranged from the family and he had asked the girls why they had recently had so little contact with their brother. The youngest one, Helen, told him that they suspected Liam of getting into the drug scene and that this meant he was both ashamed and worried about having too much to do with his sisters. They missed him and they tried to make a fuss of him when he was home briefly at Christmas, but he seemed to be worse than ever and not interested in them or what they were doing or planning to do.

All three sisters appeared genuinely sad about the situation, but somehow reconciled to it. Steve supposed that they saw this going on all around them all the time, it isn't just a working-class thing. Just as on this occasion, addiction doesn't have a defined demographic. They gave Steve a picture of Liam. It was a couple of years old, taken when he was still the poster boy of the school teams, but it was a sufficient likeness and it was all that was available. He put the picture on the desk in front of Jerry and the two of them sat down and decided how to play this.

****

DI Gregory had, while waiting for Steve to come back, gone around again to Moira's house and told the parents the grim news. They had taken it as well as could be expected. Moira's mother sat there, holding tightly to the baby, as if that were the only way she could maintain her sanity and as if that were her remaining hope for the future and Jerry surmised that it probably was. Moira's father went over and sat next to his wife, put his arm around her and cried silently, Jerry could see the tears running down his cheeks.

"It's so tough, Inspector, it just isn't fair. She was a top student at the Manor Academy before she got into drugs. She kicked that awful habit and she was so back on track. She was even going back to study. Me and Madge, we had our lovely daughter back and a granddaughter too and now some bastard has wrecked it. I guess Madge and me, I guess we have a purpose now. I think we are going to be bringing up another daughter. Let's hope we make a better job of it this time. I'm not goin' to take my eye off the ball; I'm not goin' to screw up again. Eh Madge?"

Jerry was deeply moved. These good people. This drug shit happens to good people. But Jerry had a job to do.

"I am so sorry. I really liked Moira and I think you must remember, always, to be proud of what she did for Millie. Not many people, once they are on heroin, can fight their way off it and your daughter did that. I think you can always let Millie know that her mother did that for her."

Jerry couldn't help thinking back, with guilt, to the Sunday evening when he arranged the meeting with Moira for the next day. Would it have made a difference if he had seen her that Sunday night? He knew it would not have done. He might have got more detail on her story, which obviously involved the boy, but whoever killed her would still have made an appointment the next night and would still have done exactly what they did. Moira's story, by itself, did not move the investigation forward very much; it was her murder that moved things on. He brushed the slight feelings of guilt aside.

"Please can you let me have a photograph? It might just jog someone's memory of seeing her with someone or being somewhere on the night she died. And what was her personal phone number please? We have her mobile phone and we need to get the record of her telephone calls from the company."

"Did she have a laptop or a desk top computer?"

She did, apparently.

"I am afraid we will have to take them away and look at them and we will have to come and search her room to see if we can find any hint as to who might have done this."

"That's OK, Inspector. We understand. We are going to go home now if you don't mind. I've written our address and phone numbers on this piece of paper for you. I think we need to let little Millie start to get used to her new home and somehow it hurts more to stay here." And the tears began to roll down his cheeks again. The two parents gave Jerry a set of keys and started to get their things together ready to go home.

Jerry said goodbye to the two of them, looked, with slightly sad eyes, at little Millie, and went back to the car.

****

"Right," said Jerry, "we have the phone and we have the phone number. I sent off to the phone company for the record of the telephone calls and to see if they could give us any idea of location and movement of the phone, especially over the last 24 to 48 hours. The phone is charged so we may be able to save some time if we can get in there and look at her recent call logs? I have also asked for her land line number and we can look at the log of those phone calls too."

They had been so lucky that the phone had survived the impact of the fall.

The pair of them sat and looked at the phone, still attached to the charger, and Jerry pressed the start button. The phone lit up, but it asked for a four-digit pin.

"Bugger," said Steve.

"Try 0803," said Jerry, looking down at the file on Moira, which was open on his desk.

The phone unlocked itself.

"How did you know?" said Steve.

"Little Millie's birthday," said Jerry.

They looked back at the list of recent calls. The two most recent calls were to the same number, it was Liam's number. One had been on the Saturday around 1 pm, it had lasted about three minutes, the other had been at 9.20 pm on the Sunday night and had lasted ten minutes.

"Oh my God," said Jerry. "We need that boy, now. Can we catch the late edition of the Herald?"

It was a rush, but they made it. They impressed upon the editor the urgency and he stopped the presses, reset the front page, and the version that Annie and Simon had seen, with Liam's face all over the front page, had duly been distributed.

****

Annie stood there in a degree of shock, but only for a moment. She pulled herself together quickly and took hold of the paper. What she read made a lot of sense to her, in the context of what Liam had already told her. She knew Liam had not actually killed Moira, he had been lying on the floor convulsed and cramping at about the time the murder was said to have happened. He had not killed her directly, but Annie also realised that his buying of drugs from Moira on that previous Saturday had condemned her to death, as surely as an old fashioned hanging judge wearing a black cap might have condemned a convicted murderer in the days before abolition of the death penalty. *How many more, relatively innocent, might die?* she wondered.

She was sure it was Freddie, Bruno and the others who had ordered or carried out the killing. Her guess was that, as Moira was the last person the gang knew to have seen Liam, they would have been trying to get Liam's whereabouts out of her. It was highly likely that, if they knew she, Annie, was aware of Liam's location, they would come for her and she was not sure that she could hold out, especially if they threatened Simon and Sarah as well.

The story in the paper was uninformative, unless you knew what Annie knew. The police statement was that a well-known drug addict and dealer had been killed at about 9pm on Monday evening by being thrown off the top of the Hotel development on Gloucester Road. It was believed that she had recently been dealing drugs in the vicinity of the leisure centre and that she might have sold drugs to this young man, whom they wanted to interview, as he may have been one of the last to see her alive.

The police did not think this young man to be dangerous, but he might be desperate and the public were advised not to approach him but simply to call the police, immediately, if they had any idea of his whereabouts. There was an incident number to call. There was a small reward for information leading to the arrest and conviction of anyone responsible for this murder. The telephone line would be manned night and day.

"Let me have a look," said Simon. He took the paper and put it on the table and picked up a couple of scones from the cooling rack. He cut them in half, put, first, butter, which melted into them because they were still warm, and then some jam, picking out a couple of nice big strawberries for each of the scones, and, finally, a far too big scoop of what must really have been quadruple clotted Devon cream over the top half, slapped it on the bottom half and sunk his teeth into the resulting huge stack of scone and artery blockers.

"Bloody Hell," he said and a mixture of crumbs, cream and jam and a little butter, began to dribble down his chin. He wiped it off with his finger, which was duly licked.

"Don't swear," said Annie. "And don't talk with your mouth full."

"Oh, come off it, Sis," said Simon. "How often does anyone's sister's ex-boyfriend appear on the front pages of the local paper in connection with a murder? Just wait until everyone at school hears about this. They'll all be getting on to me tonight about it on the chats."

Annie could feel the world closing in on her. Simon was right. No matter how hard she tried, she couldn't hush this up and the gang were going to find out about her sooner or later. They would soon start watching her and, if they followed her to the allotment, they would find Liam and kill him. Even if they did not follow her, they might just find a way to abduct her and question her and she was not sure if she could keep quiet.

The police would be along too, no doubt about it. They would want to question everyone who had known Liam at school, they would contact his friends, if he had made any, at University, but they would soon learn that she and Liam had once been very close and she felt sure they would focus their attentions on her. She had to think of a way to put an end, once and for all, to any idea that she might know where Liam was hiding out, but she could not immediately think of how that might be done. Meanwhile she would need to be even more careful about visiting him in his hideaway. Thank goodness she had until the morning before she needed to see him again.

"Come on Sis, I made those scones specially for you," said Simon.

And although her mouth was dry with fear, Annie took two scones, prepared them with a little more delicacy and restraint than Simon had, and managed to eat them and thank him for his kindness.

****

Back at the police station, DI Gregory and Sergeant Bronowski had just reached the same conclusion as Annie.

"Let's get the picture sent up to Loughborough and get the locals to ask around about Liam and any one he might be friends with. We can do that in the morning first thing and, if they have any promising leads, we can get up there fast and follow them up. I don't reckon the answer is going to be found up there. All the crap hitting the fan seems to be down here, so I reckon it is down here we are going to find our lead, if any." DI Gregory paused.

"OK Jerry," said Sergeant Bronowski. "And I will go and see his family again, in case he has made contact with them and then I will also try to find out about his friends and set up interviews with as many of them as seems sensible. He's quite a nice-looking lad in these photos so he is quite likely to have had a girlfriend, I'll see if I can find out who. I'll also go and talk to the guys at the leisure centre to see if they can give us anything more.

"Oh, and I'll see if they have CCTV and I can pick up anything from them. I reckon there might also be some tapes from the surrounding roads. There are a lot of cameras in that area and there's a drug surveillance camera on the back entrance, so let's get the team on it."

And with the plan of action agreed, they went off to their respective homes.

Sergeant Bronowski's wife was heavily pregnant with their first child, so he stopped at a Stops' Shop on the way home and bought a large bunch of flowers and a box of chocolates. Feeding for two was a serious business.

Inspector Gregory also went home. His wife, Marianne, and his daughter, Audrey, were currently away; Audrey at University where she was studying for a PhD in English, although Jerry thought she was more interested in drama; Marianne, "bubbling" with her parents, who were in their early seventies and were trying to be very careful in the course of this wretched pandemic. Jerry made himself a coffee, poured himself a G and T, stuck an M & S "Count on Us" mac and cheese in the microwave, looked at it, thought *hungry* and stuck a second one in, to keep it company.

He rang his son at University and was rather pleased when, just for once, the young man answered.

"Hey kid, how is it going?" James was one of the proudest things in Jerry's life, the other, perhaps, being his daughter Audrey. How Jerry and his French wife, Marianne, had managed to produce two children who were so academic was a mystery to both Jerry and Marianne. They might have expected beautiful or handsome, Jerry was quite striking in appearance and Marianne was incredibly beautiful, in a very French way. She knew how to wear clothes, she knew how to do her hair, she knew how to use make-up and she was kind and generous, Jerry often thought she was kind almost to a fault. The children had been brought up bi-lingual and Jerry himself was also fluent in French.

"It's strange, Dad," said James. "The students have been sent away and all our teaching has gone online. I spend hours on Zoom. The research in the lab has ground to a halt so I am having to do some work and write up things I had been putting off. I might even start writing up my PhD."

They chatted for a while, maybe ten minutes, neither of them was particularly good on the telephone and they usually dried up and hung up after about ten minutes, but they contacted each other frequently and had a really deep affection for each other, and, much to Jerry's surprise, an obvious respect for the professional skills of the other.

Jerry put the phone down and heaped both portions of mac and cheese on to his plate, poured himself another G and T, he had finished the first during his phone call, and settled down for the evening in front of the Sports Channel.

****

At number 42, the arrival home of Sarah had produced another round of shock and horror. Sarah looked at the front page, read the story and was, just like Simon, shocked. What can you say? She immediately tried to telephone Tara, but the O'Connor family was not answering and the call went straight through to voicemail.

"Tara, I am so sorry to see the news," said Sarah. "If you need to talk, give me a call when you get this. I am so sorry. I can't really imagine what you are going through, but if I can help in any way you know where I am and if you need the girls to come around and be out of the way for a bit just let me know, we have plenty of space. So sorry." And she hung up and turned back to talk to Simon and Annie.

"I am sure the press will get onto the fact that you and he used to be so close," said Sarah. "My strong advice is for you to say as little as possible, in fact nothing at all. And that goes for you too Simon. And don't go talking it over with your friends either. The press can do a lot of mischief with a very little material to work on."

"I never entirely understood why you two broke up and why it was so bitter afterwards. I don't think Tara did either. Do you want to talk about it? Will it help?"

Annie thought about that question for quite a long time and she decided it might be better now to come absolutely clean with Sarah and also make it clear to Simon, now that she was confident he was not going down the same path as Liam. Without being specific they needed to know that this was probably all about drugs and they should watch out for their own safety.

Sarah and Simon sat there in absolute silence while Annie told them about the prom and the drugs and how she had known, from that point on, that Liam was into the drug scene and was involved in dealing. She explained that she had kept quiet, because she felt she owed Liam something and did not want to get him into trouble and she did not want the people she loved carrying information that could be dangerous to them.

She told Simon that she had suspected the parcels he was delivering for Liam on his paper round were actually drugs for some of the customers and that she had actually confronted Liam about it once, but he had denied it. She said that they had had a blazing row, but it had all been in private, so nobody else knew just how angry she had been. She said she decided to put up with the hostility from those who thought she was treating Liam unfairly because she knew he was going off to University and she hoped everything would then be alright.

"I was worried about you, Simon, and I'm sorry if I was a bit hard on you, but I am so glad you were strong enough to stay clear of the real trouble and when Liam went, I was so glad to get my super little brother back."

Simon came over and gave her a hug and continued to hold tightly to her.

"What are we going to do, Mum?" asked Simon.

"Nothing," said Sarah. "Like I said, say as little as you can. Don't obstruct the police but don't give anything to the press and don't gossip with your friends. Have a stock line ready like 'I just don't know what all this is about. Isn't it horrible?' And then stick to it."

They all knew the next few days would be hard but two of them did not really understand just how hard it was going to be. Annie was desperate to tell the other two that the police and press might be the least of their concerns. She had the suspicion that the poor woman who had died had been murdered by the drug gang looking for Liam and the money. But she knew she couldn't tell them any detail without putting their lives in even greater danger. The detail was something she was going to have to take on all alone.

"I think it is a good guess that this is all mixed up with Liam and the drug scene," said Annie. "So I suggest we are all extra careful not to go anywhere where we might be in danger. We all know where the dealers hang out around the City, you would have to be blind not to know. At all times, keep your mobile with you. Simon, put my number on speed dial. I don't want to alarm you and I am sure it will be alright, but it is better to be safe than sorry."

Annie was far from sure it would all be alright.

"Do you think I should phone Daniel and cancel?" said Sarah.

Annie could hear the tone of disappointment in Sarah's voice and she reckoned that there was nothing to be gained by ruining all three of their evenings.

"No Mum, definitely not. I am sure Simon is big enough to look after me, besides which we don't have enough scones and cream left over for you as well as us to have as pudding. When are we going to meet Daniel anyway? Has he got any kids?"

Sarah brightened immediately, promised to introduce them to Daniel at the first opportunity, reported that he had two children, a girl call Jenny, the same age as Simon and a boy called Peter, a year younger than Simon. She then went upstairs to get ready and Annie decided she had to be a little more direct with Simon.

"These drug gangs are dangerous," said Annie. "I don't think either you or I have any idea how dangerous they are. They probably just chucked that poor woman off the top of a building. I think we need to be very careful, for a while. I don't want to have to go down to the mortuary to identify my little brother and I don't want you to have to go down there to identify me. I am a bit worried about Helen, Ruth and Alice. I expect their Mum will have warned them. I wonder if they really knew that Liam was as heavily into the drug scene as he seems to have been?"

At that moment, Sarah came back down and they all commented on how she looked great and the mood lightened considerably. A taxi pulled up outside and Sarah said goodnight to the two of them and went off on her evening date.

The rest of the evening passed uneventfully. With the responsibility of keeping an eye on Simon Annie did not go for an evening walk, and, in fact, she did quite a bit of study for the lessons that she was supposed to have the next day. She had a feeling that both the police and the press might be after them and she did not want to fall behind with her work. That place to read Maths with Physics was very much in her plans.

She lay in bed that night, awake for quite a while, trying to work out how to use an interview with the police and, if it happened, with the press, to get a message to the drug gangs, that she had absolutely no idea where Liam might be, that she had washed her hands of him ages ago and that she never wanted to see him again as long as she lived. The last part of that thought train was beginning to be more and more true.

Chapter 16

The next morning began very early, as was now the regular routine, for Annie. The climb, the jog, the moment of anxiety as she opened the door to the polytunnel. Inside the tunnel Liam was still in a bad way but she thought she could see signs that he was becoming a little more aware of his surroundings and it looked as if he had made an attempt to get himself some food.

The stench was growing ever more offensive and Annie resolved that tomorrow, if the improvement continued, she would bring some clothes, some soap and some shampoo and try to clean him up. The diarrhoea seemed to be getting better and his chapped lips were healing. His eyes looked slightly less sunken and his face, though still pinched in, was not as skeletal as it had been two days ago. The look of bewilderment in his eyes seemed to have changed to a more haunted one; there was fear there, there was desperation.

Annie went through her routine of filling the water bottles. She put down the additional offering of bread and bananas that she had brought from home. She cleaned up as much of the mess as she could without getting herself too dirty, and she again warned him to stay put in the tunnel. The temperature inside the tunnel had not fallen below 30 degrees so Liam would have been losing water all the time. She pressed the reset again on the thermometer.

"Give me your mobile," said Annie. she really did not want him at this stage to start contacting people, but she found that she need not have worried for the battery had run down completely and there was no way he could have called anyone. She took it anyway. She was not clear whether it would still be traceable, even with a dead battery and she was not going to take any chances.

She had brought an old iPad with a kindle app, fully charged, along with her and she handed it to him.

"There are quite a few books on this, but it only has Wi-Fi and you don't have Wi-Fi here," she said. He acknowledged vaguely, but his face suddenly twisted into a grimace and he clasped his stomach. A parting shot of cramps and diarrhoea? It was horrible, it was degrading, he had clearly soiled himself, again.

"I will see you tonight. I really think you are through the worst. I may be a little later because I want to be able to spend the time to clean up both you and this place. I will try to bring you something warm to eat. I reckon you ought to be able to take some hot soup now."

Annie had wondered whether to tell him about the newspaper and about the death of Moira, but she thought he was still far too fragile. It wouldn't make any difference to him anyway. He was hardly going to go and turn himself in. The gang would undoubtedly have a way to reach him, in hospital, or on remand, or simply in temporary police custody, and, when he was released, they would get him. No, she had to come up with a plan to move him away, without detection, and find him somewhere safe to live and re-establish himself, with a new identity, until he and she were sure that the gang was safely behind bars.

Given that they were undoubtedly responsible for the murder and probably a few other deaths too, once they were caught they would receive long sentences and Liam would have a lot of time to make sure that he could disappear below their radar.

But all that was for the future. For the moment, get home, get through the police interview and find out how to change the identity of one desperate human being.

Shortly after Annie reached home, went to bed and got up again for the second time, Sergeant Steve Bronowski called at the O'Connor home and confirmed that none of the women there had received any communication from Liam. Tara had already gone to work at the local hospital. Tara and Sarah both worked there and that was where they had originally met. Bronowski began to ask Liam's sisters about Liam's friends, whether he had mentioned anyone at University in particular, or had spent a lot of time, just before he went off to University, with anyone.

It soon became clear to DS Bronowski that there was no obvious lead there. It looked as if Liam had been a little bit reclusive throughout most of his final year in the sixth form. He seemed to have focussed on his leisure activities, his martial arts and, just a bit, on his study. The girls said that he always seemed to have plenty of money from his job and had been in the habit of buying the latest tech, Apple watch, iPhone, iPad, that sort of thing. Of course, he had taken all these things off to University with him.

Bronowski made a note to tell the guys up in Loughborough to make sure they got hold of the IT stuff when, as they were bound to do, they searched Liam's room at the halls of residence. It also occurred to him that the level of expenditure these girls were talking about would not easily have been sustainable on the minimum wage payments from part time work at the leisure centre.

Everything was pointing towards an involvement of this young man in the drug scene, although he was probably somewhere near the bottom of the food chain.

It might have been left at that except that, in more casual conversation, as Helen, the youngest one, was showing him out of the kitchen, where they had kindly given him a cup of coffee, socially distanced of course, while he talked to them, Bronowski said, in a chatty sort of way:

"Sounds as if your brother has been a bit of a loner then?"

"Only really in the final year at school," said Helen. "Before that, he was almost always with Annie."

"Who is Annie?" said Bronowski, immediately very interested.

"Well, you see, he had this girlfriend Annie, from when he was about 12, I suppose, and I think we all honestly thought they were going to be together forever because they were almost never apart and then something seemed to happen and after Annie went to France on holiday, with her brother and her dad and his new family, Annie came back and that was it.

"Some of the girls said she had found someone else in France, but Alice and Ruth say they don't believe that and I think they are probably right because it was way too sudden and Annie doesn't seem to say anything about a new bloke and Simon, Annie's brother, doesn't believe it either and he told me that there wasn't anyone else in France, just them and the dad's family and some really nice food and wine and scenery and things."

It all came tumbling out in a rush and Bronowski listened patiently and then pounced.

"Do you know this Annie and Simon still? Are they still around?"

"Oh yes. We still go around there. Annie's Mum and our Mum are very close friends and we all like Annie and she is a very good musician and sometimes she goes for a jog with Alice. Mind you we haven't seen Annie for a bit, because of the social distancing and Annie is working hard for her exams, because she has an offer for Maths with Physics at Cambridge. She's really clever and very nice so I wish Liam hadn't bust up with her."

Bronowski thought to himself, *Wish everyone I asked a question was as forthcoming*.

"Have you got Annie's address please and what's her other name?"

"I think it's 42 Manor Road and her other name is Grant, Annie Grant."

"And she is at the Academy?"

"Yes. So is Simon, he's in Ruth's class."

Bronowski thanked Helen, gave her one of his cards and told her that if she or any of the other girls had something to add they shouldn't hesitate to call his number.

Back in the car he radioed the switchboard and asked them to let Jerry know that he was going around to 42 Manor Road to see a girl called Annie Grant who was an ex-girlfriend of Liam O'Connor.

****

Annie was up and in her bedroom working, when Bronowski rang the doorbell. Simon answered the door.

"Sis," he yelled up the stairs, "there's a policeman here wants to talk to you."

Annie put her pen down, she always used a fountain pen for writing or for doing her calculations, paused the lesson video, collected her thoughts and went slowly, apprehensively, but with an outward appearance of composure, down the stairs.

Bronowski looked at the young lady coming down the stairs towards him. It almost took his breath away. *She is beautiful*, he thought. *That lad can't have been very happy for this one to go out of his life*. As she came down, Annie was putting on her face mask. Bronowski had already put his back on before coming into the Grants' house.

"Good morning, Miss Grant," said DS Bronowski. "Thank you for agreeing to talk to me. I am Detective Sergeant Stephen Bronowski and I am investigating the murder of Moira MacDonald. I am sure you will have read about it in the newspapers and as I believe you know Liam O'Connor we wondered if you knew anything which might be able to help us find him. Would you mind if I ask you a few questions?"

Annie smiled at him although he could only see it in her eyes.

"Not at all, Sergeant," said Annie. And Bronowski thought that there was something magical in her voice. He was captivated.

93

"Sergeant," said Annie, "is it warm outside? Because if it is, perhaps we could go and sit in the garden and talk, then we could remove our masks and it might just make things easier all around."

"That's a really good idea, Miss Grant," said Bronowski, anticipating the pleasure of talking, without the encumbrance of a mask, with this incredibly beautiful girl. Police work is sometimes hard, sometimes boring, sometimes routine, sometimes sordid, rarely is it pleasurable and Bronowski jumped at the chance of an interview which would be both informative and aesthetically pleasing.

"Would you like a cup of tea or coffee, Sergeant?" asked Annie.

"Coffee please, black, no sugar," said Bronowski.

"Simon, any chance you could make us both a cup of coffee please?" said Annie.

Simon smiled behind his mask. He had seen so many of Annie's charm offensives. He didn't recall a time when a male recipient of this offensive had been able to resist. He knew exactly what Annie was doing and he thought he knew why but, of course, he did not actually know the half of it.

Annie and the Sergeant went out into the garden. The grass had been recently cut, by Sarah, over the weekend and lots of flowers were in bloom. They sat near a trellis of jasmine and the smell of philadelphus also filled the air. New mown grass and sweet-smelling flowers in warm sunshine is a heady mixture. DS Steve Bronowski was lost in a sensory heaven.

It was possibly that which made it so easy for Annie to convince him that there was no longer any connection between herself and Liam O'Connor. As Simon might have said, she had worked her magic.

DS Bronowski asked the direct question about why, after nearly five years of being inseparable, Annie and Liam had broken up.

Annie had decided that there was nothing to be gained by hiding Liam's involvement with the drug scene. It wasn't as if the drug gang didn't know about it. They had employed him, for goodness sake.

So Annie explained that she had found out about his involvement in drugs when she came back from France, that he had offered her some marijuana and some white powder at the Prom that night and she had simply got up and walked out on him. She explained that she had never, nor would she ever, use or condone the use of these drugs but that, out of a sense of loyalty to Liam, which she now recognised may have been misguided, she had not told anyone and had chosen,

94

instead, to spread the rumour of a new boyfriend in France to explain why they were no longer together. She had hoped it was a passing phase and Liam would move on, but she did not believe that he had.

No, she had not heard anything of him since he went off to University. No, he had not even contacted her at Christmas when he called home for a few days to see his family. No, he had not contacted Simon either, as far as Annie was aware, although, obviously, it would be for the Sergeant to ask Simon himself. Yes, she and her brother were very close and she did feel quite protective of him.

At that moment Simon came out with the coffees and a couple of madeleines that he had made that morning.

DS Bronowski thought he must have died and gone to heaven. At the very least, he must have done something good in his life to have deserved this moment of peace in the middle of an unpleasant murder investigation.

"Do you think Liam is capable of being mixed up in a murder like this? Was he, to your knowledge, ever violent towards you or anyone else?"

Again, the answer was a firm no.

Then with Bronowski thoroughly softened up, Annie began to ask some questions.

Do you think Liam was directly involved in this murder? The police did not. Has he been seen around recently? Yes, he has. Can my name be kept out of the press because I am working so hard for my exams and it would be horrible to have the press crawling all over a relationship that went so sour more than a year ago? We will see what we can do. If you do find him what will happen to him? That depends on what he has to say. We think that he may have bought some drugs from Moira MacDonald over the weekend before she died and that makes him one of the last people to see her. We have no idea what the motive behind her death was. There is a rumour that someone has stolen a lot of money from one of the big gangs around here and Moira's death may have something to do with that, but we really don't know. We just want to know whether Liam saw anyone following Moira or can shed any light on why she might have been killed.

As Sergeant Bronowski spoke, Annie began to breathe a huge sigh of relief internally. *They have no idea where Liam is*, she thought, *and they have no idea that Liam stole the gang's money. They are buying that I have not seen him for almost a year. Now all I have to do is find a way to get him out of here and we could be home and dry.*

Then Bronowski said something that changed Annie's mood again.

"Miss Grant, it is possible that some of the more dangerous members of the drug cartels around here may want to talk to you. I doubt that they will use violence, or even make it obvious who they are and why they are asking you any questions that they ask, but please be a little careful until we have sorted this situation out. We are following several lines of enquiry and we are hopeful of catching the perpetrators and putting them away.

"But, in the meantime, please be careful and, if you think anyone is getting a bit too close to you, or making you feel uncomfortable by their presence, do not hesitate to call us. Here is my card."

And for the second time that morning, Sergeant Bronowski handed out his card to a charming and innocent young lady who, he rather hoped, would not need to use the information printed on it.

Sergeant Bronowski asked Simon to join them and, because of his age, Annie stayed for the interview.

It was about as neutral an interview as Annie's had been and she felt that it established in Sergeant Bronowski's mind that Simon too had had nothing to do with Liam following his departure for Uni. Simon was about to tell Bronowski about the parcel deliveries for Liam during the year before the departure, but Annie caught his eye, shook her head and Simon changed what he was going to say. Whatever it had been going to be came out simply as "I used to see him a bit at the leisure centre and walking around town when I did my paper round."

And that was about the gist of it. Bronowski finished his third madeleine, washed it down with the last of his coffee, went back to Police Headquarters. Simon went back to his GCSE course work. Annie went upstairs, sat on the bed and burst into tears, overcome by relief. Then she pulled herself together, picked up her rather beautiful silver "Cross" fountain pen and began to scribble some of those hieroglyphics that mathematicians understand and the rest of us just look at in bewilderment—STEP 2 and 3 were looming large.

Chapter 17

Back at Police Headquarters, more information was coming in. The trawl of the street CCTV cameras around the hotel site had shown a low traffic density around 9pm on the Monday. It was to be expected, with the movement restrictions in force, but there were rather more cars than DI Gregory would have liked. The Hotel site was off the main London Road and a through route for the City, that messed things up a bit. The building site cameras were no use at all.

Now that the basic construction work had been done, the site foreman had become very slack about checking the recordings and the workings of the cameras around the site. Only one camera had been working on the Monday evening and that was focussed largely on the temporary portacabin store, watching for break-ins. All that the team could see was about six inches of the back, the very back, of a light coloured saloon, that had backed into the camera field of view and remained there for about thirty minutes, around the estimated time of death.

Correlating that with the camera images from any of the approach roads drew a blank. There was not quite enough visible to be able to determine the make of the vehicle and the camera definition was sufficiently poor that the colour was also not quite clear. It might have been grey, it might have been white, or cream, or even, light blue, it was dirty. Even for the experts a few square inches of car body are not an easy make, especially with poor quality CCTV cameras.

They ran a check on all the number plates on the passing cars, but not one of them came up with a name that they knew, certainly nothing connected with the drug scene. Curiously, all the light-coloured vehicles were registered to women owners, including a couple of GLE mercs with personalised number plates. That did not look hopeful, but DI Gregory decided that they had to interview all the owners of the light coloured cars as soon as possible and the rest of the passing traffic, all hundred or so of them, on the off chance that anyone had seen anything suspicious going on.

The leisure centre car park cameras on the Saturday also gave them a number of plates to look at, but only one of these appeared on both lists and that belonged to the manager of the centre who had, presumably, been driving home from his shift on the Monday night. They checked the cameras for the Monday and the manager's car was there until about 8:30pm, they saw him get in and they saw him drive off.

The CCTV on the Saturday showed Liam meeting Moira in the Car Park and the pair of them chatting animatedly. There was no clear evidence of anything, money or drugs, changing hands, but the pair did go out of sight for a few minutes and Moira then reappeared and left the scene, but Liam remained hidden from view. About twenty minutes later, Liam again appeared on camera.

"What the bloody Hell is that clown wearing?" said Steve.

The surveillance footage showed Liam dressed in the harlequinade set of clothing he had stolen from the lockers.

"Well," said Jerry, "if we do get hold of him, at least we can hang on to him for a bit on suspicion of theft!"

The rest of the tape for the Saturday showed a few of the usual suspects drifting around the Centre. There were a few known users, one other known dealer, other than Moira, that is. Nobody else caught the eye. The external facilities were in use even if the indoor facilities were not.

"Bit disappointing," said the sergeant. "Going to get the troops organised for a bit of legwork. They can start interviewing the drivers as soon as I have printed out the list for them. I wonder where the little git has gone, I don't think he can have gone far because we've got people on the bus and train stations and the family says that he hasn't yet learnt to drive and he certainly hasn't got a car."

"What about the family and his ex-girlfriend?" asked Jerry. "Did you get anything useful from them?"

"Well," said Steve, "I got the name and address of the girlfriend, Annie Grant, from Liam's youngest sister and went around to see her. She is really a nice kid. Annie was very clear that she chucked him because she knew he was into drugs, so at least we have it confirmed that he was involved with the scene. She seems a sensible kid and I am sure she will let us know if she hears anything at all, either from him or about him. They sound like a nice family. There's a little brother who makes amazing cakes! He said he had not seen Liam either since he went off to University."

"How do you know the brother makes great cakes?"

Steve explained and DI Gregory sat there shaking his head gently from side to side.

"Why do none of the people I interview offer me cakes?" said Jerry.

"Charisma bypass?" said Steve and ducked as Jerry threw a cigarette packet at him.

****

It was lunchtime and Bruno had gone home to collect Fly, the border Collie. Bruno lived in a large detached house on the outskirts of the City in the Summerland district and had a garden of about three-quarters of an acre. It was completely fenced in and Fly had the full run of the grounds during the day, whenever Bruno was out about his business. This was one of those suburbs where neighbours had forgotten the meaning of neighbourliness and that suited Bruno very nicely.

Nobody overlooked his property, nobody cared who came or went, nobody cared whether Bruno came or went. He had a gardener who tended the grounds for him, a cleaning lady who came twice a week and did his laundry, as well as clean. An ex-public-school boy, Bruno was well spoken and both the gardener and the cleaning lady thought him to be "A proper gentleman". Bruno made it clear, to everyone, that he had inherited his wealth and that was what made it possible for him to do as much charity work as he did. He was on the Board of two local school trusts, a charity working with the homeless and another dealing with rehabilitation of addicts. He was, to all intents and purposes, a pillar of society.

Bruno and Fly got into his Range Rover, with the dog guard across the back seat, and went off to the park near the O'Connor home. Bruno was prepared to be patient about this and knew that he might have to make more than one trip to "exercise" Fly before he got what he wanted. But, as Annie and Steve had discovered earlier, it was a fine spring day and the girls went for a walk in the Park at lunchtime. Fly was guaranteed to make an introduction for Bruno to one or more of the girls. It worked. It was, of course, Helen, the youngest and most talkative of the three, who made all the running.

"Are these your sisters?" asked Bruno; elegant, athletic looking, public school accent, well versed in the social niceties.

"Yes," said Helen. "And we have a brother, but we haven't seen him for ages, not since Christmas and he is away at University now."

Bruno asked a bit about the brother, asked what Helen and the other two girls were hoping to do for a career and generally used all his public-school charm and social manners to get as much information as he could, which, in this instance, was not much. He imagined the girls were still a bit shaken by seeing their brother's face all over the front page of The Herald and he was not inclined to arouse suspicion by asking too many questions. He would have to try another approach to finding out about Liam O'Connor's friendship groups.

Bruno said goodbye to the girls and went off with Fly to walk around the perimeter of the Park. There was no hurry, he had all afternoon to make more enquiries and Fly would be cooped up in the Range Rover for much of the afternoon. A bit more exercise would be a good thing.

Bruno's next port of call was Freddie's Office.

"I am trying hard to think how we get more information about who Liam's friends were at that Academy," said Bruno. "We also need to find out who he was friends with outside school. I think we can rule out his having escaped back up to University because we have eyes at all the termini and, when we went up there, the person at the desk in the hall of residence said she didn't think he had many visitors."

"It's not like we're the police, is it?" said Freddie. "We have no legitimate excuse for barging up to people and asking them about the kid. We would only be drawing attention to ourselves and that is the last thing we want to do, especially at this time, after we just bumped off that woman."

"I think we are going to have to wait for the press to get nosy and see if we can feed off any of their scraps."

"We can keep an eye on the sisters as well. They may have friends in common with their brother. Especially after this they may well want to go and talk to other people and anyone they are close to may well know something about Liam."

So that is what they did. And it led them nowhere.

Chapter 18

That afternoon, Annie practised both instruments, finished the Maths and the Physics work for the day, including some STEP questions, and looked over the theory parts of the music "A" level she was taking, just for fun. Having finished all that she changed the internet access from the regular ISP to her VPN and began to investigate how someone could obtain a new Identity. She also looked at rehab centres within a hundred miles radius and how people might be referred to them.

Annie was becoming more and more convinced that going cold turkey, her original idea for Liam, would not work in the long term and he needed longer to free himself psychologically of the habit. From what she read Liam would need at least a month to have any chance of staying clean. While cold turkey might have been working for the first few days, she had no reason to think Liam had failed to stick to their agreement, she was convinced that he would break down and seek a fix, at any stress or strain in the next few weeks and she knew that might be fatal.

She identified a private rehab centre in the countryside, maybe 70 miles away, which explicitly stated that they did do self-referrals. The process involved an initial telephone call— "To see if you are suitable for the treatments we offer"—an acceptance or refusal, and if a refusal, a recommendation of other rehab courses that might be suitable. The organisation seemed only to require a name, an address and payment of about £6,000 up front, for a month of treatment.

She was a bit alarmed that the Google search she had done on the VPN still identified her location as being in the City and had originally given her the addresses and websites of local referral centres, but she knew that any communication was encrypted and her actions were unlikely to bring the drug lords around to her address.

Annie thought hard. The money was simple, that idiot Liam had quite a lot more than half a million in £50 notes. In a day or so he would be aware enough to make the relevant telephone call. All he needed now was an identity to use for the transaction, and bank account to make the payment from. She wondered if you could turn up at a drug rehabilitation centre with a bag of dirty fifty-pound notes. They might be used to that if they dealt with people who wanted to remain discretely below the radar.

The online sites suggested you could get a birth certificate, which is the key to getting most of your documentation, in about 24 hours. It said you needed your person's full name including any middle names, complete date of birth, father's full name, mother's full name, mother's maiden surname and the place of birth. Annie thought they could work on that and anything else, which would probably take a lot longer, they could work on when Liam was safely in rehab. However, when she looked deeper into it things now seemed much more complicated than she at first thought.

You needed to go onto a Government website and get a GRO code, a Government Record Office code and at that point Annie realised that this could create some problems that they just did not need. Most people in England go through life without hardly ever needing to confirm their identity and, if you have cash, you don't need to use credit cards for most day to day transactions. You might need a National Insurance Number if you are going to get a job, but Liam would simply be hiding out, keeping below the radar, at least for a while, and he could sort his new ID out for himself when it was safe to do so.

It might be a bit more tricky now that everyone was going COVID contactless, but, if he got into the rehab centre, the first month of food and lodging would be taken care of, and a month might be long enough to sort out a bank account. In the long run the half a million pounds should be more than enough for him to sort everything he needed and the priority now, for Annie, was to move him on to a place of safety, and, in doing so, make life safe again for his, and her, own families. They would have to use cash to pay the rehab bill in advance. Liam would need to check that was possible when he rang them up. A story about not wanting his parents to know about his addiction might just work. He had to make that phone call as soon as he was with it enough and he had to push for as early an admission as possible.

It looked to Annie as if she would have to keep Liam under wraps for at least four or five more days and it was getting more and more precarious. She really was not sure how much longer she could keep on getting away with the trellis climb each morning and the visit during her walk each evening. She felt sure something was bound to catch them out.

****

Meanwhile, back at the Police Headquarters DI Gregory had another think. He was in agreement with DS Bronowski that Annie Grant was probably telling the truth when she said she had not seen Liam since he left for University; but he also thought that Liam was likely, if he was a junkie, to need money for a fix and was very likely to contact either his family, or his ex-girlfriend, to help him out. He had picked up his last fix at the leisure centre so it would be sensible to keep an eye on those three locations. Di Gregory instructed the mobile units working the area to make regular runs past the two homes and the leisure centre, just to see if there was any sign of Liam.

DI Gregory also put the word out on the street that he was interested in any information that could explain why Moira, a relatively small cog in the machine, had been murdered. He wanted confirmation, if it were available, that it was about a theft from the big boys and that they suspected Liam of being responsible.

The detectives had also put in place the usual alerts having received permission to monitor any exchanges on Liam's two bank accounts, the current and the deposit, and on his two credit cards. There was an alert out on his telephone calls but, as they had previously discovered, the telephone had not been used since the Sunday of the murder and now appeared to be turned off and untraceable.

****

Freddie and the drug gang had similar thoughts to those of the police about what Liam might do. They did, now, believe that Liam had taken their money. They had hauled the Boxing Instructor in and softened him up a bit, bashed him around basically and he had told them that Liam was the only one to whom he had given the number. The reason they did not throw him off a different roof was that, apart from the theft by Liam, the money laundering system was working too well to dismantle it at this stage and they were sure that, having, at last, changed the combination the instructor was never going to let anyone else know it. Things were hot enough right now without another murder investigation which might just provide more links to the top of the drug food chain. If anything else came up, they could always go back and talk to Muldoon, the boxing coach, at a later date.

They were less concerned to keep an eye on the ladies, rather they were putting the word out to all the dealers and pimps to keep an eye open for Liam trying to buy drugs. As Bruno said, "I reckon that is our best chance to get the little beggar, but there's no harm in keeping an eye on the little ladies too. I think Fly and myself will take our regular exercise in the Park and might take a stroll down Manor Road from time to time too."

Annie, not at first realising it, was under surveillance, low key surveillance but, nevertheless, it added to the risks she was taking in keeping Liam at the allotment and she was aware that her slightly changed behaviour, the early morning journey in particular, might be a problem. She would see what she could do about the birth certificate in the morning.

That evening, Annie went for her evening walk and inevitably called in on Liam. She took with her a spare old T-shirt that she found in the bottom of her wardrobe, one that Liam had previously left there. Had he not been neglecting himself and losing weight over the past few months the shirt might have been too small but as it was it fitted him quite well. She also took with her some old track suit pants that Simon, who was quite tall for his age, had not worn for a long time and probably did not remember he still owned. She also took some shampoo.

Liam seemed markedly more with it and, if not upbeat, he was too psychologically stressed for that, at least able to understand what Annie told him next. She explained that she was going to give him a new identity, that she was going to take him to a rehab centre, that it was very private and discrete and that he himself would have to make the appointment. She was going to get him a new phone and it would be pay-as-you-go and, for the time being, he would not have access to the internet. He would have to top the phone up by buying vouchers in a store, but he really shouldn't be using it, except in an absolute emergency. She would give him a top up voucher when she gave him the phone.

Non-cash transactions were a real worry. Setting up a new bank account would need ID and credit history and that was not something Annie could even contemplate doing in a hurry.

Liam complained that he was beginning to find the stench of his own faeces and the cramped surroundings of the polytunnel quite oppressive and Annie, having seen that almost all the allotment holders had already gone home for supper, decided to risk allowing Liam to go and wash himself in the toilet space and put on some clean clothes. She gave him the t-shirt and track suit bottoms, plus one of the two remaining clean pairs of underpants from the packet she had bought when she first put him into the tunnel. She gave him a carrier bag to put the dirty clothes in.

While Liam was cleaning himself up, Annie attached Uncle Willy's hose to the standpipe and used it to wash down the floor of the polytunnel, washing the faeces and general detritus to the back and out under the rear door flap. She also watered the small number of tomato plants and other vegetables that Willy had planted out before lockdown and before the official shielding requirement had been placed on Aunt June. Annie finished the cleaning up by finding a small tin of Jeyes fluid; she diluted some in a bucket, and, with the outdoor brush from Willy's shed, swabbed everything down.

By the time Liam sneaked back into the polytunnel, clean and wearing the clothes Annie had bought, it smelt not of faeces, but of Jeyes fluid. Liam had taken the water bottles with him and filled them from the tap and he went quickly back and topped up the other water containers.

"I get really thirsty," he said and then remarked, "It still smells like a lavatory."

"Yes," said Annie, "but it smells like a clean lavatory and if you decide you are going to eat some of the food in that pile over there, you aren't going to be eating a load of E.coli with it, so shut-up!"

The floor was still damp, but it was drying reasonably quickly in the warmth of the tunnel and Liam sat down on the water barrel plinth and looked up at Annie.

"So! You are going to give me a new name?" he said.

"I hope so," said Annie. "I need to get some information from the local newspaper archives at the Library. I need the birth of someone around your age and the names of their mum and dad and I need to go back and find the mum's maiden name. That should work. It's just a precaution in case someone does try to check up, but I don't see why they should."

"Well, as long as you don't call me..." and Liam gave her a list of about half a dozen names that he refused to answer to.

He is getting through it, thought Annie, but she said, "Beggars can't be choosers."

Then she added, "I am a bit worried about you now. You are getting better, but you must be psychologically stressed and bored and I really worry that you are going to blow this whole thing. You must remain inside and you must be quiet and you must be patient. With any luck, we will get you out of here before the weekend is finished."

"OK," said Liam. "I won't pretend it's easy, but I really don't want to die. Can you bring me some more chips when you come tomorrow night? I think it will be risky trying to cook anything in here because the people next door might smell something. They seem to spend the whole morning and half the afternoon here. I've been looking out through the gap in the ventilation mesh and they practically bloody well live here. I am surprised they haven't come over to investigate the smell."

What Liam didn't know, and neither did Annie, that even if the neighbours had noticed the smell, the understood allotment etiquette is that you can use common pathways but you must not go onto other people's allotments unless specifically invited. Etiquette, on this occasion, may have been a lifesaver.

"OK, hot chips, and do you want any fish or sausage or something?"

"Fish please and some Coca-Cola?" Liam was almost pleading.

Annie went home for supper. The passing unmarked police car noticed her, that was their job. She was just coming out of the newsagent's. They noticed she had a carrier bag in one hand and a large bottle of Coca-Cola in the other. It all looked quite normal and they carried on with their patrol. Annie had no idea of their presence and did what she had always planned to do.

She turned left, walked down the service access between the newsagent and the adjacent dry cleaning shop, put down the Coca-Cola bottle, lifted the heavy lid of the black landfill rubbish skip, threw in the carrier bag with the faeces-stained clothing, covered it over with some of the rubbish already in the skip and resumed her walk home.

Supper that evening was a lively affair. Simon, having finished his school work early in the afternoon, and while Annie was doing her research on the birth certificate and rehab centre, had prepared his own special version of macaroni cheese; a sort of pie, with a basic three cheese sauce, Gruyere, parmesan and extra mature cheddar, and spring onions and spinach mixed with the white sauce which, in addition to the seasoning and the cheese, contained Simon's favourite ingredient, cream, as well as the milk and the eggs that thickened the sauce. He finished it on top with a thin layer of macaroni, arranged in a lattice like pattern, with a final thin layer of grated cheese, which turned golden brown and slightly crunchy, when he heated it before serving, using the fan setting, with the grill function, at the top of the oven. He served it with a salad of contrasting tomato, radicchio and red baby beet, accompanied by an extra virgin olive oil, red wine vinegar, lemon, bay leaf, sea salt and pepper dressing.

It was unusual for them to have a pudding mid-week but Simon had been in an expansive mood and had finished his work in good time and to his own satisfaction, so he had made a blackcurrant mousse with some of the frozen blackcurrants that Uncle Willy had given them from his allotment last autumn. As Simon said, "I had some cream left over and it seemed a pity to let it go to waste."

It was, of course, nicely presented, served in individual delicate crystal tumblers, with a small rosette of whipped cream and a triangular wafer biscuit, set at a jaunty angle, on each portion.

Whether it was the quality of the food, or the relief that Annie could now see her way out of the immediate crisis, or just that the two youngsters were incredibly nosy to find out about their mother's date last night, whatever it was, the conversation was very animated. Sarah must have thought that she was being subjected to an inquisition. The two youngsters were relentless in their cross examination. They wanted to know where she had been, what she had had for dinner, what she had had to drink, how long were they in the restaurant and, finally, what time did she get in this morning, for Simon had stayed awake until at least 1am, watching his YouTube videos and chatting to his friends on the computer. Sarah, by now blushing a little, admitted that they had gone back to Daniel's house and had a night cap, but refused to be drawn when Simon asked her about whether they had been kissing, "and things".

Annie came to Sarah's rescue.

"You don't ask a lady questions like that, Simon. It is not really any of our business what Mum does on a date. What we need to know is whether this is serious. Mum, is this going to lead to something do you think? Do you really like Daniel?"

Simon took the hint.

"Sorry Mum. I guess that was being a bit personal, but what I was trying to work out is exactly what Annie has just asked you. Is it serious and are we going to get to meet Daniel?"

Sarah took a deep breath. There had been a couple of people before, temporarily, in her life, but it had never been serious and there had never been any point in introducing the "boyfriend" to her children, but this was different. Daniel had been widowed about two years ago, when his wife had contracted a particularly acute and vicious leukaemia which had progressed more rapidly than might have been expected so that she was not even diagnosed until the involvement of brain and other tissues made the prognosis desperate. She had died within six weeks of diagnosis. Daniel had clearly been deeply affected by this and it was not until he and Sarah began to form a friendship, at first very platonic, but supportive, that he even began to think about going out on a date.

Both he and Sarah were wary, thinking of the old adage about separating work and pleasure, but over the past year and more especially over the past six months, they both recognised that they looked forward to meeting each other at work and both wanted to see if the relationship had any more mileage in it than a work based friendship would imply. The first "dates" had been short interludes and had involved either meeting over lunch, or for a coffee during the day, not involving leaving either sets of children at home in the evening. The first evening date had occurred when both discovered their great love of theatre, particularly musical theatre and a touring company had come to the City with a pre-West End production of *Rent*.

Through their mutual enjoyment of this slightly challenging play, the two of them began to realise that they had more in common than just a general interest in helping ill patients, they shared values and attitudes about some of the major social ills, racism, homophobia, almost any of the divisive issues that afflict our society and belittle the legitimate human behaviours of non-normative groups. This common humanity was the first platform to the deeper relationship that both were seeking. Daniel was confident enough with Sarah to explain that his wife, Freya, had shared the same basic principles and Sarah was strong enough to encourage him to talk about Freya and, finally, get ready to move on.

They had dated regularly after that, at least once a week and sometimes once in the week and at weekends too. Last night's dinner date had been the first time that they had gone back to Daniel's house and made love. It had been something special for them both. Daniel was ready to love again after his loss, Sarah was ready to trust again after her divorce. They both knew that they had to wait a little longer to be sure, but that they were both hoping that the relationship might reach the stage of becoming permanent.

There was no way any of this was going to be included in the conversation and Simon, cheeky Simon, could wait to find out if Daniel and Sarah ever kissed. He might just see it when the time was right.

Sarah spoke quietly and chose her words with care. It was important to give the children time to adjust to what might be a new chapter in all their lives. There were also sensitivities around Daniel's children. If the two families did unite there would be four children who suddenly had an extra brother and sister each.

"It is serious, Simon. I like Daniel very much and I hope that you and Annie will like him too. I think he is a good man, tolerant and open-minded. You probably need to know that he lost his wife to leukaemia about two years ago. As I said yesterday, he has two children, Jenny and Peter. Jenny is your age, Simon, in the same school year as you, and Peter is a little younger. I met them briefly, because they came into A and E one day when I was working there and they met Daniel who was taking them out to supper after his shift. I thought they seemed quite nice.

It is quite serious, we like each other very much, but both Daniel and I know it will be a big adjustment for everyone if it gets really serious so we did spend quite a lot of time last night talking about how we could introduce all these strangers to each other and we were wondering if we could all do something together this Saturday or Sunday after Annie finishes at the shop? I was going to ask Simon to cook the six of us a meal but after this evening's cordon bleu offering, I don't think I could afford his fee!"

Simon jumped straight in.

"I'll do it," he said. "It will cost you because there will be a lot of double cream and pricey ingredients, but I will do it."

Annie sat stock still and Sarah looked at her, thinking that perhaps Annie was upset about the development of this relationship with Daniel. Knowing nothing about Liam and the drama unfolding already in Annie's life, she had no idea that Annie's hesitancy was around anxiety about how she was going to juggle the job, Liam, and an important family get-together.

It was not quite panic, Annie tended not to panic, but it was an additional drain on her intellectual and emotional capacity. If only she could sort out the birth certificate tomorrow, get Liam to make his telephone call first thing on

Friday, and book himself, in his new name, into the rehab centre for either Saturday or Sunday morning, she could move him on Friday or Saturday night and get back to a slightly more normal existence.

A dinner party on Sunday evening would be the best option, it gave her two chances to move Liam on and out of her life, for the time being. Annie decided to be proactive about it. There was also the little matter of the first of the STEP exams on Monday June 15th with the second paper on the Friday, 19th. The two papers would determine whether her application to Cambridge was successful or not.

"Could we make it on Sunday?" she said with enthusiasm. "I should love to relax after my weekend exertions and it wouldn't matter if I had a bit too much to drink on the Sunday. After all, I might just hate them and need to drown my sorrows." All this said with her best beaming smile, turning on the full charm and Sarah, relieved that whatever had fleetingly troubled Annie's thoughts had nothing to do with Daniel and his children, immediately agreed that Sunday it would be.

"Can we do a shop with the posh supermarket this Friday then?" said Simon. "Good thing there are only six of us 'cos then we can sit out in the garden."

Chapter 19

Meanwhile, the police investigation was making about as much progress as the gang's hunt for Liam. There was a wall of silence around the drug scene. There were no fingerprints and no forensic clues of any significance at the crime scene. The syringe and tourniquet were completely clean. The camera evidence had given no more clues, despite the team extending the survey of CCTV tapes to the previous four weeks at the leisure centre and at the building site.

The only additional information that the regular informers had come in with was that the people at the top of the chain were anxiously trying to find out who had robbed them of a substantial sum of money in the past month or so. DI Gregory and his team had no idea who the top men might be. There was always the possibility that the drugs scene in the City was being run, at the very top, from out of the City itself, but, even then, there would have to be a relatively high-level link man, or woman, keeping an eye on things within the City.

Almost in desperation, DI Gregory contacted every one of his informers and arranged discrete meetings with them. The disused Church Hall saw more use than it had since the owner died and the congregation stopped attending. Other officers, with their own networks of informers, were asked to seek additional information but none was forthcoming.

"One thing is absolutely clear," said Jerry Gregory, "Moira's murder was a professional job. Might have been a hired hit man and, if not, it was certainly done by someone who knew their business. My bet is on a local because they knew where the cameras are and the hotel building site is rather a specific location. I think, also, that it might not have been a planned event but probably was spur of the moment and my bet is it relates to the selling of drugs by Moira to Liam O'Connor. We really will not get anywhere until we get hold of him and he seems to have vanished from the face of the earth. We need to check the tapes again on all the roads around Liam's house. Oh, and we should check on the roads around the leisure centre to see what direction he left in after picking up his drugs. We might also have a look at the area around that girl's house, just in case."

CCTV coverage in the estate and the residential area around Annie's house was far from comprehensive, but the main roads were covered and Manor Road was certainly off the main road and Stops' Shops were all on arterial ways. The shopping arcade had its own CCTV and, for the moment, the police were not particularly looking at the arcade, just the main road. Although he was taking a long shot, DI Gregory was about to get, almost, lucky.

The instruction, in the first instance, was to look for Liam O'Connor. The pictures from the leisure centre had shown a young man, dressed in ridiculous non-fitting clothes, with long untidy hair and wearing a face mask. The trained spotters looked at Liam walking away from the centre and noted his posture and his gait, his general build and appearance. There are a group of people and every police force tries to have one or two on the books, who seem to be expert at recognising the basic features of individuals and are not confused by little details like changes in hair colour, glasses, facial hair and similar popular "spy" tricks. Jerry put these people onto the task.

There was a lot of footage to go through and it was only the Saturday footage that revealed any sign of Liam. He was seen leaving the leisure centre in the direction of the London Road and he was seen on the London Road, heading South. Just after that he turned into one of the side passages, the passages with those high, dark, preservative treated, fence panels that often connect adjacent roads in the sprawling council estates of our cities. They provide privacy to the adjacent gardens and they act as a route, especially in terraced developments, for the rubbish bins and recycling bins to be taken to the front of the terrace for collection. They also let into the back-garden bicycles and anything too big to go through the front door. Unfortunately for Jerry and the team, they are also an excellent defence for burglars and other criminals against the surveillance techniques that so much crime detection relies upon.

There were no other signs of Liam at all on the Saturday but on the Sunday morning, remarkably early in the morning, around six o'clock, a youth that might have been Liam, was seen walking a very short way down the London Road from one dark passage way to another, heading north. He then disappeared. Fifteen minutes later someone quite small came along the London Road from the South carrying what looked like a couple of coffee mugs in their hands. They turned into the same dark alley down which Liam had disappeared.

It was impossible to make out much detail, because the person was wearing a mask, but they assumed that it was a young woman, if only because of the way the person walked. There was a bit of a sway in the step and the general impression was of someone with slightly wider hips than might have been expected in a young man. Hair length, especially since the 1960s, has never been a reliable indicator of gender, and this person was wearing a beanie.

From a few minutes after six, a whole pattern of joggers and early morning exercisers, many with dogs, walked through the surveillance areas. The person seen earlier came back into view about twenty-five minutes after she had first disappeared, back out of the same dark passageway. They could see more clearly that she was wearing a small backpack of some kind. She was no longer carrying the cups in her hand. The dog walkers and the joggers, showed no specific pattern of activity. They, like Liam and the girl, disappeared down different alley ways and, sometimes, reappeared further along.

So intent were the observers on looking for signs of Liam that they did not register the reappearance of the girl, this time walking with a young boy and pushing a bicycle, when, at around 7:15, she came back into view heading north again. Nor did they detect when this same girl went out in her lunch hour to purchase items and, again returned with a heavy load. The forecourt of the arcade and the cycle path from it were not covered by the main road cameras.

During the rest of the day, there was no sign of Liam, the tapes appeared to show routine traffic on both the pathways and the roads. The COVID advice meant that there was less pedestrian and motor traffic than usual, but even so nothing about the day's events recorded on camera stood out from the ordinary.

The tapes for the next few days, right up until the present, showed a similar pattern of activity, except that Liam did not appear again and the general traffic density was greater than on the Sunday. Presumably some people were still going to work rather than working from home and there were lots of school children, especially the younger ones and their parents and the pre-examination years children, walking in the direction of the Academy and its associated primary schools. The early morning girl with a bicycle did not appear again either, although there was an early morning jogger who appeared at about 6am each day heading north, sometimes with a back pack and reappeared at about 6:45, or slightly before, heading back south. The observers did not draw a connection between the girl on the Sunday and the jogger the rest of the week, which was, perhaps, fortunate for Liam and Annie.

Lots of people went for evening walks, including the young girl who jogged each morning. The observers linked the two events in their minds but did not really give them any significance. True, people were only supposed to go out and exercise once a day, but to arrest a young girl for exercising twice was likely to bring down a whole heap of wrath and indignation from the community and lead to accusations of a police state mentality. There was one day she missed her evening exercise and it turned out, when they looked carefully, that she had gone for a bicycle ride earlier in the day with a young man. That was on the Tuesday.

The perusal of the surveillance tapes was to continue, with ever waning enthusiasm, over the next few months.

That night, the Wednesday night, was again a very uncomfortable night for Liam. The stomach cramps returned, but without the loss of sphincter control and urgency that he had previously experienced. He decided that it was safe, in the middle of the night, to use the toilet block in the allotment store right next to his hideaway and he spent quite a few hours sitting on the lavatory with bad diarrhoea again. He was also desperately thirsty and he drank lots of water. He had developed a craving for some salt, so he ate his way through several packets of twiglets, which had been part of the supplies Annie had dumped on one of her visits. Every time he had a packet of twiglets it triggered another bout of diarrhoea and cramping, but he just could not stop himself from eating.

At about 3 am, the cramps died down and, realising that the store was almost light proof, much more so than the polytunnel, he went back and got the camping stove, the matches, a tin of tomato soup and a billy can together with his spoon and can opener and he made himself a hot drink, for the first time in five days. This time, when he drank the soup, it did not trigger the diarrhoea and he went back to the tunnel feeling better than he had for almost five days. He cleared up very carefully after himself and even put some disinfectant down the lavatory. The cunning survivalist in him was beginning to surface.

Liam fell asleep about 3:45 am and was still asleep when Annie arrived next morning to check up on him.

The morning visit was routine. Annie, as she had done every day, had put on her jogging gear, climbed down the trellis and gone off to check on Liam. What survival instinct had made her think of turning this journey, after the first day, into a morning jog we shall never know, but it worked. She had started to meet various other joggers en route and always gave them a wave and acknowledgement. This was another feature of her activity that put the police observers off the scent. It was not deliberate on Annie's part, just an inevitable result of her good nature and general openness to humankind.

She was pleased, and a little surprised, to see Liam asleep and clean when she arrived and the strong scent of Jeyes fluid was beginning to fade as the ventilator panels on the polytunnel did their job. She began to think that they might get away with this plan. It all depended on whether the "Marlborough" rehabilitation centre came up with the goods. Annie woke Liam gently and his look of recognition and awareness of his surroundings was immediate.

"I'll be back tonight with your new ID and your new phone," said Annie. "It will not be a smart phone, just a basic phone for you to use, in emergencies only, until you get yourself straight."

Then Annie took the newspaper clipping about Moira out of her tracksuit pocket and showed it to Liam. To this point, he had not known about Moira. It hardly seemed possible to look any more drained than he already did but Liam seemed to manage it. He went as pale as a sheet and looked at her, almost pleadingly.

"I caused that," he almost whined. "No question, if I hadn't gone and asked her to get me that fix, she would still be alive now. I would be running still but Moira would still be alive."

And Liam looked guilty and scared and apprehensive all in the same instant. It was not as if he had really expected anything else, but he now knew for certain that, if the gang caught him, he would be dead. He also now knew that the police were looking for him and, even if they believed him, that he was not directly involved in the murder, if they found him and sent him to prison on remand the gang had contacts that would make sure he never came out of prison alive. Suddenly he had a flash back in his mind to Loughborough and the sight of Bruno and Jason Miller and he remembered that he had seen them before. He couldn't quite remember where it was, but he knew it was only a matter of time before that, too, would come back to him. The gang would probably have worked out that Liam could identify at least one or two of them and that would mean that they needed to silence him, permanently.

"Oh God," said Liam. "How did I start this? How did I drag you into it? What is going to happen to Moira's baby? You know, she had a baby and she was getting completely off drugs and she just did this one last sell to me because she needed the money and I offered her well over the going price for it."

Annie had neither time nor patience for this. There was too much to be done.

"You just concentrate on how you are going to persuade the rehab centre to give you an urgent place on their programme and how you are going to persuade them that you need to pay cash. And did you bury all the money under the slab by the pill box, other than the £25K I took from you? I need to spend some of this to get your new phone and some more clothes and a hold all for you to put them in. You cannot turn up at the rehab centre in your old T-shirt and Simon's track suit bottoms.

"And you better have a story about how you got into drugs and why, now, you want to come off. These people are not going to be mugs and they will have been dealing with addicts for a long time and they will be able to tell the difference between lies and truth quite well I imagine. Best, probably, if you stick closely to the truth but think what you need to change to protect your family and my family and, as a side issue, yourself."

"How are my family doing?" said Liam. "I imagine they are taking it hard. What on earth can they be thinking. I so neglected them. They must have blanked me out of their lives and then suddenly, here I am back in their lives in a way that just brings them hurt and, I imagine, danger."

" I'm sure you are right," said Annie, "but they are close to each other, just as they used to be close to you, and I'm sure the gang will realise pretty quickly that they do not know where you are and, unless you try to contact them, I think they should be alright. Leave them alone. OK? No attempt to contact them. As far as they are concerned, you are dead.

"I am pretty sure that someone will have told the gang that we used to be close and I am sure they are keeping an eye on me, but then, so are the police. I have kept that in mind when I try to do anything related to this, like visiting you. I am going to have to think hard about how we get you out of the City and over to the rehab place. CCTV will show footage of any car movements and that is giving me a headache. I might well have to get some false number plates for Mum's car. I am so tired of having to think ten steps ahead. I shall be so pleased when you are off my hands and in rehab. What you do after that is your problem and, seriously Liam, I will not want you to contact me ever again.

"I will be back and I will bring your damn fish and chips and I will get the other stuff done. Don't die in the meantime. I should hate to have wasted all this effort."

And on that highly sarcastic note, Annie went home, climbed through the window and went back to bed.

****

At headquarters that morning, DI Gregory and DS Bronowski were talking. They were basically bemoaning the fact that, having cleared the drug scene and the child prostitution rings from the streets during the previous year, they were now still in the very early stages of trying to uncover the new chain of command of the same criminal industries. It had not done more than temporarily rebalance the balance sheet of crime and conviction. There was still the underlying problem of low employment following the relocation, or shrinking, of many of the local industries.

The major car manufacturing plant, that had formed the basis of much of the local employment throughout the twentieth and early part of the twenty first century, had been mothballed and the production of the new hybrid had been moved to Belgium. Child poverty, overcrowding, lack of amenities, all these made this city fertile ground for drug taking and prostitution of all types, including sex trafficking and underage exploitation. It was not a case of giving up, but it did always take longer than one would have liked to get to the root of the problem.

DS Bronowski decided to drive past the Grant and the O'Connor homes just once more. He didn't see anything unusual and he had no real reason for doing it, but Annie happened to be looking out of the window when he drove past her house and she saw the car slow down as it passed. She recognised the driver and was not a little concerned.

Chapter 20

When she got up, for the second time that morning, Annie sat with Simon having breakfast.

"What you up to today?" said Annie.

"Got a lot of course work for History and Media," said Simon.

"OK. I need to go and get myself a new pair of running shoes at some point." said Annie, "I might as well go today because Mum has left the car and I can get down to the Richmond Centre and look in the Sports Shops there. They have a Waitrose down there and that funny oriental food shop, so if there are some posh ingredients for the weekend I could, perhaps, pick them up for you? Make me a list and I'll see what I can do."

Simon grabbed a piece of paper and began to scribble a few of the more unusual ingredients, and, also, one or two of the things that he liked to have in his stock cupboard, now that he was becoming the frequent cook for the evening meal.

"Haven't you got any course work today?" he asked, and Annie explained that she was "absolutely" up to date and had some practice to do but it could wait. She had STEP work, but she would get to that later. She wanted the shoes first and to call in at the library.

Annie took the car keys from the peg in the cupboard, put on her flat, sensible, driving shoes, made sure she had her mask with her and headed off out.

She didn't really like Mum's car very much. It was probably a good town car, one of the smaller hybrids and it was very quiet, particularly at start up, but it was a little slow on the acceleration and the steering was not very responsive. It did, however, have one major factor going for it, Annie's Dad had paid for the increased insurance, so Annie was allowed to drive it when Mum did not need it.

Annie's first port of call was the Library. In normal times, there would have been no way she could park there, but in these stages of the pandemic there was little traffic and the parking spots were available, because the City had temporarily suspended the parking-meters, so any spare slot was free of charge.

Annie had her laptop with her and went into the reference section of the library. She had been here before to consult the newspaper archives which were kept in that section, some on microfiche and others, more recently, digitised and kept on hard disc. Her previous visits had been in connection with Geography GCSE course work, looking at the rebuilding of the local station and the public record of it in The Herald newspaper.

This time she was looking back 19 years and interested in the birth column. She found a report of the birth of a little boy about two days before Liam had been born, out of curiosity she looked to see if Liam's birth had been reported, it had.

The first birth she chose to follow up was Mark Owens. She knew Mark Owens from the Academy. He was a likeable, if slightly anonymous, lad who, if she recalled correctly, had gone to the local Regional College and was following an apprenticeship in car mechanics. The personal advert mentioned Mark's parents by name, so it was relatively easy to search the records for the announcement of their marriage, but Annie drew a blank. She knew she needed both their full names, the maiden name of the mother and their professions, if any.

Her second try was more successful. Also 19, born a day or so after Liam, Edward Simon Collins had parents named Michael Patrick Collins and Jennifer Elizabeth Jones. The bonus was that the short report on the wedding, complete with photographs, gave the occupations of the happy couple. Mr Michael Patrick Collins, a carpenter, eldest son of Mr and Mrs Joseph Collins of Warwick Walk, had married Miss Jennifer Elizabeth Jones, only daughter of Mrs Margaret Mabel Jones, widow of Mr Edward Jones. The Bride was given away by her cousin, Mr Simon Jones. Miss Elspeth Grey, a nurse at the same Hospital as Miss Jones, was the Chief Bridesmaid.

Annie knew there was not time to get this ID before taking Liam to a safer place, so she copied the information on a piece of paper in her neat clear hand and put it in an envelope to hand to Liam for him to use later, when and if he decided to go for some physical ID.

Her next port of call was the Richmond Centre. She didn't really need a new set of running shoes, there was still a good month or so of wear left in the ones she had, but she needed the excuse to go and do some shopping and the new running shoes made the best excuse she could come up with on the spur of the moment. She tried on a selection but in the end went for what she had always gone for, New Balance Ladies Running shoes, size 6, in pink.

The next thing she did was to buy the groceries and fancy condiments and things that Simon had asked for. Best to get those things out of the way before starting to equip Liam for his rehab stay.

The large local department store on the Richmond Centre complex was a partner in one of the major national department store groups and Annie systematically went through all the necessary departments. She purchased trousers, a jacket, shirts, underwear, socks, two pairs of slip-on shoes, trainers, toiletries, including some spare razor blades, a couple of cheap pens, a cheap watch, some handkerchiefs, a nondescript tie, a sweater, a pack of three T-shirts, two pairs of pyjama trousers and, last but not least, a large travelling bag, neat, but not too flashy looking. It took her two trips to get it all back to the car and she paid for it all with some of Liam's cash.

Back at the car, she packed everything into the travelling bag, removing labels and throwing the packaging away in the carpark waste bins next to the supermarket. She put the bag in the boot of the car, covered it over with the travel rug that Sarah always kept there, heaved a deep sigh and went home.

What this week had taught her, among many other things, was that getting a new identity, if you want to do it legally, is difficult. Without the basic ID, you cannot get a National Insurance Number, you cannot get a passport, you cannot get a bank account, you cannot get; actually it is probably easier to say what you can get, a takeaway from McDonald's probably sums it up and then only if you pay cash.

Once Liam comes out of rehab, thought Annie, *he is going to have to find some way to get all this sorted but perhaps, by then, there will be less vigilance and he will be less in danger. The police and the drug gangs may have given up on him?*

She started the engine and went home.

******

Back at the police station, DI Gregory and DS Bronowski were talking about Liam.

"No sign of any credit card transactions, no attempt, as far as we can tell, to buy drugs from any of the sites we have under surveillance, no cash withdrawal from his account. No CCTV footage anywhere. He must be staying put in one place and someone has got to be supplying him with food and drink and probably drugs?" said Steve.

"Yes," said Jerry. "I think you are right. And there cannot be that many places he might be hiding. I reckon we should start looking in all the likely places. There are lots of building sites, lots of derelict buildings, lots of disused premises, what with the recession and the pandemic. I think we must consider that this is all about the gang and their lost money or drugs, the stuff Moira told me about, and that this lad, Liam, might know something about that. If he has some of the money it might explain why he hasn't used a card or made a withdrawal from a cash point for over a fortnight. He was making fairly regular use of his cards while he was in Loughborough."

"Let's get a search organised," said Jerry. "Sensible to start in the south east, I reckon, because that was where he was last seen."

For the rest of that day, the Thursday, a thorough and systematic search was planned and it was agreed to begin, first thing, on Friday morning. The search would have to continue over the weekend. The force was currently short of manpower. The effects of COVID had reduced the already somewhat depleted complement, with a small number suffering the disease itself and a larger number shielding or self-isolating. It is difficult to know whether, had there been more men available, the search might have been more successful.

Steve had decided that he, himself, would go out with the men conducting the search and first he was going to go back and just check, with the Grant and the O'Connor families, whether they had heard anything at all since his last visit to them. Something in the back of his mind was telling him that a lad like Liam, with no obvious background of hardcore criminal activity, would almost certainly be reliant on amateurs to help him hide, if, indeed, he was hiding. Acting as a courier for the drugs gang, which is what Moira had told Jerry that Liam had done, did not set you up with the contacts to disappear you in the way that more hardened criminals might be able to rely upon.

Steve looked out of the window of the police station, saw it was a beautiful day, remembered the delightful cup of coffee in the garden with the delectable Miss Grant and decided that he might start by visiting her for another cup of coffee and a chat.

****

Annie had barely arrived home and was standing by the front door with her key in her hand when DS Bronowski pulled into the driveway of her house, just behind the little red hybrid. The shoebox was on the doorstep by her feet and the bag of groceries was in her other hand as she fitted the key into the lock.

Annie heard the car pull onto the tarmacked driveway and stop. She turned her head and, just briefly, went a little pale. Bronowski noticed the slightly startled response but put it down to Annie's just not expecting anyone to pull into the driveway behind her and thought no more of it for the moment. Annie quickly regained her equanimity. *There's no reason why he should know anything*, she thought. *This is just a routine visit because they haven't found Liam yet*. She was right, of course, but she still felt a little uncomfortable. She had so much to hide and a slip of the tongue might, always, happen.

Steve put his mask on, got out of the car and walked up to the porch.

"Good morning, Miss Grant," he said. "May I have a word with you, just routine?"

"Of course, Sergeant," said Annie. "Like a cup of tea or coffee? Coffee black, no sugar, isn't it? We can sit in the garden if you like, it is a beautiful day."

Steve Bronowski was flattered that Annie had remembered how he took his coffee, accepted the offer. and they went through the house to the back garden, still with the delicious scent of jasmine but now with the aroma of sweet peas added to the garden scents, following a few days of warmth and sunshine. Annie went back into the house to make the coffee; she had an espresso machine in which she used compatible compostable pods made by a different manufacturer.

Steve sat there in the garden, once again wondering how that lad Liam could ever have given up the amazing Annie for a few grains of nasty white powder. Deep down, Steve knew that circumstance and deliberate manipulation could hook almost anyone on a drug, but why anyone would go that route when they had … No point in thinking about it, he was here to just check that there had been no further news since his last visit.

Annie came out with the coffee and they sat on the garden chairs, conveniently two metres apart.

"Any news, Sergeant?" said Annie, taking the initiative.

Steve smiled.

"That, Miss Grant, is what I came to ask you," said Steve.

"Please call me Annie, Sergeant. Miss Grant makes me feel very old."

"Thank you. So, Annie, have you heard anything at all from Liam, or even about Liam, during the two or three days since I last called?"

"I am sorry, Sergeant. I just haven't heard a thing and there seems to be nothing new in the papers either. Liam just seems to have disappeared but, as I told you before, he disappeared from my life completely when he went off to Uni and we had not really been speaking to each other for almost a year before that. I do hope you can find him. I worry for him. He can't be safe if he's mixed up with the drugs and the murder of that poor woman. I guess you are looking everywhere for him but…" and Annie paused and left the end of the sentence hanging in the air.

"Well, thanks Annie. We are worried about him too. If he was the last to speak to Moira then he is in danger, he might have seen something that whoever killed Moira will not want us to know about. As I think I may already have said, we don't think he killed her, but we think he knows something which may point us in the direction of the people who did. Once again, I am sure you will let us know if you hear anything."

And Steve Bronowski finished his coffee, exchanged a few more pleasantries, gazed admiringly at Annie, put his notebook back in his pocket, bade her farewell and went off through the side gate back to the car.

Is there something I am missing? he thought. *She reminded me again about the bust up, she reminded me again that it was over six months since she had seen him at all. Is she pushing that too hard?*

Steve Bronowski had no real grounds for doing anything other than accept Annie's words at their face value, for the moment. He got back into the car and headed around to the O'Connor household.

This time, when he rang the doorbell, Tara O'Connor answered.

"Good afternoon, Mrs O'Connor. I am Detective Sergeant Bronowski," said Steve. "I am sorry not to have seen you before this, but I hope you don't mind if I talk to you now. I spoke to your three daughters a few days ago but I think it would be good if you would be kind enough to answer a few questions for me now and it might even help us to find your son. I do want to emphasise to you that we do not believe he had anything directly to do with the murder of Ms MacDonald but we do think he might have some information that will help us find the killers and that is why we are so anxious to talk to him."

Bronowski paused. Tara O'Connor looked at him straight in the eyes.

"Sergeant, I would be very happy to talk to you. I'm worried sick about Liam. I really don't know how or why he is mixed up in all this, but it must be dangerous for him. Would you like to come in and we can certainly talk about it?"

Bronowski had put his mask on to begin the meeting and, when they went inside, Tara also put on a face covering. She chose a visor and they went into the sitting room which was well ventilated, with the door open and the two large French doors onto the garden.

"Can I get you a drink, Sergeant?" said Tara.

"I just had one with Annie Grant," said the Sergeant. "I think I am alright for the moment, thank you, but please, don't let me stop you making one for yourself."

Tara went briefly into the kitchen and put the kettle on and then came back and sat down while the kettle boiled.

DS Bronowski brought her up to date with the search for Liam and explained that they were worried because the police had reason to believe that the people who had killed Moira MacDonald were also interested in finding and silencing Liam. He might well know something about why Moira was killed, and if the police knew why she was killed they might be able to determine who had killed her.

There was a pause while Tara went back into the kitchen and made herself a cup of tea. She came back and sat down and started to talk.

"It seems that you know that Liam got mixed up in drugs," said Tara. "We rather suspected that all was not well before he went away. There was the moodiness, he even hit one of his sisters on one occasion and although Annie was very loyal and never told us what went on to cause the bust up, from what we heard from some of the children through the school gossip, Sarah, Annie's Mum and I, we thought that it might have been because Annie was not prepared to get involved with drugs and Liam was getting a bit more involved.

"I don't know if you have kids, Sergeant, but as a mother I just didn't want to believe my son was doing drugs, much less that he was involved in dealing them. I was in denial. I tried to talk to him about it on a couple of occasions but just got the shut down and sullen silence and he stopped even talking to me for a few days each time I tried to bring up the subject. I was tempted to turn him in, but I didn't have any physical evidence.

"I did think he had a bit more money than I would have expected, because he was buying some pretty nice IT stuff like iPhones and things, but he would swear they were second hand and from a mate who had just bought the latest model and, to be quite honest Sergeant, I wouldn't know an old model from a new one in a month of Sundays. I had hoped that when he went to University it might stop, but my suspicion is that it got worse. We didn't hear from him at all for the first four weeks and then I think we must have had no more than half-a-dozen calls, mostly to his little sister Helen, until he came home for Christmas.

"He spent a few days with us, but he might as well not have been here. He stayed in his room, except once or twice, when he went down to see his mates at the leisure centre and that's when I thought he must be right back on the drugs because the rumour we had heard was that it was at the leisure centre that the local dealers were distributing. I thought again about telling the police and I know I should have done, but I didn't have any proof again, just a suspicion. We haven't heard from him since he went back to University, apart from another few phone calls to Helen."

Bronowski interrupted her at this point.

"Was there any particular friend he had at the centre? Was there anyone he mentioned or that you knew that you saw him with? Did you ever find any drugs in his room or his clothing when it was washed?"

"No Sergeant," said Tara. "I never found any drugs. The friends were not really friends, he never seemed to do anything outside work or school with them."

She paused for a minute.

"Although, come to think of it, there was one boy in his class, Michael, I think he was, yes, that's right, Michael O'Grady. After Liam began to work at the leisure centre, they did seem to hang out together quite a lot. In fact, now I think about it, Liam saw Michael when he came home at Christmas. Just once but I am sure he did go and see him. I was disappointed he didn't spend much time with his sisters and he didn't go and see Annie either. That didn't surprise me though, not really. The breakup had been final, no way back, I think. Probably about as acrimonious as my divorce."

Tara gave a slightly rueful looking grin. She picked up her tea and sipped it.

"Are you sure I can't get you a drink?"

Sergeant Bronowski had listened carefully and was very interested in this Michael O'Grady. Probably nothing, but it was one more person to go and talk

125

to who might be able to shed some light on Liam's disappearance and might even have had contact with him, especially as Liam had bothered to meet up with him at Christmas.

"Yes, quite sure," said the Sergeant. "I am very grateful for your honesty about this and I do understand why it is so hard for you to talk about it but you have been very helpful and please, if you do hear anything at all, or remember anything that you think might be of use then please call. I just want to reassure you that we have Liam's safety as our first concern and any use of, or even minor dealing with drugs, by Liam is not where our investigation is focussing."

As usual with Steve Bronowski, there was a small exchange of pleasantries and he took his leave. This time he did not see the three sisters, who had gone out to the park for their afternoon recreation. He just got back in the car and drove to the station. At the station, he reported back to Jerry Gregory and then telephoned the Academy to ask for the address and any information they could give him about Michael O'Grady. It turned out that Michael O'Grady was a smart kid who had gained a place to read Modern and Mediaeval Languages at Cambridge. Since October last year he had been studying French and Spanish at University. There was little chance that Liam had been in recent contact with O'Grady.

Chapter 21

After eating a cheese and pickle sandwich for her lunch, Annie jumped on her bicycle and headed down to the supermarket to pick up a mobile phone. She bought two relatively cheap pay as you go phones and paid for two £50 top up vouchers. She also bought a cheap, UK only, Satnav. The total came to just under £300 and she used six more of the £50 notes that she had taken from Liam before she moved him to the allotment. All the expenditure so far had not even dented the stack of notes and she thought there must still be at least twenty-five thousand pounds left.

Even after paying for his four weeks treatment, that should leave Liam enough to live on for at least six months. It should also give him enough money to be able to get himself some false id and start to rebuild his life. It seemed strange that he might never be able to reconnect with his real family but, perhaps, once the people that were after him had been caught, it might be possible for him to take up his life again. It was much too soon to speculate but the money he had, even though it was dirty money, did at least give him a chance to come out of this.

Annie was tempted to take the phone to him at the earliest possible opportunity, but she was too smart to succumb to that temptation. Any diversion from her current pattern of behaviour would lead to questions, and, having seen Bronowski drive past her house this morning, she knew that she was under surveillance.

From what Liam had told her she had a shrewd idea that the gang would be keeping an eye on her too. They might think that she could lead them to him. They did not know how definite and final the breakup had been and someone was bound to have told them that she and Liam had once been close.

Safely home with the phone, Annie got down to some serious practice. The concert was only a few weeks away and the *Symphonie Pathetique* was not a trivial undertaking. She spent an hour and a half on the violin and then, in a lighter mode, played a bit of Gershwin and a few other more modern pieces on the piano. Simon heard her, made her a cup of hot chocolate, with his trademark whipped cream on top, and brought it in to her in the music room. They sat and chatted and, for a moment, both were very close and very content. They finalised the delivery for the Friday evening and Simon was very careful not to let on what his plans were for the big meal on Sunday night. The only thing that Annie knew for certain was that there would be cream, double cream and clotted cream, somewhere on the menu.

****

The drug cartel members had taken the unusual step of meeting in person. The obvious place for this was Bruno's house and they had, all, discretely, driven there and parked in the tree lined parking space outside on the tarmac. They were frustrated by the lack of information about the whereabouts of one Liam O'Connor. Absolutely convinced by now that he was the thief who had taken their money from the Boxing Club locker, they were about to up the stakes in the hunt for him. They sat around the central island in Bruno's kitchen and discussed exactly how to do it.

"The first thing we can be absolutely sure about," said Bruno, "Is that he knows who I am because he must have seen me at Loughborough and that is what spooked him. What we don't know is if he remembers who any of the rest of us are, but there was that occasion when he delivered the package to us and I think he was introduced to us all then, although as I recall we were all a bit drunk at the time. If the police get him and question him and find out about me then there is a sporting chance that they are going to track things back to the rest of us."

The others agreed with him.

"Makes it imperative," said Bruno, in his smooth upper-class tones, "that we find him and silence him before he can talk. What have we done about putting the word out among our group who worked out of the leisure centre? I wonder if we ought particularly to contact the kids who were there and the other kids who were at the Academy. How many are there? Was it ten?"

Jason Miller responded, "I think it's fifteen now but at the time Liam was courier for us, it was only about eight. Six of them are still around but a couple of them have gone off to university. I think one of them is at Cambridge and one at somewhere in the Midlands. You ought to know Bruno, I bet you got the report from the CEO at the Trust Board."

Bruno responded, "That's right about the two who have left. I can't remember which College the Michael kid went to, but I can look back at the minutes and check. I think Liam might have been a bit closer to the two who went off to University than to some of the others, they were all a bit younger, some of them quite a bit younger. By the way, I have an update from the last Board meeting about the temporary and permanent exclusion kids. Might be some promising recruits there, especially a couple of the girls. Jason, I'll give you the names before you go."

At that moment, Bruno's partner, Julian, who was cook, housekeeper and chauffeur rolled into one, came into the kitchen and rather petulantly said, "You guys, are you going to come and eat or not? I don't mind cooking, but I do mind when business spoils my efforts. Now if you are not in the dining room within two minutes—and Freddie, that means you go now and empty your pathetically weak bladder, you geriatric tramp—I am going to throw it all in the bin!"

Julian flounced out, the four all looked at each other, rolled their eyes and Bruno said: "What I have to put up with. But then, he is a heavenly cook and very discrete and we have been together a long time, since boarding school, in fact! Better go and eat. We can talk more afterwards."

And they went through to a rather splendid evening meal of scallops with hazelnut butter, lamb cooked three ways, delicious seasonal vegetables with this season's Jersey royals and a salted caramel and apple tarte tatin, served with a crème fraiche infused with calvados.

The food was so good that the conversation flowed, despite the serving of only one small glass of Chateau Haut-Brion with the lamb. On these occasions the last thing any of the four wanted to do was to attract the attention of the police with a positive breathalyser test and, to keep these evening meetings secret, the participants always drove themselves and drank very sparingly.

When the dishes were cleared away and the coffee was served, all four had decaffeinated at this time of night, the business part of the meeting was resumed.

"I suggest we up the reward to ten thousand quid for anyone turning him in," said George.

George was always the quietest of the group. He was also the least intelligent and formed part of the group only because he had inherited a lot of underworld contacts from the family haulage and garage businesses. He was very useful and the haulage business was very useful to the others for moving things around. They also obtained their cars from him, at a discount.

The only debate about George's suggestion was whether it was enough. It was less than 2% of what they had lost and retaining their freedom in the light of the murder was, probably, priceless. They thought about more but decided that £10K for the people they were targeting was a substantial reward and probably, for the time being, entirely sufficient.

"OK," said Freddie, "I'll put the word out. Has there been anything from the people watching the bus and train stations?"

There had not.

"How about that girl and his family?"

Bruno went over his conversation with Liam's sisters again and reported that the people watching the girl's house had seen no sign of Liam. He made some remark about her appearing to be a perfectly normal kid apart from the fact that she seemed to be obsessional about fitness and went out for a jog or a walk at least twice a day. He also commented that she was not a normal teenager either because she seemed to get up very early for her morning jog.

"Strikes me she is a little goody two-shoes," said George.

A short while later the party broke up. The word was going out in a more reinforced way, Bruno was going to check the leaving destinations of the two school kids that used to work for them and he was going to pass on the details of the delinquent school kids, Jason was going to talk to all the county lines and other drug linked kids from the Academy and the leisure centre and, finally, Jason was going to see what might be done to recruit the delinquents, either to the drug business or, in the case of the girls, to the prostitution racket. Nobody was going to write up the minutes!

Chapter 22

That same evening, on her evening walk, Annie had gone past the "Chippy" and purchased cod and chips, laced them with salt and vinegar, purchased a large bottle of Coca-Cola and delivered them to Liam at the allotment. Physically, Liam was looking much better, but he was in a tremendous state of agitation and he kept telling Annie that he was really struggling psychologically. He was desperate for a fix. He started telling her where she could get him a fix and begged her to do so , but she gave him short shrift on that.

"Sergeant Bronowski came to see me today," said Annie. "He told me, point blank, that the police are looking for you to stop you being killed. They really believe that the gang is looking for you to kill you. They don't know what you did but they are beginning to think that they have identified you as the person who stole something from them.

"Now, do you think it sensible for me, someone who has never used drugs in my life, to go and buy some drugs from the gang? What do you think will happen if I do that? My guess is they will watch where I go and then I reckon both of us will end up dead. You can forget it. I am not dying for you and, although long term I don't give a damn, in the short term I don't want you dead either.

"So here is what you are going to do. Eat your fish and chips and listen while I tell you what has to happen, and it has to happen fast."

Annie paused. She waited for Liam to unwrap the newspaper from the polystyrene container inside and start to eat the first hot food he had eaten in five or six days. There was, on this occasion, no repeat of the stomach cramps and issues that had occurred with the soup the day before and Annie thought that the worst of the physical withdrawal was now probably over.

"Right, Liam," she said, "you need to get in touch with the Marlborough Clinic tomorrow morning, as early as you can, and you need to persuade them to take you as soon as possible. You have the burner phone, so you can call me as soon as you have an admissions date. Don't text. The companies keep a record of texts, but they only record the number for a phone call. I have put my burner phone number on your phone as speed dial 1.

"I can't help you with this but I suggest you stick as close to the real story as you can and that you say your parents have disowned you and your sister, that is me, but no names please, is helping you and you really want to come off the drugs. By all means tell them that you have just gone cold turkey and, although you are over the worst of the physical stuff, you fear that the psychological pull will be too much at the moment and you need to be somewhere where you will have support and no possible access to drugs. Is there any chance they can admit you for a month? Ask them how much that would cost and can you pay cash and, if you can, you will get your sister to bring the money to you and bring it with you, but they will have to take it all in advance because you don't trust yourself not to try to use it to buy drugs. I reckon that will do it."

Annie paused and looked at Liam, who was still eating and almost seemed to be enjoying the meal. He took a big swig directly from the Coca-Cola bottle and burped.

"'Kay, Annie. Anything you say."

Liam gave the impression he was more focussed on the food than what Annie was saying.

"Listen, you pig-headed idiot," said Annie, "I'll go over it again and focus this time."

She did go over it and this time she thought he had taken it in. When she was confident about that, she handed him the telephone, she had put about £50.00 worth of calls and texts on it. She then gave him the envelope with the piece of paper on which she had written the details of his new, temporary, identity.

"Well," she said, "from now on until you sort yourself out, you are Edward, Edward Simon Collins, and you had better learn what is on that piece of paper and we had better find you an address to use. I suggest we use a flat somewhere, a student flat with multiple occupancy, just in case they want to check up on you, but my guess is that £6,000 and a clean-looking boy like you, I think they will just take you at face value and not bother too much about background, especially as they are supposed to be very confidential and discrete. I am betting they have been given false addresses before and I doubt it will ring alarm bells, even if they do check and find that no Edward Simon Collins lives there."

Annie got out her iPhone and decided to look up a hall of residence for students in Manchester, it seemed far enough away to be a safe choice. She picked one of the larger ones and wrote down the address on Liam's piece of paper.

"That is where you live, but don't tell them unless they ask. If they want a next of kin address, you give your sister's address, Emma Collins and the phone number. I have written the number and address on your piece of paper, and the name, in case you forget. Remember, Emma, she doesn't have a middle name."

Annie thought to herself how incredibly hard it was to cover all the bases and she decided that she was now far too exhausted to even contemplate coming back tomorrow. There was no need either because Liam had enough food and was now with it enough to be able to pick his moment to sneak out through the back door of the polytunnel and collect his own water; besides which he was no longer losing vast quantities of fluid in his diarrhoea, so a top up of water before it got light should last him through until Annie could visit in the evening.

"I will not be here in the morning," she said.

A look almost of panic crossed Liam's face.

Annie explained her reasoning; she really did need a decent night's sleep. The early mornings, the late nights lying awake worrying, they were taking their toll and if she were to drive him safely to Essex one night, she really needed to be awake. She was also worried about the surveillance, both by the police and, she suspected, by the drugs people. They were so close to getting away with this that anything she could do to reduce the risk of discovery was worth thinking about. Finally, she pointed out that she was very close to some of the most important exams of her young life so far and she was not going to mess that opportunity up for a drug addict.

Liam looked a little bit ashamed. He was beginning to realise just how big a chance Annie was taking for him and he knew in his heart that he did not deserve it.

"OK, I'll call you when I know what the rehab place says."

"Remember, call, don't text. See you tomorrow evening and be careful."

And with that, Annie went home to supper and a good night's rest.

Annie could not have known how fortuitous that decision not to go early morning to see Liam would turn out to be. For no real reason except that both groups had decided to step up their hunt for Liam, an unmarked police car and a grey Mercedes were in the vicinity of 42 Manor Road at about 6 am on the Friday morning. Bronowski and Gregory, the two policemen, were on their way to an early morning rendezvous at the leisure centre with a whole army of policemen, including a few called in from neighbouring forces, who were to take part in the search. They wanted to take full advantage of all the hours of daylight and sunrise was around 5:30 am.

Freddie was just simply being nosy. He was cruising the area around the leisure centre and London Road, on the off chance of seeing something, anything, which might be of interest. He often got up early on a Friday and started work early because he usually played golf with a couple of the local councillors, former school friends, on a Friday afternoon. It was no bother to take a slightly more circuitous route to his Office. The drug gang had a picture of Annie, a slightly old one, because she had been photographed for the local paper when she got her ten grade 9 GCSE grades, the best in her school and one of the best in the area. Bruno had also managed to give them a better version, through his contact with the Academy at Board level.

Annie stayed in bed until 7:30. Freddie and the policemen missed an opportunity.

Chapter 23

The morning was uneventful on all fronts. The police search, systematic and thorough, looked at all the possible garden sheds, garages, disused buildings, derelict sites and unoccupied houses in the local vicinity. It was amazing how many there were and it was clearly going to take a lot longer, with the limited number of officers at their disposal, than the two detectives had hoped it would. They found themselves, mid-morning, sitting on a bench outside the Wolfson Road Allotments hut, drinking a cup of coffee with the Chair of the WRAS, the Wolfson Road Allotment Society, who happened to be a member of the same Polish Church as Steve Bronowski and his wife.

DS Bronowski, apropos of nothing, asked Stefan Brylewski if there had been many strangers around lately and was told that the allotment holders had been so densely working on site that there was no room at all for a stranger to sneak on and nick vegetables, or tools. Looking at the allotments and the immaculate state of almost all of them, that was easy to believe. They had a short discussion about the two or three plots that were in a bad way and Stefan said that some of these were elderly folk who were either shielding or might soon be finding the work on the allotment too much and giving up their tenancies.

It was a nice sunny day and the three of them chatted for a while and then the detectives moved on, back to the real work and to watch the members of their search team going along the passageways at the back of Wolfson Road, looking into the garages and outbuildings along the boundary.

****

Annie and Simon did their schoolwork and Annie practised her violin. A few more STEP questions and then she decided to go for a walk just before lunch. Strangely enough she had missed her early morning run and it was almost as if she was having trouble waking up properly. Funny how the body gets used to things. On the walk she noticed a couple of gardens on the estate where there were cars propped up on bricks, with the wheels removed. It was quite common for local young men to work on 'old bangers', in the hope of getting them serviceable again and then selling them on at a significant profit.

She dropped in at the newsagent's and bought a small packet of those mints that come with a hole in the middle! She walked a little further than usual today and when she was about three miles from home, approaching the local bird sanctuary on the bank of the river, a telephone rang. It was the burner phone and it was Liam.

"I spoke to them," he said, "and they said they would take me. They gave me an appointment. It was easy to convince them. I reckon they are short of custom during the COVID crisis and yes, they are willing to accept cash. They said it would be £6,500 for a month of full board, more than you said, but so what? And they told me I would not be allowed mobile phones, or the Internet. I can have a kindle or an iPad or mobile with a kindle app, but I have to load my books before I go and they will take any SIM card out and keep it, to make sure I cannot surf or make phone calls. They said they would let me call my sister Emma on the house phone once a week and more in emergency, but they warned me that they would be listening in to make sure no drug deals were being done.

"Honestly Annie, I reckon this is going to be worse than a bloody prison. Still, if I can't get out, I reckon those buggers chasing me can't get in."

He told her when the admission was going to be and what else they had said to bring and other details. They seemed to want him to have some gym type stuff, because physical activity was an important part of the rehab. Annie was rather pleased she had thought of it, but she decided to go and get an extra track suit bottom and a couple of pairs of running shorts, a swimming costume and one of those six-packs of white exercise socks. Liam had been told to report at 10am on the day of his admission.

Annie was thinking that might be a problem. But there was bound to be a way around it. She just needed time to think. She was becoming an expert liar and expert planner and very good at hiding her tracks. There was a big bit of her, her conscience, the Jiminy Cricket whispering in her ear, that really did not like the way this was changing her. She hoped the deceitful behaviour would never become permanent.

She went home and met Simon in the kitchen. They sat and shared a tub of hummus, some pickled gherkins and a wholemeal pitta each. It was Friday. That meant the grocery delivery. This week it meant two grocery deliveries. Tesco was coming with the usual stuff and the posh supermarket was bringing the ingredients for whatever it was that Simon was going to make on Sunday. Simon's excitement about this had as much to do with the cooking as with the chance to get to know Sarah's boyfriend and his children. The latter was important because both Simon and Annie were getting the distinct impression that these three strangers might be about to enter their lives permanently in a highly significant way.

"I hope they are nice," said Simon. "I can't imagine Mum going out with someone who wasn't at least half decent, but I think his children are a complete unknown. Oh!" A sudden thought came to him. "What if they have allergies or absolutely hate something?"

Annie paused for a moment.

"Do you know any recipes that don't have cream in them?" she said teasingly.

They both laughed.

"I don't see you refusing to eat it," said Simon, "but seriously, we need to check that they aren't fruitarians or pescatarians or vegans or allergic to dairy or nuts, that sort of thing. And they might have religious food taboos, lots of kids at school do. That would be fine, of course, but I need to know. I need to know now, so I can arrange to get other ingredients, if we must. The stuff on order won't be wasted, we can always freeze it, but you are working tomorrow and I don't drive, so if we need to go back to the Richmond Centre we need to do it today. I know Mum doesn't like us calling her at work, but I just have to do it this once."

And Simon called his mother who, fortunately, was on her lunch break.

Ten minutes later, she called him back.

"No allergies, no dislikes, no religious or other taboos. Omnivores, just like you ravenous beasts. In fact, Daniel said he hoped you would cook enough because Daniel says that Peter eats more than the other two of them put together. He says that you can always just give Peter more carbohydrate!"

"Thanks Mum," said Simon. "I can do better than that, but I am relieved I don't have to rethink the menu. See you this evening."

And he hung up.

The afternoon passed quietly enough. Simon went back to his room and Annie was looking for an excuse to go and buy the extra gym items for Liam when Simon suddenly shouted down the stairs.

"Can you check the order please, not the Tesco but the other one. Did I put the fresh pineapple and the langoustine on the list? And how about the clams. Can you go to the fish counter and get me some? I think I need about six langoustines, some large shell on prawns and some of those razor clams?"

Simon made his list and Annie agreed very readily to go and get these extra bits and pieces. There were a few other items too, but it seemed that the fish was the main thing. She could see why he had wanted to check up before embarking on the cooking. Seafood can be quite a problem for some people. Nuts, milk and shellfish seem to be high on the list of things that people are allergic to.

Under cover of collecting Simon's ingredients Annie went back to the Sports Shop and topped up the things that Liam would need. She also filled up with petrol and screen wash for Sarah and she got a couple of bottles of water for the car. On the way back, she called at various places and picked up a few other things that she thought she might need.

****

That evening, the Tesco delivery came, right on time. Annie and Simon unpacked. Simon carefully put aside the items he would need for the Sunday meal. Then came the special supermarket delivery and Simon, almost over the top with excitement, unpacked it lovingly. He then went back to finish cooking supper. Annie went for her evening walk. She was thinking as she walked, was it only a week ago that Liam appeared on the doorstep instead of the delivery man? It seemed like a lifetime.

She called on Liam, told him that she would not be along in the morning because there was no way she was getting up at 5am, she had the early morning start at the shop. Liam looked a bit crestfallen but was cheered a bit by the thought that his time in the polytunnel was coming to an end and by this time next week he would be comfortably ensconced in the rehab centre, with someone other than Annie responsible for his welfare and safety.

Annie had brought a few extra food items, Liam's appetite was returning with a vengeance, and she left them for him with another 2-litre bottle of Coca-Cola.

"That stuff will kill you if the druggies don't," said Annie.

****

Sarah came in after her long shift and could smell the arrabbiata sauce for a rather nice pasta dish that Simon was making. They had a pasta machine and Simon loved using it. He had made the mushroom, garlic, onion and cheese ravioli while Annie was out at the shop and the arrabbiata sauce was an absolute standard of his. He used a mixture of herbs from their own garden, the Grants had a herb planter in the back garden area and, as well as using fresh herbs in the summer months, Simon had started drying some for use in the winter and before the new season crop had matured to the point of being harvestable. He also used his own dried chillies from the plants that he grew in pots each year, Thai Dragon was one of his favourites, almost as hot as Scotch Bonnet but with a bit more flavour. He did not grow Scotch Bonnet, the occasional one was too hot for enjoyment; Thai Dragon was consistently hot and he could always judge how much to use. He liked flavour with a bit of heat.

"Hi, you two," said Sarah, "I need to clean up before I even begin to feel human. Can we hold supper for half an hour while I get a bath and change into something more comfortable? I think I need a bath tonight, not just a shower."

Simon indicated that this 'would be fine' and the supper would not be spoiled, could Sarah just 'shout down the stairs?' ten minutes before she wanted to eat. He then set about making a green salad and a suitable yoghurt dressing; yoghurt dressed salads go quite well with spicy foods.

The two youngsters sat down and waited.

Sure enough, after about twenty minutes, Sarah called down that she was nearly ready and Simon set the pan of very slightly salted water back on the boil and put the arrabbiata sauce to warm up. He waited until Sarah was downstairs and she and Annie were already seated before he put the ravioli in to cook. Simon's ravioli pasta was deliciously thin and he knew that three or four minutes would be plenty of time for the cooking, anything more might make it rubbery. He arranged the cooked ravioli on the very pretty square dinner plates, white with slightly rounded corners, dressed them with a little of the sauce and put the rest of the sauce into matching individual tiny white sauce jugs and brought them through to the table.

The salads were already there by each place and the dressing was also on the table. There was one of those big parmesan mills for those that wanted, but with a sauce as tasty and perfectly seasoned and as delicate a ravioli as Simon had made, it would have been almost sacrilegious to use it. Neither Sarah nor Annie did so.

There was almost compete silence while the first course was consumed. Then the conversation began, while Annie cleared the plates into the dishwasher.

"Only ice cream for pudding tonight and a bit of fruit with it if you want it," said Simon.

"You know," said Sarah, "I fancy a glass of dessert wine with that. Will you join me, Annie?"

"Do you mind if I don't, Mum?" said Annie. "If you open it, I will have some tomorrow, it keeps OK in the fridge, but it sometimes stops me sleeping and I want a good night's sleep tonight. I think Jane isn't working tomorrow so it will just be me and Stops and I think that is going to be tough. I think she has a birthday for one of the kids, so she should be back on Sunday."

They ate their ice cream, Sarah drank her wine, they chatted. Most of the conversation was about the impending visit of Daniel, Jenny, and Peter Carter.

Chapter 24

Back at the police station, Steve Bronowski had just gone into the video room where the team were going over the tapes from last weekend for one last time.

It had been a frustrating day. The search team had covered quite an area but, apart from a few items of electronic stuff, a couple of TVs, a couple of DVD players, things like that, which might have "fallen off a lorry" and found their way to the garden sheds of known villains, nothing had been found. There was no sign anywhere of someone inhabiting a space they should not have been in. There were a couple of squats in some of the disused properties, but the people there were all known to the police and all were able to account for their presence and to state clearly that there was no one else staying there.

Steve had a word with the video team.

"I want to come in tomorrow morning and I want you to take me through the tapes, especially the ones from last weekend around the leisure centre, the hotel building site and its access roads and the London Road. I know you did a whole month of tapes on the leisure centre and the building site, but could you just also go back a week or two earlier on the London Road and the other local main road tapes? It is possible that there is a change of pattern that is worth investigating. Is something going on this week, with Liam hiding away, that was not going on last week? I'll be back around lunchtime tomorrow for you to take me through it. Meanwhile, get some sleep. You guys have been on long shifts all week and I need you alert tomorrow."

And with that Steve Bronowski went home to Friday night fish and chips, picked up from the best Fish and Chip shop in the City, the same one at which Annie had bought Liam's cod and chips the night before. Fish and chips wrapped in newspaper. Ironically, as he picked up the bundle from the counter, he saw the picture of Moira MacDonald, with those big, blue eyes, staring back at him.

******

The next morning Annie woke as usual at 5:30 and luxuriated in not having to get up and run to the allotment. She snuggled under the sheets for a few minutes more. The slight condensation on the sash windows of the rambling early Edwardian made Annie think that there must have been a very clear sky and a high humidity. Unusual at this time of year to get the condensation. She got up, didn't bother to get dressed, but went down the stairs very quietly and made herself two slices of toast and a double espresso. She put them on a small tray, with a glass of cold mineral water and went back upstairs to get dressed.

She ate her breakfast while dressing. Sensible shoes and trousers today. With Jane off work she was going to be run off her feet. She washed her face, cleaned her teeth, brushed her hair and put on a little eye makeup. She left the house quietly, without waking the other two, mounted her bicycle and reached the shop in good time. She locked the bike under the shelter of the car port at the back of the shop.

"Morning Mr Stops," said Annie, as she walked through the unlocked back door. "Oh, I forgot my mask!" The exasperation showed in Annie's tone.

"Morning Annie," said Roger Stops, bent over the bundles of daily papers that he was strewing around the big back room.

"There's a proper mask, a cloth one, over there on the desk. It's been washed. You're welcome to use it today, but I would be grateful if you washed it overnight and brought it back tomorrow. Jane is always forgetting hers and it is useful to have a spare. I hope these kids are on time today. With Jane away, I need you out there ready to serve the customers a bit sharpish this morning."

"No problem," said Annie. "But I do have a favour to ask you. Do you think it would be alright if I finished a bit early tomorrow? Say around 5 pm? Mum's new boyfriend and his children are coming to supper and I should like to be able to go home and be sociable with them and help Mum and Simon get ready for the evening."

"That should be fine, Annie," said Roger. "Sunday afternoons get a bit dead anyway and Jane will be back tomorrow so why don't we say 4 pm? And don't worry, I won't dock your pay for the weekend!"

"Thanks," said Annie. "If it weren't for COVID I would give you a big hug! I must admit I'm a bit nervous about meeting these people, I think Mum and the dad might be getting serious."

Roger Stops laughed. "Have you got some sedatives?" he joked.

The youngsters started to arrive, the papers started to get sorted and the regular Saturday shift began.

Roger Stops had installed a protective Perspex screen around the till. Annie felt more protected, she was grateful. They had all had some COVID safety training and they wore gloves and minimised handling of goods and so forth, but people were still not sure how to handle the crisis and lots of things were still going on that later would not have been acceptable.

Sarah did cycle home at lunch time and collect her own mask. There was a wash load going on, she could see the machine was already half full, so she stuck Mr Stops' mask in the machine. She would be able to take it back, tomorrow morning, just in case Jane needed it.

****

Around noon Steve Bronowski dropped in on the video team. They went through the tapes of the previous weekend first. The tapes of the hotel building site had shown nothing out of the ordinary in the week leading up to the discovery of the body. The tiny glimpse of the rear wing of the light-coloured car was the only thing out of place. Every vehicle and person seen visiting the site during working hours was legitimately there. The leisure centre tapes had already been seen by Bronowski and there was nothing new to add.

The team and DS Bronowski looked at the Sunday morning tapes again, especially the London Road tape in which Liam appeared.

"Let's go over this again," said Bronowski. "Liam appears and disappears down a side passage. We know those side passages lead to various parts of the estate and we spent yesterday doing a thorough search of the area. Then this girl appears and goes down the same side passage as Liam. She has a backpack and a couple of cups in her hands and she comes back just under half an hour later, without the cups and still with the backpack. Then, you say, she comes back at about 7:15, walking with a different boy and pushing her bicycle.

"I don't know. Was she so thirsty she needed two cups of coffee, or was she taking a cup to someone else? Could it have been Liam? There is no evidence that the two of them are connected and she comes back later with a different boy. I know it is probably perfectly innocent, but we need to think a bit more about this. We need to find out who she is and what she was doing there on that morning.

"Does she appear in those tapes again during the week? Was she in those tapes the week before? Let's have a look at the morning tapes around 6 to 8am."

"She's there most days and sometimes she also goes in the afternoon," said one of the team.

"Show me," said Steve.

It was the Thursday afternoon tape when the penny dropped.

"It's Annie Grant," said Steve. "You say she goes every morning about 6am?"

"Yes, Sarge."

"Well, I know where I am going to be tomorrow morning then," said DS Bronowski and he called Jerry Gregory to tell him the news.

They decided not to interview Annie just yet. Waiting until the morning and then following her to see where she went, was more likely to bring a quick result and if they spooked Annie and she did not turn up, it was highly probable that Liam would just take off and they would never see him again.

Steve arranged for a backup team, on foot, to meet him the next morning In Manor Road and they would follow, at a discrete distance, as Annie went for her morning jog. The team was chosen on the basis that they needed to melt into the background among the group of regular joggers and they needed to be fit enough to keep up with Annie, who, as far as they could tell, was quite quick, more a runner than a jogger.

Steve and Jerry thought that they might be close to a breakthrough in this case, for the first time in a week.

Simon was very busy in the kitchen when Annie got back from her Saturday shift. Supper this evening was going to be for Annie or Sarah to prepare, Simon was totally wrapped up in the preparations for the next day.

Annie was a little later than usual getting home. She had gone around to the allotments on the way home and had briefly touched base with Liam who, physically at least, was beginning to feel better. But he still had this terrible craving for the drug. His mood, having been cramped up in that tiny space for a week now, was not of the best.

Annie did not stay long, she had things to do and the concert was not so far off. She reminded Liam of the need for caution and left as soon as she decently could. She told him when she would next be there.

Annie thought she noticed someone watching her as she came home. She wasn't sure, but she thought that, earlier in the week, she had seen the car parked

144

in the lay-by opposite. Her guess was that it was a policeman, but she knew it might also be someone connected with the drugs gang and she was glad that she was not planning her routine evening visit to Liam this evening.

She was right about the car. DI Gregory had arranged for someone to keep an eye on Annie's house for the rest of the day. It would be unfortunate to have something go wrong in the twelve or so hours before the big event tomorrow morning.

Annie, while not in Simon's league, was a more than passable cook and she decided to take her mind off events by making a cassoulet. She was going to cheat with pre-cooked butter beans and cannellini beans, because she did not have time to cook dried ones, but otherwise it was going to be fine. She would need a baguette, garlic baguette is a must for soaking up the juices of the cassoulet and they did not have a baguette in the house, so she decided to rush to the Richmond Centre, where there was a French style patisserie and bakery, and pick up a baguette.

"Mum, can I borrow the car? I need some French bread," she yelled.

"Yes, of course, dear," said Sarah.

Annie pulled out into the road and drove off. Sure enough, the mid-blue saloon followed her, all the way to the shop. After she picked up a couple of fresh, beautifully crusty, baguettes, she drove home by a very circuitous route and the car followed her all the way at a discrete distance.

She left the car, not in the driveway, but in the garage at the back of the house. The garage had two sets of doors. You could enter it from the driveway, or you could enter it from a service road that led out onto Maidstone Way. Annie opened the garage doors and put the car away.

In the police car, the guy on surveillance duty was not that amused. He didn't think Annie had seen him but he had gotten very excited when she went out in the car. When she came back with two French sticks, if he had been French, he might have muttered the expletive, 'merde!' He was quite sure that DI Gregory, with that charming French wife of his, would have done exactly that.

****

Supper was uneventful. Annie's cassoulet was well received and Annie and Sarah and, on this occasion, Simon did each have a small glass of a passable, if inexpensive, Beaujolais Nouveau to wash it and the garlic bread down. Everyone was very tired and tomorrow was a big day. The Grant household turned out the lights at about 9:30 pm, but not before the blue car copper, as Annie saw on looking out of the window, had gone home to bed.

Chapter 25

The next morning, Annie's haptic alarm woke her at 5:30 and she went down and made herself two cups of coffee. She put on her tracksuit and running shoes and put a couple of things in her backpack, including a small pain-aux-raisins, which she had purchased the day before at the same time as she had picked up the baguettes. She put the two coffees into her travel mugs and, with one in each hand, she ran off to the allotment.

She was not surprised to find that there were more than the usual number of joggers out there this morning. She was not surprised to note that some of them were quite tall. She was not surprised to find that they seemed to be running a relay race in the same direction as her own morning run was taking her.

She reached the allotments, went up to Uncle Willy's polytunnel, opened the door and went in. She came out again a minute later with a small 1 litre watering can, which she filled at the tap. Annie went back into the poly tunnel and started to talk, while she watered the seedlings that she had been growing there all week. Some of them were beginning to sprout, others were not yet peeking above the vermiculite.

She sat down and drank one of her coffees quickly.

She was just about to start on the other when the door behind her opened.

"Hello Annie," said Steve Bronowski.

"Hello Sergeant," said Annie, rather breezily. "What on earth are you doing here at this time of morning?"

"I might ask you that," said the Detective Sergeant.

"Well," said Annie, "this is my Uncle's allotment and he is shielding because my Aunt June has cancer and we agreed a week ago, that I would come down and plant some seeds for him in the polytunnel and generally tidy it up. I sometimes come down in the summer and help him here anyway and Simon and I water for him when he goes on holiday, so I guess it was natural for him to ask me. Sorry about the smell; Jeyes fluid is good for sterilising the floor."

Steve Bronowski's jaw dropped open. Annie reached into her backpack and took out her pain-aux-raisins.

"I've only got one of these," she said, "but you're welcome to share it with me and I haven't touched the second coffee yet so it's COVID free. Would you like it. I have to go home in a minute anyway because I am working today."

****

DS Bronowski took the coffee and the half of the pain-aux-raisins. He sat down on the upturned plinth of the water butt and took a deep breath. He had a kaleidoscope of thoughts crashing about in his head. In one way he was relieved that he was not, for the moment anyway, going to have to arrest the delightful Annie, but a bit of him wondered if he might not be being played for a fool. Surely it was too much of a coincidence that Annie had started visiting this place exactly when Liam had disappeared. He was going to check her statement very carefully.

Uncle Willy was going to get a telephone call very soon. Bronowski couldn't believe that only two days ago he had been sitting just outside this 'bloody plastic tent' drinking coffee with Stefan Brylewski. What if he had looked in? And what about all the other polytunnels on other allotment sites. You just don't think about them as places to hide things, let alone people. They are see-through, for goodness sake, or practically so. But then, he realised, they are only see-through when the light is behind them and this one of Willy Grant's was right in the corner of the site and the sun would never shine through it. If Annie had been hiding Liam here it was a very clever move.

"Do you mind if I head off now?" said Annie. "My shift starts at 7:30 and it's 6:45 already. I need to take the spinach and a couple of beets home and get my mask and my working clothes. I usually start at 7:30 on a Sunday at the paper shop and I've to leave early today because we have people coming to dinner. I don't want to be late when Mr Stops has said I can go early. You can leave the cup down here and I will pick it up with all the others when I come tomorrow morning."

Steve Bronowski looked around. There were three more travel mugs perched precariously on the rather cheap greenhouse staging at the side of the polytunnel.

"Looks as if you've had a party down here," he said.

"No," said Annie, laughing, "I have a head like a sieve sometimes and I forget to take them home, especially if I go outside and pick some veg for supper after I have watered inside, as I am going to do quickly now. I need a couple of beets for a salad and some spinach for poached eggs and spinach and there are still quite a lot growing out there. Let yourself out, but please make sure you shut the door when you go. It helps keep the temperature up and these seeds are just beginning to germinate. Bye Sergeant!"

And Annie was off.

Bronowski guessed there would really be no point in it but he put some gloves on and collected the coffee cups in an evidence bag. He then went over the inside of the tunnel very carefully looking for anything that might indicate that someone had been living here for a few days, but there was nothing. Nothing at all. And he reckoned the Jeyes fluid would have done a good job of removing any other biological clues. It kills DNA and RNA viruses and most bacteria anyway.

OK. Back to the search and the video surveillance and the enquiries. Perhaps they should have a quick look at some of the other people around early morning on the day that Liam was seen on the CCTV. But first a telephone call to Willy Grant.

****

It was shortly after 10 pm on Saturday night that Annie had gotten up quietly, checked that the lay-by opposite was empty, put on some warm clothes and gone down to the garage. She had collected the car keys off their peg and walked across the grass to the garage, being extra careful not to make any noise. The last thing she needed was to wake her own family, or any of the neighbours. This was crunch point, this was when her life was going to have a real chance of getting back to normal.

She went in through the side door of the garage and took out her iPhone. No point in putting on lights that might be seen. The torch app on her phone was more than enough. She found the screwdriver and collected the number plates she had taken from one of the cars on the estate, on the Friday afternoon on her way back from the shop. They were from one of the cars up on bricks, one of the ones that had been there for absolutely ages, with almost nothing being done to it.

The front number plate was a long flat one, the one at the back was a square one. They were not quite a perfect fit, but at night, and all her driving with them would be tonight, nobody was going to notice. She knew that the CCTV and traffic surveillance cameras would pick up that the vehicle was untaxed but by the time anyone checked up, the plates would be back up on bricks and her real plates would be back on the vehicle. She finished with the screwdriver and put it in the glove compartment of the car. She also had no reason to believe that anyone would be looking for her car to make a journey of the sort she had planned, so any likelihood of discovery was an extremely long shot, pretty much the same chance as winning big on the lottery.

This was the one time she was glad Mum had a hybrid car. It was so much quieter than the big old diesel they had owned previously.

The garage door, with its well-oiled hinges, made almost no noise as she opened the door to the Maidstone Way exit. A few minutes later she had parked up outside the garages in Wolfson Road, taken a small bundle of clothes for Liam to change into immediately and gone to meet him, as arranged earlier, at the polytunnel.

"The first thing we are going to do," said Annie, "is to make sure that we remove every trace of your having been here. Put these gloves on."

She offered him a pair of blue latex gloves in a large size. She herself was wearing a pair already. No point in leaving fingerprints on the number plates.

"You can start gathering all your junk and rubbish into this black bin liner. Everything you have used or touched in this tunnel is going to go in there. And any of the clothing that is not going with you to rehab goes in there too.

"You can keep the iPad. I don't suppose, from what you told me, that they are going to let you load any new books on it when you get to the Marlborough so, if you don't like my taste in books, tough!
"I am going to wash down the floor and the tunnel walls with Jeyes fluid. We can Jeyes fluid the coffee cups too. You just take this cloth and use it to wipe everything you even remotely might have touched. When you've finished cleaning up your rubbish, you can go into the lavatory and shave and change into some of this stuff and bring out the last of the clothes you don't want. Hang onto the anorak. I forgot to get you another coat. And then we will get going. Wipe any surface you might have touched in the lavatory before you come out."

He did as he was told and when he had finished, went into the lavatory and changed. He emerged looking a bit more like the old Liam, but, still a bit haggard and drawn.

"OK. Let's go."

And Annie got into the car and plugged the new Satnav into the cigarette lighter socket, entered the post code of the Rehab Centre, turned up the volume and set it going.

"Hold this," she said, "and don't drop it. There's some water in the side pocket and some bits of chocolate and crisps and stuff. There's also a bit of baguette, a little stale but I did freshen it up in the oven and I put some butter and ham in it. So, you can have that. I suggest you eat it because it is going to be a long night."

She looked at the dashboard clock. It was a little after 11 pm. Plenty of time to get to the nearby town and get home in good time to get a few hours' sleep.

"Now listen," said Annie, "I need to be back here as early as I can and get some sleep and then pretend that tomorrow is an ordinary day. Your appointment isn't until 10 am. There is no way I can hang around and wait until then. I need to drop you off somewhere, with money, so that you can get a taxi to the rehab centre. You have the address and the phone number is plugged into your burner phone. Once you get there, you are on your own for the month. I am assuming you will be clean when you get out. If you are not clean, just don't bother to try to come back into my life, but if you are clean, call me on the burner phone and I will arrange somewhere to collect you.

"I have given you half the money you left with me. It comes to about £15,000. You are going to need to give the Marlborough Clinic a big chunk of that. The rest is in the lining of your holdall and we hope that they are not going to pick the seams apart looking for drugs. My guess is they will just rely on surveillance to stop any drug use. If they do find the money, I suggest you just say that you cleared out your deposit account when you decided to go clean and I suggest you ask them to look after it for you."

Liam listened. He understood.

There was no conversation for the next fifty or sixty miles, only the sound of the Satnav giving directions to the rehab centre. When they got close Annie spoke up.

"We are getting near now and Stansted Airport seems like a good place to me to drop you off. I am sure there will be taxis there. There is going to be a lot of coming and going. You can wear your mask and nobody will notice. And you should be able to get something to eat or drink if you want. I am going to drop you at the bus station. I wish you luck Liam. And from now on, when we talk to each other, You are Edward, or Eddy and I am Emma Collins."

Annie followed the signs to the free drop off area and stopped, very briefly.

"Good luck, Edward," she said. "Call me when you are ready and we can work out how to get you to somewhere safe."

He stepped out of the car, picked up the bag from the backseat and went to the bus shelter to wait for the courtesy bus.

Annie drove off. She looked in the mirror and could see him standing there, looking every bit like a little lost child. A moment of sadness came over her and she almost wished she could go back and give him a hug, tell him it would be alright, but she really did not know if it would be alright, and she had had enough of living on the edge. Tomorrow should be back to normal. She would have a month to live her own life and, after the exams in a couple of weeks, work out how to get him to somewhere safe and how to try and help him reorganise his future.

Maybe the murderers would have been caught by then. That would certainly simplify things. She was very aware of the increased surveillance she was under and she had to go home and deal with that. It would be a good idea to get Sergeant Steve Bronowski and the man in the blue car, off her back. As far as she knew the druggies were not pursuing her, but she was not going to let down her guard completely. A chance word from one of her school fellows might just awaken their interest and then she could be pursued by a group unconstrained by legal procedure. That might be much harder to handle.

She turned on the radio and selected the pre-set for radio 4. At this time of morning, for it was now nearly 12:30 am, Annie preferred talk radio to music. It somehow kept her more alert.

She thought about Liam/Edward with nearly nine hours before he could get a taxi to the Rehab Centre and she hoped he would manage to stay out of trouble and away from the attentions of the airport security and police. These days that was not always easy. She had packed him some masks and she hoped he would have the sense to wear one.

Annie reached the city about an hour and a quarter later. Shortly after 1:45am she pulled up outside the house with the junk cars and put the borrowed number plates back where they belonged. She replaced the number plates on the hybrid and drove home. Her luck held and nobody saw her. She entered the garage from the Maidstone Road entrance, put back the screwdriver, shut and locked all the garage doors and crept quietly back into the house and up to bed.

The alarm woke her at 5:30. It hardly seemed to her that she had been to bed. She put on her tracksuit, made her coffee and went off to the allotment.

****

When Annie got to the shop that Sunday morning, she felt as if the cares of the world had been lifted from her shoulders. Even Roger Stops commented that she seemed particularly cheerful today, even more so than she usually did.

Annie reflected on the conversation with DS Bronowski. She was very happy with the way it had gone, exactly as she had planned it. She had known for a couple of days about the surveillance and the fact that the Rehab Clinic had given an admission date so soon was an absolute bonus. She could not imagine how she could have got away with it if the date had been postponed to the following week. She now thought that she could give her full attention to the dinner this evening and, after that, the serious business of ensuring she made her Cambridge offer.

Jane breezed in later, without her mask, and Annie was rather relieved that she had washed and dried the one that Mr Stops had lent her yesterday. It was only yesterday.

Roger Stops suggested that, if Annie wanted to work through her lunch hour, she could go home even earlier. This Sunday, with COVID rearing its ugly head, trade was even more quiet than usual. Annie jumped at the offer and just managed to stop herself giving him a hug. She was trying to be careful about social distancing.

At about 3 pm, she left and went home. She went upstairs to her room, shut the door and promptly fell asleep on the bed.

Chapter 26

Freddie and the gang were playing a long game. Bruno had obtained all the information they had asked for, about the people that Liam had worked with in the county lines and in the leisure centre enterprise and the gang had made a short list of four people that they wanted to talk to. Michael O'Grady, the boy who was now at Cambridge, was one of these.

The others were the boy, Shaun, who had taken over from Liam as the weekend part timer at the leisure centre, a fellow martial arts student from the Boxing Club, named Darren, and, inevitably, Annie Grant. They knew they would need different approaches to Annie from the other three. Annie was not connected directly to the drugs scene, so they had no hold over her, while the other three were at the mercy of blackmail if it were needed.

****

It was Freddie who had gone up to Cambridge to interview Michael. He caught him coming out of College on the way to the Market, which was still open. Centre of town College, cheap and fresh vegetables and a stall holder who had good supplies of marijuana, if you knew how to ask him. Michael was not on heroin, he occasionally used cocaine and he dabbled in some of the recreational drugs that come and go in fashion. The gang of four were at the top of the network that supplied Michael and it gave him a nice little earner and them a way into the student scene.

Freddie took Michael to 'El Patio', a sort of retro coffee shop with decent pastries and very good coffee. He asked Michael bluntly if he had heard from Liam and Michael told him equally bluntly and convincingly, that he had heard nothing about Liam at all for a year, other than one meeting at Christmas, until the murder and the newspaper headlines last week. His mother had told him about it and he had gone online and read the articles.

"I don't think he would have murdered that woman Moira," said Michael. "I know he was dealing, just like me, but he was a fairly decent bloke under all that. I don't think he would be capable of killing anyone."

Freddie smiled inwardly to himself and began to explain why he was interested in Liam.

"The thing is, Mike; you don't mind if I call you Mike? The thing is that he has something of ours and we want it back. We had almost forgotten about it, written it off as a business loss, until he came back across our radar and now we want to find him and ask him, nicely of course, to return our property."

"Oh!" said Michael. "I get it. Look. The only people he was really close with in school were that Annie Grant, although they bust up huge more than a year ago, nearly two years now I guess and she doesn't even do alcohol much, let alone any other stuff. I don't reckon she would know anything. And then there were a few people at the martial arts place, I think it's called the 'Boxing Club', he spent a lot of time down there and he was really friendly with the coach there, oh, and a guy called Shaun, I don't know his other name."

They chatted a little more, finished their coffees and, as a parting shot, Freddie said: "Very helpful, Mike. We'll keep you supplied. You're doing an OK job for us. We may have other jobs for you soon. If we do, I will be in touch. Meanwhile, I was never here, OK?"

****

It was one of Bruno's rough boys who had dealt with Shaun and Darren. It had involved grabbing them from the roadside as they were walking home one night, hooding them and taking them to the same place where they had first questioned Moira. The thugs had made it very clear to the two lads that, if they told anyone about this, or if they found out anything about Liam and kept it to themselves, they were likely to fall off a similar height building to the one Moira had "accidentally" fallen off. Not surprisingly the boys were scared and there was no danger of their talking to anyone.

These interrogations, unlike the meeting with Michael, had yielded nothing new by way of information.

Bruno had been given the task of finding a way to talk to Annie. He was going to try to manage that on one of his visits to the Academy as a Trustee of the Academy Board. But that was put on hold for the time being.

155

From these enquiries the most significant new information was that Liam had been particularly friendly with the Boxing Club coach. The gang decided that the Boxing Club coach, since the money had disappeared from his personal locker and he had been the link between Liam, as courier, and the money mule, was now worth a little more investigation. That would happen sooner rather than later. George was looking forward to trying to find out if there had been any collusion between Liam and the coach.

George had obtained his scar in a knife fight, he had a scar, his opponent had a small piece of ground in the local cemetery. George was very adept at hurting people with his knives without doing irreparable damage. It was quite rare for George to conduct an interview without getting to the truth. He was very fair, he would stop hurting people if he believed what they had told him and he carried a box of butterfly sutures, non-stick gauze swabs and non-allergenic tape so that, when they put their clothes back on, their underwear, shirts and trousers did not get blood stained. He often helped them clean up too; George had been a medic in the army for about ten years, until he decided he had had enough of doing as he was told and left to take over the family businesses.

Chapter 27

Annie woke with a start at about 5:30 pm. She had slept deeply and woke thoroughly refreshed when Simon stuck his head around her door, with a cup of tea and a ginger biscuit.

"I don't want to spoil your appetite, but I just thought you might like some time to wake up and get ready. They will be here in about an hour and a bit. I stuck my head around your door earlier and you were out like a light. Have you not been sleeping well?"

"Thanks Simon," said Annie. "You are wonderful. I have been missing a bit of sleep lately, not sure why, but I feel good now, quite ready for whatever the evening brings. I hope we all get on. A ginger biscuit is fab." And she gave him a hug and a kiss on the cheek.

Simon was busy with the final preparations. He had made tagliatelle with his favourite pasta machine, he had prepped all the sea food, including the langoustines. He was going to make tagliatelle all'Almafitana, using the langoustines, some large king prawns, calamari, and the razor clams, as the seafood component. The sauce ingredients were chopped and the manzanilla sherry was ready to add to the sauce at the right moment. He had the saucepans ready and had put the plates ready for plating out. He wanted to arrange the seafood on the tagliatelle himself.

There was an art to arranging seafood on a pasta base and Simon wanted to practise it. He had made the dressing for a green salad, to be served as a palate cleanser after the seafood, and he had chopped and mixed the leaves, celery, green apple, cucumber, and chives for the salad itself. The pasta dish needed to be made and served immediately, to stop the seafood going rubbery and tasteless.

There were large doors that could be opened between the kitchen and the garden. It would be fine for Simon to be completing the cooking while everyone else was seated at the table. There were olives, gherkins, ciabatta bread, olive oil and balsamic vinegar for starters while the banquet was being prepared.

They had set up the gazebo in the garden and were planning to eat there. It was warm and the COVID regulations did allow it.

Simon had taken time in preparing the place settings. Sarah thought he might be practising for running his own restaurant one day.

The dessert, a pavlova with mango, pineapple, kiwi and passion fruit and a mixture of mascarpone and double cream, with a hint of maple syrup, had already been prepared and was in the refrigerator. He would sprinkle a few red pomegranate seeds on it at the last moment. Simon had also made a classic French lemon tart. The lemon tart and the cassoulet that Annie had made on the Friday evening, had become firm favourites since the two children had spent that summer in France with their father Henry and his family. That was also where they had become introduced to langoustines.

It had crossed Sarah's mind that the langoustines and the French lemon tart might just be subconsciously a way for Simon to remind himself that he did have a father.

Strangely enough, it also occurred to Annie, when she learnt what they were going to be eating. She herself was acutely aware of the strangeness of the situation. It was all very well to point out that hundreds of other families had experienced this potential move into "step-relative-hood" but, when it comes to experiencing the situation yourself, it is bound to trigger concern. Annie was just hoping that they would all like each other as people.

It was very important to her that no undue pressures or expectations were placed on anyone. As she had remarked to Simon on the Friday evening when they sat in the kitchen talking, whatever happened, Henry was still their father, Sarah was still their mother and Jenny and Peter would surely feel the same about their mother and Daniel.

Sarah and Simon had bathed and changed earlier, while Annie was still asleep, so she was able to go into the bathroom and soak, luxuriously, with some bath salts that one of the year 10 Business Enterprise Teams at the Academy had sold as part of their project. She nearly fell asleep again. The reaction to no longer having to watch out for Liam and no longer having to disrupt her normal life pattern, had somehow caused her whole body to go into a relaxed mode, which would probably allow her to sleep for a week, if she let it.

Fortunately, she did not drown; she managed to shave her legs, wash and dry her curly black hair, put on some very simple make-up and get dressed in a navy blue Jolie Moi swing dress that she had bought from John Lewis in the January sales. It showed off her beautiful neck, and the two tiny light chocolate coloured moles, just above her left collar bone, were more effective than any necklace might have been, in drawing attention to the milky smoothness and warm cream colour, of her skin. She looked stunning, without being overstated. She slipped on a pair of navy sling sandals, delicate, with a stiletto heel, thin heel strap and a single thin band across the toes. She had varnished her toenails blue. Even her feet looked beautiful.

Simon was wearing a freshly ironed white shirt, open necked, with long sleeves and gold cufflinks. He had a neatly pressed pair of dark grey trousers and black shoes, which he had polished to a dazzling shine. He also had available a chef's apron, which he often wore while cooking. Annie was staggered to see that that apron too had been washed and pressed!

Sarah, dark complexioned like Annie, was wearing a red cocktail dress in red lace, with a more plunging neckline than Annie's. She had also chosen to wear a gold necklace with a heart locket and matching small gold stud earrings. She had on red sandals with a mid-block heel and slightly thicker ankle and toe bands. She too looked stunning.

The three of them sat there.

Sarah started to laugh.

"Here we sit like we are all going out on a first date," she said. "It must seem all the wrong way around to you. I think the usual thing is for mum and dad to sit there, waiting for child to bring home a potential partner and hoping like Hell that he or she will not be a complete dork. On this occasion, there are three of us sitting here, and three of them in a car, hoping like Hell that none of the others is a complete dork."

It certainly broke the tension and all three of them were laughing happily when the doorbell rang. Almost so much so that they missed the first ring and it was only when Daniel pressed the bell for a second time that Sarah leapt to her feet and went to let in their guests.

The opposition too had gotten it, absolutely, right. Once their coats were duly removed and hung up on the pegs in the hallway, it was possible to see exactly what they were wearing.

Daniel was wearing a well cut mid-grey suit with a plain white shirt and an open neck. Peter could have been dressed by the same tailor as Simon, and Jenny, a little younger than Annie and almost as blonde as Annie was dark, looked stunning. Her hair was piled high on her head, held in place with a simple pink hair ornament. She too had a cocktail dress, cut high at the neck, slightly flared in the skirt and with long sleeves. It was a delicate shade of pink and she had found a pair of tiny earrings which matched it perfectly. It had a satin waistband, tied in a bow at one side. She was wearing pink sandals, similar in style to Annie's.

There is no doubt that the two groups were eyeing each other up.

Simon, bless him, broke the ice.

"I'm Simon. This is Annie and this is my mum, Sarah."

"I'm Jenny."

"I'm Peter."

"I'm Daniel."

And Simon did it again; he walked up to Peter and gave him a fist bump and he walked up to Jenny and gave her a hug, then he turned to everyone and said, looking at Jenny: "I'm so sorry. I forgot and you looked so nice, I just wanted to hug you."

And both Simon and Jenny blushed a darker pink than her dress.

And the ice was broken completely.

The further introductions were completed and everyone sat down to chat.

It was still relatively early after the first COVID wave, local infection rates were going down, but by eating outside, they were doing their best to minimise possible cross infection, and, by way of compensation, the evening scent of the sweet peas and some early blooming honeysuckle made the setting almost perfect.

To even a casual observer, it was obvious that Simon and Jenny were spending a lot of time looking at each other. Simon's hug seemed to have ignited, in them both, a bit of a spark. They were chatting away animatedly, and, being the nice kids that they were, they were including Peter in everything.

Annie, that bit older and that bit more sophisticated, was included in the adult conversation with Sarah and Daniel. Daniel asked about Annie's plans, he asked about her music, he asked about her job, he could not have been more charming. Annie found that she really liked him. He was kind and thoughtful and he had the same sense of social awareness as Sarah and Annie.

Perhaps surprisingly, or perhaps not, Daniel quickly told Annie that he realised that his coming into their mother's life might be hard for them and Annie immediately said she thought it might be hard for everyone, because none of them knew exactly what to do or how to behave.

"I guess Peter and Jenny will find it very strange if Sarah and a ready-made pair of older family members come charging in on their lives," said Annie.

"But, you know, Mr Carter, I think it is, probably, necessary for each of us to think about what all the others of us might be feeling. And I promise not to be perfect. I will be me and I know I have faults and I can do a very good row and even a sulk, if I must. So just be warned." And Annie smiled.

"Thanks Annie," said Daniel. "First thing to be done is for you and Simon to call me Dan."

Annie smiled.

"Second thing is for you to know that, if things progress between Sarah and me, we will try to find the right role for me in your lives too, the right role for Sarah in my children's lives and the right role for you and them in each other's lives. And we won't try too hard. With any luck we will be able to just let it happen.

"What's guiding me in all this is that Sarah and I have begun to find real happiness with each other, and I guess we want to share that happiness for a long time and to share that happiness with all of our children.

"I don't know if she has told you, but Sarah and I have spent hours reading advice on being step-parents and it seems to be all pretty rubbish except for two things. One is not to rush the development of the relationships, let them evolve naturally and if they don't evolve naturally then just accept it. The other is to recognise where everyone is coming from, so if you will allow me, not tonight, this is meant to be a fun evening and Simon seems to have done a huge amount of work to make it special, not least giving Jenny that hug…"

They both failed to suppress a grin.

"…If you will allow me, on some occasion," continued Daniel, "I would like to talk to you about our family and how it was and is and for you to talk to me about your family and how it was and is. Okay. Sorry for the heavy stuff. I can do heavy for England at times, so I hope you will excuse that!"

They looked at each other, Annie and Daniel, and both somehow knew it was going to be alright.

"Would you please take your places at the table, supper is served," said Simon.

Simon had put place cards on the table, but, unbeknownst to him, Annie had rearranged them quickly when he wasn't looking. He was now sitting next to

Jenny rather than diagonally opposite her. He looked at Annie, blushed rather sweetly, but said nothing.

The dinner was a resounding success. Even the ciabatta bread, olives and gherkins were enjoyed by all. *Quality counts*, thought Simon, making a mental note for his restaurant of the future. The tagliatelle was beautifully presented and the langoustine, once the two Carter children had learnt how to handle them, were declared delicious. Finger bowls, for dealing with messy fingers after the prawns and langoustine, simply added to the fun. There was parmesan on the table, but nobody wanted to spoil the subtle flavours of the dish and the parmesan grinder remained untouched.

Sarah, not an expert on wine, had taken the advice of the local wine merchant and had served a Melissa Bianco "Asylia" 2017, a white wine from Calabria, according to the wine merchant. It went well with the clams and the sea food. Daniel drank very little, he was driving, but Annie, relieved of all that tension, had maybe a little more than was usual.

They cleared away the finger bowls and the little dishes with the prawn, clam, and langoustine shells.

The green salad, with a slightly citrus dressing, was considered a triumph, and remembering what Daniel had said about Peter's appetite, Simon had given Jenny, who had joined him in the kitchen to help bring through the dishes, some more ciabatta for Peter. It did, of course, demand some more olive oil and balsamic vinegar.

When Simon offered pavlova or lemon tart, there were one or two long faces. When he said: "Let me rephrase that. Which would you like first, some pavlova or some lemon tart?" they all started laughing.

The bottle of Sauternes that Sarah had opened earlier in the weekend had kept well in the fridge and everyone had a small glass with their pavlova.

Simon had insisted that all good meals not only involve cream but also end with cheese. He had a three-year-old Cornish cheddar, a Brie and a Jarlsberg, with wholegrain crackers, digestive biscuits and unsalted butter, which he insisted on putting before everyone. There was one major taker, Peter, but the others all had a little of the cheese as well.

Over coffee, decaf of course, the conversation became quieter and some were clearly getting drowsy. Annie made a special effort to talk to Peter and she found that he, like her, was interested in science, but, for the moment, he was not sure whether he wanted to be an engineer or a medic. And then he whispered, very conspiratorially, "But I might really like to be an actor."

That was a bit unexpected, but Annie thought it was amazing. She told him that she herself was thinking that she might even want to be a musician. Annie asked Peter about his dramatic career and was surprised to learn that he had played several parts in the local amateur dramatic scene, including the part of the boy, Jeremy, in a local version of Chitty-Chitty Bang-Bang. It turned out that he could sing and he could dance. He had been having dancing lessons since he was six. He had first gone to watch Jenny doing ballet and had asked if he could join in. He soon became more interested in performing modern dance than ballet, although he still loved to watch ballet.

About 10 pm and all thought that time had flown, Daniel clapped his hands and said: "Really sorry to break up the party, guys, but I have an early ward round in the morning and I think all the rest of you probably have things to do too. I think Sarah is on an early tomorrow as well."

Sarah nodded.

"Next gathering will be at our place. Please tell me you want a next gathering."

And he looked in the direction of Simon and Jenny, who were beginning to appear oblivious to the rest of the world.

"Do you two think we should meet again?"

Daniel winked surreptitiously at Annie. Annie managed, just, to keep a straight face.

It was agreed, Sarah and Daniel were instructed by the youngsters to find a date for all of them to meet again.

"Unless you are going to come and cook at our place, Simon, you will have to put up with a takeaway. Chinese or Indian?" asked Daniel.

"If we make it Thai, it will be sort of both," said Jenny.

"I vote for Thai then," said Simon.

"I guess we will be eating outdoors again," said Daniel. "Let's hope it stays warm."

"Well, the Government said that two families with one parent and children under 18 could form a social bubble from the 13th of June and that would mean that we could eat indoors if it chucks it down with rain," said Sarah.

"And we could all go out together somewhere too, in the same car," said Jenny.

163

"Not in our little hybrid," said Simon, "but I fancy a ride in your nice big Merc."

"Not so fast!" said Sarah. "Let's just leave it that Dan and I will come up with some ideas and we can take it from there. We need to remember that Annie has some important exams on the Monday and the Friday of that week. Shall we arrange our next dinner party together for June 20th?"

Everyone was too polite to remark when Simon gave Jenny another, and this time, slightly longer hug, before a fist bump for Peter and Daniel, as the Carters left for home.

Chapter 28

On the Monday morning at the Hospital, both Daniel and Sarah were on the early shift. Daniel did the quick check, after handover, of all the patients in A and E and in the holding ward, in which patients were sorted before going off to the wards or, in many cases, before being discharged to the care of their own GP. Sunday night had been remarkably busy and it was a good hour and a half before he had finished sorting out the bits and pieces of the cases that had been left for him.

Rounds these days were not simple. The first thing you had to do was to put on all that PPE. Fortunately, this being the main hub of the local NHS Trust, the provision of PPE was good. Daniel was aware that this was not the case everywhere. Daniel was used to PPE, he had been a very junior doctor during the SARS crisis in the early 2000s and everyone had been well trained in the use of PPE at that point, and there had been a repeat occasion, when he had been designated infectious diseases officer during the Ebola outbreak that started in 2013. Most hospital trusts had someone who had that role to deal with, among other things, Ebola, if it came in on a flying visit.

One of the hard things about PPE is that it gives you a barrier between yourself and the patient. This crisis had shown to all those involved in providing NHS care to the public, just how important facial expressions are to communication. The staff, medical and ancillary, were having to learn new ways to impart confidence in their patients. Probably the hardest thing was dealing with children. For children hospitals are frightening enough, without having someone dressed like Darth Vader coming into a room to talk to them or to examine them.

With all these constraints and the constant sterilisation of surfaces and spaces, a round that might have taken forty minutes before COVID now took twice as long.

For Sarah too, the organisation of casualty was a different experience. Triage had new complexity. There was still the basic principle that "life threatening" emergency had to be seen immediately and dealt with, but then it got complicated. Anyone receiving patients in A and E had some degree of PPE protection, but at this early stage in the pandemic, procedures were not as well worked out as would, later, be the case. COVID symptom patients were seen in a separate area from those who had none of the symptoms of COVID and that meant more demands on staffing. It was not much fun and very hard work.

About two hours into the shift Sarah and Daniel sat down to share a coffee break. Both were writing up notes as they sat. They both declared themselves delighted with how the first meeting of the families had gone and both commented on the amazing impact that Jenny had had on Simon and Simon on Jenny. They exchanged compliments about each other's children and agreed that 20th June, a Saturday, would be great for a rematch. Daniel again repeated that it would be a Thai takeaway but Sarah suggested that they let Simon cook again for them and that they should all meet at the Grants' house again. Daniel said yes to that.

"There will be cream," laughed Sarah.

"I want this to progress quickly now. You know I love you," said Daniel. "I can see a time coming when 6 people will not be allowed to mix again, even outdoors, especially if this virus gets a hold, and I don't think I could stand that. Certainly, by the winter, the virus will be rampant. We have never seen anything like it and the measures the Government is taking are very tentative. I think they're in an impossible position; you can see that ICU is filling up with COVID patients, but the economy is taking a hit. I personally wish they would shut down air travel and close the borders.

"That Shakespeare quote, about being 'set in a silver sea' and the sea serving 'in the office of a moat'. We could do it, you know. It wouldn't be easy to get into Britain if we decided to shut the airports and halt Eurostar and the passenger ferries. We get so much food from Europe that they would have to allow freight, but we could test the drivers. I know things are looking up at the moment, but the virus hasn't gone away, and, come the winter and with all these people going away on summer holidays, I think we have not even begun the second wave and history tells us there will be a second wave."

"I agree and I love you too," said Sarah. "I wonder if we should think of some formal arrangement to make it possible for us all to continue to meet. There has been some talk about forming support bubbles in order not to be separated. Should we put it to the kids? I think my kids are smart and mature enough to understand what the problem is and, provided we can guarantee them some head space and physical space, I think they would go for it. How about your two? As I mentioned last night, from what I gather from what the press is leaking, two families with children under eighteen and only one parent in each household, can form support bubbles, live in their own homes, but visit, stay overnight, the same car and everything. You aren't in any sort of arrangement like that now, are you? We certainly aren't."

"No," said Daniel. "I suggest we put it to the youngsters tonight and then call each other."

"I have another Shakespeare quote for you," Sarah said. "I think it is from Julius Caesar. 'There is a tide in the affairs of men' and, if I remember rightly, it says if you take advantage of that tide, you get your fortune and, if not, it all goes pear-shaped. I don't think he actually said pear-shaped, but you get what I mean."

They both laughed.

"The little beggars better say yes," said Daniel. "Otherwise they'll be leaving school and earning their own keep!"

And with that they went back out into the department.

****

Twenty minutes later, a boxing and martial arts coach walked into casualty, his shirt and trousers covered in blood. His injuries were not life threatening, but they were extensive and Mr Carter was called to see him.

It was obvious from the examination that multiple relatively shallow cuts had been inflicted with a very sharp knife, possibly one of those Stanley knives, what the Americans call a box cutter, or even a scalpel. There were dozens of them, all just deep enough to draw blood and require closure with a suture of some sort, none deep enough to have damaged a major vessel.

Daniel was quite sure that these had been inflicted on Bryan Muldoon, that was the coaches name, by someone else. There was no way that some of those cuts on his back could have been made by Bryan himself.

Not only his body skin had been cut, but also his scrotum and penis had been damaged by the knife. A circular cut around the penis was particularly unusual

167

in any self-harm setting and rang alarm bells with Daniel immediately. He stepped out of the cubicle briefly and asked the receptionist to call security.

He went back into the cubicle and began to ask the patient, who was clearly in a lot of pain, what had happened.

"I fell through a glass roof, doc. I was clearing out the gutters and I saw a couple of tennis balls what someone had hit up there and I went up the roof to try and get them down and I slipped and fell and I went through the glass roof into the changing room."

Daniel knew that this was utter bullshit. First, the glass roof would have been reinforced glass; second, there was, as far as he could see, no bruising, just cuts; third, the cuts were clean and there was no tearing of the upper layers away from the lower layers as would have happened with a cut that had lateral force on it, a lateral force due, in the case of a fall through a glass roof, to gravity.

"I'm sorry, Mr Muldoon, your injuries are not compatible with that explanation. Someone has been cutting you. I think we need to call the police. Have I your permission to do so?"

Muldoon looked terrified.

"No Doc. No fuckin' way. I fell through the roof. I swear it. Can't you just stitch me up and let me go? Please?"

"You know, if we don't report this the people who did it may come back and do something even worse to you?"

"OK Doc. I admit someone cut me up, but if I tell the police then not only me but my wife and kids are going to get done too. I may get a few scars but I think they are goin' to leave me alone now. I think they are done with me. Please Doc. Patch me up, give me something for the pain."

Daniel thought about the new GMC guidelines. He had no choice but to follow Bryan Muldoon's wishes.

"OK. I will report to the police that someone came into the department with cuts all over his body, but I do have to respect your confidentiality, so the police will not know it was you who got carved up like this. There is so much fine suturing needed, a lot of the cuts will just heal, they are very superficial, but there are lots that are too deep and I am going to suggest that we get our plastic surgeon in to deal with you. He will be under the same constraints of confidentiality as I am, and he sews much better than I do. I see they left your face and hands alone. That helps a lot.

168

"May we take some photos of the injuries, before and after the sewing up? It may be very useful for teaching purposes and I will let you look at them and delete anything that you think might be able to identify you. I would also like to show them to the police. This is a very serious issue. I would not photograph any area with any of your tattoos."

"OK Doc. You can take the photos if it helps with training. Thanks. Please don't show them to the cops." And Muldoon began to cry, deep, deep sobs.

Daniel gave him some Entonox as a temporary pain killer and contacted the plastics team and the duty anaesthetist. He went back to the office, wondering who had been responsible for this horrible torture and why they had done it. Patient autonomy, one of the four pillars of ethics. Patient autonomy, on this occasion leading to the confidentiality clause.

The Government was "minded" to introduce a requirement for doctors to report the detail of knife crimes, but the argument against was simple; if patients could not rely on confidentiality they might seek treatment elsewhere, or no treatment at all, and then a lot of deaths might follow from infection or botched surgery. Daniel had been at a post-mortem once, for a backstreet abortion in which the patient developed gas gangrene, you only needed to smell that stench once to never want to smell it again.

Daniel made his careful case notes, including the diagram chart of the injuries. He anonymised a second copy of the report to show the police, if asked.

****

George had spent a heavy night drinking on the Sunday evening. Had he been breathalysed on his way to work he would certainly have been done for drunk driving. His work this morning had been to find out from Bryan Muldoon if he really had been colluding with Liam over the heist.

They had snatched Bryan Muldoon as he left home on the Monday morning to walk to work. A Range Rover with blacked out windows had pulled up beside Muldoon; two masked men had jumped out, grabbed him from behind, hooded him, shoved him on the floor in the back of the car and had taken him to the warehouse for a "quiet word". Muldoon had consistently denied any involvement in the theft. He had already admitted stupidity in giving his locker number to Liam, but he had no knowledge of Liam's whereabouts nor did he know where the money was.

It was probably the alcohol that made George, on this occasion, get it wrong on all counts.

First, he didn't believe Muldoon's denial until he had done much more damage than was necessary. Second, his normally delicate control of the scalpels he used was severely compromised by his being hungover. Far too many of the cuts were deep and by the time George accepted that Muldoon had been stupid and not wilful, the guy was too much of a mess to patch up with butterfly sutures and sticking plasters. So, when George did, eventually, stop the torture, he had to warn him that, if he said anything to the police, not only he but his wife and kids, would be in trouble.

Instead of taking him home, George and his driver dropped Bryan Muldoon off near the A and E department and Bryan Muldoon walked into the hospital.

****

The afternoon briefing contained the information about the knife crime and about an increase in the supplies of heroin and ketamine in the local area. Some particularly high-grade heroin seemed to be circulating and there had been a couple of overdoses, one of them fatal, because the users had not recognised the strength of what they were injecting. There was still nothing on Liam O'Connor and links to the death of Moira MacDonald seemed to have dried up.

The police were keeping a watching brief on Annie Grant's house and on the O'Connor family home, but they were more and more concerned that Liam had evaded them and was now somewhere else, probably a long way away. The CCTV tapes had shown that Annie had only started her early morning runs on the Sunday of last week, the day that Liam disappeared. Bronowski, after his confrontation with Annie in the polytunnel on the Sunday morning, decided to make that telephone call to Annie's Uncle Willy, he wanted to check that Annie really had been asked to look after the allotment. Willy confirmed that he had asked Annie, last Saturday evening, to keep an eye on the allotment for him. His exact words were:

"Yes, we agreed that she would plant some seeds for me in the polytunnel and generally keep an eye on things down there. She's a good girl, you know, she often helps me out."

What Willy did not say, because he was not asked, was that it was Annie who had rung and suggested the arrangement. It was probably a good thing for Annie that he did not.

****

Annie and Simon had spent a very normal day, working, practising and relaxing. Annie was glad to be getting on with some academic study and Simon was also working diligently on his GCSEs. For Annie there was a relief in having moved Liam on and she was quite pleased when she got a voicemail, on the burner phone, which said:

"Hi Emma. Just wanted to say that the place is alright, I am sure I am going to be well looked after, love, Edward."

She did not expect to hear from him other than once a week for a month now. She could get on with making sure she got her grades. More than ever now, she wanted Cambridge.

There was also the small matter of Sarah and Daniel to think about. Annie suggested to Simon that, having heard the preliminary announcements about forming support bubbles, this might be the only way that Sarah and Daniel could progress their relationship and allow the four younger ones to get to know each other.

"I wouldn't mind that," said Annie. "But with any luck, I will be off to Cambridge in October and that leaves you behind on your own. I think this really has to be your call as far as we are concerned."

"I look at it this way," said Simon. "It doesn't really make a big difference to me if we are a bubble. I can't see my other friends much anyway and you will be gone, and it might be quite nice to have Peter and Jenny and Daniel to give me and Mum something else to think about other than how much we miss you."

They both agreed that it was important for Sarah and Daniel and that, with all this COVID rubbish going on, it was the only way the two families would be able to see each other in a way that was necessary. It was going to take far more than one dinner party to prove compatibility, although Simon confessed to being very attracted to Jenny, and liking Peter, and Annie said she thought there was more to all three of the Carters than met the eye.

****

171

The report of the knife crime came through to the police station in mid-afternoon. It was so unusual, that extent of injury so deliberately inflicted, that it triggered alarm bells immediately with the duty officer who informed the Chief Superintendent. It sounded like something to do with serious crime and not just a routine knife crime. The duty officer felt a bit depressed that he should be thinking of stabbings as routine and, therefore, signalling this out as different.

Steve Bronowski was sent immediately to talk to Mr Carter, the surgeon who had reported the case to them.

The interview added little to the report that Daniel Carter had sent in earlier but talking to him Steve thought it became even clearer that this was torture, and, without disclosing any detail likely to identify the victim, Daniel was able to confirm that the man had been frightened, had refused to go to the police because he was scared of receiving further visits from those who had done this to him.

Daniel also told Steve, in response to a direct question, that he thought the man would not be able to walk very far with those injuries, at least not for a day or two. It was partly the pain and partly the tightness of the stitching on the upper parts of the leg and in the groin. There would be a feeling of tension as the man moved and it would make him very tentative about those movements.

As soon as Steve got back to the station and reported to Jerry and the Chief, they called all available senior staff on duty to a briefing in the Ops room. Daniel had respected Muldoon's confidentiality and had not shown the photographs to the police but the diagrams he had drawn left everyone who saw them in no doubt that this was torture, for the purposes of gaining information about something in the criminal underworld, or punishing someone who had transgressed. There was nothing that could identify the victim, so Daniel had respected Muldoon's wishes.

"We think this might be connected to the MacDonald murder," said Jerry Gregory. "We know there is clearly something going down with the crime gangs that they are trying to get to the bottom of, and Moira told me, at our last rendezvous before she was killed, that they were going on about some missing money? Could be a pretty big sum, especially with this level of violence."

"I think that, for the moment, we should assume it is linked and if we can find who did it, we might be getting closer to finding who killed Moira MacDonald and who is in the new set-up behind the drug and sex rings; we might assume this guy they tortured is one of the bottom feeders in the food chain. Can we find out who he is? I suggest we start with the fact that the A and E team said the guy walked in. With those injuries, I don't expect he walked very far. The surgeon said he could probably only have walked a couple of hundred metres at most. Let's get the CCTV from outside the hospital and work back from there."

There was a little more to add. The rumour mill among the underworld informers had it that several people at the bottom of the food chain had been picked up and interviewed about something that was worrying the top of the food-chain. They had been roughed up a little, apparently, and then told to say nothing. It was only that the victim of one assault was still fresh from the beating that caused him to say anything at all. What he did say to the informant was that they were trying to find Liam and were "interviewing" any acquaintances of Liam, which was why they had picked him up. The informant would not give a name, but he said the bloke was scared out of his wits and, almost as soon as he said something, he realised he was heading for trouble and shut up like a clam.

"Sounds as if the guy who was carved up might have been an acquaintance of Liam O'Connor too?" said Bronowski. "I think we had better have another look at Liam's male associates, especially the ones during his time in the final year at school. Think I will go and ask at the leisure centre again. I might be seeing the clientele that Liam dealt with if I go at the weekend. I wish we knew how Liam got into drugs; he was clearly clean until a few months before his bust up with Annie Grant."

Steve and Jerry sat there after the conference drinking a cup of coffee; Jerry was smoking a cigarette, so Steve was sitting by the open window.

It is easy with hindsight to have 20:20 vision, perhaps even better vision than that. The two of them wondered if they should have been pushing the newly agreed line of inquiry harder in the past week, but there had not really been any reason to do so and the reason why Moira died had not been as obvious as was now beginning to emerge. The top of the food chain was beginning to make mistakes and one might think that the team should have investigated some of these things before.

Well, they clearly had done it, but in a different context. Now they had a different focus. What they were looking for now was not someone who had been contacted by Liam in the past ten days or so but someone who had been part of his life before that, someone who had been with him on the addiction trail or, at the very least, had watched him go down the addiction trail.

Moira's murder was beginning to look less like a premeditated murder and more like an interrogation that had gone wrong. An interrogation linked to the desire of the crime lords to find Liam and probably whatever he had stolen from them. That death had been their first big mistake. Perhaps the knife crime was their second.

****

That evening, after supper, Sarah broached the subject of the possible forming of a support bubble with the Carters. The children were a little naughty because they let her tie herself in knots a bit before confessing that they had gotten there already that afternoon. There was some mock crossness, but Sarah was far too relieved to be too annoyed by their teasing.

Meanwhile, in the Carter household, a similar, but not totally congruous, discussion was going on.

"Dad," said Jenny, "is it bad of me to like Sarah and Annie and Simon so much that I almost forgot about Mum? I sort of feel that she would want us to move on, but I don't want to forget her; I think she would want you to be happy as well. I don't think forming a bubble with the Grants would make as much difference as all that. It would allow us all to get to know each other and that is not going to happen if we stay separate families. We wouldn't be able to see our grandparents, I suppose, but we can't really see them now anyway. Nan and Gramps live in Cornwall and we hardly ever see them and your Mum and Dad are isolating."

She paused for a moment and Daniel waited.

"I am worried that this is all going to be so nice that it will squeeze Mum out of my thoughts, and I do miss her, almost every day."

"Freya is still your mother. That will always be, and we will make sure we don't forget her. I've talked to Sarah about Freya and she understands, both that I loved her very much and still miss her and that you two do too. I really don't think Sarah wants to be your mother. I am sure she will want to care for you and look after you and I expect, knowing her nature, that she will come to love you; but all her thoughts will be for you as people and not for you as her children. And as for Freya, you and I both know that she would want us all to be happy.

"Love isn't rationed. It is organic, it grows. The more you love, the more capable you become of loving. The more you give, the more capable you become of giving. I would like to give it a try, getting to know these three and having them getting to know us."

174

Jenny gave a little smile and said: "Thanks Dad. I guess my vote is for forming a bubble. And, before you say anything, Peter, it is not just because I fancy Simon!"

"I know, but you do, don't you? Dad, I think we have to do it, if they'll have us," said Peter. "You know, Dad, Jen is right, it doesn't make that much difference to us in every day terms, but it does mean we can all get to know each other, and, the most important thing is you and Sarah can work on your relationship."

And then, being very practical, Peter said: "We won't have to go around there or have them around here every day, will we?"

Daniel just looked at him and gave a wry grin.

"OK, better make that phone call," said Daniel, just as the phone rang.

"Hello Sarah," said Daniel, "I was just about to call you." There was a pause. "Wonderful." Another pause. "Let's fix the next engagement, shall we? Bubbling starts on Saturday 13th June, according to the latest bulletin. Can we start our bubble from the following Saturday?"

It was agreed that they would.

After a bit more chatter, he hung up.

There was excitement in both families. After the isolation and social distancing of lockdown, having a new group of social contacts was quite a refreshing change, but there was also apprehension and Annie, following all that had happened recently, was aware that three more people were being brought into the circle of danger. *Damn you, Liam,* she thought, *why did you have to come back into my life?*

Chapter 29

At the Rehab Centre, Liam, under the alias of Edward, was having an interesting time. Had a supply of the drug been available to him he would, almost certainly, have used it, but, as it was not available, he was trying, with varying success, to put that out of his mind. The physical withdrawal symptoms, the shakes, the sweats, the cramps the diarrhoea, had long gone and now it was just the occasional emptiness in his head and the craving for the highs he remembered from the early days of his using. He was reflecting on how, at first, he had used the drug for pleasure and how, later, he had simply used it to stave off the withdrawal symptoms. He was almost resolved never to touch the stuff again, almost!

He was being well fed. The inmates had all had those nose swab COVID tests and he, as a newcomer, had had a swab taken, which proved negative, but he was in isolation for a quarantine period. There was no internet Wi-Fi that he could access, but he was able to charge up the old iPad with the kindle app and the Centre also had some "in-house" kindles which had lots of detective stories, classics, and spy-thrillers on them. They also had some kindles loaded with Mills and Boon, but Edward politely said no thank you, with a face that was, perhaps, less than polite.

He had a personal trainer allocated to him and she had assessed him and was planning his physical rehabilitation to go alongside the mental.

He had a psychologist attached to him to talk him through his addiction history and help him with his recovery. He was told that they had a number of types of therapy available and he would have a chance to talk them through with the psychologist and then the psychologist would either continue with Edward's treatment or refer him to a colleague more practised in the chosen therapy. On first review of the options Edward decided that CBT, Cognitive Behavioural Therapy, was the one he would go for.

It was, in many ways, the least invasive into the personal history and the most forward focussed. He thought he could lie his way more consistently through that therapy than through anything with a more psycho-analytical approach. He promised himself a lot of fun inventing who he was now. He might even be more successful academically, he might come from a wealthy family, he might have some brothers instead of three sisters. The family he knew most about, other than his own, was Annie's, so he would draw heavily on the Grants for his own family background.

To be fair to Edward, he was, deep down, afraid, and this interlude, of a month, was going to give him time to decide where and how he would go from here. It was unfortunate that he could not use the internet. He knew that the building had Wi-Fi. He could be doing a bit more research, if he could get access to a suitable device, especially into how to forge a false identity. He was convinced he was going to need a false identity when he did eventually leave this place and start to rebuild his life.

For the time being, he had no way of finding out if there were possibilities of internet access. Isolation for ten days was the admission rule so he would have to contain his impatience and plan strategically, which he could do in his head. The operational detail would come later. If the worst came to the worst he could always get back home and collect some more money to tide him over while he worked things out. The thing that was beginning to worry him most about that was something he saw on the news bulletins.

There was a TV in his bedroom, limited to Free serve channels, and he was aware that COVID was making people turn more and more to contactless transactions. He still had his credit card and debit card and his bank accounts, but he was aware that any transaction on those cards and accounts would bring the police down on him like a ton of bricks and, not far behind the police, along would come some hit man with the intention of finding where the money had been hidden and, failing that, a clear instruction to kill him. He did not like pain, he liked the idea of death even less than that.

****

The surveillance team had looked at Monday's tapes around the Hospital and had seen a man, with what looked like bloodstained clothing, walking towards the A and E entrance doors. They noted the direction he had been coming from and traced the relevant CCTV cameras backwards from the site. Eventually they found the point at which the man had been, unceremoniously, dumped out of a slightly battered looking Range Rover with blacked out windows. It was a very old model, with 2004 number plates.

Not surprisingly, those number plates turned out to be false. There was no glimpse of the driver or any other person in the car, but they did get quite a good picture of the man pushed out of the car, his face contorted with pain. Nobody recognised the man, he was not a known criminal, at least he was not known to the local police force. The force was also involved in a National Crime Initiative trial of facial recognition software, so they ran the picture through that. Again, it did not come up with any matches to known criminals.

This was a bit of a surprise to Jerry and Steve who were quite convinced that the victim must be part of the criminal community. They were right, of course, but Muldoon had never been in trouble and had only started taking money for allowing the gang to use his locker as a drop-box when his third child had been born and the money was getting really low. If they were going to spot him as the victim, it would have to be by a different route.

They downloaded stills and distributed them around the force asking them to watch out for this individual. It stood to reason that he was a local and someone, a copper on the beat, one of the mobile patrols, might just catch sight of him.

The repeat visit to the leisure centre was a little more helpful. The two detectives decided not to wait for the weekend to follow up on their thoughts from yesterday and, instead, went straight to the leisure centre to ask the manager again about Liam's associates and to which people he had been a personal trainer. They got some new names and gave their team a list of new people to be interviewed. They asked about Shaun, the boy who had taken over from Liam, and were told that he had come from the Boxing Club, just as Liam had. They had never had any inkling that the Boxing Club was involved in the drug scene, for them it was a place that did good youth work, but now it clearly merited a visit.

The manager of the leisure centre swore, 'on the bible', that there was no drug dealing going on, and it seemed to both Jerry and Steve that he was simply naïve and not devious. They asked him if they could have a copy of the attendance records for the past two years and, for the same time-period, a copy of the duty register. He had it in electronic form, which was going to make the searching through it rather easier than it would otherwise have been. He downloaded it immediately onto a flash drive that Steve 'just happened to have' in his pocket.

"He really hasn't a clue about the drugs, has he?" said Steve as they left, with a clear intention to come back at the weekend and interview anyone who emerged, after they reviewed the records, as a possible significant contact.

The foot soldiers in the detective team had completed, quite a few days earlier, all the interviews of the owners of light-coloured cars seen in the vicinity of the hotel murder site and all the ladies had been thoroughly respectable. Steve and Jerry could find no way of connecting any of them to the drug scene or crime in general. The owners of the larger cars, the Mercedes and the Audi owners, were, all five, married to respectable businessmen, a solicitor, the owner of a retail chain in the city, a commuting to London banker, a stockbroker and a senior local government official. The smaller car owners were just eminently respectable and had no criminal records, not even a speeding ticket between them.

The trail was going cold on the murder front. Jerry and Steve both thought that their only chance to solve the murder was to find out what the gang were making waves about, what had been taken, who had it, what Liam knew about it; in short, they had to find Liam.

On the Monday morning, after the fiasco with the polytunnel, the search of the city areas had resumed, spreading out in the general direction of the southern suburbs, moving now to the south west quadrant. Liam had only ever lived at 23 Grange Road and had spent most of his youth in the vicinity of his home and the primary and secondary schools which he had attended. Neither Steve nor Jerry expected him to have gone very far away from familiar territory.

They were scrutinising the general crime scene for any evidence of the sort of theft that might indicate someone in hiding was stealing to get food or clothing, but all they had really seen was the sort of low-level crime committed by junkies and young delinquents, damaging enough to the victims but, very often, with no chance of resulting in an arrest or conviction.

Other crimes were beginning to take up their time. A couple of very big robberies, an attempted rape, a stabbing at a pub, a possible arson attack, all the sort of things that happen too often in a large city.

Trying to identify the victim of the knife torture, trying to trace further contacts through the leisure centre and the Boxing Club, and, just in case, keeping a very unobtrusive surveillance of Annie and the three O'Connor girls, these were probably the most useful things to do at the moment.

Chapter 30

Right now, Annie's first important exam was under a week away, on Monday June 15th. She was much more rested without having to worry about Liam, but she was still getting up early to run. She found the early morning jog had become a great way of waking up, getting the blood flowing to the brain and setting her up for a good morning's work. Jane, at the shop, had apparently called in sick and so Mr Stops was short of one pair of hands and had asked Annie if she could help. They discussed it and Annie said she could do a couple of hours each afternoon or early evening for him but, in return, she would like this Sunday off because of the exam the next day.

It was a no-brainer, of course and Roger Stops readily agreed. He asked her whether she might do a couple of weeks for him and, perhaps resume her weekends on 20th June. Some people, when exams approach, simply run faster and faster on the treadmill and get themselves worked up into quite a frenzy, but Annie had always been well prepared, well in advance, and she always thought that sleep and focussed revision was the answer to doing well. She welcomed the idea of structure to the day.

During COVID and distance learning, structure was something that she and Simon and all the other school kids had struggled with. It was easy to let time drift and find yourself not actually doing the work you needed to do, because you had left it too late. For the next fortnight, she would have a regular pattern. A jog, breakfast, work, lunch, music practice, shop, supper, after dinner stroll, sleep. Time off for good behaviour on Saturday and Sunday this week!

Annie knew that, with mathematics, you need to be able to think. There is some basic theory you need, but, in the end, you either have the mathematical instincts or you do not. The essential difference between the "A" level maths papers and the STEP papers is that you can do well on the "A" level papers if you learn the theory and do lots of questions to get used to applying the theory, it being obvious which theory you need to apply to any particular question, but, with STEP, it is not always obvious which theory is needed and, sometimes, a very out of the box, almost instinctual, approach is needed.

She thought back to her mathematics interview at Cambridge last December. She knew she did not get everything right, but she also knew that some of what she had done had convinced the interviewers that she had a way of thinking mathematically. There had been a question about the fairground game where you roll pennies down a slot onto a board with numbered squares, it was a probability question; there had been a stacking problem, there had been graph analysis, there had been trigonometry, there had been calculus, but all of it requiring her to think how to approach the problem. She had felt right out of her comfort zone but had enjoyed every minute of it. She wanted more and she was trying her best to make damn sure she got it.

Her morning jog, or her evening walk, took her past Uncle Willy's allotment because Aunt June's shielding was still in force and he had asked her to carry on helping.

She did not think of Liam very much during this period. The more pressing matters were the exams and the relationship between the Grants and the Carters, especially the two parents. Sarah and Daniel were spending together any evening on which they were free. On one of those evenings Jenny and Peter came around to Manor Road and the four of them, Jenny, Peter, Simon, and Annie, sat out in the garden chatting about life in general.

Simon and Jenny were concerned about the upcoming GCSE results and thinking about their "A" level choices. Peter was thinking hard about his GCSE choices but spent a lot of the evening talking to Annie about musical theatre, he had a remarkable knowledge of the genre and was really into Sondheim, which resonated with Annie. They sang a couple of duets, just because they could. The relationships were developing well.

Sarah and Daniel were moving closer and closer to deciding that they would get married and they were looking forward to being able to meet as a group of six more frequently and without social distancing, from the 20th.

Even the weather was kind.

****

Steve Bronowski's interview with Shaun from the leisure centre on the Tuesday morning gave him more pause for thought. They interviewed Shaun

Baker at the police station, an attempt to put a little more heat on the lad. It worked, in a way.

"So, how did you get the job at the leisure centre?" asked Steve.

"Liam told me he was leaving and introduced me to the manager and the manager gave me the job," said Shaun.

"How do you know Liam?" asked Steve.

"Met him at the Boxing Club," said Shaun.

"Did you know he was doing drugs?"

"They all were," said Shaun.

"Are you?"

Shaun looked uncomfortable, looked away, fidgeted with his hands.

"'Course not," said Shaun.

"What did you do at the Boxing Club?"

"Mostly Martial Arts, same as Liam. That's how I met him really, we were in the same Taekwondo group. We were both in the club team and we used to go to competitions together."

"Was he any good?" said Steve.

"He was alright. He got better when he started taking anabolics. You could tell he was taking anabolics 'cos he got very bad acne and he became a bit aggressive. All the ones that did alright took anabolics."

"Where did he get the drugs from?" asked Steve.

"I don't know," said Shaun.

"So, you are telling me that there was a drug culture at the club, is that right?" said Steve.

"I guess so."

"But you never used drugs?" asked Steve.

"No."

"Do you still go to the Club? Do you still compete?"

"I do and I still fight for the Club."

"Do you do alright?"

"I get by."

"You told me that all the ones that do alright take drugs, but you get by and don't take drugs?" said Steve.

"I have nothing to do with drugs," said Shaun, beginning to squirm in his seat.

"How do they get the drugs at the club?" asked Steve.

"Don't know, I never asked them." More squirming in his seat, beginning to sweat.

"Does anyone at the leisure centre do drugs?" asked Steve.

The sweat was pouring off Shaun now and Steve could almost feel the fear. Time to back off. He had his answers. Shaun was mixed up in the drug scene and was filling the Liam role of supplying at the leisure centre. They could revisit that later but, in the meantime, Shaun would just be someone useful to keep an eye on. And the confirmation that the Boxing Club was a place where drugs were used was something to build on. Tiny cracks in the wall, but Steve could not have known how significant the Boxing Club link was going to become.

Time to let the lad off the hook, put him back in the water.

"Thanks Shaun, you have been most helpful. Very sensible of you not to get involved in all that drug stuff. There are some nasty big fish out there would eat up small fry like you."

Steve popped outside for a second and made a phone call to the duty officer.

"A young lad is about to leave my office. I don't think it will help a lot, but can you stick a tail on him, just to see where he goes. Needn't hang around all day."

When he came back, Steve delivered the sting in the tail.

"If we need to talk to you again, we will be in touch. You can run along now lad. You have been a great help."

Shaun got up and left, almost ran out of the door, without another word or a backward glance. He was hoping desperately that the gang did not know he had been picked up and taken to the station for questioning, but he rather thought they would find out and then another uncomfortable interview might happen. He was almost tempted to come clean, but he knew it wouldn't help the police get the leaders and it would almost certainly get him into a lot of trouble. He decided to go to the Boxing Club to warn Bryan.

****

Sergeant Ahmed followed the boy Shaun as he left the station. The lad made no attempt to see if he was being followed, he just put his head down and ran away as fast as he could. Ahmed almost lost Shaun in the traffic around the transport hub, the bus and train stations in the centre of the city, but he caught sight of Shaun leaving the main shopping concourse by the south exit and the policeman managed to get on his tail again. It was about a twenty-minute walk to the Boxing Club.

The club was officially still closed, because of the COVID restrictions, but Shaun rang the bell and a man, walking slowly, as if in pain, came to the door. Shaun quickly stepped inside, looking over his shoulder before he did so. A big argument seemed to ensue. The older man who had answered the door seemed to be very angry and was shouting at the boy. Sergeant Ahmed was near enough to hear a few words, "Why the fuck did you come here?" seemed to be the focus of the anger.

The boy said something Ahmed couldn't catch and the older man put his hands on his head and looked to be very distressed. In doing so, he showed his face more clearly than before and the Sergeant recognised the slightly contorted features of a man whose picture had been distributed only that afternoon. The man who had been cut and tortured and stitched up at the Hospital only the day before. He took out his radio and called the information in.

Five minutes after the call came in, Jerry Gregory and Steve Bronowski were in an unmarked police car heading for the Boxing Club.

"Do you reckon this is our breakthrough?" asked Steve.

"Could be," said Jerry. "But I am worried about what might happen to the guy if we do things too high profile. We need to tread carefully. I suggest we interview him very quietly inside and we try to make sure no one sees us go in. They might know some of our unmarked cars, these guys. So, let's park a few hundred yards away and walk. You're getting fat anyway so the walk will do you good."

"At least I don't smoke," said Steve. "When are you going to give that up?"

They parked in Elm Street and walked separately to the Boxing Club. Steve rang the bell first and went in, Jerry followed. The Boxing Club coach led them through to his large office next to the gym. The office had plenty of internal windows looking out on to the gym and was air conditioned and they were able to keep a good distance apart. The two detectives did not know what effort it must have taken for Muldoon to walk normally, it must have been agony for him, but there was no way from his behaviour that, if they hadn't already known, they would have recognised him as the torture victim.

"Let me introduce myself," said Jerry. "I am DI Jerry Gregory and this is DS Steve Bronowski. May we have the pleasure of knowing to whom we are talking?"

185

"I'm Bryan Muldoon. I'm the chief boxing and martial arts coach here. Why are you here?"

Muldoon looked very nervous. This was going to be a tricky interview.

"Well, let me explain. We had a report from the Hospital that someone had been badly injured in a knife incident and had gone to A and E at the Queen Katharine for treatment. We always get reports from the hospital of knife crime, although the doctors do respect the confidentiality of patients, but the report we got on this crime was so horrendous that we thought we had to try and find out who the victim was and why the attack had taken place."

"OK. I understand, but what has that got to do with me?" asked Muldoon.

"Well, we asked the doctor how far the bloke could have walked with the injuries he had, and the doc said not very far, so we had a look at all the local CCTV cameras and we saw someone with blood-stained clothing getting out of a car on the Victoria Road approach to the Hospital. We didn't recognise him, but we were making enquiries in connection with the murder of Moira MacDonald and questioning people about Liam O'Connor, I am sure you saw The Herald about 10 days ago. We are trying to talk to anyone who knew Liam."

"Well, to cut a long story short the name of this place came up when we were questioning the lad who took over from Liam at the leisure centre so we thought we would come and talk to you to see if you knew anything. We were very surprised when you turned out to be the person who was captured on CCTV getting thrown out of the car that morning."

The colour had drained from Bryan Muldoon's face. On reflection, Steve thought that Muldoon had already been a bit pale, probably from some loss of blood, and now he was ashen grey.

"I must have a double."

"No, Mr Muldoon," said Jerry. "This picture is you." And Jerry took one of the photos out of his pocket and showed it.

Muldoon's head dropped into his hands. He could see no way out of this. The instant he rolled up a sleeve, took off a shirt or put on a pair of boxing shorts, the multiple scars were going to show. He had already known that for the foreseeable future he would have to conduct his work wearing long sleeves and tracksuit trousers.

"It was you, wasn't it?" said Steve.

Muldoon didn't deny it. He simply said nothing.

"Who did it? Why did they cut you up so badly?" asked Jerry.

There was a long pause. Muldoon knew he could not deny he had been cut but he was going to play dumb about the reasons and give nothing away.

"I don't know why they did it. They just grabbed me from behind and shoved a hood over my head and put me in the back of a car on the floor. They drove me to this place and marched me inside and then they stripped me and strapped me to a sort of medical couch thing and then they took my hood off and began to ask me questions.

"Every time I gave an answer, they said I was lying and this horrible guy, they were wearing masks so I couldn't see them, he just started to cut me. It bloody well hurt. It went on for ages. Then, suddenly, the one with the scalpels said something about believing I didn't know anything of any use to them and they untied me, got me dressed and bunged me back in the car. Drove me to the Victoria Road near the Hospital and threw me out."

Neither Jerry nor Steve believed him. Not this level of violence without something more behind it. So, Jerry began asking questions.

"OK. Well, let's get a couple of things straight. The fact that you didn't report this and the fact that they used such violent torture on you, they mean you are lying to us. You know why they did this. You must do. And we will go on questioning you until you do tell us what it is about. Where did they pick you up?"

"Right outside my house in Madras Lane," said Muldoon.

"How long did they drive for before they got to this place where they took you?"

"I reckon no more than ten minutes. There wasn't much traffic 'cos of lockdown, so it was a pretty steady drive," said Muldoon.

"How about when they dropped you in Victoria Road?"

"I was in too much pain to think about that, but it wasn't very long. Probably a bit less than ten minutes that time."

Muldoon began to think of a way to get out of this and keep the police from knowing that he had been involved in any of the drugs racket, specifically the money laundering.

"I think that Liam must have done something. I think they thought I knew where Liam was. He used to be a member here. They seemed to be really after him because they kept asking me where is Liam and where is the money? I had no idea what they were talking about. They asked me if I had helped Liam take the money and I kept saying what money and they kept saying you know what money and I didn't. I don't know why they thought I had anything to do with it. Liam was only one of loads of boys who came here so what made them come after me I don't know."

The only bit of that statement that made any sense to the two policemen was that Liam must have done something to the drug guys and, probably, it was a very large theft from the drugs cartel. The idea that Muldoon was a random victim made no sense. There must have been something that linked Liam and Muldoon.

Then Jerry remembered what Moira had said about how the drugs and money were handled at the leisure centre and he thought he might just have an idea of what had gone down here at the Boxing Club.

He started to probe.

"Does everyone have a locker here?" The sweat began to appear on Muldoon's brow.

"Yes, they do," said Muldoon.

"Do you have a locker?" The sweat began to almost drip off the end of Muldoon's nose.

"Of course I have a locker," said Muldoon.

"Would you mind showing us?"

They went through to the locker room and Muldoon showed them his own double width and full height locker, complete with combination lock.

"Does anyone else know the combination to your locker?" asked Jerry.

"No," said Muldoon, rather too rapidly for Jerry's liking.

"Are you sure your locker isn't used as a drop box for drugs?" asked Jerry.

Close, but no cigar, thought Muldoon. *I do not like this.*

"How about money?" said Jerry.

"Why would you think that?" asked Muldoon. "All I am is a bloody martial arts coach. Not some drug tycoon."

"Then why didn't you report the knife attack on you? What hold do the people who cut you up have over you?"

Muldoon replied, "They said if I told the police, I would find my wife and kids badly hurt, probably an accident with a car one day."

"And you believed them?" asked Jerry.

"Of course, I believed them. If they could do what they did to me, a simple thing like running over a kid with a car is going to be nothing to them. I really wish you hadn't come here. I bet those guys have spies everywhere and if they know who you are and you have been talking to me, I reckon I am going to be in trouble."

"Right," said Steve, "can we look inside your locker?"

Muldoon dialled the combination and opened it up. The detectives looked inside. For a locker belonging to a martial arts coach, it was rather empty.

"Would you mind if we arranged to have the locker swabbed for drugs?" asked Steve.

"Go ahead," said Muldoon.

"Let's go back through to your office shall we. Just a few more points to clear up," said Jerry. And they went back and sat down.

"Is there anything you can tell us about the warehouse where they tortured you?" asked Steve.

"I could hear some heavy machinery working nearby while they did it," said Muldoon. "It sounded like a demolition crane or something because I kept hearing breaking glass and crunching metal and a sound almost like a bulldozer. I think it must have been quite a way from a main road because I didn't hear any normal traffic sounds. It had bare grey concrete walls and some breeze block partitions inside with steel girders, I reckon that I was quite high up because I do remember being in a lift. It had electric light because they had a light on while they were doing it to me."

"No logos? No labels anywhere? Any other details?"

"No, sorry," said Muldoon.

"Right. Well, there's just one thing more you can do for us. Do you have CCTV and do you have a record of all attendances?" asked Steve.

"We have CCTV but since lockdown we have had it turned off. Didn't seem any point when we were locked up so tight anyway. And the records of entry are recorded in a book. The entry is by a keypad door lock. Everyone signs in when they come in. I can let you have any of the books for the last year or so now, but anything before that is kept in my filing cabinet at home."

"When did you last change the combination? Could Liam have come in here recently? Could he have slept here at night?" asked Jerry.

Muldoon looked a bit shamefaced.

"I'm afraid our security is rubbish. We haven't changed the keypad code since the place opened about three years ago. So, I suppose the answer to your questions is yes, he could have got in and yes, he could have slept here but there has been no sign of it. The place has, apart from me, been empty I think."

"Mr Muldoon. Are you sure you are not holding something back from us? I still think the level of torture is too much for there not to be something more to your involvement with the thugs who did it. I am going to give you overnight to sleep on it and one of our officers will be back tomorrow to get a signed statement from you about the whole incident. You might like to think whether there is something more you want to add. I doubt whether your silence will buy you safety. I think you and your family's only chance of safety is for us to put the people who did this to you and whoever is behind them, in prison for a very long time.

"I don't believe your statement, Mr Muldoon, not about the randomness anyway. Too many things say you are involved and you can be sure that, even if we do not have the concrete evidence for saying that at present, we will find it and it would be much better for you if you were helping us, rather than obstructing us, in our hunt for the nasty pieces of work behind the drug scene in our city. Someone will be back tomorrow. Good day to you, Mr Muldoon." And with that, Jerry turned on his heels and left, closely followed by Steve.

One of Jason Miller's county gang children saw them leave and, anxious to make a bit of cash, reported it to Jason. The lad knew a policeman when he saw one, even a plainclothes copper like these two.

That evening, about six o'clock Bryan Muldoon was walking back home. His mind was in a daze. He had sat there all afternoon after the police had gone trying to decide what to do and he had reached the conclusion that his only option was to tell the truth. He would tell them about the locker drop and Liam's involvement and that his only involvement was to put the rucksack in the locker. He walked slowly towards home, still in some pain but feeling that maybe there was a way out of all this. Even a short prison sentence was better than the idea of a life looking over his shoulder. He forgot to look over his shoulder.

The eyewitnesses said that a dirty old Range Rover with early noughties number plates came out of nowhere at a very high speed and smashed into Muldoon as he walked slowly across the road. The car stopped, reversed back over the man lying on the ground, lined up its offside front tyre with his head and went back over him once more. It drove off fast in a southerly direction.

Twenty-five minutes later, George drove the vehicle into the wrecking yard, next to the lorry depot, the second-hand car lot, and the empty warehouse. Not long after that, the car that had picked up Muldoon on Monday morning, and finished him off on Tuesday evening, was reduced to a metal shell, crushed into a block and loaded onto a lorry, with several other blocks of metal, on its way to the recycling yard.

The news of the hit and run came through to Jerry and Steve as they were conducting their case review shortly before going off duty.

"Oh, shit!" said Jerry. "I was pretty sure he was going to tell us what the big deal is with Liam. I think I am going to assume that Liam stole something very big. I reckon a month's takings in this City would be in the millions and we don't know for sure how much of that would be laundered through something Liam would have access to, but for the drug lords to take this much trouble it must be a lot. So, I think we focus even more on finding Liam. Everything points to him."

They put in train the usual CCTV search, but Madras Lane was not covered by CCTV and George knew all the roads to take to minimise CCTV coverage of his journey back to the breakers yard. They did spot the battered old Range Rover a few random times, but not enough to identify where it had gone. The South East sector was probably the best they could do and well out into the suburbs into the bargain.

This was all beginning to be a bit of a headache. Every limb of the enquiry seemed to be cut off just as it looked like bearing fruit. But sometimes, police work requires patience.

"Don't worry, Jerry," said Steve. "They are making mistakes; they will make others. We'll get them."

Chapter 31

The activity in both the Grant and Carter households had settled back into its regular groove. The cancellation of the summer exams had lifted a load off everyone's shoulders, except, of course for Annie. But Annie was sorted! Just enough adrenaline to perform well, not enough to create anxiety. The only triggers to anxiety were the once a week voicemail calls from Liam.

One call, in the first week of his stay at the rehab centre, sent a little shiver of alarm down Annie's spine.

"Good evening, Emma, Edward here. Just wanted to let you know that I come out of quarantine next week and I can then start to mix with the other rehab folk. I am sure some of them will be able to help me with the things we talked about before. I hope your preparation for your exams is going well, they must be due next week. I am almost over the worst cravings now and the CBT is good. I have a great therapist. I will see you in about three weeks. Love from Edward."

"Oh, God!" thought Annie. "If he is talking about what I think he is talking about, he is going to be tapping up junkies for information about false ID; that could be really dangerous. And I wish he had not mentioned my exams being next week. The people at the rehab place are going to ask him about those exams and the only exams I know of taking place next week are the STEP papers. I hope he doesn't say it is University entrance requirement exams.

"Please God, let him say it is my University exams. And seeing me in three weeks. I need that like a hole in the head. I am going to have to cover up any journeys I might make from Daniel's family as well as my own and that just makes it even trickier to get away. I need to think about how to handle that problem as soon as my exams are finished."

The concert had been postponed until late July. That was one piece of relief. It made more sense because the orchestra could practise together a bit more and it would mark the end of the school year more effectively. Annie was looking forward to meeting up with her friends again to rehearse, even though it would be socially distanced.

So, apart from beginning to wish that Liam had been strangled at birth, Annie was back on track.

She was finding the short stint in the shop very therapeutic. She was also aware that the amount of surveillance of her home and her activities in general had declined and she was grateful for that. She did catch a glimpse of that blue police car a couple of times, mostly when she went for her morning jog, and she also noticed a grey Mercedes slowing down as it passed her house a couple of times. She wondered if she was, perhaps, becoming paranoid.

****

The Boxing Club was closed off to all visitors and designated a crime scene. The police went in and removed all the records they could find and all the old CCTV tapes. The search of the leisure centre records and CCTV, was also continued.

Jerry asked for a summary of what had come out of the leisure centre records. The CCTV did not go back far enough to be of interest because they kept their tapes only two months. They had a tape backup routine that involved storing everything on a daily tape, a weekly tape and a monthly tape so that there was always a second copy of everything, but only back as far as two months ago. The police had already reviewed the relevant footage around the time of Liam's last visit there.

The electronic records had been more interesting. It seemed that the known dealers all came to the centre on Wednesday or Thursday before 6pm. Liam and Shaun both worked at the weekends and both worked on Thursday evening, from 6pm-8pm, just a couple of hours. From this, added to what Moira had told Jerry, the detectives reckoned that the courier, either Liam or Shaun, was bringing the drugs in at the weekend and leaving them in a locker, the dealers were collecting their stash and leaving the money on the Wednesday or Thursday and, presumably, Shaun or Liam took the money away on the Thursday evening and delivered it somewhere on the Friday, or Saturday when they collected the next load of drugs. If the Boxing Club was involved, then a focus on Friday and Saturday at the Club seemed a good place to start.

It proved to be a good starting point. There were two important facts. Shaun and Liam both always visited the Boxing Club on Friday. Significantly Shaun had not been a regular Friday visitor until he took over from Liam at the Centre. Then there was always, on the Friday, about half an hour after Liam or Shaun arrived, a person who appeared, signed in, and left about thirty minutes later. It was a different person every week. That person only ever came once and that person's name could not be found in the register of club members.

A search of the electoral roll showed that at least some of these people did not exist. Of course, a couple of the assumed names did appear on the register, but there are a lot of people in a big city and random choice of names is always going to mean that some real person will have that name. The key point was that some of those names did not exist.

"I think I've got it," said Steve. "The drug deals are done at the smaller centres by the Wednesday or Thursday. The couriers, like Liam and Shaun, pick up the Money on the Thursday evening from their locker where the dealers have left it. They take it to the Boxing Club on the Friday and put it in a Locker there before 7 pm. At around 7:30 to 8:00 pm, a bigger fish arrives and collects the money from the locker and takes it to a central place to be laundered. That bigger fish also drops off the drug supplies for Liam or Shaun to take to the leisure centre for the next week's delivery.

"I think, if we look hard enough, we will find traces of drugs in some of the lockers at each of those places. And, if we do, we at least know what Liam must have done. He must have gone back to the Boxing Club and nicked the money that Shaun had dropped off there. But for the gang to have made such a fuss it was probably more than one small centre's takings. I wonder if there are other centres we can identify where they also go to the Boxing Club to drop off the cash and pick up the next stash of drugs? Or is the leisure centre the focus and are the dealers who go there the second tier, supplying the front-line pushers?

"I bet, either way, some kid who is a member of the Boxing Club, but also has a part time job somewhere where lots of people go, is involved. Nobody would think it unusual if a kid with a part-time job was also going to a leisure centre or a gym. I reckon it has to be an afterschool and weekend job and whoever it is will not be working Friday but will be at the club on a Friday or the leisure centre on a Thursday."

"OK," said Jerry. "Let's get the lockers swabbed and tested and let's get the guys on finding out which kids fit the pattern you have suggested. We might then have a few leads to follow up. What I really want is this gang, the big guys. We need to be careful not to spook them, but we need to get on with this. I am afraid we might just pick up the smaller fish again. Our big hope is that someone we nail will have seen at least one of the big fish and through one of the big fish we might find their associates."

It was beginning to feel a lot better. They had a hypothesis to go on, it fitted the known facts, they had a plan of action which was less than random. They would never have thought of the leisure centre if the gang had not bumped off Moira shortly after she had talked to Jerry. They would never have thought of the Boxing Club if the gang had not carved up, and then killed, Muldoon. What might their next mistake be, or, could this be enough. Lots of patient detective work to be done.

****

Chapter 32

Life happened over the next few days. The police continued to build up a picture of the work and leisure activities of the youngsters using the Boxing Club. The search of disused buildings and hiding places, where Liam might be, was concluded, with no success. Moira's parents had the body released to them and they arranged a funeral. The only people attending would be the parents, the baby and Jerry Gregory.

Bryan Muldoon's wife began to look at life as a single mother with three young children, did not like what she saw and decided to put her house up for sale and move back to Gloucester to be near her parents. Such a move would take time to arrange but it would give her peace of mind and the children a chance of happiness.

The gang of crooks began to think that this was all going to blow over but recognised that they were going to have to find a new route for laundering their cash in the south of the city. They had interim measures in place, based on the way they ran things elsewhere in the city, but none of those measures left them quite as distanced from the point of delivery as the leisure centre and Boxing Club had and they were wondering about all the arrangements they had in place. It was time, perhaps, for a major overhaul of supply routes and money laundering.

Tesco delivered on the Friday. Simon cooked on Saturday and Sunday. Sarah and Daniel went to work, came home, relaxed.

Annie sailed on serenely, as always.

Around her, the inter-family relationships progressed. The exams she was going to take on the Monday and Friday were online and she needed to practise using the system it was being run on. She had received details of how to conduct a practice run after she had registered way back in May, and she had had a preliminary look at what was required, but she had another and more systematic look over the weekend.

On Monday 15th June, at the appointed time, Annie headed off to the testing centre at the Academy, sat down at her appointed desk, logged on to a computer, and began the three-hour examination. She had plenty of fluid, plenty of fast glucose fixes and peace and quiet.

When she finished at shortly after noon she went straight home where Simon was waiting with a big hot chocolate with whipped cream and some delicious brandysnaps he had made that morning.

"How did it go?" asked Simon.

"It was OK," said Annie. "I think I answered enough questions. There was nothing there that struck me as out of order. To some extent, it is all going to be about whether I attempted the right questions."

Annie never enjoyed post-mortems on exam papers and Simon respected that. He knew perfectly well that if Annie said it was OK, it probably meant she had aced the paper. He didn't know what she would have said if she had done badly because, in her entire life, she never had done badly. As one of her friends remarked: "She even passed her bloody driving test first time and, I bet, if they gave them, she would have gotten a distinction."

Annie gave herself the afternoon off. A walk, some violin practice, and the evening shift at Stops' Shop.

When she came home, Sarah asked her about the exam and Daniel called to check all was OK. *That's nice of him*, thought Annie.

Meanwhile, a pattern was beginning to emerge from the police station enquiries around youngsters who were members of the Boxing Club. In the south of the city the part time jobs were largely leisure related. The leisure centre, a couple of gym clubs and evening work at a couple of indoor pools associated with the two major secondary schools, employed eight youngsters who were regular members of the Boxing Club and turned up there at the club on Fridays.

Another group of eleven youngsters had evening and weekend jobs at a series of fast food and oriental takeaways owned by a man called Jason Miller. On making enquiries the police discovered that Jason Miller had taken over the family fish and chip shop from his father sometime in the late 1980s and, by a series of shrewd acquisitions of disused shops and pubs, when they came on sale cheaply during periods of high street recession, had built a minor empire. He converted them to takeaways and seemed to be doing very well. He tended to let them out to different ethnic groups to run as family businesses, with a variety of cuisines, and he was clearly making a lot of money from his share of the turnover.

There had been no reports of any problems with Mr Miller and the law. He seemed to be a pillar of society; he had even provided free meals on one occasion for some of the homeless during the COVID crisis.

Jerry and Steve, however, began to speculate. Once their minds had started to move in this direction, they were thinking that maybe a takeaway was a pretty good place for two kinds of business. First it involved a lot of random people coming to buy legitimate goods and could therefore be a cover for distribution of less legitimate items; second it could be a cover for prostitution, because young people, not given to cooking evening meals, often hung around there socialising over food and that too could be a cover for less legal socialising.

It did seem a bit of a stretch to pick on Jason Miller at this point. One obvious interpretation was that he was simply providing work opportunities for less advantaged members of the community, for youngsters to make a bit of cash.

There were ideas forming. Ideas worth just developing. Observation, solid police work. That was needed now. Just a note to people to keep an eye on the retail outlets and the youngsters with the part time jobs.

The issue here and now was that the places with the part time jobs were shut, except the takeaways, and people were not hanging around those in the way that they used to. Nobody was going to give a warrant to search the Miller places just on the hypothesis that Jerry and Steve had come up with. Patience was called for, again.

Development of some of these lines of enquiry would need a post-COVID environment in which more normal social interaction was taking place.

"I wonder what that machinery noise Muldoon mentioned was all about," said Steve.

The report of the hit and run in The Herald had brought no useful information from the public. The timing of the hit and the route taken by the car, meant that the vehicle had not attracted the attention of the public once it had got away from the immediate scene. The lack of recent CCTV footage at the Boxing Club was unhelpful. The false names at the Boxing Club were random and showed no ethnic bias. No clues there. The police just carried on. They had done the obvious things, like putting out an alert to all the bodywork firms and garages, including George's, but there was no return from that line of investigation.

Keeping tabs on Shaun was equally fruitless. In fact, the whole drug scene was so far underground during COVID, no casual meetings, no obvious dealing; everything must be online and to order. It would be the police on cyber-watch who might just pick up something there and that was outside Jerry's and Steve's paygrade.

Jerry and Steve knew which group was responsible for both the murders of the past month but were no further forward in putting names or faces to the members of that group.

****

On Wednesday 17th June Liam came out of isolation and started to mix with the other inmates. Everyone in the Rehab Centre had tested negative for COVID and so the social distancing rules were rather loosely applied. The team at the Rehab Centre felt that it was important not to relax the rules completely, because the inmates would be going out into a COVID world when they left the Centre and would need to be, at least a little, tuned in to the National guidelines.

Liam, Edward as he now tried to think of himself, had two main obsessions. The first was to find a way to access the Internet; surely someone in the place had worked that out; and the second was to find out how to access effective, if forged, ID. He was convinced that someone in the group here trying to quit the drug scene would have knowledge of how to do both these things.

He had to be careful about how he approached the issues.

He got lucky on the first of his quests very early on in his re-introduction into society. It was in his first morning coffee break and he got chatting to a very attractive young woman called Grace, who was about a couple of years older than Liam himself.

The pair of them were sitting at a table by the window, looking out on the rather splendid grounds, with lots of rhododendrons and azaleas still in bloom, although some of the earliest had begun to fade. The family that had built the house in the last part of the Victorian era, had served in British India, and, as had so many such families, had planned their grounds around the plants that had captured their imagination during their period of service.

"I would love to take a picture of those plants and send it to my sister," said Edward. "But we don't have Internet and I don't have a sim card in my phone or my ancient iPad. They took them out when I got here. As far as I can see, the Wi-Fi is password protected so that does it for me."

Grace laughed.

"Listen Edward," she said. "Do you really think that a bunch of badass junkies will have allowed themselves to be cut off from the Internet by some techie amateurs? If you are nice to me, I will give you the username and password, but you must use it sparingly. If they notice a huge increase in internet traffic, they are going to start changing passwords and that could be a pain. What do you want it for anyway?"

Edward decided to take a gamble.

"I badly upset my drug suppliers and I think they will be after me when I get out of here, so I need to disappear. I took my cash out of my bank accounts before I came in here and I have hidden that cash somewhere safe, but I need a new bank account. As far as I can see, everything is going contactless, so without a bank account I am stuffed. I can't just use the cash. I need to get some new ID."

"Oh. Well, there you go," said Grace. "I may be able to help you there too. I changed my ID when I escaped from an abusive stepfather. It cost me about £2,000 to get the fake papers. Can you afford that?"

"Just about," lied Edward.

"Well, first things first," said Grace. "The username is 'rhododendron' and the password is 'azalea'. How "blooming" original. I wonder if they change it to 'crocus' and 'snowdrop' in the spring." And Grace began to laugh at her own little joke.

"I am supposed to leave here in about two weeks, I came in a few days before you. Just before I go, I will give you the names and contact details for the guys who will sell you the false ID. You will need to give them a name you want to use and a few details, the ones you would use for getting real ID. You can find out on the Internet what info is needed. Be careful. They are sharp. Don't part with your money until you see the paperwork. Give them a deposit but keep back at least half, and preferably a bit more, for payment on delivery."

Edward was a lucky boy. At least Edward thought so. Only time would tell whether he was right.

****

The next significant event in that week in Annie's life was the second STEP paper on Friday 19th June. Once again, she took it in her stride and managed a good night's sleep the night before, a decent breakfast of nutty muesli with some Greek yoghurt, accompanied by a strong coffee made in the espresso machine.

She took herself off again to the Academy and sat the online exam. This time, when she finished, she almost allowed herself a smile.

The exam could not have gone better. It was not a case of hunting around for questions she could do, or even questions she could do best, but for the ones she would most enjoy doing. It was that aptitude, that flair, that excitement for the challenge of difficult mathematical problems, that the academics interviewing her the previous December had detected. It was because of that talent that they had made her an offer.

Simon asked her how it went.

"I enjoyed it," said Annie.

"Here's your hot chocolate," said Simon. They gave each other a hug.

"And now it's your turn to help me. Tomorrow, we start to bubble with Jenny's family."

Jenny's family? thought Annie. *I see where this is going.*

Simon continued: "I really can't let an occasion like that go without doing something special in the kitchen. I am going to make just some simple things, but we are not going to have a Thai takeaway, even from Mr Miller's best Thai restaurant. But they want something spicy and flavourful, so I am going to make a curry myself. It will not be Thai, but it will have my own spices and that is where you come in. Please will you go to the Oriental supermarket at the Richmond Centre and pick up this list of ingredients? The basic ingredients, the chicken, the spinach, the rice and all that, they are coming tonight in the Tesco order, but the spices I need from the specialist shop. Would that be alright, Annie? And," with a smile, "the double cream is coming tonight too."

Annie smiled back and sipped her hot chocolate. How come Simon made hot chocolate taste like nectar? When Annie made it, it was lumpy and a bit bland. She was determined to make some money early in her career and invest it in his restaurant. Would be a lot better investment than some ISA paying 0.1%.

Annie finished her drink, got the car keys and went on her shopping trip. Last time she had come here to the centre, it had been all about Liam. Now it was all about Simon and Sarah and herself and their future. She was slightly anxiously hoping that she had not misjudged her performance in the two exams this week. There were still two months before the results would be announced. Something like August 13th was the date in the electronic paperwork she had received. She rarely, if ever, misjudged her own performance, but this was the toughest maths test she had ever done.

The college she had chosen, St Joseph's, had a strong puritan tradition and was one of the group of colleges founded around the time of the Tudors. She had fallen in love with its grounds and its buildings on her visit there and the porters, the people who are at the interface between the College and the city, and who welcome arrivals, had clinched it for her. If you judge helpfulness and kindness on scales of one to ten, with ten being the best, the lady head porter and her two assistants would have got at least twelve on both scales.

Some of the spices were not easy to find in the store so she had to ask the assistant for help. Despite the mask she was wearing, the aroma in the shop was exotic and exciting. It made Annie think about all those history lessons on eighteenth and nineteenth century imperialism. Not the most politically correct period of British history but interesting, nevertheless. She remembered that History interview question that her friend Kim had been asked at her Cambridge interview. 'How can we begin to understand the history of the colonised when we are the colonisers?' It was something like that anyway.

Kim seemed to have done quite well on it because she got an offer. Given that Kim was predicted 2A*s and an A and the offer was for 1 A* and 2 As, Annie was pretty sure that Kim would be at Cambridge next October. If only Annie could get there too it would be a welcome support, particularly as COVID was going to make forming new friendships a bit tricky.

When she stopped daydreaming, Annie gathered up the spices, and the packets of wonton soup mix and frozen wontons that she had added for herself and went back to the car. As she drove home, she anticipated the aroma of roasting spices and intense cooking effort that would fill the house tomorrow, probably all day.

The Tesco delivery came. Associating the delivery with Liam was beginning to fade, but Annie did spare a thought for how he was getting on. Just a brief thought. She knew that, in a couple of weeks, she might have to do one last thing to move him on out of her life but, for now, she was going to cut herself some slack, enjoy the moment and not do any more blooming maths! Just before supper the sounds of some Gershwin came from the piano in the music room and Sarah and Simon knew that Annie was, for the moment, at her ease.

****

Meanwhile, the drug tests at the Boxing Club and the leisure centre had shown traces of cocaine, heroin, and some other drugs in the locker allocated to Shaun, previously allocated to Liam, as well as in Muldoon's locker at the Brook Street gym, where the Boxing Club met.

Jerry and Steve debated bringing in Shaun again for questioning but were concerned that, because they could not prove it was he who had put any drugs in that locker, all they would do would be to spook him again and someone else might just end up dead. Far better to wait, watch, and see, when post-lockdown drug dealing picked up again, where Shaun went to pick up his drug supply and drop off the money. It was always possible that the drug gang would move the activity elsewhere, but the two policemen were sure that Shaun would have been "debriefed" and the gang would know that his questioning was all about Liam and Liam's whereabouts, so they might be reluctant to do anything more than move the drop off and collection point to a new venue, keeping the leisure centre part of the activity intact.

It was worth making that assumption for now and, if after a few months no activity had resumed, the police could start to look for a similar pattern elsewhere in the City. Two separate hubs, with overlapping clientele including youngsters, where distribution and collection could be separated. Ideas about some possible locations were already beginning to surface and Jerry and Steve asked the team to keep a particular eye on those places.

Chapter 33

The Saturday morning came, Saturday 20th June. After Simon got back from his paper round there were lots of telephone calls between the Grants and the Carters, mostly on the lines of welcome to the Bubble. Annie was out at the shop doing her regular weekend shifts, but she did manage to talk to people on the phone over the lunch hour and said she was looking forward to the evening. Annie and Peter just chatted about theatre and music and ballet. Simon stopped short of declaring undying love for Jenny but made it very clear that he was looking forward to being able to see and hug her, legally, and she made it clear that she had similar thoughts. Sarah and Daniel were just excited.

Sarah and Daniel had discussed whether this time there should be a sleepover and had suggested it to the children. All had agreed that it would be nice, but Annie and Simon did point out that they would be off in the morning to their newsagent related jobs. Daniel's comment was that Jenny and Peter hardly knew that there was early morning on a Sunday and would be likely to sleep in until at least lunchtime.

For most of the day, the Grant house was filled with the smell of roasting spices and cooking curry. Sarah busied herself preparing the spare bedrooms.

There was not the apprehensive tension of the first dinner shared by the two families a couple of weeks earlier. Annie was greeted by the aromas as she returned home from the shop and her stomach began to rumble.

The Carters arrived on time and because rain had been forecast and they were now a two-family bubble, the table was laid out in the dining room. There was no attempt at social distancing, it no longer applied. There were lots of hugs and lots of physical contact, kisses on the cheek, in some cases, and simply kisses in other cases! The desire for human contact that had built over months made each hug and each touch of the hand very special.

The meal did the occasion justice. A Punjabi chicken curry, simple but delicious, with onion Bhajis, homemade naan, aloo gobi saag, chutneys and saffron pilau rice, made a filling but delicious meal, even Peter's prodigious appetite was satisfied. This meal was served with Cobra beer, the beer produced by a firm founded by a Cambridge graduate, who wanted a beer that would complement curry and not either drown it or lose out to it.

Simon had spent ages looking for a suitable Indian dessert and he came up with one he had found on the web, gulab jamun parfait. It was colourful and not too heavy and Simon had cheated a little by buying the gulab jamun, those little balls of milk solids and flour soaked in rose-flavoured syrup, from the shop in the Richmond centre. He had layered the sliced gulab jamun with a parfait he made, from yoghurt and cream, with a little honey, and decorated it with quartered gulab jamun, strawberry and pistachios.

Another triumph for Simon. And a sweet wine and some decaf left everyone feeling sleepy. This time it was not a case of Daniel declaring it time to go home. This time there was to be a sleepover. Annie and Simon were caught a bit by surprise but not upset by it. Jenny, Peter, and Daniel had brought overnight bags with them and were shown to their rooms. Nobody seemed to want the evening to end but Annie was tired from the mental tension and exertion of the week, Peter was tired from growing, and Simon and Jenny were tired from the excitement of just seeing each other, so, shortly before midnight, everyone went to turn in, leaving the two adults alone downstairs.

Sarah and Daniel had wondered about sharing a bed on this occasion but had decided that it was something that everyone would have to get used to sooner or later and not to do so would make more of a statement and issue than doing so. Besides which, the practicalities were that Jenny and Peter needed a lie-in and Annie and Simon were getting up early. Strangely shyly, Sarah and Daniel also went to bed together, to sleep together for the very first time.

It was strange for everyone the next day to wake up with all six people in the same house. Annie and Simon went off to their jobs and the others woke to a leisurely breakfast. Simon was back around 9:30 and he, Jenny and Peter went for a walk, leaving Sarah and Daniel to enjoy a leisurely breakfast together. It was now obvious to both that the relationship was not only going to work, on a practical level, but they were very much in love and it was going to make them very happy.

The Carters stayed for some tea, a simple baked potato to which they added either cheese, tuna, or baked beans, or, in Peter's case, all three. Simon made a salad and as always, it tasted good, with a classic vinaigrette.

As they went home, no further plans were made. Everyone had everyone else's mobile phone number and they were simply going to offer companionship on different things that they wanted to do and thought that one or more of the others might want to join in.

And that is how things progressed for the next few weeks. Annie was in winding down mode, all her schoolwork had been completed and the STEP hurdle was behind her. Mr Stops asked her to help him out more at the shop and, mindful of the expense of university, she readily accepted. The fifteen thousand or so pounds she still had of Liam's stolen money was not something she intended spending. It was going back to Liam as soon as she could hand it over. At some point soon, only about two weeks away now, Liam was going to need a little bit more of her attention but, after that, he would have to fend for himself.

Liam's telephone call in the week after Annie's exams was frighteningly cheerful. Annie could not help thinking that Liam's overconfidence was a prelude to a fall.

"Emma, I am doing really well here," said Liam. "The CBT is brilliant and so helpful and I am not having any cravings now. I think the physical activity is helpful and I will want to join a gym when I come out. I have become a vegetarian as well and that is making me feel tons better. I am not a vegan; I like eggs and cheese too much to become vegan, and, anyway, from what I have found out, veganism is too difficult for someone like me who is not well organised. Perfectly fine if you know what you are doing. but you know me Emma."

"Well, Edward," said Annie, "I'll believe you when I see you turn down a bacon butty. I am glad you are doing OK. I guess you will be coming out on Monday, 6th July?"

"Yes, Emma," said Liam. "I will call you when I know exactly what time."

Annie thought about this. Three days after her birthday, at a weekend. Now, with five other people and not just Simon and Sarah to keep in the dark, what on earth could she do? They would all want to make a fuss of her 18th. Her original intention had been to tell everyone she was going to Cambridge to look at St Joseph's again, and she could then pick up Liam and take him to a safe train station and send him on his way. If she tried that, the whole lot of them would want to come with her to Cambridge, or at least the youngsters would. She should have thought of it before.

If she could switch things to a Monday then she might be able to fix something up, but did she really need to see him at all. She knew where she thought he would find it easiest to hide, it had to be a big city. She wanted to get more of his money to him to tide him over. He really could not afford to come back home because of the high risks involved. He had managed to get from Stansted to the rehab centre; surely he could get himself back to Stansted and then a train to Cambridge, and on to almost anywhere.

The more Annie thought about it, the more she thought she had to find a way to get a message to him. He had Internet, apparently, and he had her old iPad on which Internet was running. Maybe she could message him. But how would she get the money to him? Left luggage offices were clearly not an option, because of the open bag policy, and Cambridge Railway Stations and Coach Stations did not have left luggage lockers anyway. It was all a bit complicated, but a plan was beginning to form. The first thing was to establish a line of internet communication with Liam.

Annie called the Marlborough Centre and asked the receptionist if she could either speak to 'Edward' or get a message to him. She was told that she could not speak to him because the rule was only one telephone call a week and they had had theirs already this week, but any reasonable message could be passed on.

"Please would you tell him that I need his username and password for the computer at home because I need to download the invoice for the printer we bought together; it has gone wrong, and I want to claim on the warranty? I am happy for him to give it to me next time we talk. I've tried all the old accounts he had so I think he must have set up a new one to use on this computer."

She just hoped that would be enough to let Liam know what she really wanted was for him to set up a Gmail account and be ready to receive messages. She could try hinting a bit harder, when they next spoke, if he had not already been in touch.

Annie knew what she was going to do about the money. She knew where she was going to send him, but that was for later.

Annie turned over in her mind whether to try and get him some more money from the stash. She decided that another ten thousand would probably make quite a big difference, especially if he had to obtain false ID. It would involve another night-time climb down that blasted trellis and a slightly risky walk to the pill box by the canal bridge. She would take the tyre lever from the car with her to lift up the paving slab, grab a few handfuls of notes, she was beginning to understand what ten thousand in fifty-pound notes looked like, and then she would have to hope that it rained to cover her tracks. *Please rain in the next few days*, she thought. A quick look at the forecast suggested overnight rain on the 23rd so that would be a first chance to try and make the pick-up.

Why was it all so difficult? The answer was simple; it was so difficult because she had to do it without being discovered or she would be in trouble and Liam might end up dead.

On the evening of Tuesday, 23rd June, the likelihood of rain certainly seemed very high. Simon had spent most of the evening on the telephone to Jenny. The two of them spent hours on the phone talking together and Annie remembered back to when she and Liam were just the same, almost never apart and always talking on the phone when they were apart. It seemed like a different world.

Peter had called Annie briefly to ask about some school related maths problem and Annie had explained it to him in a way that he understood, but in a way that made him feel that he had worked the answer out for himself. Sarah and Daniel had gone out to dinner and told Annie that they would be staying at the Carter's House after the dinner and 'not to wait up'.

Once Simon was asleep, which was about 10 pm, Annie climbed out of the window and down the trellis, went to the Garage, which she had left unlocked, and removed a large tyre lever. It was not the tyre lever from their current little car but one from the big old diesel that they had previously owned and which had been sold for £50 for scrap. They still saw that big old machine driving around. Annie thought one of the youths on the estate had probably taken it and done it up. The insurance, although it probably was not insured, would have been about twenty times the value of the old heap itself.

The tyre lever was certainly big enough to give Annie the mechanical advantage she needed to lift that darn paving slab.

Annie was wearing a very old anorak with a hood over her head and she wore a mask to make sure that her face was not visible. She knew there were CCTV cameras on the way to the canal bridge and she tried, as far as possible, to keep to the minor roads without CCTV coverage. Although she could not know it at the time, it worked, because at no point did her presence register on camera in a way that might have drawn attention. There was a very brief glimpse of a figure huddled up under a hooded anorak making its way rapidly down the London

Road for about 50 metres or so and then it went out of camera and never reappeared.

The irony of her walk across the grass to the canal bank and down towards the pillbox was not lost on Annie. She gave a rueful grin, then she checked that nobody was watching and slipped down the bank to the pillbox entrance. There were no signs that the paving slab had ever been moved, although it was only a few weeks since Liam had hidden the money there. Annie scraped away around one of the edges and pushed the tyre lever down into the ground. She found another large stone to act as a fulcrum for her lever and jammed it in place. She then put her whole weight on the lever and was greatly relieved when the slab lifted, relatively easily. She let the slab back down and went to find a thick stick to use to prop the slab up so that she could look underneath.

There were plenty of trees here and the debris from a storm about five weeks ago had not yet been cleared, probably because many of the park keepers and council ground staff were being furloughed. She brought back to the spot a couple of stout branches, lifted the slab again and propped it up with those two branches. The rucksack, as Liam had described, was clearly visible. She simply undid the neck of the bag, grabbed two large stacks of fifty-pound notes, stuffed them in the pockets of her anorak, closed the neck of the rucksack carefully and removed the props. There was what seemed to Annie a very loud bang as the slab dropped back into place. It really was not loud and would have been masked, even a few feet away, by the sound of the wind and of the rain, which was now falling heavily on the leaves.

Annie scrabbled around for some dirt and some bits of twig and grass and filled in the large indentations she had made with the lever and the props. She noticed that there were, nearby, two or three large plastic takeaway containers that had filled up with water. She poured the water over the top of the slab to wash away footprints and mud and left the scene. She was satisfied that no one, looking at the slab, would know that it had been moved, nor would anyone suspect what lay underneath it. She threw the two props into the canal, picked up her tyre lever and headed for home.

There was the small matter of a soaking wet anorak, soaking wet trousers and soaking wet shoes so she decided to strip to her underwear in the garage, shove the notes into her knickers and bra, leave the wet items in the garage to dry out overnight and climb barefoot up the trellis and into her bedroom. She reckoned that, with Sarah away at Daniel's house and Simon not able to drive, no one would go to the garage, so no one would discover the wet clothes before she had time to move them tomorrow.

Back in her room, Annie took off the rest of her clothes and crept through to the bathroom to collect a towel. She dried herself carefully and counted the money. There was about twenty-five thousand pounds, far more than she had intended. She already had about fifteen thousand hidden away so forty thousand in total was a huge sum. And Liam would have had left some of the money he had already taken with him. She decided there and then that she was going to pass all of it to Liam.

He needed to open a bank account with his false ID and tell the manager some story that would let him put five thousand into the account immediately. He could set up four bank accounts at separate banks with more than £10K in each...

Annie suddenly realised she was sitting on the bed naked and it was raining outside and she was getting cold and bed might be a very good idea. She put on a t-shirt and some knickers and tucked herself in under the sheets.

There was nothing to do now except to wait for Liam, aka Edward, to make his next telephone call to her.

Chapter 34

With the period of serious lockdown beginning to ease, the police were hoping that increased overt activity on the drug scene might begin to help them crack the MacDonald case and the Muldoon hit-and-run. Large numbers of the policemen were going square eyed looking on computer screens at CCTV footage. There were a lot also on stakeouts, or wandering around the known drug dealing areas, trying to spot dealers and customers that might somehow tie in with the main investigation, but it all remained very elusive.

Children, known already to be linked into the county lines scene, a few low grade dealers back on the street, some suspicious activity around the leisure centre, although there were no new visitors, only Shaun and the known dealers; that was the limit of what they were picking up. The only new information was around Miller's takeaways. Some of the leisure centre regulars seemed to have developed an increased appetite for fish and chips, burgers, takeaway curries and the like. They were also hanging around at many of the places, because a lot of Miller's outlets had an associated dining area often outdoors, so eating out was beginning to happen again.

Against that was the problem that home deliveries were hugely increasing and Steve and Jerry suspected that if the takeaways were involved in the drug scene, home delivery was going to be a big part of the distribution system. Every one of Miller's shops was running home delivery.

To sum it all up, the surveillance was completely messed up by COVID. Boredom was affecting the CCTV teams. Coppers on the beat were faced with masked civilians and villains alike. New behaviour patterns were emerging to distort the background on which behavioural change could trigger alarm bells.

Gradually, a pattern did emerge. The known dealers tended to eat in, 'eating out to help out'. Not enough evidence to justify a raid, but enough to start to look at Mr Jason Miller to see if he really was squeaky clean. Jerry set a few people on that, to investigate his background and his financial dealings. They also had a brief to find out who his friends and associates were and what type of dealings he had with them.

Edward, meanwhile, was slightly intrigued by the message from his "sister". He knew that Annie had the details of his previous email account, username and password, because they had not kept secrets from each other. He knew, or thought he knew, Annie's account details, so he tried to have a look, but he soon found out that she had changed every password, and, on Facebook and Instagram and anywhere else it was possible, her username. He thought about it and, not having lost all his reasoning ability, decided to set up a new Gmail account, with a new password, with username and password relating to his new identity in the same way as his old username and password related to his true identity.

Annie had the detail of his new identity, she had given it to him, so all he would have to do on Thursday, when his next call 'home' was allowed, would be to tell her that she was silly to have forgotten it, it was his name and birthday, like it had always been. Annie would get that.

He played the ideal rehab patient to a T. He was being very careful about time online. He piggybacked on Grace's VPN; Grace already knew that he dared not use his own credit card because the drug people were still after him. He used the VPN to make sure that the ID application was nailed down and he saved as much as he could to the iPad. He changed the six-digit pin on the iPad for greater security. He was beginning to put confidential information on it that might just let someone get to him if they could hack it. It would certainly reveal his new assumed identity.

He created his email account and set up two tier verification using his mobile number as the second layer. He invented the answers to the verification questions, using totally fictitious schools and mother's maiden names and the rest, and wrote them down in "Note" on the iPad, in case he forgot! He then sent an email to Annie. It went through. She had not changed her email address, just the password access to the Gmail account. The mail simply said, "Love from Ed".

The rest of the time he spent with Grace and doing various forms of therapy and physical exercise and reading detective stories from Annie's Kindle library. He left her Mathematics and Philosophy books well alone. He tried one and it made him realise that, even without the drug problem, he and Annie would have grown apart. Annie was far too clever for him and he would eventually have resented that. He felt sad and, for the first time in a few days, desperate for a fix.

Annie got the email as she sat eating her afternoon rock bun at the shop on her short afternoon break. She was thinking back to the night before and reflecting that, once again, the gods had smiled upon her. They sent rain at the right time, they made sure nobody was out walking and nobody saw her. This was not going to last but, for the time being, all was on track.

A plan had formed in her mind. She thought it to be a good one. It would mean Liam making his own way to the city she thought would be safest for him to hide out in, but he would have more than forty-thousand pounds to hide away with and, surely, not even Liam could mess that up?

****

As planned, "Edward" called "Emma" on the Thursday evening and told her that she knew already what his username and password were.

"Oh. I feel so stupid," said Emma. "I remember now. Silly me." They then began a banal conversation and it was just as well because, although the rehab staff did not listen in to every telephone call, they listened at random when they were not too busy; this one was monitored. With the email line of communication established, plans and instructions could now be dealt with in total secrecy.

"Edward" and "Emma" signed off in a typically brother and sister slightly smarmy way and the switchboard operator put down her headset. She turned to the manageress who happened to be in the office and remarked that "Edward" seemed to be doing well.

The manageress simply said: "Humph. A bit too well for me. I think he is a bit too perfect. He and that Grace Chandler girl. I think they are becoming an item and I think they are both going to be bad for each other. I wonder if they realise that, for years, I have watched couples disappear together into the long grass and some of the girls have even gotten pregnant."

But £6,500 is a sum that tends to buy silence and cause the blind eye to be turned and at least the two people in question were going to leave the Marlborough clean, however temporary that might be. A month is not long enough to fix such a deep problem and a referral to continuing therapy was always needed if the departing inmates were to remain clean.

****

There was nothing obvious turning up among the associates of Jason Miller. His solicitor, who dealt with all the property deals was F. O. Seeley and Partners, a very respectable local firm; he bought his cars from the local Rover dealership; he was a member of the Rotary Club and, as far as Jerry could tell, was also prominent in the local Freemason's Lodge. In addition to the properties in the City he had a small cottage in the Village of Ringstead, in Norfolk, and a timeshare in the Dordogne area of France. Absolutely nothing to go on there.

The team just kept working away trying to accumulate data which, might, in the fullness of time, begin to reveal a pattern. There was nothing so far to disprove the theory that the Miller empire was being used to distribute drugs but failing to disprove a theory and proving a theory are two entirely different things.

When he came off the telephone to Annie, Liam decided to talk to Grace. He and Grace were beginning to form a close relationship. It was partly their shared experience of drug addiction and their shared experience of getting clean. It was partly simple proximity and what the French call 'en l'absence de mieux', but Grace was also, once off the drugs and beginning to adopt a more healthy life style, a very pretty young woman, and "Edward" was beginning to look a little more like his former self. There was physical attraction and companionship to be had here.

"Edward" decided to take a big chance. He had already mentioned about the need for false ID and Grace had offered to help him with that and she knew he was in trouble with the drug suppliers, so it would be no new revelation to explain why. He was not going to come straight out and talk about the huge sum of money he had stolen but he would explain that he had stolen some of their money and they were looking for him and he needed somewhere to hide up until the heat died down. He was not yet ready to reveal his real name either.

It was too soon to be sure that Grace did not have any links to his hometown or to the drug scene there. She came, according to what she had told him, from a City less than forty miles from his and it did seem entirely possible that there were overlaps between the drug scenes in both cities. If nothing else people would be moving frequently between the two locations and information transfer was quite likely.

"Grace," said Edward, "the trouble I got into with my suppliers was that I stole some money from them and they want it back. I took it about a month ago and they have sent the heavy mob after me ever since. I saw them at my Hall of

Residence, I was at Uni and simply ran. They won't just take the money back either, they are going to hurt me badly when they take it, if they catch me."

"Oh my god," said Grace. "That may have been very dumb. These guys are nasty. But we are where we are. Have you got any of it left?"

"Yes. About £40,000," said Edward. "It should be enough to hide away until the heat is off, but I really don't know how to do that."

"You've got the right girl here," said Grace. "When I escaped from that stepfather who was abusing me, I hid out for about three years without getting found. I only stopped hiding when I heard he had been arrested as part of a sex crime ring and been given fifteen years in prison. I managed it without any capital. With £40K, you should be laughing.

"You will need false ID, I bought mine with cash and sex, but you can simply pay cash. I know it might sound like a crazy idea, but will you think it over. I really like you and I think you like me. I am afraid I am going to go back on it when I get out, especially if I go back to living on my own. I would need to get a job and that is fine, but especially during COVID I would be so lonely. I honestly think that having you with me could be the difference between staying clean and going back on heroin. I can help you and just having you with me would help me."

Edward paused for a moment and thought about it. The silence began to stretch out. Grace began to think that this was not a good sign. Then Edward said: "Would you really do that? It puts you at risk too, you know."

"I would do it," said Grace. "£40K is a lot of money to us but not to them. I reckon they will give up looking for you before too long and in time you will have changed, cut your hair, dyed it a different colour, grown a beard, I don't mind beards, all sorts of things like that change your appearance. If we can sit out the first few months, we will be home and dry."

Edward thought to himself, *£40K is one thing, upwards of half a million is quite another*. Liam's natural selfish streak suppressed any desire to let Grace know how much more serious the situation was.

"I am making arrangements, for when I come out, to pick up the money before I go into hiding. A friend of mine is going to take it to somewhere that I can collect it. I have a bit more money than that. At this moment I have about eight thousand with me, its stitched in the lining of my bag. That should let us get to anywhere we need to get to. What do you think?"

"So, who is this friend? Are they trustworthy?" asked Grace.

"She is someone who hid me for a week when the heat was really on. She is totally trustworthy. Once I let her know exactly when I am coming out of this place, she will set up an arrangement that lets me get the money. Then she has said she wants me out of her life forever. She means it."

"OK. Well, it is always easier to hide somewhere that you know. We need somewhere with job opportunities. We need to be able to get false ID there. My thought would be to go back to where I hid for the three years I was hiding from my stepfather. It's on the mainline between London and the Northwest. I suggest we go to…" and Grace mentioned a town in the Midlands which Edward vaguely knew of.

"By the way," said Edward, "my real name is Liam, but I suggest you forget that because once we get the false ID, I am going to be Edward Simon Collins."

"My real name," said Grace, "is Grace!"

That evening, Liam sent an email to Annie filling her in on his conversation with Grace. Annie had very mixed feelings about it. On the one hand, she was relieved that Liam was going to be moving out of her life and going somewhere different. He did not tell her in detail the city he was going to, just that it was somewhere off the cross-country route to Liverpool from Stanstead. It sounded as if the person he had picked up with, Grace, was a lot more streetwise than Liam, who was, after all, only a schoolboy who had gotten mixed up in something which had taken him well out of his depth.

She didn't see any irony in the fact that she herself was just a schoolgirl who had gotten mixed up in the same way and yet, was managing to keep her head and his, above water. She began to set her plans around the possible routes for Liam and Grace to their planned destination, but she was glad that she did not know exactly where he was going to. It was clear that Grace knew her way around getting false ID, which would be useful, and Annie asked if Grace had a usable credit card and bank account, because the plan she had in mind would be a lot easier if she did.

The reply came back positive and Grace assured Liam that she had more than enough funds to cover two tickets to anywhere, one for each of them. Mobile tickets were the easiest and Grace had an iPhone and Liam an iPad, so they would be able to travel. They would give some story about travelling for work and they could sort the story out over the next day or two. There was no reason why Grace's card should be identified with travel by Liam. It would be the young man called Edward Simon Collins with whom Grace Victoria Chandler would be travelling.

Grace and Liam booked their tickets for the Monday, 6th July, off peak. Grace had arrived at the Marlborough a little before Liam so she asked if she might stay a few days longer so that she could leave with and look out for "Edward". Liam gave her cash from his room to cover the difference. Annie told them to book one ticket each to Ely, in Cambridgeshire and one from Ely to their destination. After Ely she was hoping to be done with him.

****

As far as the police and the local drug lords were concerned the hunt for Liam was getting nowhere and they both decided to scale it down.

Annie noticed that she saw the blue police car less frequently and she was no longer aware of the feeling of being watched as she went about her daily business.

The big event coming up was her Birthday. In times of COVID, what would have been a huge 18th Birthday celebration had dwindled to a lunch time drink and buffet with some school friends, Kim and a couple of others, on the Saturday, the day that meetings of six people from different households, outdoors, were to be allowed, and a day trip to Ely on Monday 6th, with Simon, Jenny and Peter. Annie had wanted to go to Cambridge but thought it might be a little premature. She still did not know for certain if she had gotten in.

The bubbled households were going to celebrate her actual birthday on the 3rd and the two households were planning mostly to stay together over that weekend.

Annie had a couple of things to buy in anticipation of the Birthday Weekend. She was still running, still playing music and still helping Uncle Willy on the allotment. Jenny, Peter and Simon were coming on several evenings to help. If it was not raining, and for the moment the weather was glorious, it was quite pleasant for the four of them to wander down there after an evening meal and sit in Willy's plastic chairs and drink a light beer or a sparkling water and just enjoy the long summer evenings. Jenny sometimes came on Annie's early morning jog. They were both quite athletic girls and enjoyed the exercise, which kept them fit now that the team sports that they both enjoyed had ceased to happen.

There was a final telephone call from Liam on Annie's birthday. Liam had completely forgotten that it was Annie's birthday, which made Annie feel even more comfortable about her plan to have him move out of her life. Annie told "her brother" how pleased she was to be seeing him on Monday, there was a bit more exchange of trivia and they hung up.

Immediately, Annie emailed Liam with the final details of the plan. He was happy with the simplicity and the cleverness of it but decided not to tell Grace until they were on the train to Ely.

When he turned off the computer, he went through to the reception area and asked the receptionist to order him a taxi from the Marlborough to Stansted Railway Station for the discharge time on Monday morning.

Annie went back to her "birthday party". The six of them in the bubble were now completely relaxed in each other's company. Annie had insisted that Simon was not to make too much fuss about cooking. The weather was too good for that and he was too busy spending time with Jenny. The only concessions to major celebration were a very nice Dom Perignon 2010 champagne, which must have cost Daniel well over £150, and a rather nice Cotes Du Roussillon which went very well with the cassoulet that Annie had asked for. Garlic bread filled the ever-hungry Peter. Simon had also made a cake for dessert. It was a classic red velvet. It was, of course, delicious.

The meals eaten together by the six were now becoming more comfortable and familiar and they were all beginning to be very fond of their "soon to be" stepsiblings. It was clear that the country was beginning to loosen restrictions, a little, and, although the six of them were very careful about COVID, the panic of the previous few months was beginning to recede in the country at large. Daniel and Sarah still got very cross with people who flouted the COVID rules and Daniel was still convinced that a second wave was coming and would be a lot worse to endure because it would be in winter, without the evenings for people to go out and take their exercise.

The Tesco man came on Annie's birthday and, included in the shopping, were some party-style and picnic-style items for the Monday trip to Ely. Jenny had been looking at architectural styles in one of the pieces of work she was doing for her exams. The Cathedral at Ely, "The Ship of the Fens" was on her list of places to visit. Peterborough Cathedral was also on her list, because Katherine of Aragon was buried there, but Ely had a river and some riverside pubs that were now allowed to open and that, together, with Hereward the Wake, swung the decision Ely's way.

Annie had heard that you could walk from Cambridge to Ely along the riverbank. She looked it up. It was about 17 miles. She wondered if she would ever be doing that over the next few years. She thought it might be a good idea to book a table at one of the riverside restaurants. She intended to park in Ship Lane Car Park, parking there was free all day and she booked a table for four at The Cutter Inn for 1pm. Her estimate was that, if they left home around 10am, they would be there in good time and could have a look at the Cathedral on their way to eat. The reviews for the restaurant were good and it did seem to have a river frontage, which they all wanted, coming from a landlocked city.

Annie sent one last email to Liam and hoped like Hell that he would get this right.

****

At the Marlborough, both Grace and Edward were getting excited. They were ready to leave. They made their final arrangements, using Grace's credit card. After every transaction she made, Liam gave her an equivalent amount in cash. He really did not want her to feel used in any way. As more and more of her story had been revealed to him, he began to realise how important it was to her to feel valued and appreciated, much more important than it might have been to some other women.

The final message from Annie came through. They were now ready to make their journey to anonymity and freedom. There was the whole of Sunday to wait. It would have been almost unbearable were it not that they had each other for company.

Annie and Simon simply went to work on Sunday as usual. Sarah was working a weekend and Daniel was not. More and more the Carters were staying the night at the Grant's house and this weekend they had been there since Friday evening. Sarah and Daniel always shared a bedroom, Jenny and Peter were gradually bringing things over from their own house and turning the rooms they had slept in, on that first overnight stay, into their own private spaces. They were all taking turns in doing the chores, although Simon and Annie still did the majority because Peter and Jenny still had things to do at their own home. Simon was teaching Jenny to cook and had his nose put out of joint a little when she managed to make a Victoria sponge lighter and fluffier and tastier than his. It may have been only marginally so, but it was better.

Peter was beginning to take more interest in his music again and, with Annie to help him, was beginning to make real strides. The pair of them would often sing duets and solos from popular musicals, for themselves and for the rest of the family, and Daniel would sometimes ask Annie to play some jazz piano for him.

The weekend passed and the day of the great expedition to Ely dawned.

At the Marlborough, Grace and Edward ate a good breakfast. There were eggs, mushrooms, grilled tomatoes and vegetarian bacon strips. As always, the coffee was good. The sourdough toast, toasted on one of those awful machines that either just warm up the bread or incinerate it as it goes around on a conveyor belt, was duly smothered in lots of butter and strawberry jam, and two very well fed ex-inmates picked up their luggage from their rooms and went, with their masks in their pockets, out to the entrance porch to await their transport. There was tension in the wait. The Marlborough knew their destination was Stansted but, beyond that, the trail would go cold for anyone who stumbled, however that might be, on the fact that Edward and Grace had once been patients here.

The cab arrived a little early and Grace and Edward got in. They kept the holdall with the money with them, but Grace's bag was put in the boot.

Stansted was reassuringly busy. The impending lifting of restrictions for re-entry from the end of the week meant that many businesspeople, who had been putting off travel because of the need to quarantine on return, had decided to make those long-postponed trips. Wearing their masks and carrying their luggage, Grace and Edward went to the railway station, flashed their e-tickets and moved to the platform from which the cross-country train to Birmingham was due to depart. Even the spartan grey empty platform did not dampen their spirits. The sun was shining and they were off on a new part of their lives.

The train was waiting at the platform, but the doors were temporarily closed. The minute they opened the two rushed to get on board and sat, opposite each other, at a table by the window on the side away from the sun.

"I'm going to need a new smart phone, an iPhone," said Liam.

"Yeah! Right!" said Grace.

"Well, I can't keep waving this bloody great slab around every time I want to do something and a new iPhone with my new ID seems the best thing to do. Annie kept my old one and she wouldn't give it back to me because she didn't trust me."

"Who's Annie?" asked Grace.

Liam felt guilty, he should not have mentioned the name. It just was not fair to Annie, especially after she had done so much for him.

"The friend I told you about, but please just forget I told you her name."

"OK. I just hope she looks like the back of a bus," said Grace. "But I bet she doesn't."

They settled back to enjoy the Journey.

The train stopped at Audley End, Cambridge and then pulled into Ely where the two alighted. It was still quite early and Annie had told Liam that she would probably be arriving shortly before noon and so he should plan to go to the car park any time between 12:30 and 1:30. It was still not yet 11:15, so, with more than an hour to kill, Grace and Liam decided to go and look at the Cathedral. It would be less conspicuous than sitting around at the Station and, with the beginning of the lifting of restrictions, there were quite a few visitors milling around. The walk from the Station was not very far and they spent maybe forty minutes wandering around outside and sticking their heads inside, before leaving to head South down the hill, at about ten minutes past noon.

Chapter 35

Annie had filled up with petrol the day before, just to be on the safe side. She checked that everyone had their masks and she put a packet of those grotty blue ones in the glove compartment, just in case.

She set the Satnav for The Ship Lane Carpark in Ely and the four of them set off. The journey was a little quicker than they anticipated, so they arrived at about 11:30.

"Let's go and look at the Cathedral now," said Jenny. "It looks really impressive up there on the Hill."

"I need the loo first," said Annie, who had started her period that morning. After breaking off with Liam, she had come off the pill and was now menstruating normally. She could not know how fortunate it was that she diverted them all back down the hill to the nearest public convenience. It meant that the Grants and the Carters approached the Cathedral at about 12:05 from the North side. Peter had decided he was already hungry, so they had stopped, very briefly, to get a takeaway coffee and donut from one of the stalls in the grounds of the Cathedral. These little roadside enterprises had sprouted like mushrooms during the COVID lockdown.

As they were approaching from the North, a very attractive mixed-race girl, in a striking apricot orange dress, and a young man, left the Cathedral doors and turned South. Simon looked, thought to himself, *Is that Liam? No*, and he dismissed it from his mind. When he looked again, the couple had disappeared around the corner and out of sight.

Annie had purchased entry tickets for the four of them the day before and they spent about 40 minutes walking around inside. Ely is long, the third longest Cathedral in the country. It is a Norman church, in essence, built in 1083. It has a lot of stained glass, courtesy of the Victorians, who seemed to like stained glass everywhere. The entry fee, which was quite high, included the guided tour, so they took advantage of that while, especially in Peter's case, waiting for their lunch.

While the Carters and the Grants wandered around Ely Cathedral, Grace, in her beautiful apricot dress, and Liam, went to find the Ship Lane Carpark. Liam spotted Annie's car, the red hybrid that she really did not like. He went over to it and as per instruction, reached under the offside rear wheel arch and removed the little key box that Annie had placed there the day before. He opened the boot and lifted the travel rug to find the small rucksack containing the money. He removed it, replaced the travel rug, locked the door, put the key back in its box and reattached the box to the underside of the wheel arch.

He and Grace went back to the station and waited for their train. Liam knew that this was the end of an era. He knew that he would probably never see or hear from Annie again. A moment of sadness affected him, but he looked at Grace, absolutely sparkling in the sunlight, her coffee-coloured skin glowing with life, and he knew that he was ready to move on. He thought that, at some stage, he would go back for the money he had left under the slab by the pillbox, but for the time being, it was important to keep a low profile and sort out a new life for Grace and himself.

Annie had also seen Grace and Liam leaving the West door of the Cathedral and had hoped like mad that Simon would not recognise them. She cursed Liam for his bad timing, but, on reflection, thought that he had only done the sensible thing and that she herself had nearly created the crisis by not getting her timing right. She thought about Edward Lorenz and his butterflies. A sighting of Liam by Simon could have been the very thing that brought her world crashing down in chaos. She liked Chaos Theory, but this had been a little too close for comfort.

"Come on," said Annie, "let's go and see what The Cutter Inn has to offer."

It was whitebait and burgers all around, seated at a table outside with an excellent view of the river. Simon had a lager, Annie had an alcohol-free beer, Jenny and Peter both had lemonade shandy. They diverged on the dessert. Inevitably Peter had apple pie and triple ice-cream, the others just had the ice-cream.

They lingered over the coffee and dessert, just soaking up the sunshine and revelling in being outdoors and at a restaurant for the first time in months. They all took advantage of the lavatory facilities at the Inn before heading back to the car.

Back at the car, Annie let them all get seated and then, surreptitiously, removed the key box and stuck it in her pocket. For Annie too, this was almost a symbol of the end of an era. She hoped and believed that the episode with Liam O'Connor was a thing of the past.

They drove home in high spirits, Annie and Simon dropping the Carters off at their own home before heading back to 42 Manor Road to peace and quiet.

****

Liam and Grace boarded the train for Birmingham at Ely Station. Grace was now in charge. She arranged to take herself and Liam back to the landlady she had stayed with when she first left home to run away from the abuse. She had been confident that Lavinia would take her back in, especially if she introduced "Edward" as her fiancé. She and Liam had already decided that they would be an item to the outside world, these days "my partner" was as common an expression, if not more so, than "my husband" or "my wife". She had contacted Lavinia to ask if they could stay and Lavinia had been very excited.

"Grace, darling," Lavinia had said, "I have been so alone here during lockdown. Will you and your fiancé, Edward, was it? Will you be staying long? Will you be happy to share a room, the big one at the front? The little old room at the back is really damp now."

Grace assured Lavinia that sharing a room was exactly what she had in mind and Lavinia giggled and said that she was not surprised. There was a bit more conversation about how pleased the two would be to see each other again and could Grace and Edward bring some extra milk and bread from the supermarket and something for high tea.

After an uneventful journey up through the Fens, the train eventually reached their destination. The two of them left the train and picked up the food items at the supermarket outlet on the Station complex. Grace, perhaps the element of Caribbean ancestry driving it, liked spicy food, so they chose a spicy vegetarian curry with some veggie sides for high tea. They took a taxi from the Station to Lavinia's house.

Lavinia's house was one of those small terraced houses that you find in so many of our Midlands towns and cities. It was probably built in the mid-Victorian era for factory workers or railway workers, it had the distinct feel of the work force housing of that era. Lavinia's house was an end terrace and had a small side passage, accessed through a separate gate, into a walled back yard, as well as the front door on the street, with its raised doorstep and the boot scraper built into it.

Lavinia herself was large and homely and welcoming. She smothered first Grace and then Edward in her immense bosom and started talking. It was as if a dam had been breached. Lavinia had clearly been lonely beyond belief during the COVID crisis. All her regular activities, the Gospel Choir, The Church, The Women's Institute, The Afro-Caribbean Society, the Lunch canteen where she helped three days a week, all these had ceased to function during lockdown. She was lonely and she was making up for lost time.

Edward and Grace settled themselves in the room. Edward impressed on Grace once again that the true reason for his presence here must not be revealed at any cost.

"Besides which," he said, "the real reason I am here now is to start to build a life with you."

They went down to the parlour and sat around the kitchen table and started to plan with Lavinia how much they would pay for rent and board, who would get the shopping, what they liked to eat and what they did not like to eat. Both Grace and Edward had had enough of vegetarianism and decided that fish and chicken would be alright, much to Lavinia's relief.

Back up in their room the two youngsters came up with their plan of action. Tomorrow Grace would take Edward to meet the guys who had helped her with false ID all those years ago. That was top priority. Grace would go to the local bank, which was still the one where her bank account was registered, she had never bothered to change it, and she would deposit some of the money, perhaps £500, explaining that she had been paid in cash for some furniture she had sold, and they would work out how to gradually put more in over time.

Using fifty-pound notes for relatively small purchases at the local supermarket was one way to go. There were four huge supermarkets in the immediate vicinity, so four chances to change the fifties meant the money could be made useful, and they decided to arrange with Lavinia that they would buy the groceries and other items for the house and she could transfer money to Grace's account, or set off the purchases against the rent they had agreed.

Grace would get Edward that iPhone, paying cash, which was 'a birthday present from his grandmother'!

That night they slept together in the same bed for the first time, but they were so tired that that was all they did; making love was the furthest thing from either of their minds.

At breakfast the next morning, Lavinia was in fine voice. Gospel song after Gospel song filled the house, for the first time since lockdown began Lavinia had company and was enjoying it. Grace suggested to Edward that they go out together to meet the people who had got her the ID on which she was now living. The important thing was that it could get him a bank account and that would let him get a credit card and then he could begin to live a bit. He would also get a social security number so that he could work, if there were any jobs available. A false driving licence was useful because of the small picture and the fact that nobody ever checked it with central records. You just flashed it as photo ID and that was that.

From what she could gather, the best ID was for a genuine person who had been born at roughly the same time as the person requiring the false ID, and that meant a lot of checks were passed without any question. She had, in several years of using her ID never had a problem. She thought getting a passport might be a bit trickier, but she had never tried, and, just for the moment, it was not on her to do list. She called the guys on their mobile and arranged a meeting time and place.

They left the house with a shopping list for later in the day and a pocket stuffed full of fifty-pound notes. The route to the rendezvous passed through the central marketplace and they picked up a coffee from the kiosk near the fountain in the centre of the Market square. The woman running the kiosk said a few choice words when they tried to pay with a fifty pound note but, when Grace said that Edward had just come out of hospital and that was all he had been given, she lightened up and gave change, especially when Grace told her to round up the price to four quid.

Everyone was masked up on the street because this city had a high infection rate and caution was the best policy. The notes and coins from the transaction went into Grace's purse to be transferred later to what the pair of them were calling their fighting fund. Fifty-pound notes are all very well, but twenties and smaller are easier to spend.

They reached the rendezvous exactly on time. It was in the "beer garden" of a small pub in Fenton Street, "The Fenton Arms". The well-dressed man who approached them was very business-like. He wanted to know what the ID was to be used for and they told him. He had no desire to know why Edward needed a change of identity. He took the piece of paper on which the details about Edward Collins were written and asked Edward why he needed this name on his ID. Edward explained that he had already adopted the pseudonym, having looked it up in a paper, he did not mention Annie and he explained that the person was a genuine person and the details of the parents and their occupations were also correct.

The business-like young man told Edward that he could not guarantee that the documents would be for Edward Simon Collins, he would have to run his own checks. He told Edward to look at him and not smile and he took a few pictures, from which one could be selected and cropped for photo ID purposes. Edward noticed that the man had made sure the background was a blank whitewashed wall on the side of the pub. They haggled over price, but not much, and settled on one thousand pounds for each document, so with birth certificate, National Insurance card, driving licence and a passport and an extra thousand pounds for a new passport for Grace, it came to a total of five thousand. Edward handed over half the money up front with the rest to be paid on delivery.

He asked the man how he could guarantee the documents would not be rejected and was told not to worry about that, it was why the price was a thousand a document. He also asked whether it would be possible, in due course, to renew any of these documents by the normal legal channels and, much to his surprise, he was told that it would. He asked how that might be, given all the checks, and was told: "That's for me to know and you to be grateful for!"

A passport photo was then taken of Grace.

"Be back here on Friday with the rest of the money," said the suit. "Thank you for your custom."

Edward could not believe what had just happened. It seemed too good to be true, but Grace had survived all these years with false ID from this source without ever having experienced any hitches and it all pointed to the probability that this was going to work.

Looking around them as they walked back through the city, they could see the tell-tale signs of drug dealing going on and it would only be true to say that both of them felt, for a moment, the desire to spend some of this cash on a really good fix, but the two of them together were stronger than either alone and they made it to the supermarket without succumbing to temptation.

Edward forgot to put his mask back on when he tried to go into the shop and the security guard stopped him. For a moment Edward started to panic. How did the security guard know? Then he realised what was the matter, smiled, apologised and masked up.

They bought the items that Lavinia had asked for and headed back to the house. Both knew that they would need to find some sort of employment, especially in these difficult times, if they were to keep themselves occupied enough to avoid boredom and cravings. The only job that Edward had ever done was at the leisure centre, so he was going to look for a similar job here. Failing that, he was young and strong and now healthy looking, so almost any form of physical labour might work. Once he had the National Insurance Number, he might be able to start looking. Grace had done several jobs, mostly in retail, and she would see if any of the supermarkets was looking for someone, picking, stacking shelves, working the till, or doing whatever was available these days.

Eking out the things they had to do they decided that tomorrow they would go to Grace's Bank and put some money in, on Thursday they would go and purchase a new iPhone for Edward and on Friday, armed with their new ID they would go to a different bank and open a separate account for Edward and a joint account between the two of them.

It did not sound rivetingly exciting, but, when they got bored, they could always go home and make love. That was more exciting.

Somehow the Friday came. Lavinia was like a mother hen looking after them and Edward was beginning to like her as much as Grace clearly did. In the evenings, when they all sat together watching TV, Lavinia would open up to Edward about this little scrap of a teenager, battered and damaged, who had come to her for help and support, and how that little scrap had grown up into this beautiful woman. Lavinia also made it clear that she had known that Grace was not keeping the best of company and that she was probably earning money by turning tricks and dealing drugs:

"But I prayed to the Lord every day, every week, that my little one would see the error of her ways and come through it a better person, and I can see that my prayers have been answered."

Somehow Edward did not want to know what had driven this little waif out of her home. He was sure it would be painful in the telling and it would need the relationship between himself and Grace to have cemented more strongly before Grace would have the confidence to tell him, if she ever did decide to do so.

228

After breakfast Grace and Edward took another two thousand five hundred pounds out of the rucksack for the documents, and three and a half thousand for deposits to open new accounts and to top up Graces existing account. Grace could not believe that the pile of money hardly seemed to have diminished at all.

At the Fenton Arms they exchanged the money for the five documents and Grace looked delighted with her new passport. Edward was, indeed, Edward Simon Collins. The suit told him that they had checked and the basic homework that Edward had done was absolutely first class. Edward knew that he had Annie to thank for that.

So, Edward Simon Collins opened a bank account with a deposit of twelve hundred pounds and applied for a debit card and a credit card. He did not know, nor did he want to know, how his credit rating was sufficient that the card was agreed instantly, it would take four days to arrive. Grace Victoria Chandler added £500 to her account, money that was 'proceeds from her sale of furniture as she moved in with her partner'. Grace and Edward opened a joint account, with another two thousand pounds that they had 'put together from their separate savings accounts'. Grace flashed her eyes at the teller dealing with them, it was not necessary, but she enjoyed doing it anyway.

They went to the Apple Store and bought Edward his iPhone. He went immediately to the river and dropped the burner phone Annie had given him into the deepest part.

Liam O'Connor was, for the moment, no more.

Chapter 36

Back at 42 Manor Road, life settled back into a comfortable routine. Annie was practising hard for her concert. She was spending time on the violin, but she was also spending quite a lot of time on the piano these days and nobody in the bubble knew why. It was simply that she had been asked by her music teacher at school to play a piano solo in the end of term concert. They had asked her to play, Gershwin's Rhapsody in Blue. It was no hardship, she loved it and played it all the time just for pleasure.

She enjoyed the online rehearsals for the Pathetique and, starting after July 10th, they had been allowed to meet up socially distanced to rehearse together. It was strange wearing masks and being seated so far apart, but it was better than nothing and it gave her a final chance to say goodbye to some people she had known almost all her life. Of course, some people asked her about Liam. Although the papers had stopped reporting on him some weeks previously, the students had all either been busy with exams, or just not meeting up together and this was the first chance for many to ask Annie for her thoughts. Close friends, like Kim, had kept in touch and they had gossiped a bit, but others were just renewing acquaintance for the first time.

A couple of other girls and four of the boys had done STEP papers, so that was also a topic of conversation. The concert was on Friday, July 24th, the day after the summer term ended. It would then be just over three weeks, on August 13th, when the results of the A level exams and the STEP papers would be released. GCSE results would be out a week later, on August 20th. It all seemed so strange this year. Teacher-assessed grades and then moderation and then the Government not seeming to know whether it was on its base or its apex.

Annie almost felt fortunate that she was relying on an examination to determine whether she made her offer or not. Her back-up offer was a much lower one for Mathematics with Physics in the Natural Sciences programme at

Durham. Much as she liked Durham—it too had a splendid Cathedral, just like Ely—it was on St Joseph's College Cambridge that her heart was set.

COVID was not going away and, even if she made her offer, Annie was unsure whether she would be going up to Cambridge. She knew that the Cambridge Exams had all gone online and that some had been completely postponed. Her hope was that, if she got in, the University would have in place measures to allow students to return safely in October. For the time being there was nothing to do but wait and enjoy the summer to the extent that she could. She quite liked tennis, she loved her morning runs, she enjoyed her music, and she was beginning to enjoy the company of Jenny and Peter, as well as Simon. She resolved, if ever she were in position to do so, to have four children herself; she hated thinking it, but it was more fun than just being a twosome.

The concert duly took place. All Annie's now extended family attended and her father Henry even came up from London to be there. It was a very strange meeting, as much for its rarity as anything else, but Annie thought that Henry was perhaps relieved to see Sarah and Daniel so happy together and his children also looking happy with the situation, and he was nothing if not charming, to everyone.

For most of the audience, the highlight was the Gershwin Rhapsody. It was not just the technical mastery, that was almost a given, but the exuberance, the vitality, the shear musicality of the performance that captivated the entire audience. There was a feeling that, one day, you might be saying to the World, I was there when she played the Gershwin.

The entire Academy Board was present for the Concert and, afterwards, most of them came up to congratulate Annie. One, a very athletic looking man with a remarkably smooth manner and a cutglass accent, a man called Francis Calder-Warren, asked her if she had any intention of trying to go professional as a musician. Annie replied that she was hoping to go to Cambridge to study Mathematics with Physics, but she would keep up her playing and decide later. Francis Calder-Warren called Sir George Grover and a few other members of the Board to join them, socially distanced outdoors and with masks of course, and the conversation came to a natural end with everyone simply congratulating Annie again for a very musical rendition of one of most people's favourite pieces.

Henry left after the concert and the Carters and the Grants went back to 42 Manor Road, to sit in the garden and drink some cold white wine and eat a few nibbles.

A few days later, a rather lovely letter arrived from Henry addressed to both of his children, assuring them of his continuing support and simply saying that they were always welcome to stay with him and his family, either in London, or at the family farmhouse in France, and he hoped that soon they might meet their half brother and sister and form a friendship. He, Henry, would love to think of Simon and Annie as role models for his new family.

Sarah was not disturbed by this, she had moved on completely and she knew that whatever Henry wrote, Annie's and Simon's first loyalty would be to her, and so she was content. She thought it good of Henry to have made the attempt to present the olive branch.

Annie's results duly came out on the 13th. She went online and there they were. Inevitably the results were stunning. The four "A" levels were A*, Music, Maths, Further Maths and Physics but the jewel in the crown was two "S" grades at STEP 2 and STEP 3. Not only had she scored S grades but her marks, 112 and 115, put her in the top 2% of all those sitting the paper, in each paper and probably much higher than that on the two-paper aggregate. Annie had her place.

One would not have believed it possible for someone as bright and full of life as Annie to glow even more brightly, but she did. When she first looked at the results, she allowed herself a small tear of happiness and excitement, then she wiped her eyes and went to give the news to the family. She called Henry to let him know and she could tell that he was deeply moved and very happy for her. She rang Kim and there were squeals of delight, for Kim, with her 1A* and two As offer, had made 3A*s and would be joining Annie on the trip to Cambridge in October. Kim was going to an all-female College, St Mary's, a little further out of town than St Joseph's and, because of the history of the failure to admit women to Cambridge until the middle of the nineteenth century, a much newer college. Annie remembered the conversation they had had.

"I get plumbing and central heating and double glazing," Kim had said.

"I get four hundred years of history and a cold bum in the winter," said Annie.

Confirmation letters were sent from the respective Colleges. The University had decided to have all lectures online but to take the students back for the small group teaching, as much as possible of which would be face-to-face. They hoped also to build the sense of collegiality that is so much a feature of Cambridge Colleges, by having the students in residence. As more communication took place it became clear that the University was going to establish a system of households, whereby students would live, eat, and socialise in groups.

The University had also arranged that each household would have regular COVID testing and this would be random, not symptom driven. It would involve everyone in a household isolating if one tested positive. Kim's College had slightly different arrangements, the accommodation structure was more block than staircase, but the principle of small family type groups living together was applied across the board.

Annie and Kim were both looking forward to some teaching, which had been very restricted in the past few months, and to some peer-to-peer interaction, both at a social level and an intellectual level.

They celebrated Simon's Birthday on August 16th, just three days after the A and STEP results and then they celebrated again on the 20th when he and Jenny got their GCSE results. They both had 8 Grade 9s and a grade 7, but Simon's grade 7 was in Religious Studies and Jenny's was in Media.

There were a lot of happy faces.

For Annie, there were things to buy and things to do to prepare. She had an email from her College parents, two undergraduates assigned to offer helpful advice to the incoming freshers. It told her what she would really need and what she might get away without. It was one of the most useful communications she received all summer.

Annie started to clean out her room. She came across things like Liam's old iPhone, that she had virtually confiscated when she stuffed him in the polytunnel, and, she really did not know why, she decided to keep it and some of his other stuff, the old T shirt for example, in case he should ever get himself straight and come back to claim those items. She put them in a desk drawer in her room and forgot about them for the time being.

Of the five bedrooms, Annie's room was not the largest nor even the one with the nicest view. The best view was the master bedroom, with its own bathroom, which Sarah and Daniel were sharing with increasing regularity. There was a debate about whether Annie would keep her room when she went off to University and it was agreed that she would. Annie found that strangely comforting; she was not yet ready to leave the nest without a backward glance.

About the end of August, less than three months after the two-family bubble had formed, everyone was ready to take things a stage further. The Carters were spending more and more time with the Grants in Manor Road and it made sense to move in completely. Daniel decided to hang onto his house for the moment with a view to selling it in about a year's time when, he hoped, the vaccine programme would have brought COVID under control. He had high hopes for the vaccines, especially the Oxford-Astra-Zeneca one, and he and Sarah agreed that once the pandemic seemed to be under control they would get married and celebrate all the COVID battered birthdays at the same time.

As Daniel said, "I think everyone is going to have a COVID birthday and some poor so-and-sos will have two, so let us get married and have a huge rave up all at the same time."

He was thinking of Peter, with a March 31st birthday and Jenny with a May 31st birthday. He thought Annie might be lucky and get away with just one COVID birthday, and Simon also.

Chapter 37

Grace and Edward were making real progress in sorting out the finances and establishing Edward's identity. Edward had managed to get a job in the agriculture sector. It was hard work and it involved quite long and antisocial hours, but it was something to keep him busy and help him get fit. He was helping with the harvesting of several crops. He and a group of others were collected in a transport from the Market Square each day and driven out to the fields to work. It was clearly seasonal, but for the time being, it kept him away from temptation, although the desire to relapse was growing less with time. He hoped to be able to go back to study one day and he enrolled in some free online courses at the local regional college. Grace had never studied beyond GCSE and had only very limited formal qualifications, not that they were of any use to her with her new identity. She did, however, manage to get a job as a receptionist at a local firm where she had worked previously. Her track record there had been good and they were happy to re-employ her when their current employee decided to resign to look after her family during the pandemic.

Life almost became normal and it might have remained that way had not two things happened. Edward saw, in the online edition of the Herald newspaper, that Annie had got into Cambridge, to St Joseph's College, and Grace, a much longer "user" than Liam had been, began to find the absence of drugs more and more difficult. It was the drug issue that first reared its head. With access to plenty of money Grace was able to contact a supplier and get herself small but regular supplies of marijuana. At first, she kept it from Edward but soon he began to be suspicious and Grace eventually confessed to what was going on. Rather than put a stop to it Edward decided that marijuana was not dangerous and he would enjoy some too.

To be fair to them both, it might well have stopped at marijuana had not Grace and Edward had an enormous row. Edward got a postcard and wrote to Annie with the intention of sending it to her at St Joseph's. Grace found the postcard before it could be sent and ripped it in little pieces and dropped it on Edward's side of the bed so that he would find it. Edward was furious. All the postcard had said was:

"Well done, Annie, you're a great girl and you deserve it, L."

The row had two results. One was that Grace decided to comfort herself with a shot of heroin. The other was that Edward decided to get another postcard and make sure that this time he did post it to Annie, about a week after the beginning of her first Cambridge term.

Annie was part of the cohort of students who arrived at St Joseph's on Sunday 4th October. She had been allocated a room in the court known as West Court. An early 20th century block built around a sunken garden with some very famous chimera trees planted in it. Annie could not help smiling about Kim's comments about the plumbing because the College had carefully refurbished every part of this court, over a period of about seven years, a staircase at a time. All the rooms had central heating, a wash basin and double glazing. The other thing about these rooms was that they had been built at a time when space was at less of a premium and they were spacious and well-lit by natural light. Annie was on the first floor of Q staircase, a staircase with 24 rooms in total.

The 24 students on Q staircase formed a single household, but they were divided into three smaller units of 8 rooms, for the purpose of accessing toilet and cooking facilities. There had been no attempt to allocate students to staircases by the subject they were studying. Annie's group contained two medical students, an historian, an English student, a linguist, a biologist and another mathematician. Mathematics with Physics is very much a mathematical topic at Cambridge whereas Physical Natural Sciences, in which it is also possible to study physics, is a little less mathematical.

Everyone was COVID swabbed on arrival and given their instructions about how to behave around the grounds. There was a huge marquee which had been erected on the large grass area known as 'The Rec', because it was normally used for all sorts of games in the summer. There were, usually, rather rough grass tennis courts, croquet pitches, volleyball nets and the like set out on the area for casual use, and the relevant equipment was kept in the Porter's Lodge for use by students. Even at this early stage Annie, like so many others, was hoping that by the summer The Rec would be a 'rec' again.

It was impossible not to have seen in the National news that Universities were having a bad time bringing back their students. It was a case of fresher's 'flu' but, of course, far worse. Students from all over the country converging on a single place and living in very close proximity to each other. It seemed to Annie that St Joseph's and the other Colleges were determined not to let that happen here.

Fresher's week was going to be entirely online and there was a timetable of events, the best that could be managed under the circumstances.

The Porters' Lodge was staffed, as Annie remembered, by kind and helpful people, including the Lady Head Porter. Annie was a little pleased to find that the Porters remembered her from the interviews. She had no idea how stunningly beautiful she was, and that anyone, male or female, would find it hard to forget such an exquisite human being.

The Autumn coolness was beginning to close in and a cheerful fire burned in the grate in the Lodge. Students were not allowed to enter the Lodge but spoke to the Porters through a couple of Perspex windows in the Lodge doors. There were socially distanced markings on the court outside the lodge and in the entrance archway. Annie was impressed by how thoughtful and observant of the rules everyone was. St Joseph's had provided every student with two linen shopping bags and two well-made cloth face masks, marked with a hammer and pliers on one of each and a mallet and chisel on the other. It was a way of greeting the freshers and welcoming back the older students that was much appreciated.

There was, throughout the College, a one-way system at every one of the bottlenecks or pinch points on the routes around College. This applied particularly strongly to the refectory where students came in through one door, walked around the service area to pick up their food and left through a different door. The exit route was into a separate court, which then meant people having to walk about seventy yards to get back to The Rec, where the marquee and the dining tables were situated.

The other piece of basic information that all students needed was the location of the individual post boxes, known as the pigeon-holes. Under normal conditions the room containing these was a little way along the cloister from the Lodge, next to the public lavatories that were just inside the College entrance from the street. Like many other parts of the College the pigeonhole room had CCTV so that the porters could keep an eye on the post.

Large items, such as parcels, were not put in the pigeonholes but kept behind the Lodge Screens. A slip announcing the arrival of the item would be put in the pigeonhole, with an identifying number and the slip could be exchanged for the parcel at a suitable moment. In these difficult COVID times the pigeonholes had been moved outdoors, simply placed along the wall, next to the Porter's Lodge. The Cloister provided adequate protection from the rain, but the surveillance of the pigeonholes now relied upon the openness of their situation, the CCTV was not moved.

As the Bursar had said: "We will only have to put it back once the vaccination programme has worked."

There were times of year, like Valentine's Day, when the Lodge became an auxiliary florist and chocolate shop. But that was something for the future as far as the freshers were concerned.

The students tended to eat in blocks of four. They went to the kitchen, where good hot meals and salads had been prepared in advance. They collected the food in reusable plastic containers and took it away to the marquee, where they could sit in their groupings, or to their own room, where they could eat alone. They took the empty cartons back to the kitchen when they had finished their meal and the items were recycled through a very efficient automatic washing system.

The system at Cambridge provides every student with a tutor, who looks after their welfare and interacts on their behalf with the University authorities when that is required. They also have a Director of Studies, who is someone expert in the discipline that they are studying. The DoS, as she or he is usually known, is responsible for directing their academic progression through the system. In Annie's case her principal DoS was a jovial, if slightly eccentric, mathematician who looked after all the mathematicians at St Joseph's and was a man much loved by his students.

Directors of Studies are of two types, one type does the bare minimum, the other type and George Latimer was that type, take not only an academic interest in their students and help them academically as much as they can, but also show concern for their welfare and, in many instances, become the first port of call, even before the tutor, for students with welfare or wellbeing issues. Annie also piggy-backed on the Natural Sciences programme and the Physical Natural Sciences DoS, Kathryn Lambert, would help organise Physics teaching for her alongside the mathematics teaching organised by George Latimer.

Much less formally now, but still embedded in the regulations, students are required to be in residence in Cambridge for nine terms to get an honours degree. In the past this was certified by the Tutor who saw the student at the beginning of term and signed them in and then gave them permission to leave at the end of term, that permission being in the form of a piece of paper called an exeat, which the student presented to the porters to signify their departure, the porters then registering the departure and closing the student's room for the vacation.

For those who know Cambridge Station, it is only recently that Cambridge has had a second and a third proper platform on the far side of the railway track to London. For more than a century the single platform, long and unencumbered, allowed the University Police, the Constables, to stop "the young gentlemen" escaping to London without permission. Anyone wishing to go to London had to show the Constables their exeat from the college.

The beginning of term interviews for Annie were all face to face this year, or, in some instances, mask to mask. Just as the students had generously spacious rooms so did the tutors, although some of the tutors' rooms were in older and less well-lit and ventilated parts of the college. Even so, each tutor had tried to open windows and doors to create ventilation; the staircases, where possible, had a one-way system, and tutors sterilised the chairs and surfaces between student interviews. Most of the tutors were wearing visors as face coverings, rather than masks, the University current guidance being that visors, with ventilation and social distancing, were acceptable.

Annie's tutor was a very pleasant young linguist. Elspeth Gray's thesis had been on the Spanish Theatre in the twentieth century, she adored Lorca. Elspeth was impressed with the young woman who came to see her, the calm and collected bearing, the easy conversation. Elspeth immediately knew that Annie was one of those students with whom she would form a very good working relationship and whose career she would want to follow long after the Cambridge days were over.

Annie, for her part, was delighted to find a young don with whom she felt immediate rapport. They talked about theatre and Elspeth warned Annie not to get too involved too quickly, although she made the slightly wry comment that there was currently no theatre in Cambridge because of COVID. Annie reassured Elspeth that she did intend to work but that music was an important thing she did. Elspeth promised to ask the Director of Music for permission for Annie to use the Steinway Grand in the music practice room, a permission reserved only for the most talented musicians in the College.

Annie told Elspeth that she was planning to apply for an Instrumental Award, probably with the piano as her instrument, and to join the University Orchestra playing the violin. She would also like to sing in the Choir, but that, of course, was on hold for the time being. Annie asked Elspeth about her research and Elspeth was about to begin to describe her interests before she realised that the interview had already overrun and there were more than fifty other pupils, either to welcome, or to welcome back, over the next few days.

Annie left the study and went to her pigeonhole, from which she extracted a whole load of circulars and one personal letter, which happened to be from Simon. She went back to her room and made herself a cup of instant coffee and sat down to read the letter. It appeared that everyone was missing her already.

The morning was given over to tutor meetings for the whole fresher intake, but the afternoons belonged to the Directors of Studies. Annie went to her Physics DoS meeting with Kathryn Lambert first and learnt that she had been allocated to a supervision group with another student from St Joseph's, one Rupert Smyth. They would be supervised by a graduate student of the College called James Gregory and the supervisions would be once a week, in the East Court supervision room. Annie thought to herself, *One down two to go*, as she headed off to her meeting with the Maths DoS.

George Latimer looked at the young lady sitting opposite him and suspended disbelief. Someone that petite and beautiful could not be as brilliant a mathematician as this girl, from her track record, clearly was. Then George just began to feel privileged that she had chosen his college. It was, perhaps, fortunate that Annie had not done the Maths Olympiad, for if she had, another college would have gotten to know about her and would, probably, have hoovered her up.

George asked Annie why she had not done the Olympiad and she explained that she had not really heard about it and, anyway, she was too busy with her music and her part time job and enjoying her own reading around mathematics and philosophy. George asked Annie about her reading and was amazed by the variety and depth of it. He, George, did not usually supervise first year students but he knew that, on this occasion, he could not resist the chance to work with so much raw talent.

Blast, thought George, *Sophie is going to kill me. Bang goes my Thursday. Who can I pair her with?*

Sophie was George's wife and George already supervised three nights a week, so adding Thursday would be a slight concern. Perhaps he could, in times of COVID, find a daytime slot? But he was worried about finding someone who would not be overawed and perhaps destroyed, by sharing a supervision group.

Mathematics is the ultimate competitive academic field and intimidation, however unintentional, has demoralised many a perfectly adequate student. There are students, who have sufficiently strong personalities and high EQs, that thrive on the challenge of being with someone who has an understanding that they cannot, alone, achieve. There was one student, with an S and a high grade 1 at STEP, who might just be able to cope, and George wondered whether this Annie Grant might not just be someone who, with such obvious joy in learning, could motivate Ashok to achieve things that he would never, otherwise, have thought possible.

We'll try it, thought George.

"Annie, I want you to share maths supervisions with a young man called Ashok Ahmed. The two of you will see Professor Jackson at St Helen's College, her room is A5 in the front court there, she will cover the Applied Maths. I will take the pair of you for Pure Maths here in St Joe's, on Thursday. I would like to supervise you during the day if that is possible. Let's look up your timetable and see if there is a spare slot."

Professor Latimer opened the timetable on Moodle and looked at the first-year lecture schedule, first for Maths and then for Physics.

"I wouldn't normally take time out of your day if we were in COVID free times, but we aren't and I suspect you are going to be sitting around a lot anyway rather than doing your violin, piano, tennis and everything else you do, so it looks as if there is no scheduled online teaching for Thursday at 2 pm. Could you bear to have a supervision then?"

It was agreed and Annie went off back to her room with her timetable worked out and looking forward to starting some work.

George Latimer and Kathryn Lambert had sent the mathematicians some work to do in advance of the first supervision, so Annie sat down to look at it. It was not difficult, but it was fun and what with that, regular exercise, a book she was reading about Popper, another one by a famous crime writer, and lots of playing music, Annie managed to fill most of her time. She enjoyed going with her "housemates" to collect lunch and dinner, but she was being very careful not to begin to put on the freshers five kilos that tend to bedevil UK students during their first year at university.

Her College Mum was a runner and took Annie with her on a couple of decent runs from the college which were safe during the hours of daylight, well populated without any isolated danger spots. They did one run out along the riverbank to Baits Bite lock. That was about six miles in total. Daytime only that one, and with a partner; part of the run was well out of town and only the rowers on the Cam and fellow runners, would be there to monitor your safety. Annie did always try to run with someone so, if she could not find a St Joe's student to run with her, she would sometime call Kim and arrange to meet outside St Mary's.

The first online lectures in all subjects began on Thursday of that week and Annie sat patiently through them. She made notes where appropriate and followed up on anything she had not quite grasped first time around. For each of the subjects there were examples sheets to be worked through, either set by the faculty or by her own supervisors.

The first supervisions that she had were all that she could have dreamed of. Her first was with Professor Jackson and she and Ashok went together to go over the examples. Ash was clearly a good student for he, like Annie, had managed to complete all the examples and that gave Agnes Jackson the chance to introduce additional material that stretched the understanding of both her students. The supervision with George Latimer consisted of George finding out that both these two had finished the example set and wanted more.

It turned out that Annie and Ashok had gotten together online and there had been a couple of things that Ashok didn't quite get, until he had talked it over with Annie, but then he did get it and he didn't quite realise how he had got there. That was to happen a lot over the rest of the term.

The Physics supervision was with a different partner and was memorable for a very different reason.

Annie and Rupert Smyth went to the supervision room in East Court where Jim Gregory was waiting for them. They knocked and went in. Jim Gregory stopped what he was doing, stood up and stared. He covered it up quickly. He started to speak, but initially all he managed was a croak. Then he cleared his throat and asked the two students to sit down. He couldn't take his eyes off Annie as she moved to sit down. Jim mentally pinched himself and switched to professional mode.

The supervision room was spacious and had a floor to ceiling glass wall on to the central courtyard. It also had excellent air conditioning and ventilation, with external air intake and no recirculation. It was one of the safest rooms in College in which to supervise. When the two students came in Jim was just sanitising the surfaces and wiping everything down. He was wearing a visor, in

242

accordance with University guidelines for indoor face to face teaching, and both Annie and Rupert were also wearing visors.

Annie thought Jim looked a little young to be a supervisor, barely a handful of years older than herself, but she trusted Professor Lambert and soon found that, not only did Jim Gregory know his material, but he was also excellent at explaining things. Once he got over the croak, he also had a rather pleasant voice, resonant and clear. *Besides which*, thought Annie, *he's quite good-looking.*

Chapter 38

Early in that second week of October, the Academy Board held another Zoom meeting with Sir George Glover presiding. It was, principally, a meeting to receive a report from the Education sub-committee on examination results and outcomes. It also received a preliminary report of the Business and Resources Committee on the budget and audit, a report on safeguarding and an update of the Trust safeguarding policy in the light of COVID, the interim report of the Strategy Sub-Committee, and the Risk Assessment. The success of five students in getting into Cambridge was noted and the announcement was made that each of these students, plus eleven others who had obtained places at outstanding universities, had received one-off grants of £1000 from the Bishop Bryanston Trust Fund.

The meeting was dull, but fortunately very brief. Sir George went back to the report on his desk about the proposed acquisition by his company of a series of prime High Street sites that might be available as the result of COVID induced business failures.

Bruno left the Academy Trust Board meeting and immediately telephoned Freddie.

"That girl, Annie Grant. She got into St Joseph's College. Just a heads-up. We still haven't found that kid who stole our money and, you never know, he may try to contact her. I thought you said you had someone who might be able to keep an eye on her?"

"I do," said Freddie. "Michael O'Grady."

Freddie got on the phone to Michael O'Grady.

"Michael, how are you, dear boy? Do you remember that I said we might have another little job or two for you soon? You do? Good. It shouldn't be too onerous, but we would really like you to keep an eye on Annie Grant for us. See if you can find out who she is friends with and, if possible, see if she gets any post? I know these Colleges have pigeonholes; I was at one of the colleges myself. You will do that for us? It's St Joseph's. Thank you, dear boy. Expect a little something in the post, for your trouble. Bye."

It was that weekend that Edward sent the postcard to Annie. Just like the one Grace had torn up, it simply said:

"Well done, Annie, you're a great girl and you deserve it, L."

On the front was a picture of the Cathedral in the City, on the back was a postmark confirming the location. The postcard arrived in Annie's pigeonhole on the Tuesday morning.

On Tuesday morning Annie called Kim and arranged to go for a run along the riverbank. She looked in her pigeonhole briefly before she left the college and noted a brown envelope, which probably meant more intra-college bumf, on top of the pile, and a small typewritten slip of paper, on its edge beside it. She was a bit late for her meeting with Kim, so she decided to leave it there until she came back from the run.

Perhaps surprisingly during lockdown both Annie and Kim were getting to be very fit. They were taking their exercise seriously and were also glad of it as an excuse to meet up. There was no doubt that this current student experience was more a crock of manure at the end of the admissions rainbow than a crock of gold. Kim was enjoying one on one zoom discussions with her supervisors and some classes about how you used evidence in historical study. Kim was frustrated by the lack of social opportunity that COVID was creating. She shared the evidence classes with some students from other Colleges. She quite liked the look of one of them and was planning to try to meet up, socially distanced, of course.

Annie told Kim about this rather handsome and very pleasant young supervisor called Jim Gregory that was doing her Physics supervisions, and, as she talked, she realised that she had, indeed, thought him rather attractive and that she was looking forward to their next meeting on Friday, for rather more than just the academic interaction.

"He has very nice blue eyes," said Annie and then she thought, *Where did that come from?*

When Annie got back to St Joe's, having left Kim at her own college, she went to the pigeonhole and immediately wondered if someone had been going through it. The slip of paper was now on the bottom of the pile and on the top there was a postcard, with a picture of a famous Cathedral on the front.

Annie went pale with shock and almost fainted. She read the message on the back:

"Well done, Annie, you're a great girl and you deserve it, L."

Paul, one of the porters, saw her and immediately asked if she was alright.

"I'm OK," said Annie. "I just got back from a run to Baits Bite and I felt a little faint. I need a cup of hot chocolate and a biscuit, that's all."

"I just boiled the kettle," said Paul. "You stand there a second and I'll be right back."

Annie waited and three minutes later, Paul emerged with a big Liverpool FC mug, full of steaming hot chocolate, and a small pack of ginger biscuits. He was wearing gloves and a mask. He handed them to her.

"Now just you run along and get yourself a shower and a sit down, and drink that chocolate and get your energy levels up," said Paul. "By the way, did that friend of yours find you?"

"No," said Annie. "Which friend?"

"That boy called Michael who said he was at school with you. He asked me where your pigeonhole was so that he could leave a note for you."

Annie felt very afraid. Michael. The only Michael she knew was Michael O'Grady and there were rumours that he had been mixed up in drugs, like Liam; and Liam had been sort of friends with him. It was quite possible that he was still in touch with the gang of four.

"Thanks Paul." Annie forced herself to speak. "He didn't find me, but I expect he'll try again. Must run and get that shower now. Do me a favour and don't let him know what room I am in. He was a bit of a pest at school, always wanting a date, and I had a boyfriend."

It was the best she could think of on the spur of the moment and Paul, of course, could quite understand how some boy might become a bit obsessed with Annie Grant. He spoke to the Head Porter and she left a note on the desk that nobody was to be given Annie Grant's room number without Annie's specific permission.

Michael O'Grady went back to his room and called Freddie.

"Mr Seeley, I think I have some information you might want. I looked in Annie Grant's pigeonhole this morning and she had a postcard from someone signing himself L. I think that could be Liam O'Connor, so I thought I should let you know. The postcard was of the Cathedral at..." He mentioned the city. "The postmark was the same city. It was posted on Sunday."

Freddie rang his fellow gang leaders and the four of them agreed to meet that evening at Bruno's residence. They knew now where to search for Liam and, they hoped the missing half a million.

Liam might still have been alright. The city was large enough, a few million people, for Liam to have been difficult to find but for one thing. Grace had relapsed and was again buying drugs.

The gang of four met and decided to make contact, on the off chance, with the drug dealers in the other city. They would ask for cooperation in finding Liam and anticipated that the other group would, recognising the importance of punishing people who stole from a properly organised crime setup, be only too glad to help.

It was not long before someone reported that there was a woman who was buying heroin regularly with fifty-pound notes. It was about two weeks after the postcard that this information got back to the gang of four. Freddie was despatched to deal with the matter and find out where the lad was hiding out.

During that two weeks, Annie was watching over her shoulder everywhere she went. She only ever ran with a partner and she never left the college after the hours of darkness. She and Kim talked quite a bit. They were both enjoying the academic work. Kim had sent a chat message to the boy in her supervision group and they had started to meet a little, socially distanced, of course.

****

Annie found herself looking forward more and more to the Physics supervisions and she and Jim would linger and chat after the formal session ended. Rupert Smyth was always rushing off to row or do gym or something, he was a Blues level athlete, so the window of opportunity presented itself. Jim and Annie found that they had a great deal in common. There was love of the core mathematical aspects of physics, for a start. But there was also a love of music and the theatre and cassoulet, one must not forget the love of cassoulet.

Jim explained that his mother was French and that he was bilingual and had spent many happy holidays in France with relatives, and Annie explained that she had simply come to love French food during a brief holiday there with her Father a couple of years ago. Annie also explained that her brother was a superb cook and had an ambition to open his own restaurant one day.

"When this COVID stuff is over, would you ask him to cook for me?" asked Jim, almost before he could help himself.

It was awkward. Academics are not supposed to become involved with their students. But Jim did not have a current girlfriend and Annie Grant had poleaxed him when she came into the room those three weeks ago. He would just have to remain on good terms, for the time being, and try to get through the year without moving the relationship to a different level. If he stopped supervising her next year, then maybe he could ask her out? Could he wait that long. He was going to have to talk to someone about the ethics of this.

Meanwhile, Annie was going through a similar dilemma. You were not supposed to fall for your teachers. But it was already too late. Perhaps she could ask to change supervisors and then maybe it would be OK. She had read the College's sexual harassment policy, but this wasn't harassment.

And all the while, in the background, was this nagging fear that the drug gang might be after her again.

****

Grace had gone home that lunch hour to pick up two more fifty-pound notes for her next purchase. That evening on the way home, she went to the dealer's place and made her buy. Freddie followed her home and sat and waited.

At about 7 pm that evening a tall and fit-looking young man walked back towards the house from the direction of the Market Square.

"Got you. You little shit!" said Freddie to himself.

****

"So, the woman has been buying drugs with nice crisp fifty-pound notes?" said Bruno.

"Indeed," said Freddie.

"I think that must mean she knows where the money is hidden and he has got it with him there," said Jason Miller.

"No wonder he managed to hide out for so long. Could stay below the radar and just pay cash for everything. No way any of our people would have spotted him."

"I am a bit puzzled," said Freddie. "He looked totally fit and totally clean to me. I don't think she was buying for them both, just to feed her own habit. I think we would have found him anyway, but her habit made it one whole lot easier. I left some of our guys over there to watch the place and make sure he didn't get spooked and run. How do we want to deal with this?"

George almost started to salivate in anticipation.

"I still have my knives," he said.

So, they agreed. Another battered Range Rover with false number plates would drive the short distance to pick up these two people and then bring them back to George's warehouse to "work on a solution".

And so it was that, just a few days later, on the Friday, at the time when Annie was going to her fourth supervision with Jim Gregory, a battered Khaki Range Rover parked itself in the road next to Lavinia's end terrace house and waited.

Grace was grabbed first. From behind, with a bag put straight over her head. She kicked out backwards quite viciously and Jason nearly lost his hold on her, but George knocked her unconscious with a sand-filled blackjack and they bundled her into the back of the vehicle and tied her up. They also removed the hood, while she was still unconscious, and gagged her, before putting the bag over her head again.

"Put her in the recovery position," said George, his medical training showing. "We don't want her to croak before we find out where the money is."

They waited. After about thirty minutes, Grace began to struggle and muffled sounds started to emerge from under the bag. The two drug lords ignored it all.

At about 7 pm, Liam came back and was just putting his key in the lock when George, who could move very stealthily when he wanted to, came up behind him and hit him with the blackjack. Jason picked up Liam's feet, George got his shoulders and they unceremoniously dumped him in the back with Grace, tying up his hands and feet and gagging and hooding him too.

An hour later, Liam came around to find himself tied, naked, to the same table in the same warehouse to which Bryan Muldoon had been strapped two or three months ago.

The same sadistic bastard with the knives was standing over him.

They sat Grace in a chair, tied her to it, so that she could watch every detail of what was happening.

"You little bastard," said George. "You've led us a right dance. But we have you now. We can do this the easy way or the hard way. Where's our money?"

Liam's gag had been removed and he simply said: "I can't remember."

Liam had worked out already that if he told them where the money was, both he and Grace would be dead. He also knew that if he told them a lie then there would be a lot of pain to follow. He really did not know what to do. His immediate thought was that he might be able to use the money as a bargaining chip to get Grace freed. Then he realised that, by removing the bag over her head, they had let her see them and he immediately knew that Grace and he would both be killed anyway. He had another, somewhat bizarre thought. If he did not tell them where the money was hidden, then maybe Annie would get it. He remembered telling her where it was and that she had brought him some of it when he went to Ely that day.

George started to lose patience.

"Come on, you little shit, where is the money?"

Liam again claimed loss of memory.

George started to cut him.

Liam screamed. Grace struggled and writhed in her chair, so very upset. The noise of the machinery, a mixture of engine whirr and screeches of metal on metal, more than drowned out the scream.

"Listen, you little shit. I will ask you again and every time you refuse to answer, I will cut you again," said George.

After about ten minutes and when Liam's torso was beginning to look like a series of bloody noughts and crosses grids, George stopped cutting and asking questions and went over to the corner to make a cup of tea.

"Cup of tea, Jason?" said George.

"Please," said Jason.

George made four cups of tea.

"Thought we should give the kids one each too," said George. And promptly poured the boiling hot cups, first over Grace, who screamed ineffectively into her gag, and then over Liam's torso.

Liam screamed and screamed with the pain and went unconscious.

"Now, young lady," said George. "I am going to remove your gag and ask you a couple of questions. If you scream, I will start to cut you up and put your gag back on. Do you understand?"

Grace nodded.

Jason ripped the duct-tape gag off.

Grace let out a string of expletives and started to sob.

"Naughty, naughty," said George. "Now, do you know where the money is?"

And Grace, poor deluded Grace, thought that she did, and she offered to take them to it if they would leave Edward, for she still thought of him as Edward, alone.

"We have a result," said George. And then, to Jason, "You stay here with young Liam and when I get the money, I will call you and you can let him get dressed and leave. Just warn him, before he leaves, what will happen to his family if he ever talks to anyone about this."

And with the charade played out, George turned to Grace and said: "You will take me to the money. If you make any trouble, I will press the speed dial button on this phone and Jason here will kill Liam. I will kill you. Do you understand?"

"Yes," said Grace meekly. The pain from her neck and shoulders was beginning to be almost unbearable and the skin was starting to blister. There was no fight left in her. She followed George meekly to the car, got in and fastened her seatbelt.

"Where is it?" asked George.

"At home," said Grace.

They drove back to Lavinia's house.

When they got there, George said, "Do you think you can manage to carry it?"

Grace thought that a little bit strange, but she simply said "Of course."

"Well, I suggest you go in and get it and come out here with it. We don't want to get anyone else involved, do we? And if anyone else saw me, I might have to hurt them."

Grace did as she was told. Lavinia, busy in the kitchen, called out to Grace as she came in, but Grace, anxious to keep Lavinia safe, called out that she was just popping up to her room to collect something and she was going out and would be back later. She collected Edward's rucksack and went out to the car.

George looked at the rucksack and knew immediately that it contained a tiny fraction of the missing money. It was back to the warehouse.

In the conversation on the way back to the warehouse, it soon became clear to George that Grace truly believed that the money in the rucksack was all that Liam had taken and was what George and Jason wanted to recover. That knowledge signed Grace's death warrant.

While George was away, Jason had gone behind a partition for a pee and while he was there, Liam had worked away at loosening his bonds. He had not been able to break free, but he had managed to loosen some of the straps that were holding him and a plan had formed in his mind. His head was relatively free of restraint and with effort and the effects of the blood on his bindings, he had managed to get himself about three inches of upper body movement.

George brought Grace back to the scene of the torture and strapped her back in her chair. By now it was obvious to all of them that Grace had no idea how much money Liam had stolen.

"You didn't tell her about the real money, did you?" said George.

Grace's eyes opened wide.

"This little shit stole more than half a million from us, didn't you?" said George.

Liam said nothing.

That was when Grace knew she was dead. The anticipation preceded the event, but only just.

George stepped behind her, grabbed her hair, pulled it out of the way and cut her throat with a single vicious swipe of the scalpel. There was a gurgling sound, a lot of blood and Grace died very quickly, her eyes wide and staring.

Liam was, by now, completely numb.

George changed scalpels.

"I think that was getting a little blunt," he said. "A nice clean very sharp new blade for you, I think."

He came over to Liam and started again.

"I think that now, we will work up the neck a little," said George.

And he held the scalpel over Liam's neck, above the jugular vein and the carotid artery. It was the moment Liam had been waiting for. Liam timed it perfectly. Just as George was bringing down the new sharp blade to make one of his perfect shallow cuts, Liam raised his body convulsively off the table that precious three inches and impaled his carotid artery on the blade. He then waggled his neck from side to side as hard as he could.

George snatched the scalpel away and flung it on the floor. He clamped his hands over the bleeding artery and vein, but he had no grip—there was blood everywhere. George had come prepared with his usual butterfly sutures and gauze but an artery with a blood flow of several hundred millilitres a minute is

252

hardly going to be closed with a butterfly suture.

Liam bled out in a few minutes.

There was nothing for George and Jason to do but to clean up. Twenty-five thousand pounds was not enough to have warranted this wholesale slaughter, but they were where they were.

George went down to his yard and collected two big heavy-duty rubbish sacks. One body ended up in each one.

There was a fire hose on each floor in this building and George used it to wash all the blood he could down the drains. He also washed himself and Jason, for the spurting carotid arteries, first from Grace, and then from Liam, had covered both Jason and him in bright red arterial blood.

"Strip," said George. Jason stripped to his slightly grubby underpants.

"Put your stuff in the bag with the girl," said George.

George also stripped and, making sure he had no blood on him, put all his clothes in the bag with Liam. George went down to the wrecking yard office and collected two sets of overalls, safety boots and safety helmets.

"Put this lot on," said George.

They put the body bags and George's "medical equipment" in the lift and took it down to the garage. It was all transferred to the Range Rover.

George drove Jason home.

Jason had a bit of trouble explaining to his wife that he had had an accident while visiting his friend George's recycling plant and had to borrow these clothes, but she was so busy laughing at how ridiculous he looked that the matter was soon passed over.

George called Freddie and arranged with Freddie to meet at the Garage in about an hour. He went home and changed into more normal everyday clothes and ran the wrecking yard stuff back to the office.

He collected a couple of jerry cans of petrol and put them in the back of the Range Rover and he then drove to his rendezvous with Freddie. They drove, in convoy, back to the city where Grace and Liam had been hiding out. George knew of a place where he could carry out his plan to get rid of the bodies without them being identified.

This spot was on the road right next to a quarry. Vehicles had, more than once, gone off the cliff here and simply gone up in flames as they hit the ground.

They soaked the Range Rover and the two bodies in petrol and put a large amount of it in each of the black heavy duty waste sacks, then they pointed the car in the right direction, started the engine, jammed a plastic bottle on the accelerator, set light to a bundle of rags, threw it in the back of the Range Rover and shoved the car into drive, leaping clear as it took off. About ten seconds later, there was the most satisfactory explosion from the bottom of the quarry and Freddie and George had cleared the scene, almost before the noise of the explosion reached the farm nearby.

"What do we do now?" asked George.

"We have one more go at that Annie Grant girl," said Freddie. "Just a little go. Just a little muscle. She might know something."

****

Annie was completely unaware of all that happened to Grace and Liam. She was beginning to enjoy the rather strange existence in Cambridge. A couple of the households had been forced to isolate because the random testing, of symptomless and mild symptoms alike, had yielded positive COVID results. Isolation was a bit grim, but nothing like as grim as the isolation arrangements in some of the halls of residence at other Universities. The fencing barricades, the stale cheese butty, the miserable packet of crisps. At St Joseph's and the other Cambridge colleges, isolation meant confined to room, if you were the one testing positive, and confined to household, if you were negative but in the same grouping as a positive test.

However, the porters and the general college staff and volunteers from among your peer group would bring milk and cereal and a croissant or Danish pastry to your room in the morning, with butter and jam if you asked for it, a hot meal or a salad at lunchtime and hot meal or salad again in the evening, whichever you preferred. The college students' union, working with the governing body of the college, also arranged goody bags of snacks and cold drinks. It was only the isolation that was a problem.

You also were not missing out on any of the teaching because the colleges had excellent IT and all lectures were online. There were some live practical classes, for subjects like medicine, and if you had to miss one of these because you were isolating, the fact that the group sizes at University level had, of necessity, been made smaller, meant that there would always be a session outside your isolation period to which you could go to catch up. Supervisions were beginning to move online for some people, it was some of the older supervisors who chose that because of the greater COVID risk to the more elderly, especially the older men.

The supervisors were also getting very adept at mixed online and live supervision classes, using IT for the non-attenders and socially distanced face to face contact for the rest of the group. It was not too bad. Everyone became quite skilful at using whiteboards and there was the advantage with larger supervision groups that nobody could hide because their full face was permanently on camera.

Annie, and Jim Gregory too, hoped that the weekly face to face supervisions would continue. For both of them it was beginning to be one of the highlights of the week. Yes, the work was great, but it was the chat afterwards, when Rupert had left to do his physical exercise, that was what both valued most. Annie knew that, for the first time since she broke up with Liam, here was someone she really wanted to be with. As for Jim, cupid had shot his arrow in the first two seconds that he had seen Annie. He had talked to his dad and mum, who simply warned him to be a little careful about the ethics of dating a pupil, and he had talked to the senior tutor of the college, who raised an eyebrow and said: "Caesar's wife. Behave until Christmas, keep it formal. If you and from what you are saying, she, want to carry on seeing each other after Christmas, tell Prof Lambert to get her another supervisor. You will know by then if that is the right thing to do or the crush has burnt itself out."

******

Back in the city to which Grace and Liam had moved, Lavinia had reported the pair of them missing. She gave their names to the local police who came around and asked her about when she had last seen them and whether they might have run away together. The usual thing. But Lavinia was insistent that the pair had been very much in love and had been planning a life together, that things were going well in the city and that she had expected them to stay with her and support her for a very long time.

The police had also received the report of the car going over the edge of the quarry and they at least wondered if the two events were linked.

Two deeply charred bodies had been found in the wreckage of the Range Rover, with fragments of two large jerry cans, which had exploded with the heat of the fire, destroying everything, except the teeth and bones, which might be used to identify the occupants. It was still possible to identify various engine numbers and things on the vehicle and it turned out it was a vehicle which had been sold for scrap in a neighbouring town some years ago.

One would normally have expected the components to have been melted down and recycled at a suitable recycling plant, but the reclaimed vehicle had clearly been driven up to the quarry, either by the occupants or by someone else. The other remarkable thing was that the two charred corpses had almost perfect teeth, suggesting that they were quite young. The forensic investigators were convinced that this was not a simple accident, the intensity and extent of the blaze was much greater than might have followed a simple crash.

The only things which might allow identification were a gold bracelet, with several small charms attached, and a pair of small gold ear studs; even with the heat of a petrol fire gold survives the flames. The detectives took the gold objects to show Lavinia and she burst into tears immediately. She recognised the bracelet as one that Edward had recently given to Grace on her birthday.

The local police now believed the burnt bodies were the missing couple and so, while one group worked hard at trying to trace the car's movements on the night it crashed, the other group set about obtaining usable forensic material to compare with anything that came out of the crash investigation. They took fingerprints from the couple's bedroom and they checked their passports, driver's licences, bank accounts and credit cards. They also found some fifty-pound notes and some heroin.

It soon became apparent that Edward Simon Collins had not existed until a few months ago. It also became apparent that Grace Victoria Chandler was a very recent arrival in the world, only a few years before Edward.

The quest began to find out exactly who these two people truly were. With Grace, it proved simple; her fingerprints were on file following a robbery in 2016, drug related. Grace Victoria Chandler was Grace Elisabeth Jones, originally from Cardiff.

Perusal of the credit card accounts showed very little activity recently, just normal transactions for food and the like. They were not very optimistic about getting any DNA or other biological evidence from the scene.

Grace's account showed the details of the stay at the Marlborough rehabilitation Centre and the ticket purchases from there, via Ely, to the present location.

For the moment, these facts were all a mystery—how did they fit together and who was Edward?

The detectives decided that all this was very suspicious. They had very good recent photos of the two missing people and decided to seek help finding them. They sent copies to all the local forces and they asked the local newspaper to put out a request for information. They also decided to ask the local television station to show the pictures on the evening bulletin.

It was shortly after the local six o'clock news bulletin that the telephone calls began to come in.

Edward and Liam were identified as one and the same.

Jerry Gregory and Steve Bronowski watched the news bulletin and saw the photo sent by their colleagues. They knew immediately that the search for Liam was over.

"I wonder if it was someone from here who went and picked up those two kids? Let's see if there is any evidence of a Range Rover travelling from here to there on the evening in question," said Jerry. "It's a long shot but long shots are all we have at the moment."

Simon, having watched the evening news bulletin, rang Annie to tell her that the hunt for Liam had now switched to the other city and that two badly burned bodies had been found in a burnt out car in a disused quarry. He explained that Liam had gone missing with a young woman and he reminded her that he, Simon, thought he had seen Liam and a girl when they went to Ely that day. Annie said she remembered that but she herself had thought it was someone else.

"Well," said Annie, "you may have been right. Why don't you call it in?"

Simon did call, but the police just said thank you and did not question him further.

Annie was deeply shocked. She was reflecting on the incident with the postcard. She was convinced that the postcard had let the drugs gang trace Liam to the new city, and, in that, she was correct. At the time, she wondered what on earth had possessed him to send that postcard. She was almost sure that one of the bodies in the burnt-out car would turn out to be Liam's.

Chapter 39

Annie had started to go for a regular long run on the Friday before her supervision with Jim. She had got into the habit of running to Baits Bite and back on the north side of the river. She almost always ran with Kim. It was a classic mistake made by someone under surveillance, not to vary their routine. To be fair to Annie, the identification of Liam as having moved to another town was sufficient, to an innocent way of thinking, for her to believe that she was now out of danger, and off the radar, for the drug gang.

That should have been a correct assumption, but Freddie in particular was still very cross about the loss of half a million and, although he knew that Liam and the girl he had teamed up with were now dead, he wanted one more shot, a long shot, that perhaps Liam O'Connor had told the Grant girl where he had hidden the money before he went off to hide. He was going to send a couple of frighteners, just the once, to see what she knew.

On Friday November 13th, Annie went for her afternoon run along the riverbank to Baits Bite. Kim had a rearranged History supervision so, on this occasion, for the very first time, Annie was running alone. It was a bit cold, a bit damp. There were fewer runners than usual and as she reached the bend opposite the Plough Inn, someone jumped out of the bushes and grabbed her. He had a stocking mask on and a very nasty looking stiletto knife in his hand. He pulled her through a gap in the hedge into the field beyond. Annie's immediate thought was that this was going to be a sexual assault.

She was wearing running gear, only a sports bra, singlet and shorts. It was the obvious conclusion to draw, but just at that moment several large rowers came running past; one shouted loudly to the rest: "I need a bloody piss", and he came barrelling through the gap in the hedge into the field where the guy with the knife was holding it against Annie's stomach. Annie's stomach was cut by the knife as the attacker leapt to his feet and hightailed it through the gate at the other side of the field, while the burly rower stood there staring at Annie.

"Bloody hell," he said. "Thank God I needed a pee. Come on, I'll get the boys and we'll see you safely home. We need to let the police know. Have you got a mobile with you; I left mine at the boathouse."

Annie called the police and reported the attack. She rang Jim and asked him if they could postpone the supervision until later. She did not tell him why at that point. Jim readily agreed but said that Rupert was coming at the normal time so it would be a one-to-one supervision at 6 pm and it would have to be in his room in the college hostel, if Annie could stand it. Annie could stand it.

The police were very good. They took Annie's statement. The warning about a sex attacker on the loose was sent around to all the colleges, along with a reminder, to women, especially, not to run alone in isolated places. Annie felt a bit stupid. She had gotten complacent in this lovely place called Cambridge. Lovely the place might have been, but people are people wherever you are and some of them are not very nice.

The senior tutor asked to see her and Annie explained that she had never had any trouble before in five or six years of early morning and late afternoon running. She was on the verge of saying that she thought this was not a sexual assault, but something stopped her. She did not want her time at Cambridge to be linked to that drug scene that Liam had so nearly dragged her into. What she remembered, now that the initial fear had subsided, was that the bastard with the knife had called her by name when he grabbed her and pulled her through the hedge. How did the bastard know her name if he was not connected to that drug scene? It was too soon after the fresh publicity around Liam for this to be a coincidence.

By the time Annie got to Jim Gregory's room at 6 pm, it was pitch black and still raining. Jim had made some coffee and had a couple of ginger biscuits which he offered Annie. They sat and started to talk about the work when Jim suddenly said: "There was a girl assaulted on the towpath on the way to Baits Bite this afternoon. Was it you?"

Annie looked at him in complete surprise. "Yes," she said.

"I thought it had to be. I know you do that run every Friday and I couldn't think of any other reason why you would postpone the supervision. Did he hurt you?"

Annie explained the details of what had happened and then she decided to take a very big decision and tell Jim what she thought was behind the attack. It was sort of important to her for him to know that it was not a sex attack.

"I think the attack was to do with something that happened when I was at school. I think it was an attack by a gang who want to find a former boyfriend of mine and want to kill him."

There are bombshells and there are megaton bombshells. This was somewhere close to the latter. Jim's mouth dropped open.

Annie told him the whole story. How she had this boyfriend when she was 12 until she was about 16. She had grown up with him, but he had gone into drugs when he went into the sixth form and she had then chucked him immediately she found out. She said that she knew that he had got in with this very powerful drug syndicate and that somehow, he had double-crossed them and they wanted to find him. She said that the police were also looking for this man, he was called Liam.

The police had asked her if she knew where Liam was because of her previous connection with him, but she had not seen him since he left school to go to University well over a year ago. She was sure that the drug syndicate had also been watching her to see if Liam would contact her. She had not told the police all this yet because she had only just remembered about the name thing.

"You poor thing," said Jim. "Look, you must give them a call now and let them know, OK. Did the guy hurt you?"

"I just got a little cut," said Annie. And without thinking, she pulled up her jumper and showed Jim the gauze patch that the police first aider had stuck over the cut.

Jim didn't look at the cut, not really; he was just mesmerised by the sight of Annie's flawless skin and perfect figure.

"I hope it won't scar," said Jim.

"They don't think it will," said Annie. "They put a couple of butterfly sutures just for extra protection."

"I just want to hug you," said Jim.

"Humph," said Annie. "What does that do for social distancing? Hadn't we better finish this supervision work first? I'll tell the police in the morning."

They did finish the supervision work first and then Jim did give Annie a hug and then Annie kissed him. And then they sat there and talked until 1am. And then Annie went back to her Q staircase and Jim went to bed. Annie never did tell the police.

Term was ending early this year; everyone was going home in the first week of December.

The rate of infection within the University had shrunk considerably from the early days of the term. The random testing and isolation of cases was doing a good job of allowing the Authorities to keep things under control. Cases in the city were surging a bit and there was a bit of an outbreak among some of the students, attributable to a combination of Halloween illegal parties and bonfire night.

Annie was making plans to go home to her double bubble, as they were now calling it. She had kept in touch with everyone and they were all doing well. Sarah told Annie that she was convinced that Jenny and Simon were an item and both were thriving on it. She and Daniel were growing closer than ever and Peter was becoming very excited about his "big sister" Annie soon returning home.

As far as Annie was concerned, the only fly in the ointment was that she would have six weeks without seeing Jim.

On the Thursday before the last supervision, she was working late in the library and about 10 pm, she shut her books and started to walk back along the path by the pond to West Court. The old-fashioned streetlamps used to light the path were a nice feature but, on this occasion, two of them had failed and as she came around the corner from the path, through the small thicket of bamboo and shrubs, two very large men wearing stocking masks grabbed her from behind, slapped some duct tape over her mouth and dragged her deeper into the thicket.

This time she felt for certain that it was related to Liam. They knew exactly what they were doing and where they were going to take her. They went to the garages behind the maintenance department, picked the door lock and went in. They sat her on a wooden chair and strapped her ankles, with more duct tape, to the chair, and duct taped her arms behind her back. Then they started to talk.

"We don't need you to tell us where your lousy ex-boyfriend is," said one of them. "We've dealt with him. What we need to know is where the money is. And we think you know."

Annie was shaking her head vigorously.

"We think you do know, but we are going to be very generous. We are going to give you a fortnight to decide to tell us and, if you do, we will go away and you will never see us again. If you don't then we have a list of people we are going to have to talk to and probably hurt quite badly. Let me show you a few pictures."

And the second thug produced an iPhone and showed Annie pictures of Simon, Sarah, Daniel, Jenny, Peter, Kim and Jim.

"I didn't include a picture of you because you know we are going to hurt you as well if you don't talk. And in case you are wondering, if you go to the police, we will start to hurt these people anyway. Oh, and in case you are still wondering, we did kill that ex-boyfriend of yours and his little girlfriend. Apparently, they made a lovely bonfire."

"And just to show you we mean business, we reckon you need a few slaps to remember us by."

And the two thugs got out some birch canes and started to beat Annie about her thighs and stomach. Annie experienced quite a bit of pain that night.

By the time they stopped, the tears were rolling down Annie's cheeks and the thugs were obviously well content with their night's work.

"So, remember, little lady, talk to anyone about this and you will find this was a picnic compared with what we will do to you and those friends of yours. Say nothing and tell us what we want to know and you might just have a chance of surviving."

They cut the duct tape from the chair legs and dragged Annie to her feet. They freed her arms, they blindfolded her with her own face mask and marched her into the middle of the bamboo thicket and they left her standing there. It was a couple of minutes before she realised that they had gone. She removed her blindfold, pulled the duct tape from her mouth and for almost the first time in her life, she started to swear.

She thought to herself: *They killed Liam and his new girlfriend; they probably killed that poor woman right at the beginning. I have no idea how many other people they have killed. But they are not going to kill me or mine. I am going to get them. I am so going to get them.*

Annie took them at their word, they would leave her alone for a fortnight. By that time, she would be home and she had some ideas about what she was going to do. Some involved the money, others… That nice policeman Steve Bronowski figured quite large in what she intended.

The pain of the beating was beginning to fade. When she got home and undressed and looked in the mirror, there were red weals where the birch canes had hit her, but the skin was not broken and they would heal. The pain would go away but the anger she felt would not, not until she had sorted it.

After the last supervision the next day with Jim, she stayed, as usual, to chat. She said she was going home on the 4th. They exchanged mobile numbers and Jim said he would give her a call over Christmas.

Chapter 40

On December 4th, Daniel drove down to collect Annie and she packed up her music and her violin and her books and her clothes and went back to 42 Manor Road.

They were so pleased to see her, all the family. She popped her mask on and went around to see Mr Stops and he asked her if she wanted to do any shifts over Christmas and she said she would. She rang Kim, who was also home and they talked for a long time.

Simon had cooked supper, a simple chicken with mushroom sauce dish, and Annie was really pleased to be eating off proper plates again and with real cutlery, instead of the disposable knives and forks they had been eating with in Cambridge.

Sarah, Daniel and Annie chatted quite late, but the others went to bed around 10:30 because school was still functioning.

Before she went to bed Annie fished Liam's old iPhone out of the drawer and put it on to charge. She had heard the two thugs telling her that Liam was dead and she wanted to get a few photographs off the phone, to remember him by and to see if there were any clues to who might have killed him. If she charged it overnight, she could look in the morning. She remembered his six-digit pin was his birthday.

Annie had a great night's sleep and woke refreshed rather late in the morning. Everyone else had left the house and she was by herself. She made some toast and spread butter and strawberry jam thickly on it. She made some real coffee. The only time she had real coffee in Cambridge was when Jim made it for her. She missed him. She should have asked him where he lived but that sort of personal detail was probably not right for a teacher and pupil relationship. Probably that was why both had kept off the topic. She made up her mind to ask for a different supervisor next term so that she could go out with Jim. She knew it was what they both wanted. Then she could ask those personal questions.

After that ridiculously late breakfast, Annie went back up to the bedroom and picked up the now fully charged iPhone. She entered the six-digit pin and the phone sprang into life.

She flicked through a few pictures, nothing remarkable there, then she saw there was a recorded message. She dialled 121.

There was some background noise and then a woman's voice said:

"Why did you bring me here in the grey Merc of yours. Is that a personalised number plate, FOS 69?"

The rest of a conversation followed.

That was the point at which Annie realised she had the drug bastards nailed.

Annie found a pair of latex gloves and put them on. She unlocked Liam's phone so that it could be accessed by anyone, wiped off her fingerprints and put the phone in an envelope. She wrote a note on the computer.

Dear Detectives,

I found this phone by the leisure centre in Dudley Road. There was a voice mail on it and I played it to try to identify the owner and give it back. It sounded like something you ought to listen to. It was a woman's voice and it gave a car number, FOS 69. She said it was a grey Mercedes Benz. There are some pictures on it. I think they are of that boy you were looking for last summer, something O'Connor was his name I think.

She printed out the message and put it in the envelope. She made an address label out to Sergeant Bronowski and stuck it on the front. She sealed the envelope and put it in her pocket.

Later that day, a girl in a mask that covered almost all her face, wearing large dark glasses, walked past the police station. She had long blonde hair.

Twenty minutes later, Bronowski opened the envelope that some unknown person had dropped off at the duty desk.

Fifteen minutes later, the identity of Moira MacDonald's killer was known.

Bronowski and Gregory pulled the thread that unravelled the whole network. Frederick Oliver Seeley, whose wife, Mary Seely, owned a grey Mercedes Benz, registration FOS69, was brought into the station for questioning. The two detectives played him the recording from Liam's iPhone and Freddie crumbled. He demanded that his own solicitor be present and there was a pause while they waited for the lawyer to arrive.

Suddenly, all the police activity that had been slowly accumulating evidence began to fall into place. The CCTV work-ups, the surveillance of the takeaway shops, the disappearance of vehicles without trace, these all began to have a possible meaning and explanation.

The first element in the solution of all the unsolved mysteries was the arrest, on suspicion of murder, of Frederick Oliver Seeley, the husband of the woman who 'owned', for tax purposes, the grey Mercedes Benz with the personalised number plate. Many things fell out from that, especially later, when F. O. Seeley saw the game was up and began to sing like a canary.

A search of the car would yield plenty of forensic evidence that Moira had been in the car at some point in the past. But that was a little way in the future.

Paradoxically, the solution of all these crimes started with the discovery of Liam O'Connor's missing phone. The observation that Liam O'Connor had gone missing, at the same time as a car, with two unknown victims, had burned to a cinder in the quarry, intensified the search of CCTV footage on the night of the murder. The police now had a number plate to look for.

Frederick Seeley had purchased his wife's Mercedes and his own cars from George Todd's garage. George was a well-known local "rough diamond" who had built a big motorcar business, ranging from high-end luxury cars to second-hand wrecks and, ultimately, a car recycling business for the irreparably damaged vehicles. It was certainly worth looking at the CCTV around the Todd garages, and the detectives struck gold.

Looking back at all the key dates, they found that a battered Range Rover, with false number plates, had been in the vicinity of the main Todd complex, shortly before Bryan Muldoon was killed by a hit and run driver, It was just possible to make out two people in the car, although there was no detail in the images. The same car was on the same stretch of road, heading in the opposite direction, shortly after the death, and was never seen again.

On the night of the quarry incineration, a different battered Range Rover, also with false plates, was seen on that stretch of road, leaving at around 5pm and returning at about 8pm. It appeared to have two occupants when it left and when it returned. It left again a little while later and again returned nearly two hours later. There was a period of about an hour before, shortly before midnight, this car left again with two occupants. It returned a short while later with a single occupant and then left again, also with a single occupant, and never returned.

Again, acting on a hunch, Jerry and Steve got the CCTV guys to look at the main road between the two cities and it turned out that this vehicle had made the return journey between the two cities on both the occasions when it had returned. CCTV in the other city showed it heading towards the area of the terraced house from which Liam and Grace had disappeared. The footage did not cover Lavinia's house and the road next to it.

On the third occasion that the Range Rover had made the intercity journey, it had been followed, at a distance, by a grey Mercedes Benz, FOS 69. On this journey, both the cars had a single occupant, the driver. On the return journey, FOS 69 had two occupants.

This was enough to demand the CCTV footage from the Todd premises, but, hardly to anyone's surprise, the tapes from the relevant nights were missing.

There was one other interesting thing about the journey of the Range Rover on the night of the disappearance. On the third occasion it had left the vicinity of the Todd garages it had gone to the home of Jason Miller, and Mr Miller, in a set of Todd works overalls and safety gear, had gone into his house. A few minutes later he had come out and thrown the working gear into the back of the Range Rover and gone in again. The Range Rover had then driven off and shortly after was seen in the vicinity of the garage again.

This was more than enough for the team to require a word with George Todd and to obtain a warrant to search his premises. In the offices of his warehouse they found a remarkable collection of scalpels and surgical cutting instruments. Inside the bag a 'luminal' test was positive. The blood was later shown to have been that of Grace Jones. George had missed a splash of blood, from her slashed throat and forgotten that his bag was open at the time. It proved to be a crucial error on his part.

George and Freddie were nailed, but the visit to the Miller household turned the spotlight on Jason Miller himself. His solicitor was F. O. Seeley, his cars were purchased from George Todd. It was time to bring in some of the people that the surveillance on "Miller's Meals" had flagged up as possible cogs in the wheels of the drug distribution system.

Once the word got around that two of the big boys had been arrested and a third was under investigation the dawn chorus turned into a whole day sing song. The number of people who provided evidence in return for a degree of clemency was in high double figures. Miller was totally implicated. Not mentally the strongest of the four, he started to confess. He confessed to heading up the prostitution side of the business too and he explained one of the ways in which he obtained suggestions for vulnerable girls he might target.

The two detectives wondered about the identity of the unknown blonde who had delivered the phone to the police station. They went to see Annie and the O'Connor family and were satisfied that these girls, all dark haired, and in the case of the O'Connors, very dark skinned, had nothing to do with it. They accepted that the phone was a random find and they kicked themselves for not having searched the area around the leisure centre properly at the time of the earlier investigation.

Annie breathed a sigh of relief when the detectives left her.

The O'Connors were very distressed by the confirmation of their brother's death and Tara O'Connor asked if she could arrange a funeral for the burial of the charred remains of Liam's body. The funeral duly took place in the week leading up to Christmas and Annie and her extended family were among the mourners. It marked closure for Annie; sad but now ready to move on.

The Academy Trust Board held a "wrap up meeting" on the Friday after Annie came home and they asked her to join them, by Zoom, to talk about her experiences at Cambridge and to join a discussion about how the trust might modify their sixth-form provision to encourage more students, like Annie herself, to apply to top universities.

DI Gregory was to give an update on the gang crime and drug scene in the area.

Bruno, Francis Calder-Warren, had been out of the area for a few days on business but he was now at his home and he joined the meeting from there.

Afterwards, everyone said it was the most interesting and exciting, but also embarrassing, meeting they had been to.

Sir George Grover asked DI Gregory to speak to the meeting.

DI Gregory began:

"I want to update you on where we have gotten to with the drug and prostitution rackets in this City. I want to report to you today that we are on the verge of destroying the principal syndicate running both these enterprises. We have three of the principal protagonists in custody and are about to arrest the fourth. I cannot give you his name at this moment, but you will find it in The Herald tomorrow evening.

"Our officers are on the way to arrest him now, as I speak. I am afraid you will be unhappy when you discover who it is, but I want to assure you that there is nothing any of us could have done to get to the point of arresting him until a very brave informer managed to find a way to tip us off about a murder and the whole tissue of lies came falling down."

It may have been a Zoom meeting, but Annie could almost feel DI Gregory's eyes boring into her. She showed not a flicker of emotion. It was guesswork on his part, she was sure of that, and he would never find out from her that she had played any part in the downfall of the gang of four.

But the truth was, DI Gregory was thinking about Moira MacDonald and her quick-witted bravery, knowing she was going to die, in making that voice-mail call.

At that moment, there was the noise of a police siren in the background and it went silent when Francis Calder-Warren turned off his audio, gave a wry grin at the camera and left the meeting.

Epilogue

It would be several months later, at the Crown Court, when the entire gang of four received sentences, totalling 80 years, for a multitude of crimes relating to murder, prostitution and drug dealing. Mr and Mrs MacDonald, Moira's Mum and Dad, would stand there, holding little Millie, proud in the knowledge that their beautiful daughter had been the agency whereby this evil gang had been brought to justice.

On Christmas Eve, Annie was working in the Stops' Shop, a special shift to help Roger Stops. Two men walked into the shop, masked and wearing big heavy raincoats.

"Annie!" said DI Gregory.

"Inspector!" said Annie.

"Annie?" said the other man.

"Jim?" said Annie. "What are you doing for Christmas?"

Six months later, the vaccination programme was in full swing. Annie had not been allowed to go back to Cambridge when the Lent Term, the term that precedes Easter, began, and all her teaching was online.

Jim and Annie had spent Christmas Day together, since Boris Johnson had declared Christmas Day a day when there could be some cross-bubble mixing. Because Jim was doing a Theoretical Physics PhD, he did not go back to Cambridge either and so he and Annie were able to see a lot of each other. In fact, they moved in together, on a temporary basis, into the Carter home, as house-sitters.

Little else of note happened. There was a very quiet period on the drugs front, it lasted about four months and then the trade started to pick up again. Jerry Gregory and Steve Bronowski sat there again, talking about chopping the head off the monster, only for it to grow again.

C000004269

Collaborative Leadership in Financial Services

Collaborative Leadership in Financial Services

PHILIP ULLAH

GOWER

© Philip Ullah 2011

All rights reserved. No part of this publication may be reproduced, stored in a retrieval system or transmitted in any form or by any means, electronic, mechanical, photocopying, recording or otherwise without the prior permission of the publisher.

Philip Ullah has asserted his moral right under the Copyright, Designs and Patents Act, 1988, to be identified as the author of this work.

Published by
Gower Publishing Limited
Wey Court East
Union Road
Farnham
Surrey, GU9 7PT
England

Gower Publishing Company
Suite 420
101 Cherry Street
Burlington,
VT 05401-4405
USA

www.gowerpublishing.com

British Library Cataloguing in Publication Data
Ullah, Philip.
    Collaborative leadership in financial services.
    1. Financial services industry — Management. 2. Teams in the workplace. 3. Leadership.
    I. Title
    332.1′0684 — dc22

Library of Congress Cataloging-in-Publication Data
Ullah, Philip.
    Collaborative leadership in financial services / Philip Ullah.
       p. cm.
    Includes bibliographical references and index.
    ISBN 978-0-566-08988-6 (hbk. : alk. paper) – ISBN 978-1-4094-3609-6 (ebook)
    1. Financial services industry – Management. 2. Leadership. 3. Organizational effectiveness.
I. Title.

    HG173.U45 2011
    332.1068′4–dc22

                                  2011017153

ISBN 9780566089886 (hbk)
ISBN 9781409441755 (pbk)
ISBN 9781409436096 (ebk)

MIX
Paper from
responsible sources
FSC
www.fsc.org   FSC® C018575

Printed and bound in Great Britain by the
MPG Books Group, UK

Contents

List of Figures

List of Tables

About the Author

Philip Ullah holds a PhD in Psychology, and was Senior Lecturer in Organisational Psychology at the University of Western Australia from 1987 to 1992. Since then he has worked for a number of management consultancies based in the UK, and is currently Managing Consultant at Catalyst Development.

Philip has published widely in a number of psychological and management journals, and is co-author (with Mike Robson) of *A Practical Guide to Business Process Re-engineering*, and co-author (with Michael Banks) of *Youth Unemployment in the 1980s*. He has also edited (with David Fryer) *Unemployed People: Social and Psychological Perspectives*.

Preface

The inspiration for this book came on a beach in Antigua, on a short break from delivering leadership development programmes for Catalyst Development, a specialist consultancy in the financial services sector. For about a year I had been drawn to the growing research and management literature on 'collaboration'. Leading thinkers were aligned in their view that building collaboration across an organization was critical to its success. This in itself is not remarkable. They would hardly argue for the reverse. What was different was the recognition that trends across many diverse industries were rendering this more and more difficult to achieve. Globalization, advances in technology, and increases in scale and complexity meant that getting all parties in a supply chain to work together seamlessly was extraordinarily difficult. At the same time it was becoming obvious that this goal was critical to success, and could be a market differentiator.

This was particularly true in Catalyst's client base: the investment banks and hedge funds within what are called the capital markets. For the technologists charged with bringing leading edge technologies to the desks of the traders they support in the Front Office, and for the operations specialists in the Middle Office, it was vital that all parties collaborated in the pursuit of common goals.

Catalyst's leadership and management development programmes bring me in direct contact with people facing these challenges on a daily basis. As an organizational psychologist I am familiar with a significant range of tools and techniques from the leadership research literature that can help people meet these challenges. Drawing on these to develop the skills and capabilities of senior managers is an integral part of our development programmes.

In the spring of 2008 on that warm beach it was becoming clear that massive upheaval was headed for the financial services. In this context it seemed to me that effective leadership was needed to steer a path through the turmoil.

At the same time I also questioned the leadership models that had strongly influenced how this was defined. The gung-ho approach of many charismatic leaders within the industry seemed to be contributing to the problem rather than helping steer a course to avoid it.

A new style of leadership seemed appropriate, and I was intrigued by the possibility of combining this with the collaboration skills that were proving essential within the industry. This book is the result of that combination. It takes the various tools and skills that help people develop collaborative behaviours in themselves and others, and combines (or 'mashes' to use the current vernacular) these with a leadership perspective. The outcome is a guide to help people develop a style of leading that I believe is better suited to the climate that now exists within the financial services.

This book is intended as a practical guide to help people in leadership roles develop a collaborative style and approach, and to inculcate it in the people they lead. I hope you find it useful.

Acknowledgements

Over the years of working at Catalyst I have been lucky to have as colleagues people with exceptional skills and industry knowledge. I have learnt a tremendous amount from these people, and much of that is reflected in the pages that follow. I would like to say thank you to them all.

Two colleagues in particular warrant special mention. Chris Cooke and Chris FitzHenry have been my closest friends and colleagues and I never cease to be impressed by the skill and commitment they bring to the task of helping others develop their own skills and confidence. Many of the techniques and approaches I expand upon in this book are directly drawn from the work and experience of Chris and Chris, and I humbly acknowledge their contribution to the contents of this book. I also wish to thank them for making my job so enjoyable.

My biggest thanks and appreciation go to my family: Anne, James, Philippa, Richard and Jane, and to the next generation beginning with Mia, Joe and Phoebe. Anne in particular has provided support and encouragement throughout the time I have worked on this book, especially during our holidays. I want to thank her for this and for all the happiness she has given to me.

Introduction

The crisis in the financial services that emerged towards the end of 2008 has produced change and uncertainty on a scale the sector has rarely witnessed. After ten years of increasing growth and optimism, banks are virtually having to build their businesses from scratch, this time under the influence of governments and the intense scrutiny of the regulators.

If ever there was a time for clear and effective leadership within these organizations, it is during this period. One would imagine this might involve strong and charismatic individuals who can take the reins and forge a way ahead through unchartered territories. With the future so uncertain, those leaders who can provide a clear and compelling vision that aligns and motivates others to follow seem to be the answer.

This is very much the model of leadership that has prevailed during the early part of this century. But is it the right one going forward?

In one of the most influential articles on the subject, leadership guru John Kotter argued that a leader's role is to do three things: set direction (by developing a vision of the future), align others behind it and inspire them to achieve it ('What leaders really do', *Harvard Business Review*, 2001). While useful as a way of distinguishing leaders from managers (the main thrust of Kotter's article) this list of tasks promotes the view that leaders very definitely lead from the front in a highly individual and often charismatic way. It is the role of others to follow.

Yet this 'heroic' model of leadership sits uneasily with the demands of modern organizational life (Alimo-Metcalfe and Alban-Metcalfe, 2008). One might even argue that the individualism implicit in this approach lies behind many of the problems experienced by the world's leading financial institutions following the 2008 crash. The 'star trader' model of success is likely to have permeated many aspects of a bank's culture, defining what is appropriate behaviour in other departments and functions. One might surmise that this kind of individualism has led to a weakening of the controls that now seems to have lain behind some of the worst excesses witnessed in the industry.

However, there are other, more concrete reasons to doubt the efficacy of this approach to leadership in the current economic crisis. Over the last ten years I and my colleagues at Catalyst Development have run leadership programmes for some of the world's leading investment banks and financial institutions. Our work has been conducted largely within the technology and operations functions, away from the dealing floors and trading desks. The interconnected nature of banking functions and the importance of technology as a strategic weapon in the industry means they are as much at the heart of their company's performance as any single trader.

Through our knowledge of the industry, and through coaching many hundreds of senior technologists and Middle Office business heads, we have observed the increasing importance of collaboration to a bank's performance. Given this, people in leadership (and management) roles have to be able to collaborate effectively with others if they are to maintain an advantage in a highly competitive market.

This book outlines the tools, skills and techniques that many of the people attending these programmes have found helpful in developing their ability to lead collaboratively. The techniques are described in a simple and practical way that will hopefully help you put them into use. They will be brought to life with stories from people who have attended these programmes, showing how they have used them to deal with some of the leadership challenges they face in their jobs. Interviews with other senior figures within these firms also give an insight into their understanding of collaboration and why it is so important in today's global financial institutions.

The Need for Greater Collaboration

The huge changes seen in the way investment banks operate over the last 10–15 years have highlighted the need for greater collaboration. These changes include:

- Globalization.
  Investment banks operate on a global scale and their Middle and Back Office functions reflect that. Virtual teams contain people based in different continents, who have to overcome the barriers of different time zones, cultures and languages to operate as one smoothly functioning team. The need to drive down costs has led to many processing functions being outsourced to third-party vendors, again in different continents. The increased need for compliance to government regulations following the introduction of the Sarbanes-Oxley Act has added an additional dimension to this mix. The result has been a phenomenal increase in the complexity of end-to-end business processes. It is vital that all these different parties collaborate across the whole value chain if these complex processes are to operate smoothly and clients are to receive an integrated service.

- The emerging importance of technology.
  The latter part of the twentieth century saw an exponential increase in the volume of trades processed. Volume, the speed of transaction and the level of automation with which both are achieved have become key differentiators in the quest for competitive advantage. The emergence of electronic trading in the late 1990s also meant that much of this technology had to be capable of operating from client desktops. Innovation in technology, and the speed at which it can be built and deployed, means that technology departments have moved from being a relatively lowly support function to being strategic partners with the businesses they serve. Both parties need to collaborate to ensure technology investments return real business value.

- Project and programme management.
  Middle and Back Office operations can be differentiated into those that keep things running smoothly (often referred to as 'run the bank' or RTB) and those that bring about a change designed to do this more effectively and efficiently ('change the bank', or CTB). Recent years have seen a growth in the latter activities, since this can be a key source of competitive advantage. Technology projects to build and deploy new applications can individually run up costs of tens of millions of dollars. Some initiatives comprise of multiple projects and are managed as major change programmes involving

many hundreds of people. Once again these can involve multiple parties and vendors on different continents who need to collaborate effectively if projects are to deliver on time and on budget.

- Increased competition.
  The fierce competition that now exists between what is known as the 'Tier One' banks has resulted in an ongoing race on three fronts: lower costs, better technology and smarter people. Yet a lead on any one of these tends to be short lived. Costs can only be driven down so far before there is a detrimental impact on performance and client service. Advances in technology are quickly picked up by competitors, leading to a leapfrog pattern similar to that observed across mobile phone companies. Hiring the most talented individuals is effective only until those individuals decide to take their services elsewhere. Amid this constant battle to do things better, quicker and cheaper, increasing the degree of collaboration across people and departments is proving to be an effective way of improving performance without increasing resources.

These changes have raised the importance of collaboration as a means of operating effectively in the ever-changing capital markets.

At Merrill Lynch during the early 2000s, for example, collaboration was seen as the key to maintaining the quality of their equity research while instigating a vicious cost-cutting programme and fending off the challenge of the rising number of hedge funds (Groysberg and Vargas, 2005). Merrill Lynch initiated several projects to create a more collaborative culture that was less hierarchical and more inclusive. While recognizing the greater efforts, increased time and significant risks involved in working collaboratively on research, most senior executives in the bank spoke positively of the benefits.

D'Silva and Nalbantoglu (2007) describe how the investment banking industry as a whole needs to work more collaboratively if it is to meet clients' growing demand for integrated services. When clients have several lines of business with a single bank, they expect each person they deal with to have a single and common view of the relationship. Banks find this is increasingly difficult given the specialist nature of each of their product lines. The authors argue that collaboration between silos, rather than knocking the silos down, is the only way to achieve an integrated service.

More generally, collaboration is recognized as increasingly important to the goals of many different kinds of commercial and non-profit making organization. In their book *Wikinomics*, Tapscott and Williams (2008) examine the role of the internet (and in particular Web 2.0) in creating mass collaboration opportunities. They describe the process of 'peer production' as one where 'masses of people and firms collaborate openly to drive innovation and growth in their industries' (p.11). Everyday examples include MySpace, flickr, YouTube, Linux and Wikipedia. The authors also show how more established firms in 'traditional' industries have tapped into the power of collaboration to speed up the innovation process, solve complex problems and create value.

Elsewhere there seems to be a growing recognition that collaboration is a key to survival in increasingly competitive environments. Rosabeth Moss Kanter, from the Harvard Business School, studied over 20 organizations undergoing a complete turnaround of their business. She found that increasing the degree of cross-unit collaboration was one of four critical factors in gaining the commitment and engagement of their staff (Kantor, 2003).

Warren Bennis, one of the top leadership thinkers of our time, said that 'today's information driven organizations need to be more collaborative and less hierarchical to be at their most effective'. In the Harvard Business Review of 2005, Jeff Weiss and Jonathon Hughes wrote, 'Getting collaboration right promises tremendous benefits: a unified face to customers, faster internal decision making, reduced costs through shared resource, and the development of more innovative products' (Weiss and Hughes, 2005). Towards the end of 2008, the same journal asked several noted thinkers, 'What best practice challenges the conventional wisdom about what to do in a downturn?' Tamara Erikson, a leading specialist on organization theory, responded, 'Don't cut out meetings, intensify internal competition, or reduce investments in learning. Increase your firm's collaborative capacity by building relationships and encouraging the exchange of knowledge' (Erikson, 2008).

Collaboration is seen as key to innovation (Amabile and Khaire, 2008), smoothly functioning supply chains (Thompson, Eisenstein and Stratman, 2007), major cultural change (Heifetz and Laurie, 2001), flawless execution (Edmondson, 2008) and lean production techniques (Evans and Wolf, 2005).

The Benefits of Collaboration

These, and many other studies like them, point to the increasing importance of collaboration for today's financial institutions undergoing the biggest disruption ever experienced in the industry. But what are the benefits to the individual? Why should *you* become a collaborative leader?

First, and perhaps foremost, an organization will find it extraordinarily difficult to promote collaborative working if its leaders don't practice this themselves. To obtain the organizational benefits of innovation, speed, staff engagement and so on, individuals in positions of power need to be role models for collaborative working.

Secondly, the technical skills that may have helped a person climb the organizational ladder become less relevant the higher he or she goes. In their place, management and relationship skills become more important as a way of getting things done through others. Being able to collaborate with key stakeholders across different organizational silos becomes an imperative for people holding senior positions.

Thirdly, collaborative leaders seem to be better able to generate what Lynda Gratton of the London Business School calls 'hot spots' – people and teams that burst with energy, creativity and commitment. Collaborative leaders create happy, committed employees prepared to go the 'extra mile'.

Fourthly, people become better team players if they are able to collaborate effectively. Leaders are part of a team of peers and top teams need to work together collaboratively if they are to be effective. Yves Doz and Mikko Kosonen, reporting in the 2007 Harvard Business Review, found that those companies that were best able to adapt their strategy quickly to market changes were led by top teams where the key players collaborated with each other rather than operate as 'semi-autonomous feudal barons' (Doz and Kosonen, 2007).

About this Book

The rest of this book focuses on how to become a collaborative leader. Of course, a book can only convey part of the story, since we are talking about the development of quite complex skills. Ideally, this book will serve as an accompaniment to a more comprehensive development programme that involves practice and feedback. But there are many things that can be learned from adopting the guidelines drawn from the powerful tools and techniques that will be outlined here. We will also hear the stories of those who have put these techniques into practice, since these real life applications can bring to life models that are grounded in academic and management theory.

My aim has been to produce a book that can be used as a source guide rather than read like a novel. Following Chapter 1, which outlines what is meant by 'collaborative leadership', each subsequent chapter covers different tools and techniques, and can be read without having to read the previous or following chapters.

I have also been liberal with the term 'leader'. This is not a book only for CIOs or COOs. In my experience of training hundreds of people within the investment banking and capital markets industry, better leadership can and should be an important goal of anyone responsible for the performance of others.

However, instead of adopting the traditional command and control model of leadership, or the 'leader as hero' model that has dominated in the last decade or so, I believe that people aspiring to develop their leadership capabilities will benefit from the model of collaborative leadership outlined here.

Collaborative Leadership: A Model for the Twenty-First Century

1

I think that collaborative organizations which foster collaboration are likely to be more successful than those who don't. It's also quite difficult to achieve.

Peter Clarke, CEO, Man

Collaboration, properly used, is really the right tool for creating complex change. I daresay we can think of some simple occasions where it's not necessary but those are typically small scale problems.

Stephen Norman, CIO, Global Banking & Markets, The Royal Bank of Scotland

In 1990 the BBC produced a documentary in its *Horizon* series. Titled *The Wrong Stuff*, it was based on an analysis of human error in the cockpit of commercial aircraft. The programme pointed out that until fairly recently, American airlines had largely recruited their pilots from the US Air Force. The programme's main hypothesis was that the individual characteristics that had made pilots most suitable for a single seat fighter aircraft – a rugged individualism known as 'the right stuff' – were the least suitable in the cockpit of a commercial aircraft where good teamwork among the crew of pilot, co-pilot and navigator, was more important. The right stuff was, in fact, the wrong stuff.

This idea has gained more currency recently with the publication of Malcolm Gladwell's book *Outliers*. In this he describes a similar problem within some Asian airlines, where the unquestioning obedience of the crew to the pilot has resulted in a number of catastrophic accidents (Gladwell, 2008).

Despite this, we love a hero. Chesley Sullenberger III attracted celebrity-like status when he skillfully landed a stricken US Airways A320 on the Hudson River in January 2009. He provides the model for what we have traditionally expected our leaders to be: individuals who will single-handedly save the day.

This chapter outlines a model of leadership that is radically different from this 'heroic' model of leadership. I and my colleagues at Catalyst have developed this model based on many years of designing and running leadership development programmes in the investment banking and capital markets sector of the financial services. *Collaborative* leadership is based on the notion that talented and influential people create value when they connect with each other across organizational silos and create synergies. This requires a style of leadership based on achieving win–win outcomes rather than the traditional leadership qualities of charisma, vision and a determination to set the direction for others to follow.

There is an old adage that states that if I give you $10 and you give me $10, then we both walk away with $10. But if I give you an idea, and you give me an idea, then we both walk away with two ideas.

This captures one of the benefits of collaboration – it results in a net gain. In terms of the exchange of ideas, it may be that you take my idea and develop it to new heights. Or maybe my idea is not fully formed, but through collaborating you help round it out, filling in the gaps.

Collaboration also works beyond the realm of ideas. It allows people to complement their skills, multiply efforts and save important resources like time. In a world where customer requirements are driving increasing amounts of specialization and complexity, organizations have only recently come to see the need for collaboration. Getting people to work effectively across silos, rather than tearing down those silos, is becoming a key differentiator.

First, let's be clear what the traditional approach entails and why it is not suited to today's troubled environment within the financial services. Until very recently, leadership models could be categorized into what are termed 'transactional' models and 'transformational' models.

The former refer to styles of leading others that, at a basic level, involve some sort of give and take. The leader makes rewards (or punishments) contingent on the behaviour of his or her followers. This approach is best characterized by the management-by-objectives (MBO) approach that found popularity in the 1970s and 1980s. It is also at the heart of many other leadership theories, such as contingency theory, path–goal theory and leader–member exchange theory (see Northouse, 2007 for an excellent review of these).

During the 1980s, James MacGregor Burns and Bernard Bass developed an alternative: transformational leadership. This focused on the charismatic qualities of leaders who, by the strength of their character, vision and communication skills, were able to transform ailing organizations. These leaders appealed to values and emotions when influencing their followers. People like Ghandi, Martin Luther King and Nelson Mandela were held up as prime examples of transformational leaders. The massive changes experienced in many industries at the time, and the exponential increase in mergers and acquisitions, prompted many organizations to adopt this model of leadership.

There is a lot to like about this approach to leadership. In particular, it emphasizes the need for leaders to make a strong emotional connection with their followers, through inspiring them with a compelling vision of the future, encouraging innovation and creativity, and showing concern for the needs of followers.

More recently, however, transformational leadership has been questioned by some commentators. Beverley Alimo-Metcalfe and John Alban-Metcalf published an excellent review in 2008 for the Chartered Institute of Personnel and Development. They quoted scholars who see transformational leadership as engendering a kind of 'toxic leadership', where people use their authority for personal gain (Lipman-Blumen, 2004). Henry Mintzberg, in an article titled 'Managing Quietly' (1999), likened the emphasis on the leader who single-handedly turns around a company as a reflection of the current obsession with celebrity. In a later article in the *Financial Times*, he wrote of the dangers of 'managers who sit on "top," pronouncing their great visions, grand strategies, and abstract performance standards while everyone else is supposed to scurry around "implementing"'.

Given these concerns, and the huge changes seen in the financial services recently, the transactional and transformational approaches to effective leadership appear somewhat wanting. At a time when the public standing of bankers and traders is at an all-time low, there is a real need for a style of leadership that does not entail excessive risk taking and testosterone-fuelled decisions driven by the need for quick wins.

Before going on to outline the model of collaborative leadership, it is worth stating what is not meant by this term. It is not a form of consensual decision making, similar to that found in some European banks. There is no assumption that decisions need to be watered down to the lowest common denominator in a lengthy process of reaching a compromise that is acceptable to all parties. Neither does it imply the absence of a vision that can inspire people to change or drive an organization in a new direction. The broadening of the perspective from the person at the top to a more diffused cross-section of people does not mean that 'everyone can be a leader'.

The definition of collaboration to be used here is drawn from studies of conflict behaviour and in particular the Thomas–Kilmann model of conflict resolution (see Figure 1.1). In this model the authors define collaboration as the combination of both assertive and cooperative behaviours. In other words, collaboration occurs when individuals are motivated to seek the best outcome for themselves while still satisfying the needs of others. This is different from compromise behaviour, where both parties give some ground, and is more akin to seeking a genuine win–win outcome.

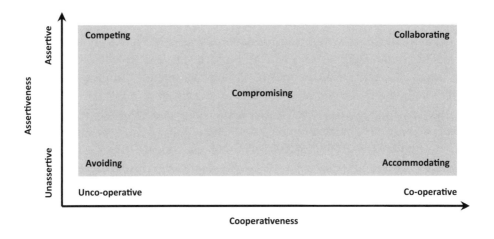

Figure 1.1   The Thomas–Kilmann conflict model

Source: Kilmann, R.H. and Thomas, K.W. (1975) Interpersonal conflict-handling behavior as reflections of Jungian personality dimensions, *Psychological Reports*, 37, pp. 315–318.

Given this use of the term, collaboration entails an active and often difficult process of working with other stakeholders to achieve a common and shared outcome. When leaders collaborate, they do not give up their right to make decisions. Instead they work with others to gain buy-in and commitment to their decisions. The same is true for the process of developing a vision. This is not a lone activity, but a process of working with key stakeholders to define and communicate a shared vision.

Peter Clarke, the CEO of Man, one of the world's largest hedge funds, described to me how he achieved this when restructuring the company following the financial crisis of late 2008:

> In the past we have said, 'this is what we're going to do,' but then you get the ultimate silo effect with everyone ignoring it. People need to understand why it is a good idea and, when the world is in a state of tremendous turmoil, especially the financial world, then it's much easier to get things done in an environment where people can see change is necessary.

The restructuring of Man involved combining three separate investment managers into one, a process fraught with difficulties and the potential to encounter resistance and opposition. Peter Clarke's approach involved a combination of setting out his future vision while working closely with key individuals to get them on side:

> It was a function of convincing people of the logic, which they accepted, and then working on a proposition which they could sell from a personal position within the firm. I don't think that's an ultimate version of collaboration, because at no point was a vote taken, because if a vote had been taken, it would have been not to proceed.

A feature of the Thomas–Kilmann model is that it does not promote any single approach to handling conflict. Different styles will be appropriate in different situations. Similarly, there will be many occasions when people in leadership positions will need to take a stance on an issue (compete) or choose not to fight some battles (accommodate). Just as transformational leadership was not intended to rule out any recourse to transactional approaches, collaborative leadership is not being promoted here as the *only* way of leading effectively.

However, there is growing evidence today that transformational approaches fail to produce the level of engagement and motivation that a more collaborative approach can achieve.

Collaborative Leadership: A New Approach

The new style of leadership required to meet the challenges of financial markets differs from the traditional, directive style of leadership in a number of key ways:

Table 1.1 **The difference between collaborative and directive leadership**

	Collaborative Leadership	Directive Leadership
Vision	Build and share a vision	Set and sell a vision
Influence	Facilitate	Motivate
Domain	Informal networks	Organizational silos
Focus	Ideas and knowledge	Business transformation

VISION

Much has been written about the role of vision in the leader's armoury. By setting a vision of a compelling future state and then aligning others behind it, a leader can tap into their commitment and passion. Followers then know how their efforts contribute to the bigger picture and can see a purpose behind senior management decisions. They can psychologically buy in to the firm rather than just provide their labour. The task of setting and selling a vision is the essence of directive leadership.

Both collaborative and directive styles of leading involve appeals to a vision. However, directive leadership emphasizes the role of the leader and involves setting a vision that reflects his or her dream of the future or solution to current problems. The directive leader's role is to convince others that the vision, and the change of direction it often implies, is the answer. In contrast, collaborative leaders work with others to build that vision, and collectively they share it with others in the organization, adapting it if need be.

Scott Marcar is one of the rising stars of the technology function within The Royal Bank of Scotland's investment banking division, Global Banking & Markets. Scott has been successful in turning round weaker parts of the function. He does this by bringing together the managers and key influencers within a function and getting them to contribute to the change agenda:

> *What we've done is try to be more collaborative than people at lower levels. We gathered forty people into a room to collectively drive the agenda for our function. That was empowering, and made people feel they were having a real say in the strategy. People came away from that thinking 'this is great, we've had a say'. Our objectives as a team this year are very much driven from what came out of that day.*

Scott Marcar's collaborative approach has built a genuine sense of involvement and commitment, though it has not always been easy. His role has been to define the broad agenda, leaving the details 'wooly' so that his team can add these. This requires trust on his part and a genuine commitment to collaboration.

This approach can also be practiced on a smaller scale, by people who hold less senior positions but who can still benefit from the input of their direct reports. A technologist from one of our leadership programmes told me:

> *Collaboration is about working together towards a common goal where you're interested in getting the right outcome, not your personal agenda or your ego or whatever. That, to me, is what defines collaboration, and I think in my role I need to be collaborative with my direct reports, not just my peers, because I need their view on things rather than it be just my view.*

INFLUENCE

Directive leaders influence through the position they hold. They motivate their direct reports through a combination of transactional and transformational styles. The former involves making rewards contingent on performance. The latter involves tapping into internal reservoirs of commitment and effort through appeals to vision and values.

However, in today's matrix organization, lines of authority are not so clearly cut. Influence cannot always flow from position. Collaborative leaders rely on their ability to influence through facilitating the efforts of others. This requires a quite different skill set: an ability to listen, to coach, to find points of agreement, and to ensure ownership of ideas and actions is shared among those involved. The collaborative leader's values are similar to the core values of facilitation, as outlined by Schwarz (1994), of providing valid information to others and allowing them to make a free and informed choice about how they will respond to it.

DOMAIN

Directive leaders operate in the domain of a function or line of business. Their role is to optimize the performance of their domain and ensure it is aligned to others in the value chain. They do this through driving efficiency gains and, where necessary, negotiating with others in the value chain.

Collaborative leaders are more diffused throughout an organization and operate within informal networks that span these organizational silos. These networks are often transient, reflecting specific projects or programmes. Collaborative leaders spend more of their time building relationships within these informal networks. When unencumbered by the ties of rank or seniority that make this kind of networking difficult, collaborative leaders are able to operate beneath the organizational radar. Here they can develop ideas, solve problems, gather information and build alliances without attracting too much unhelpful attention.

FOCUS

Influential works on leadership during the 1990s and early 2000s highlighted business transformation as the rightful focus for leaders. This involved realigning an organization in a different direction, turning everything round to support the new vision. Yet during that time, and even more so today, financial institutions, especially their technology and operations arms, have been more focused on driving down costs and improving efficiency through the adoption of techniques such as six sigma, lean production and agile development.

The reality for many people in leadership roles has been more to do with promoting these methods than developing grand visions. And in doing this, they have focused on promoting formal and informal connections between people to solve problems. The main 'deliverables' from these networks are ideas and value-creating propositions, rather than alignment behind a vision.

At their heart lies collaboration and people in leadership roles promote this through demonstrating this behaviour themselves.

The contrast between collaborative leadership and the traditional directive styles of leadership serves the purpose of clarifying what is meant by the former. With this in mind, the central message of this book is that collaborative leadership is better suited to the conditions faced within many financial institutions as they adapt to new ways of doing business. In practice, however, people in leadership roles will often have to move between these two poles. A general rule of thumb is that the more choices you have at your disposal, the more effective and influential you can be.

A Hierarchy of Change

What, then, is required if a person is to adopt a more collaborative style of leadership? An effective way of answering this question is to start with a framework originally developed by Robert Dilts, one of the foremost practitioners of neuro-linguistic programming. According to Dilts, we can think of personal change as something that can take place at several different levels (see Figure 1.2).

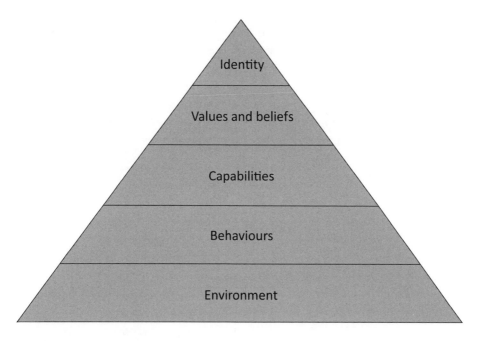

Figure 1.2   A hierarchy of personal change

This idea is useful because it gives us a framework for defining what exactly is involved in leading collaboratively. Thus, at the most basic level, we can define the environmental conditions in which collaboration takes place (for example, across silos, within teams and so on). Moving up the scale, we can describe the behaviours that constitute effective collaboration and outline the skills that ensure these behaviours are effectively deployed. At the level above this, we can identify the values and beliefs that characterize collaborative leaders. Finally, at the level of identity, we can explore how these leaders see themselves and their role and show how this differs from those who lead in more traditional ways.

In the chapters that follow, this framework will be loosely used to help organize the material. For the reader planning on adopting a more collaborative style of leading, it can help focus efforts where they will have most effect or help identify the obstacles that need to be overcome.

I start with the skills that lie behind collaborative leadership. What does a person need to be good at to lead collaboratively? This is followed with some of the tools and techniques that can really help unlock difficult situations, allowing a genuinely collaborative approach. In this sense, the focus is on some of the behaviours that will help you become a collaborative leader. Finally, I consider the cognitive processes that lie behind collaborative leadership and in particular how collaborative leaders think of themselves and their role. This is discussed under the heading of 'leadership brand'.

Throughout what follows, the various approaches are illustrated with stories and quotes from people who have put these techniques into practice. This is important because it emphasizes that to become an effective collaborative leader you have to apply the techniques. It is not enough just to absorb the material and store it for potential future use. The people quoted here have put their knowledge into practice and I hope you will learn much from their accounts.

2

Building Relationships

Collaboration is like a relationship. You have to think about it, work at it, and make it real.

Hedge Fund Manager, Man

Over the last ten years or so, banking operations have become increasingly more complex. At the same time technology and operations have experienced relentless pressure to cut their operational costs. These two forces have led to greater specialization and the fragmentation of business processes. In particular, end-to-end processes now span continents and multiple external vendors. Many of the larger banks have also executed aggressive growth plans through acquisition, resulting in even more complex organizational charts. To operate effectively and efficiently, relationships between all these different parties need to be strong and healthy. The ability to build and maintain relationships has become a critical skill for people in leadership roles or for those aspiring to such a role. From the point of view of leading collaboratively, the ability to develop a network of relationships is an essential skill.

You can do a quick assessment of your ability to build and maintain relationships. First, consider your network of contacts. Who are the people you turn to for information, ideas and help with problems? Is this is a relatively closed and narrow network, consisting mainly of people within your function or department? Without doubting the quality of these relationships, it's relatively easy to build good relationships with people you work with every day. A narrow network may mean you need to develop your relationship-building skills.

A second test involves considering the nature of the relationships you have with those in different parts of the value chain, especially third parties. Are these relationships largely transactional, with strong adherence to rules and procedures, and little in the way of trust or genuine partnership? What happens when things go wrong? Is there blame, recrimination and defensiveness?

If so, the quality of your relationships may not be high enough to enable you to collaborate effectively with such parties.

The benefit of this type of relationship was articulated to me by Scott Marcar from The Royal Bank of Scotland, who described how strong relationships allow him to confront and challenge others in pursuit of a genuinely collaborative solution:

> *My management style is quite direct, and you can't do that with people you don't know or who don't like you. If you've got a management style that is direct, but not dominant, I think you have to get on with the people you're managing with, and this often involves working on the social side of the relationship.*

Although he recognized he was a 'reasonably natural networker', he now sees it as a central part of his job and something that cannot be left to chance:

> *Actually managing a network is something I've done more of as I've risen through the ranks. I've managed the process much more.*

If 'building relationships' is something you are happy to practise only with your close colleagues, and 'arms-length' best characterizes your relationship with those outside your immediate circle, then this is something you need to work on to become a collaborative leader.

Collaborative leaders make an active effort to invest in building relationships with a wide variety of people. They see it as an important and necessary part of their job and they put time into it. For some it may come naturally, but for many it is a skill they have had to learn and work at. In general, moving up the organizational hierarchy involves spending more time networking and less time 'working', and while many people at lower levels recognize it is something they will have to do more of if they are to climb this ladder, in my experience few are comfortable with it.

Mention the word 'networking' to many technologists and they recoil in dread. This is especially so for people who are yet to rise to the heights of senior management. Technologists are often burdened with the 'geek' stereotype and the image of the lone techie working in a basement easily comes to mind. Such people, it is assumed, prefer the company of their computers to other people.

This chapter outlines some of the skills and techniques that can help. To become an effective networker does not mean becoming an extrovert, so no personality change is needed. Instead there are a few simple things than can help make a difference and can be used by almost anyone to improve the way they build relationships and extend their personal network.

Identifying your Limiting Beliefs

A simple exercise we run in our leadership development programmes at Catalyst involves asking the group of attendees to imagine a line running across the floor of the training room. At each end is a flipchart, one labelled with a '+', the other with a '-'. The line represents their ability and degree of comfort with networking and the two flipcharts indicate the poles of this dimension.

We then invite people to stand somewhere along this continuum according to their own approach to networking. Typically there is a normal distribution, with most of the group clustered somewhere around the centre and a few people close to either pole. Those in the negative half of the continuum are then asked to list on the flipchart all the reasons why they find networking uncomfortable. Those in the positive half list tips and advice to the 'negative' group.

First, let's look at a typical list that was generated at a recent programme, ahead of a networking evening to be attended by a number of senior executives. This list was drawn up by those standing in the negative half of the continuum.

- can't remember names and faces;

- engaging in small talk;

- being seen as boring;

- I'm shy/an introvert;

- awkward silences;

- finding a suitable topic of conversation;

- intimidated by senior people;

- can't be bothered/it seems pointless;

- I don't have anything to say to break the ice.

The most striking feature of this list is the negative opinion these people seem to have of themselves. They imagine the people they talk to will become quickly bored. That they themselves will run out of things to say and there will follow long embarrassing silences. Discussing these with the group reveals they remain convinced of these outcomes. In their view these are not negative imaginings, they are 'facts', based on numerous real-life experiences.

Psychologists call these 'limiting beliefs', for fairly obvious reasons. Armed with such beliefs, it is little wonder these people find the task of initiating a conversation difficult. Becoming more effective at this task involves in the first instance challenging these beliefs and replacing them with new beliefs and behaviours. This is a three-step process.

First, the person has to develop an alternative set of beliefs. Many beliefs exist at a subconscious level. They have become so internalized the holder initially has trouble articulating them. A consequence of this is the belief is rarely questioned. The very process of voicing the beliefs and writing them down starts the process of questioning their validity. In the stark light of day, some of the things listed on the flipcharts can look improbable to say the least. Will it really be the case that the other person looks upon you as boring, given that they have responded positively to your request for a meeting or your introduction? Will it be such a big problem if you forget their name or can you make light of it in a form of self-deprecating humour that will at the very least convey your humility and self-awareness?

Beliefs can be remarkably hard to dislodge though. One reason for this, outlined by David Rock in his book *Quiet Leadership* (2006), is that they become hard-wired in our brains. Like a stream that has eaten into the earth over thousands of years, some beliefs are deeply worn into our brains and the more we try to change them the more entrenched they become. The solution, says Rock, is to develop the equivalent of a new stream that will divert the flow of water. The aim should be to build new beliefs that over time become internalized at a subconscious level.

In our group exercise this is helped by the ideas and suggestions of those who are more positive in their approach to networking and building relationships. Take a look at the list these people generated, under the heading of 'Tips and Advice':

- be approachable;

- show interest;

- speak up! Don't mumble;

- ask the other person about non-work related subjects;

- be personable – have an open conversation;

- find common ground;

- show respect. Listen to what they say;

- bring others into the discussion;

- relax, be informal.

These suggestions do not require the rejection of some of the beliefs held by the negative group. In fact, one of the interesting things to emerge from an exercise like this is how similar the two groups are 'below the surface'. The 'positive' group often admit to being shy or introverted. They often report having felt the same way as the other group in the past. The difference is that they have invested time and energy to practising certain behaviours that seem to work and now have additional beliefs about their ability to strike up and hold a conversation.

This can be a revelation to the 'negative' group, who assume that the 'positive' group consists of gregarious extroverts. Once they understand their task is not to change their underlying personality, but to practise a few behaviours that others have found useful, they become much more open to the changes they need to make.

The second step involves putting into place a few behaviours that often work well. One is to use the time in a first meeting to find common ground. The goal is to find something you have in common with the other person in a five-minute conversation. It prompts lots of questions about non-work interests, children, education, holidays, places you have both lived and so on. Even if nothing is found, it will have been an active, two-way conversation.

Sometimes people say they have difficulty finding an interesting topic to talk about. The conversation goes through the usual topics of the weather, job role and small talk before drying up. My advice is that they should focus on the topic which the other person finds more interesting than anything else: themselves! Again, this prompts questions and, if not entirely interesting to the person doing the networking, at least the other person will come away with a positive impression of them.

Both of these techniques highlight an important skill when initiating a conversation at a networking event: focus on the other person not yourself. All too often, people fill their heads with negative thoughts about what will happen if they run out of conversation, or whether the other person is finding them boring, or whatever. They are so busy thinking about themselves and the impression they are conveying, they stop listening. Quite naturally, the conversation doesn't go well.

The third step is to hone the opening and closing remarks. Many people find the first few sentences upon striking up a conversation difficult. Even more so is drawing the conversation to a close. Typically, both parties end up looking around the room at other people seemingly enjoying themselves.

So, it makes sense to practise a few opening lines. Avoid anything 'cheesy'. This should just be a quick introduction, followed by a simple question, such as, 'I don't think we've met before, have we?' Then quickly move onto the goal of finding common ground.

Closing a conversation down at a networking event should be just as quick and seamless. Some people find this difficult because they think they are being rude when moving on to meet other people. I tell them it is what the other person expects at a networking event and conveys a smooth and professional approach. Again, a few well-rehearsed phrases come in handy. Once again the aim is to make it clean and simple: 'Well, it's been really nice talking with you. I'm going to mingle with a few other people here I don't really know yet.' A quick shake of the hand and move on.

Not all relationships are initiated at networking events of course and new relationships are often initiated in less contrived settings. However, building a network of relationships across organizational boundaries requires a proactive approach,and people are often held back from doing this by similar limiting beliefs and awkwardness when it comes to the first contact. By practising these few simple guidelines you can become much more adept and confident when it comes to establishing new relationships.

Energizers and De-energizers

In their book on the analysis of social networks within organizations, Rob Cross and Andrew Parker (2004) discovered a common theme among the people they interviewed. Many talked about finding some people in their organization remarkably easy to have a constructive conversation with, while others seemed the exact opposite. What was common was the way people felt after conversations with both types. Often they came away from conversations with the former feeling energized; interactions with the latter left them feeling de-energized.

Developing this theme into a research hypothesis, Cross and Parker decided to investigate how widespread the experiences were and what differentiated the two types of person. The results provide interesting reading for anyone wishing to extend their network of contacts and relationships.

First, they found that the experience was indeed a common one and that the terms 'energizer' and 'de-energizer' seemed to resonate with people's experiences of interacting with both types of people. Energizers left people feeling mobilized for action. They could bounce their ideas off them and see their thoughts develop and grow into something more tangible and well-formed. De-energizers, in contrast, left people feeling drained, as if all the energy and enthusiasm had been sucked out of them.

Secondly, they found that in addition to producing highly consistent reactions, there was also a high degree of similarity in the way they did this. Cross and Parker identified the following five characteristics that differentiated the two types of person.

Firstly, energizers have lots of optimism; they see the potential in an idea and look to how they can make it work. De-energizers, in contrast, see all the pitfalls. While a degree of realism and practicality can be a big help, there is something about the energizers that makes their optimism more useful.

In particular, they seem to have more faith in people and their ability to see an idea through to fruition. It is this confidence in the ability of others that makes the energizers popular figures.

When talking to energizers, people also feel they are really being listened to. They feel they have their full attention and get a strong sense that their ideas are valued by the energizer. Even if the energizer disagrees with the idea being proposed, they disagree with the idea rather than criticize the person voicing it. In contrast, de-energizers often seem to be preoccupied when approached by others and do not create the space in a conversation for the other person to feel heard.

Thirdly, energizers engage fully in a conversation, contributing their own ideas and suggestions and creating a real synergy of thought. They maintain eye contact and their animated body language reveals they are fully participating. So they do more than just listen – they build on the ideas of the other person and this quickly turns into 'double act', resulting in new insights and ideas from the person initiating the conversation. This leads to the fourth difference between energizers and de-engergizers: the conversation feels as if it is going somewhere and there is a strong sense of progress. De-energizers either provide little structure to the conversation, or provide too much, guiding the conversation to where *they* think it ought to go and leaving the other person feeling ambushed.

Finally, energizers behave with honesty and integrity, creating the belief that they can be relied upon to do what they have said they will do and that the goal is achievable. In contrast, de-energizers often engage in political behaviours that leave others doubting their word. This has the effect of dashing people's hopes.

In my own work I have found people easily identify with the two descriptions. Almost everyone has experienced both types of person. And this gives them the motivation to avoid being seen by others as de-energizers. But it is more than just an idea. The distinction drawn by Cross and Parker, and borne out by their research, highlights an important skill to be developed if you wish to become a collaborative leader. You need to work at the way you respond when others come to you with partly-formed ideas. Look for possibilities rather than constraints, mentally and physically engage in the conversation, and be flexible enough to adapt to the ideas of others. If you do disagree, focus on the idea rather than the person and value their initiative. None of these behaviours are that hard to practise, though some may come more easily than others.

There is more reason to practise these behaviours than simply being seen in a positive light by others. Cross and Parker found that energizers were consistently higher performers than de-energizers when performance data were compared. They also tended to be promoted earlier and were more mobile in their careers. This is because they are better at getting others to act on their own ideas; they also get more from those around them and they attract other high performers, building their reputation in an organization. As a consequence, Cross and Parker emphasize the importance of weaving relationship development into your daily work routine.

Managing Stakeholders

The techniques covered so far, and the new beliefs they generate, help enormously when initiating a conversation with someone you have just met or don't know very well. But working collaboratively involves more than networking effectively. The person aspiring to lead in a more collaborative way has to be comfortable with the whole arena of what is commonly referred to as stakeholder management.

Ask any project manager which part of their role they find most difficult and many will tell you it is managing the various people who have a stake in the project. What often makes this so difficult is that these stakeholders have different, sometimes competing goals. Usually, but not always, they belong to different reporting lines, so the project manager has little direct authority over them. Often stakeholders can slow down a project, becoming bottlenecks.

However, not all stakeholders prove to be so difficult. Some can be real allies and can help move a project along through their influence over others. In this final section, I will outline two techniques that can help you navigate the difficult world of stakeholder management. The techniques are firm favourites among clients of Catalyst, partly because they are so intuitive and easy to use. There is no magic formula involved, but they really do work and involve little practise before becoming a useful tool in the collaborative leader's armoury.

The first is called the Stakeholder Planning tool. Surprisingly, although managing key stakeholders is an important part of a large project, very few people plan how they will do this. Most have a fairly clear idea of who their stakeholders are, and how they can impact on a project's success, but that's about as far as it goes. Interactions with them tend to be ad hoc and often occur when problems arise. Stakeholders are usually kept informed, but again this tends to be instigated when a specific need occurs, such as their backing being required. Sometimes this is just too late and the project manager has extra work to do to overcome obstacles that are already in place.

The Stakeholder Planning tool takes the randomness out of managing key stakeholders. It involves determining who these people are at the outset and planning how to engage with them. What makes it most useful is that it encourages the user to think more broadly than might otherwise be the case. All too often we focus on too small a number of key stakeholders, limited to people that we directly depend on for support. Sometimes we tend not to think too much about those who might be troublesome or difficult to enlist and direct our attention to where we know we are likely to get a pay-off. The consequence of this somewhat optimistic approach to stakeholder management is that we fail to take action where it is most needed: with people who might block or curtail our efforts. We somehow hope that if we ignore them, they will do the same to us!

The first step in using the tool involves listing all the possible stakeholders, good or bad, using the list of labels shown in Figure 2.1. These labels may sound a little odd, but they help the user think more broadly about their potential stakeholders than might otherwise be the case.

For example, 'helpers' are people who hold resources you need, such as manpower, technology or finance. 'Informers' hold key information. You don't need to know specifically what this information is at the outset, only who might fall into this category. For example, knowing how your project is viewed vis-à-vis other initiatives could be important in pitching for extra resources.

You should continue to list all the stakeholders by name and role, not being too hung up by some of the labels used. They exist to help you think broadly and creatively, and not for public consumption. So, 'competitors' and 'enemies' are people who could cause your project to be delayed or derailed in some way, not because they are genuine adversaries but because they have different goals or have to balance your needs against other demands.

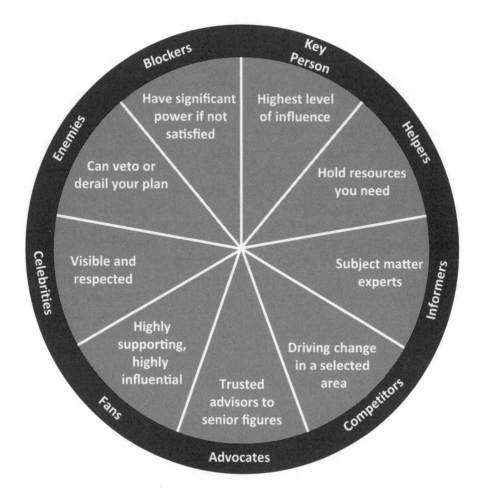

Figure 2.1   Stakeholder planning

The more positive roles, such as 'advocates' and 'celebrities', point you in the direction of people who you need to keep onside because they can influence others. Don't worry if a person holds more than one role, this simply reflects the complexity of stakeholder management.

The second step in using the tool involves identifying, as far as you can, what you need from each of these people. When you have completed both steps, capture you work in the form of chart or spreadsheet, with names, roles, what is needed from each and how you might obtain it listed in the first four columns (see Figure 2.2).

Roles	Who	What you need from them	How you can get it
Key person	Mark	Active sponsorship	Regular updates
Helpers	DC Manager	Technical support	Raise awareness of importance of project
Informers	Gary	Expert advice	Initial briefing
Competitors	Susan	Support	Build relationship and trust
Advocates			
Fans	Ops Manager	Project resources	Formal request
Celebrities	HR Manager	Nothing specific yet	Keep informed
Enemies			
Blockers	CFO	Budget approval	Get onside early

Figure 2.2   Identify the goal for each stakeholder

The third step involves plotting out the events or actions along a timeline for each person, giving you a plan for managing all your stakeholders (see Figure 2.3).

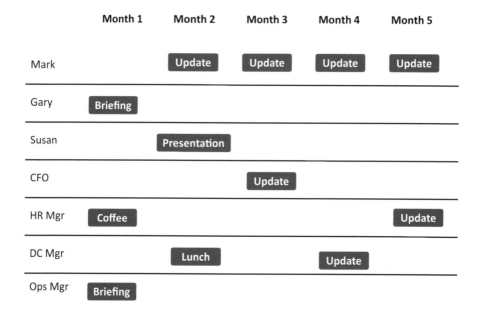

Figure 2.3   A completed Stakeholder Plan

Unlike a project plan, however, do not fill in the main body of the chart with timelines and milestones. Instead add events: what you plan to do with that stakeholder that will help you get from them what you need. These can range from meetings, to presentations, or even to coffee or lunch. The aim is to build up a plan of activities where you engage with your stakeholders regularly and ahead of problems arising. By looking across the chart for any particular role, you can see whether you are keeping close enough to them on a regular basis. Checking down the chart helps you focus on what you are doing in any single week and planning the time accordingly so you can avoid failing to get time in their diaries.

The Stakeholder Planning tool is useful for capturing on paper what you probably know anyway, but which may not get actioned. It is best to complete it with one or two members of your project team, as they will bring additional perspectives to the task. The tool moves stakeholder management into a planned and carefully managed activity, ensuring you tackle it professionally.

The second tool to be presented here is the Power Map. Like the Stakeholder Planning tool, it helps organize your thoughts and provide structure to how you might gain influence over others. The following chapter has more about techniques for influencing people, but for now we'll look at the source of influence: power.

The distribution of power within an organization is often complex and depends in part on the nature of the power being wielded. In terms of building relationships, it is useful to have a visual representation of this and this is where the Power Map comes in useful.

The first step in developing a Power Map is to represent yourself (or your project team) as a circle in the centre of what will become your map. Next, draw another circle to represent the key person you may wish to influence with regards to your project. If you have already completed a Stakeholder Plan, this will be the same key person identified there.

Represent the degree of influence you have over the key person by drawing lines between the two circles. One line means the degree of influence is quite weak, two refers to moderate influence and three lines indicate a high degree of influence.

Continue to build out the diagram, representing other individuals and the degree of influence you have over them. Then, draw lines between these various stakeholders, showing the power relations that exist between them (see Figure 2.4).

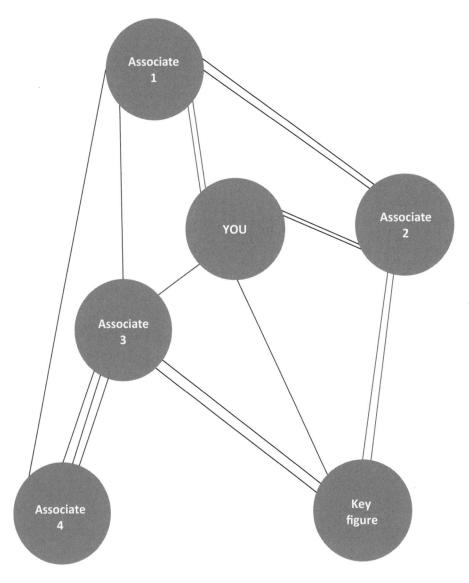

Figure 2.4   Power Map

Don't worry too much if you are not able confidently to estimate the strength of the various relationships. Make an educated guess that can later be researched. If it helps add clarity to your diagram, use arrowed lines to show the direction of influence, though be wary of producing too complex a diagram that it becomes unwieldy or unworkable. Ideally, as with the Stakeholder Plan, this should be done with others from your project team, so that you can discuss and agree the accuracy of the diagram.

Typically, and somewhat annoyingly, the key person is rarely someone you have a lot of power over. One of the strengths of the Power Map is that it highlights how you might exploit other relationships that exist. So, for example, is there an intermediary who does have some influence over the key person and over whom you have some degree of influence yourself? It can be far more effective to enlist this person's help in influencing your key person than try to do this directly. This stems largely from the fact you are likely to have a degree of self-interest, whereas the intermediary may not. People who work in sales know how powerful it can be to have someone within a potential client organization speak on their behalf to a prospective buyer and the Power Map helps you make use of advocates by identifying those you could call upon for this role.

Even if these relationships are weak or non-existent, the Power Map can come in handy by highlighting this fact. It shows which relationships you need to develop, and when used in conjunction with the Stakeholder Plan, brings a professional and planned approach to building out your personal relationships and network.

In summary, building relationships is a vital requirement for people who want to lead collaboratively. This is in contrast to the 'heroic' style of leadership that now seems inappropriate in the financial services. Henry Mintzberg, in his *Financial Times* article on 'communityship' outlined the problems with this approach to leadership when he criticized 'managers who sit on "top"… It is leadership apart.'

If this is leadership apart, then what I have outlined here is an approach to 'leadership among'. The beauty is it can be practised by many people, even if they do not hold the most senior role within an organization. In order to do this yourself, it is important that you invest time in building strong and healthy relationships outside your immediate sphere of influence and across various lines of business. You may not immediately warm to this, especially if you prefer to focus on the technical aspects of your job. But if you are to lead as well as manage, then I hope I have shown here how you may go about overcoming some of your obstacles and make an effective start.

3

Influencing

Heroic leaders are often people who don't take challenge well. I think the best leaders are those who are clearly strong-minded but are also simultaneously letting go of a lot. There are a lot of people who forget the letting go piece.

Peter Clarke, CEO, Man

You're more likely to get something done quicker in the heroic approach, riding in on your white horse, but you're also likely to fall down faster as well. Once you have that fall from grace, everyone you alienated on the way will be all over you.

Scott Marcar, Head of Risk & Finance Technology in The Royal Bank of Scotland's Global Banking & Markets division

In this chapter we focus on one of the key roles of a leader – that of influencing people. Approaches to leadership based on the 'heroic' model have tended to portray influence as stemming from a leader's charisma. John Kotter wrote in his Harvard Business Review article that leaders 'set direction' by developing a compelling vision of the future and communicating it in such a way that others are inspired to follow. This model of influence is often supported by pen portraits of charismatic leaders who have turned failing companies around by influencing others to follow them in a new direction.

Influencing other people in a way that builds and maintains collaboration is an essential aspect of leading collaboratively. Indeed it is difficult to see how one can adopt a collaborative style of leadership without changing the way one normally influences people.

This chapter outlines an approach that is applicable not only to people who hold very senior roles, but also to those in more modest positions. The approach allows you to increase your influence, while at the same time ensuring collaboration continues to take place and that relationships are enhanced rather than damaged in the process. The benefit of this is that it ensures better quality solutions and decisions through greater collaboration. It also increases buy-in and commitment to a course of action.

In the midst of an economic recession and turmoil in the financial markets, it is tempting to see the need for 'heroic' leadership as a way out of the uncertainty that prevails. Someone who, through their vision and strength of character, will set a new direction that inspires their organization to follow. The reality is that this approach is unlikely to meet the real needs of financial organizations or to get them out of their current troubles. No single person is likely to have all the answers, and a new vision, however compelling, cannot address the detailed problems of cutting costs, generating growth in a jittery market or curbing excessive risk taking.

Stephen Norman, the CIO at The Royal Bank of Scotland's investment banking division put it very humbly to me when he explained how the complexity of the modern world demanded a more collaborative approach than that which characterized the early part of his career:

> I was a great deal more controlling than I am today, and I've come to the view that the problems that we face inside capital markets, and probably in any modern global enterprise, are so complex. For example the integration of two large organizations can present problems that are so complex that you cannot centrally plan it in detail. You can't impose an inflexible plan for something like that. You must have clear high level goals and an organization that understands what we are trying to get to and the role others play. You also need to let people get on with it at the micro level. That's the only way to solve these very complex problems. So my journey towards my present leadership style was very much driven by the complexity of the world that we live in.

It is easy to assume that influence stems naturally from a leader's position in the organizational hierarchy. Those at lower levels might quite naturally believe that rising to such a level will give them access to greater influence, without them having to do too much to gain it.

In fact, people in even the most senior positions often find it extremely difficult to exert their influence in the way they would like. Convincing those they lead to follow a course of action is unlikely to be achieved simply by developing a vision.

Then there is the difficulty of influencing peers, who themselves may be responsible for managing large parts of the business and have their own agendas to pursue. It is becoming increasingly clear that in order to influence others, whether across organizational boundaries or within them, people in leadership roles have to work collaboratively with these people rather than rely on their position in the pecking order.

In my experience of working with technologists, the importance of being able to influence outside one's domain is never far from their minds. This is especially pronounced when it comes to managing complex projects, where the compliance of other stakeholders can crucially impact on milestones being hit.

Working with business partners is another area where the ability to influence is important but usually difficult. Technologists often need to say no to requests from the business that are likely to cause more problems than they will solve or which make little commercial or technical sense. Traditionally, traders have viewed Technology as a support function to assist them in their pursuit of revenue, and therefore expect technologists to do their bidding. While most now accept the need for a real partnership, there is still an implicit assumption that the technologist does what the trader says, not the reverse.

Even in relationships across technology functions, it can be difficult to exert influence. Post-merger integration often involves working with people from different 'heritage' organizations who have their own strong opinions about how things should be done. While everyone might accept they all work for the same company now, influencing people to do things differently, or to accept that your way is the best way, can seem like an impossible goal.

All of these situations point to the importance of being able to influence across organizational boundaries and to be able to do this in a collaborative way. One reason this is often so difficult is that people who belong to different 'groups' think and behave differently and often have goals that compete with our own. Working across organizational boundaries brings out our tribal instincts and we are generally much more comfortable working with people from our own group where we have common values and standards of behaviour.

We saw in the last chapter that the process of collaboration starts with building strong relationships based on trust and mutual understanding, but how do you take it to the next stage where you achieve your goals without falling into the quagmire of win–lose tactics?

Traditional Approaches to Exerting Influence

Traditional approaches to increasing our ability to influence another person tend to be based on techniques that can be used to gain compliance. Their starting point is the adoption of a win–lose strategy, where the aim is to ensure we succeed in influencing another person. Such approaches to the development of influencing skills can have a distinct flavour of sales training rather than leadership development and are unlikely to promote greater collaboration.

For example, most of what we know about influence, and how to exert it 'successfully', comes from the field of social psychology, where there have been countless research studies into persuasion and influence. The recognized authority in this space is Robert Cialdini, Professor of Psychology at the Arizona State University. He has developed six principles of persuasion that are based on decades of research into the factors that determine whether a person complies with a request. The six principles are:

1.   Reciprocation: people feel obligated to reciprocate a favour, so one way to influence them is to do them a favour first.

2.   Commitment: having made a small commitment to a course of action, a person is more likely to make a bigger one. This essentially is the 'foot-in-the-door' technique and involves gaining compliance.

3.   Social proof: if we can prove that other people tend to behave in a particular way, we are more likely to persuade someone to behave that way too.

4.   Authority: if we can demonstrate expertise and credibility, our degree of influence will increase.

5.   Scarcity: the more scarce something is, the more attractive it appears. Appealing to this principle therefore involves convincing the other party that what we are offering is in demand.

6.   Liking: people are more likely to be influenced by someone they like than dislike or feel neutral towards. Therefore, increasing our attractiveness to others will increase our ability to influence them.

While Cialdini's principles are based on sound research, and can make a real difference, they do not really promote collaboration. Instead they provide a way of getting your own way, providing of course the other party is not aware of Cialdini's work.

A similar field of study is based on the analysis of power and the various types of power that one can draw upon in a bid to influence others. If we can gain or exploit a source of power, we can then use this in our attempts to influence the other party.

While we tend to assume that power is gained from our seniority in an organization, there are in fact numerous sources of power, only one of which is directly related to position. The other types of power are:

- *Expert Power*: power stemming from expertise and experience.

- *Information Power*: resulting from access to valuable information.

- *Referent Power*: the power that comes from your presence and likeability.

- *Reward Power*: the ability to provide benefits or remove negatives.

- *Connection Power*: the power that comes from being connected to powerful others.

- *Coercive Power*: the power to introduce sanctions or remove benefits.

- *Dependency Power*: having control over scarce resources.

- *Centrality Power*: being centrally linked to other people or departments.

- *Substitutability Power*: the extent to which your role cannot easily be performed by others.

- *Uncertainty Power*: the ability to introduce unexpected changes or remove uncertainty.

This approach might seem attractive in situations where we feel we lack the power to tell someone what to do, as it can highlight alternative sources of power we can draw upon. However, it is not difficult to see how this can easily descend into the type of transactional encounter that is the opposite of collaboration. Introducing an unexpected change might unsteady the other party, allowing you to gain valuable leverage over them, but this is hardly likely to result in a win–win outcome.

The above list highlights the significant power that technology organizations can hold over other parts of their business. A system crash can result in lost trades that can cost a firm hundreds of thousands of dollars in a very short period of time and in such situations businesses are totally dependent on technologists to get things moving again. Having the power to fix costly problems, and the power to control what is a very specialized resource, can lead technologists to exploit their hold over business partners, though this rarely happens.

Influencing Collaboratively

Instead of approaching the topic of influence the traditional way, we need to approach it as a collaborative venture. In financial organizations, even if you are not the head of a major function such as Technology or Operations, or one of the trading desks, you will still need to work collaboratively with people in other parts of your organization, as well as external parties forming part of the value chain. This means finding a way forward that has a genuine win–win feel about it and which preserves, if not enhances, your reputation as someone to do business with. It also requires a smattering of humility, so that people become aware of their own role in forging a way ahead rather than see progress as a result of your own charisma or manipulation. Finally, and perhaps most significantly, influence has to be achieved where there is no formal power mechanism that allows you to give your orders and expect others to comply by virtue of the authority you hold over them.

PLAN FOR COLLABORATION

The first stage in this process involves planning how you will handle an encounter with a person whom you wish to influence. Failing to plan in advance means we act in the heat of the moment, usually when someone resists our initial attempt at persuasion and we are suddenly required to try a different approach. More often than not we simply state our original request, this time more assertively, in the hope that what didn't work the first time might work this time with a slightly different emphasis on it. Or, we outline the consequences of non-compliance, but this can easily be interpreted by the other person as a threat, making them dig their heels even deeper.

This situation can be avoided if you do some simple planning in advance. In time you will build up a set of techniques that become habitual and require little advance thought. When this happens these techniques can be drawn upon quickly when needed, resulting in smooth interactions in 'real time'.

1. Set a collaborative outcome

The first step in planning is to be absolutely clear on the outcome you want to achieve and defining what a collaborative outcome would look like. There is a range of possible outcomes that can result from an attempt to influence a person, and unless you set one that is genuinely collaborative, you are unlikely to achieve it. Some questions to help you think about your desired outcome are:

- How important is it that you maintain a good relationship with the other party?

- How prepared are you to compromise? By how much?

- Is there a quid pro quo? What are you prepared to give in return for compliance?

- How specific is your request? Does it matter *when* the person complies or *how* they comply?

- What are the specific behaviours you want from the other party?

- Are you prepared to accept a rejection if there are sound reasons? How negotiable is this in the full scheme of things?

- Is it acceptable if the person agrees in principle, but wants time before confirming they will comply?

So, for example, suppose you require the manager of another function to meet a deadline that has important implications for you but which conflicts with some of her priorities. You need to influence her to ensure one of her direct reports delivers on time. A good outcome might be:

She agrees to ensure this person meets your deadline, which requires her to free up enough of his time to do this. She also agrees that he will attend two of your status meetings to give updates on his progress. Although not entirely happy with this, the manager understands the importance of the deadline for you and comes away from your meeting feeling the outcome is a fair one and knows you are appreciative of her efforts. There is no 'bad feeling' that can carry over to future meetings and the relationship you have with her has not been damaged.

A good example of this type of approach was described to me by David, a manager within a hedge fund. A problem had arisen that required people in another part of the firm to help him iron out inconsistencies in some key data:

> It's setting a mission statement in effect: 'this is where we need to get to'. And everyone agrees with that. They had issues, because they didn't have the resources or some of the knowledge, but some of that knowledge resided in my team. So it was more about collaboration, working out how you can empower different parts of the organization to deliver a result bigger than they could deliver on their own.

By focusing on an aim that, in his words, 'everyone can agree with in the organization, and we know everyone else is trying to achieve', he was able to resolve a potential problem by agreeing on a genuinely collaborative outcome that both parties would benefit from.

2. Decide on the right method of communication

Once you are clear about your outcome you can decide on how you will communicate your request. Many situations that have the potential to escalate into conflict will require a face-to-face meeting, but this is not always easy to arrange. The other person may be based in another country or it might be difficult to get time in their busy schedule, especially if they are more senior than you. Some requests might be best made through a formal presentation to the other party, such as when you are attempting to secure funds. Others can be achieved by a phone call. Some, though not many, might be conducted via email, but here you have to be very careful and spend time composing your message in a way that avoids them replying with a simple 'no'. If you are attempting to influence the other person at a meeting that will be attended by a number of other people, you need to ask yourself whether this could put them on the spot and lead to some loss of face if they comply.

You need to consider all these options and choose the approach that is most likely to achieve your outcome. This may mean making extra arrangements that will help a less than ideal option. For example, if your request is to be made at a regular update meeting, you could meet or call the person beforehand to discuss it and get a sense of what their objections might be and what their response is contingent upon. This will avoid the other person feeling they have been 'hijacked' at the meeting, which can often lead to a denial of your request.

3. Know your audience

If you are 'pitching' an idea or proposal to a specific audience, it helps to know the 'hot buttons' of your audience. What is currently important to them? What are their big concerns? If you can show that your proposals can help them in these matters, they are more likely to give you a sympathetic hearing. A CIO with a big cost-cutting agenda, for example, will want to know how your proposals are going to save money, even if this is not the main thrust of your argument.

Not long ago I ran a session on presentation skills during a development programme attended by top technologists at an investment bank. My emphasis was on avoiding some of the well-documented mistakes that arise from an over-reliance on PowerPoint when constructing presentation slides: excessive use of bullet points, too much text, too much detail, over-complexity and so on. As an alternative I suggested making more use of the visual dimension offered by slides – a simple diagram to replace long passages of text, the removal of unnecessary detail from charts and the judicious use of pictures to convey a metaphor.

Unfortunately, the message was too readily taken to heart by the group. During the programme, project teams were required to give a short presentation to the CIO on their work. I watched in horror as slide after slide appeared, almost bereft of any detail on what they had done, replaced instead by pictures and cryptic one-liners. The CIO was not impressed and said that it was impossible to sign-off the proposals without the detailed costs and technical information he required. It was a stark lesson in knowing your audience and tailoring your content accordingly.

You should also consider the values and beliefs of your audience and play to these. Do they place a high priority on fairness and integrity? Is doing the right thing more important to them than making a quick financial return? Do they place a high value on innovation? Do they shirk from anything that smacks of 'soft-heartedness'?

All of these things can be important in tailoring your message. Knowing where your audience stands can help you avoid overlooking something that is important to them and which might tilt the balance away from you.

You should also take into account their stylistic preferences. Do they like detail, like the CIO described above, or are they more influenced by the 'big picture'? Do they want to know the long-term vision or the short-term tactical steps required?

The best way to discover these preferences is to talk to people who know the person well. Find out from these people what he or she likes and dislikes when receiving a pitch or presentation. What gets them really annoyed? Their peers are likely to know and most will be happy to advise you if your intent is honourable.

4. Anticipate questions and objections

A key part of your planning should involve identifying the questions or objections you are likely to face and deciding how you would respond to these. Planning a response that keeps collaboration open means you are more likely to avoid conflict should the other party resist your original proposal.

Planning how to deal with difficult questions also helps in your own delivery. When coaching people who want to improve their presentations skills, for example, I often find that their biggest concern is not being able to answer questions from the audience. This leads to some degree of apprehension and consequently a less than polished delivery.

There is a simple way of dealing with this that has the benefit of preparing you for difficult conversations and reducing any pre-meeting nerves. At Catalyst we call this technique the Dirty Dozen and it involves listing the 12 most difficult questions or objections you might be asked by your audience (it doesn't have to be 12, but this helps you focus on more than the obvious few).

The technique works best when done in a small team, as you are more likely to generate a good range of questions. The next step involves planning your answers to each of these questions. Even though the questions are, by definition, those you hope you do not get asked, it is usually not too difficult to work out how you might answer them in a convincing way. Again, working with others can improve the quality of your work.

This technique has the effect of 'inoculating' you against difficult questions or objections. While it is undoubtedly more challenging to deal with these in a 'live' situation, the very fact that you have rehearsed your response in a safer environment will go some way to preparing you to deal with the real thing. Another benefit is that it reduces pre-meeting nerves, which usually stem from anticipation of the unknown. As a result, you can give a more confident and polished performance, which in turn improves your ability to influence.

5. Adopt the right mindset

The final part of your planning involves getting yourself in the right frame of mind to achieve a collaborative outcome. You cannot achieve such an outcome if you are feeling angry or aggressive towards the other person.

Instead you need to be patient, empathetic and sensitive to the other person's needs, and this requires a specific mindset. You need to be genuinely interested in their thoughts and views. You cannot do this if all you are thinking about is your own point of view or how they are wrong to take the stand they have. You also have to be open-minded and prepared to change your own position if what they say has some merit.

EARN A HEARING

The second stage of achieving a collaborative outcome focuses on how you initiate the actual conversation and this requires a radically different approach to the kind you may be used to when attempting to influence another person.

Usually when we want to influence another person we start by laying out our goals and supporting arguments. This approach works fine when we are making a formal presentation (such as a 'pitch'). It does not work so well when the conversation is less structured or formal or where the other party does not want to be influenced. In these situations it can easily send the message that we are approaching the situation with a win–lose outcome in mind and forestall a collaborative outcome right from the start.

In these situations it can be more effective to begin with a different approach. Your goal should be for the other person really to hear what you have to say, free from opposing thoughts and assumptions, and to be open to your proposals. While this does not guarantee they will comply with your request, you are unlikely to influence them without this openness on their part. The essence of this approach involves you *earning* this hearing, rather than demanding or assuming it. The way you do this is by first giving *them* a hearing, demonstrating the kind of behaviours you want to elicit in return.

Earning a hearing requires you to do three things (see Figure 3.1):

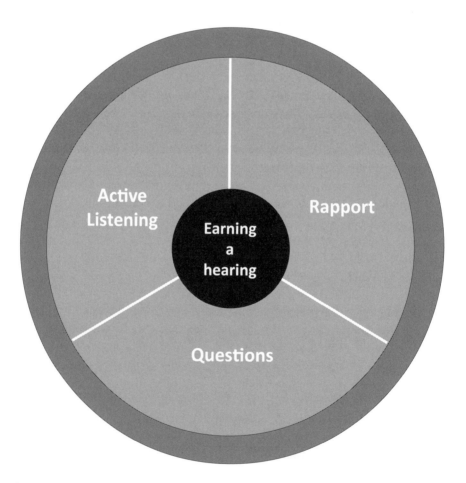

Figure 3.1   Earning a hearing

BUILD RAPPORT

This involves making a connection with the other person. There are a number of ways you can do this. An obvious one is finding some common ground. Imagine two people who are on their first date. The conversation typically involves looking for shared experiences, attitudes or interests as a way of building a connection with the other person. Their aim is to find something they have in common so that they can convince the other person to like them. Psychologists investigating the causes of personal attraction have found that the single most decisive factor is the degree of similarity between two people. This can apply to almost anything they share in common. So the art of building rapport involves discovering and emphasizing these similarities as a way of building the relationship.

A second way of establishing rapport is to match or 'mirror' the other person's behaviour in some way. People familiar with this concept often treat it with an element of scepticism, imagining it means copying the other person's movements and gestures in such an obvious way that it looks somewhat contrived. Instead, the aim should be to get broadly 'in sync' with the other person through adopting a similar posture and stance. If they are sitting back, looking relaxed, then sit back and relax yourself. If they are leaning forward, you should lean into them. When practised in a subtle way the technique really can work. If you are not convinced of its effectiveness, take a look at two people deeply engrossed in a conversation and you will see that very often they have unconsciously adopted mirrored postures and positions.

Mirroring can take place at different levels and does not just apply to posture or gestures. The less obvious it is, the more likely you are to build a connection at a subconscious level and this in turn means it will be more effective in establishing rapport. Pay attention to the way the other person is speaking. Are they talking quickly or in measured tones? Is their voice pitched high or low? Do they use a lot of visual imagery, referring to things like 'the big picture' or 'seeing the wood from the trees'? Or do they talk at the level of feelings, emphasizing their emotions with expressions like 'I feel we both need to be happy with the decision we make today'? As with body mirroring, you need to match the other person in subtle ways that make them feel at ease with you. A person who is highly animated and talking at a fast pace will, at some level, feel less connected with you if you are talking slowly in a deep tone and with little behavioural expression.

ASK QUESTIONS

The second step in earning a hearing involves finding out as much as you can about their views on the subject of your proposal. This can be very difficult when we have strong views ourselves and want to bring the other person around to our way of thinking. Remember, you will have the opportunity to express your views shortly and your aim here is to get the other person to the point where they genuinely want to hear them. The most effective way to do this is to demonstrate genuine interest in their views.

Open questions that allow you to get to the heart of what the other person believes, and why they believe it, will allow you to do this. Aim to discover what is important to them, what their concerns are and what led them to adopt this position. Good questioning will encourage them to open up and show something of the person that lies behind the viewpoint. When this happens it can be very tempting to take issue with what they say, especially if it contradicts your own views. Do not rise to this temptation. If you do, the conversation can quickly turn into an argument and you will have lost the opportunity to earn a hearing.

Also be careful about asking leading questions. When I train people in this technique they sometimes try to marry the approach of asking questions with their need to express their own viewpoint, resulting in questions like, 'Don't you think it would make more sense to do what I am proposing?' Needless to say, this does not help the conversation go smoothly.

One surprising outcome of asking questions is that the other person is required to think through their own position more carefully. When they do this they may see the limitations of their position and if you have held back on expressing your own views they will not feel the need to defend themselves. As a result they often come round to your way of thinking and you will have succeeded in influencing them. Again, avoid the temptation to say, 'Aha, I told you so!'

ACTIVELY LISTEN

Most of us are familiar with the concept of active listening, yet many people find it an extraordinarily difficult thing to do. This is especially so when we oppose what the other person is saying. Building on the process of asking questions to discover what lies at the heart of the other person's views, the aim of listening actively is to demonstrate understanding. To do this authentically you once again have to see the world through their eyes. You have to imagine what it would feel like if you were in their position. This involves more than saying things like, 'I see where you're coming from.' It means experiencing the same emotions they are experiencing through genuinely empathizing with them and demonstrating this by what you say. If you find this too difficult because you are so polarized on the topic, then it can help just to summarize their argument to show that at least you have heard and understood it.

You may find that if you really are able to empathize with the other person, you start to question your own position. This does not mean you have lost the argument. It can be an important step in finding a way ahead that may mean you give ground on some points of contention and you do not achieve the outcome you originally intended. While you may not have influenced the other person to come around to your way of thinking, in the bigger scheme of things you will have reached agreement and avoided a conflict from which no one wins. Paradoxically, you will not have presented yourself as a 'pushover' but as someone who is reasonable and likeable. This in turn will increase your ability to influence the other person in any future disagreements.

However, let's assume that you don't change your views even though you understand fully the position adopted by the other person. By working through these three steps you will often find the other person then starts asking about your own position. At this point you will have earned yourself a hearing.

When this happens you must avoid the temptation to think, 'Right, I've listened to you, now you listen to me' and go in with all guns blazing. Answer the question you have been asked, holding back other information so that the other person follows up with additional questions. If you have done a good job of earning a hearing, they will have got everything off their chest and will have little left to say about their own views. More often than not they will be genuinely interested in hearing what you have to say. Having set a tone for the conversation that is based on sharing and understanding rather than a tone that is oppositional and opinionated, you are in a great position to put your views across and explain the reasoning behind your own thinking. Because the other person will have already made all their own points known, they are less likely to oppose yours with counter-arguments.

STATE YOUR CASE

Having earned a hearing, you need to outline your proposal in a way that makes a collaborative outcome most likely. When making your views known, always try to relate them back to what the other person has said. Show how your point can address their concerns or how it avoids the consequences they might fear. This will help you to be much more persuasive, but you can only do this if you have really given them the opportunity fully to express their views and you have listened to what they have said.

There are several other important factors that can help you position your proposal in a way that gains the other person's compliance.

1. Appeal to logic and emotion

In the hard-nosed world of finance there is little room for emotionally-driven behaviour (though it often can be observed!). Presentations are expected to be logical and rational, laying out the facts and making sound commercial sense.

Unfortunately, people often need something more to win them over. I remember once meeting with a manager who had been charged with drastically reducing headcount in Production Support. The function had grown over the years, due partly to the need to support error-ridden applications. He had built a sound business case showing how, with greater investment in the development phase, fewer errors would be written into the software code. Greater accuracy in development would mean fewer people were required in the Support function.

Although the logic of his argument was compelling, he needed the support of the heads of the various business lines. It was their people who would be cut from Production Support and they were understandably nervous about providing their business partners with a reduced level of service. When I met him he had been unable to influence them to support the reductions in headcount.

It struck me that he had built a case for change that appealed wholly to rational arguments and that there was no 'emotional' content. When I voiced this impression it was like a light had literally been switched on in his head. 'You're right,' he said, 'I've completely ignored the emotional element, yet that is where their main opposition lies!' His new approach combined a strong business case with an equal emphasis on the concerns of the business heads and reassurances about levels of service.

When attempting to influence another person, you should build in an emotional element to any logical arguments. Refer to people's fears or concerns when attempting to dissuade someone against a planned course of action. Emphasize the positive emotions that will be experienced if your proposals are adopted. Tell a story or use anecdotes that make people smile or strike a chord.

Don't overdo it though! For emotional appeals to work, they should avoid the extreme of a 'doom and gloom' message. Research has shown that people block out messages that are too negative to contemplate, so remember to keep things in perspective.

2. Use imagery and metaphors

While you want to avoid falling into the trap of the project teams described above, there is little doubt that leaders who use powerful images and metaphors can exert a strong influence on their audience. This does not mean you should try to adopt the style and presence of a modern day Martin Luther King. What it does mean is that you should consider powerful ways to convey your key messages.

For example, a project team that was proposing a method to make better use of disk storage space likened their firm's current approach to owning a 160 gigabyte iPod with only half a dozen songs stored on it. A guest speaker at one of Catalyst's development programmes conveyed the number of lines of code in a certain application by referring to how many books would be needed to contain all these lines. If placed one on top of the other they would be the height of the Empire State Building.

These and other metaphors make your presentation memorable and get your message across in a compelling way.

3. State the benefits for both of you

A genuinely collaborative outcome will have benefits for both you and the other party. It helps to clearly state these, focusing especially on the benefits to them.

People often make the error of stating the details of what they are proposing rather than the benefits, especially in technical presentations. The distinction between features and benefits is a common element in most sales training. Unfortunately, the error of simply listing features is often made.

The benefits of your proposal should relate to things that are important to the other person. For example, simply saying that your proposal will result in a faster processing time does not outline why this might be important to them. The benefit might be that it allows them to process more trades or reduce downtime. This might seem obvious to you, but to be able to identify the benefits you need to see the world from their point of view.

This relates back to the earlier point of knowing their 'hot buttons'. You then need to show clearly and explicitly how your proposal will help them achieve their goals.

4. Deal with objections

The Dirty Dozen technique can help you respond quickly to difficult questions, but often your audience may simply state objections to your proposal rather than ask questions. When this happens we often respond too quickly, pushing back on their objections in a way that can make them more entrenched.

In these situations, it is important to remember that opposing an objection is very unlikely to make it go away. Instead you have to discover what lies beneath the objection and you do this by more questioning and listening.

Usually, an objection disguises something important to the other person that lies beneath the surface of their remark. This might be a concern about how their own stakeholders may react if your proposal is accepted, or a fear of rising costs, or new risks being introduced. Unless you know what their concern is, simply refuting their objection won't resolve it in their mind. So, you need to find out more by asking good open questions and listening for what lies beneath the words. Testing your assumptions through asking further questions for clarification will show your audience you are really listening and that you can see the world from their point of view.

Only when you have identified their concerns can you start to address them. If you've done your homework and your proposal is sound, this should not be too difficult. But if their point is valid you should concede it rather than lose credibility by denying it. This does not mean all will be lost and that you have failed in your attempt to persuade them. Instead you should work with the other person to find a way ahead that addresses their concerns. By engaging them in joint problem solving, you will be working collaboratively to find a solution to what could be a real problem.

Making a Pitch

At Catalyst we refer to the above approach as 'pull influencing', since it relies on drawing out the other person's thoughts and reasoning, rather than 'pushing' your proposal at them. It is more likely to result in a collaborative outcome and will usually help maintain a good relationship with the other party.

There may be times, however, when you are required to make a specific proposal to an audience or another person. This is more akin to a 'push' style of influencing, since it requires you to make a strong case for your proposals. It is also possible the other party has no competing agenda, so a 'pull' approach is unlikely to work.

Whatever it is you are proposing to your audience, if it requires their approval it is also likely to require an investment of funds. In this respect, you can think of your attempt to influence them as a 'pitch'.

Making a pitch represents a special case of influencing where your goal is to persuade the other person to invest money, time, commitment and other resources into your proposal (and ultimately in you).

There are some very useful guides on how to do this effectively and if you want to improve the quality of presentations where you are making a pitch you should consider the advice they offer. Jerry Weissman, for example, has advised on over 500 IPOs, including some of the biggest IPOs over the last decade or so. He offers a very structured approach and even has a template to help you stick to it. Every pitch, he argues, should follow this tried and tested format (Weissman, 2006).

Stephen Bayley and Roger Mavity offer an alternative approach. They argue that we are essentially making a pitch every time we attempt to influence a person, whether it is a marriage proposal, a job application or the sale of a house. All of these can be thought of as pitches, hence the clever title of their book, *Life's A Pitch* (Bayley and Mavity, 2007). They offer some great advice and although it is based on their experience of making commercial pitches in the advertising industry, it can be applied to many presentations in business life.

At Catalyst we advise people to follow a simple structure that is easy to remember and which focuses on getting your point across clearly and persuasively. We refer to it through its acronym, PROEP. Not something that easily trips off the tongue, though people do seem to remember it.

Proposal: Open your presentation with a clear statement of your proposal. What do you want the other person to do? Start with this and use simple language that gets straight to the point. People will appreciate you being 'up front' when you are making a request of them.

Rationale: Why are you proposing this? What are the benefits for you and for them? What are the consequences of not doing this (be careful not to exaggerate these or to make what can be interpreted as threats)?

Objections: Show that you understand their position and the objections they might have. This might require some homework on your part, but often it can be achieved by the Dirty Dozen technique outlined above.

Examples: Demonstrate, with examples, how you can avoid or address these objections.

Proposal: Close with a restatement of your proposal.

The beauty of this simple structure is that it can be applied to many forms of delivery. It can be used to structure a formal presentation, or an email message, or a conversation (including a telephone conversation). While the structure on its own does not guarantee success, it allows you to present your message in a clear way while showing understanding of the concerns the other person may have.

MAKING A SUCCESSFUL PITCH: THE VIEWS OF ONE CIO

Many of Catalyst's development programmes require participants to develop ideas and proposals which they then pitch to members of the senior management team. Their brief is to solve a problem or develop a proposal that will significantly enhance revenue or reduce costs. The exercise provides a good opportunity to gain valuable experience making a pitch and tests their ability to influence through a 'push' approach.

The advice given by one CIO at the conclusion of a number of pitches to him is worth reproducing here as it gives a good insight into what people at this level of seniority look for in proposals from technologists. Many of the points outlined above appear in this CIO's feedback, along with other points that relate more specifically to a technology function. You may find the advice helpful when in a similar position of making a pitch to senior figures.

1. Show the fit to the strategy.
    How does your proposal enable the business strategy? How important and significant is your idea in relation to the strategy? Demonstrate to your audience that you understand what the strategy is and the important elements of it.

2. Get into the details.
    Benefits and value should be demonstrated in very specific terms. How much time or money can be saved? Where? When? It is acceptable to give estimates if actual figures cannot be given, but support this with some indication of probability. CIOs have to choose where to invest their budget, so give them the information they need to make an informed choice.

3. Tell a compelling story of the benefits.
    After presenting the benefits in detail, identify where action needs to be targeted to reap these. Avoid sounding like a vendor saying he can solve all your problems and instead focus on the specific problems you will solve. Cite the evidence to support what you are saying and show the engineering required to do this.

4.　Focus on business processes.
Rather than look at the problem from an application perspective, you should show how business processes need to change to resolve the issue and how your solution will enable these process changes.

5.　Find the specific issue to be solved.
Focus on the core problem and build your solution from this, rather than propose a generic model that you hope will solve a number of unspecified problems. This reflects how strategies evolve in practise – through tackling these problems one at a time rather than developing a grand scheme that will solve everything.

6.　Reference the knowledge that exists within the organization.
Refer to what is already known on this topic. Have there been previous attempts to solve the problem? Evaluate what others have done in this space and show you have adopted an organization-wide approach to your work.

7.　Demonstrate engineering expertise.
Aim to wow your audience with engineering excellence rather than flashy presentational slides. Show how you have applied your specialist knowledge and experience to the problem.

Pitches or formal presentations requiring a decision from the audience make it difficult to achieve a collaborative outcome. By their very nature they are more transactional than collaborative. The audience will want to test and probe your proposal to discover any weaknesses in it, and you, quite naturally, will want to put up a good defence. Sometimes you may be competing against other proposals, bringing a strong element of competitiveness to the whole proceedings.

When there is little opportunity to influence the formal structure of such situations you can still work towards a collaborative solution by introducing some subtle yet effective elements to your presentation.

Start by defining a collaborative outcome and use this to shape how you approach the situation. If, in your own mind, the outcome is to win the pitch then you may overstate your case or defend it too rigorously against challenges from the audience. A better outcome is that the audience makes the right decision. This can include rejecting your proposal, but if this is the right decision it is as much in your interests as in theirs.

With this outcome in mind, think about how you will frame and structure the meeting. What is the best way of achieving the outcome? How can you communicate and gain the audience's commitment to this outcome? How will you deal with questions and challenges?

The PROEP structure can still be used, but your proposal may now include ideas on how to help the audience make the right decision. Instead of stating what you think are their objections and how you can meet them head on, invite objections and together test their validity. This can create a genuine dialogue between you and the audience, rather than the Q & A format that all too quickly descends into an attack–defend format.

In addition to this outline structure, you should also plan how you will open the conversation. The technical term for this is 'framing' and it can have a major impact on the way the conversation unfolds.

Framing the conversation as a problem or conflict, through use of words like 'difficult', 'disagreement', 'but' or 'issue' can put the other person on the defensive right from the start of the conversation. It is far better to frame it as an opportunity, a chance to work together and a positive step forward.

'I'm really pleased you agreed to this meeting as I believe we can make some good progress today' is a better way to open a conversation than, 'I know you disagree with me on this, but we have to confront this problem head-on if I'm to meet my deadlines.'

Working out how to frame the conversation will also put you in a more positive state of mind. Our own, unconscious, frame can often be a negative one – we think of all the things that can go wrong and we dread the meeting that lies ahead. It is little wonder, therefore, that this comes across when we actually meet up with the person.

When planning how to structure a meeting with a person we want to influence it helps to create an agenda that captures the broad sequence of how we want the meeting to go. Even if this agenda is not used or communicated formally, it will help get the sequence clear in your own mind. It also helps us keep control of the conversation if we can agree this sequence with the person at the start of the meeting. It is harder to be derailed and we can always refer back to the agreed sequence if we feel the meeting is going in an unplanned direction.

Summary

All effective leaders are able to exert their influence. But most of the time they do this in subtle ways rather than through commanding others to follow their instructions. Great leaders influence people through appealing to hearts and minds, through working with people to find a way forward that all parties can agree on. They can do this most effectively through collaborating with them to achieve a genuine win–win outcome. A 'pull' approach can help when there is strong initial opposition to the proposals being made. In situations where a 'push' approach is required, such as when making a pitch for funds, a collaborative outcome can still be achieved by following the tips outlined above.

4

Communicating

Collaborative leaders are able to connect with their followers in a way that is markedly different from those who lead in a more traditional, directive way. This difference often shows itself in the way they communicate, both formally (such as when giving a presentation) and informally, in an interpersonal context. In both situations, the communication feels more like a two-way dialogue than a one-way message. Those on the receiving end feel more involved and engaged. Differences in status and hierarchy seem to melt away and quite junior people feel relaxed in the presence of senior figures within their firm.

Stephen Norman at The Royal Bank of Scotland and Peter Clarke, the CEO at Man, both have this quality. On a number of occasions I have seen them giving presentations to small and large audiences alike within their respective companies. They are both able to connect with their employees in a way that creates a sense of common purpose and genuine collaboration in the pursuit of company goals. Afterwards, when mingling with their audience, their informal conversations have a similar feel and have the effect of putting people at ease.

This chapter outlines practical ways to improve the way you communicate with others, both formally through presentations and informally through conversations. The starting point is that leading in a collaborative way involves a very different style of communication than has traditionally been the case within the financial services. If you are to develop your skills as a collaborative leader, then you may need to learn how to communicate in a different way, one that facilitates a collaborative relationship with your followers. This applies to the person leading a small team, as well as a CIO leading an organization of thousands.

When we think of great and charismatic leaders, we tend to think of great communicators. We conjure up images of presidents, civil rights leaders or dynamic CEOs standing at a podium delivering rousing oratory to a mesmerized audience. Fortunately, collaborative leadership does not require this kind of delivery. However, it does require a style of communication that is still often far removed from the style many people are used to in financial institutions. More often than not the norm is a long and overly complex PowerPoint presentation that does little to inform let alone inspire or a leader whom people find it difficult to really engage with in a genuine two-way dialogue.

Another common problem is the gap that exists between technology and the business it supports. The latter want to know how technology can help them increase their revenues or stay within the parameters of financial regulation and risk control. The language they speak is a commercial one. Unfortunately, many technologists find it difficult to translate complex technical ideas into simple commercial messages. It's very difficult to collaborate when it feels like you are both talking in different languages.

Collaborative leaders have a way of communicating that invites others to contribute their ideas and work towards shared outcomes. The way they communicate is genuinely two-way, even when they are giving a formal presentation to a large audience. It feels like a dialogue rather than monologue and there is a real sense of collaboration between them and their audience.

In turbulent times effective communication is even more important, and, annoyingly, more difficult. The financial crisis of 2008/9 has led to high levels of uncertainty about what the future holds for many financial institutions. Many responded by laying off large numbers of people and by restructuring their operations. All this fuelled anxieties among staff about their own job security, leading to an insatiable need for information. Many managers found themselves in the position of trying to keep their teams informed, while being just as unsure themselves about what is likely to happen in the future. Communicating effectively during change and uncertainty is therefore a crucial skill in today's fast-changing environment.

Effective communication is the very essence of leadership and without an ability to communicate effectively it seems unlikely one can inspire genuine followership. Yet the term 'communication' is also so vague and all-encompassing that it can often lose its meaning and usefulness. I have lost count of the times I have heard the ills of an organization being put down to 'poor communication', a claim that tells us nothing really.

In this chapter we will focus on three specific types of communication:

1. presentations;

2. communicating during change and uncertainty;

3. interpersonal communication.

With each type I will outline some of the common failings and describe some simple tools and techniques that can improve the way you communicate and facilitate greater collaboration between you and your audience.

Presentations

Some years ago a merger between two investment banks led to the CIO of the smaller bank being given the role of heading up the new, combined technology organization. His new management team consisted largely of members of his previous management team. In practice this meant these managers quickly had to adapt from leading relatively small lines of business to being part of a much larger organization, responsible for literally thousands of people.

At an early 'town hall' meeting they each introduced themselves to the large number of employees present and gave a brief presentation of their plans to grow the business. These managers were not by any means 'career' managers. They had risen up the management layers of a relatively small technology organization, largely through their technical brilliance rather than their ability to manage people. I don't believe any of them had been through any form of management development programme at that time. Giving any sort of presentation was not one of their strengths. But this particular presentation required them to create a powerful first impression among their new legions of reports and to inspire their confidence.

Although I was not personally present, I heard from a number of people in the audience how poor the presentations were. The managers had apparently spent little time preparing their presentations and mumbled inaudibly about their plans for the future. They were nervous and hesitant, and failed in the central task of building confidence among the people who were now being led by them. Word soon spread that the new technology organization of the merged bank was being run by a bunch of amateurs.

The managers themselves had never aspired to be great presenters, but now they were being judged by their lack of this skill. Their considerable technical skills, which were absolutely central to the bank's aggressive plans for growth, seemed to count for very little in the eyes of their followers. It was a hard lesson for these managers to learn.

FINDING THE CORE OF YOUR MESSAGE

I often see great technical people struggling when it comes to giving a presentation. It is frequently mentioned by people I coach as a skill they need to improve if they are to scale the heights of their organization. Many of these people hate giving presentations. Their plight is even more pronounced when they are giving a presentation to non-technical audiences and operating outside their comfort zones.

Some of this is to do with their delivery style and I will say more about how to improve this later in the chapter. For now, I will focus on the content and in particular the process of translating an idea into a message that is then communicated to an audience through a presentation. The reason is that if this process is performed effectively, it can make it much easier to deliver the message in an engaging way. It can also avoid some of the problems to be found when the message gets lost in a mass of slides that contain more information than can ever be assimilated and remembered by an audience.

One of the best approaches to thinking about how to communicate your message is contained in a book titled *Made to Stick*, by Chip and Dan Heath (2007). Their book is a goldmine of ideas, suggestions, tips and advice that can transform any kind of communication. In essence though, their book poses two questions to anyone with a message to communicate: What is the single most important point of your message (the core)? And, how can you communicate it in a way that makes it memorable (sticky)? Address these two questions and your ability to connect with your audience can be drastically improved.

Articulating the core of your message is not as easy as it may sound. It involves stripping out all the points you want to make, all the messages you may want to convey, until you are left with one, the single most important. This forced prioritization does not dilute your core message. Rather, it lets it shine through, uncluttered by any other thoughts or messages.

To help in this process, Chip and Dan Heath suggest answering the question, 'If there is just one thing you want your audience to remember and take away from your presentation, what would it be?'

MAKING YOUR MESSAGE STICK

Finding the core of your message allows you to be really clear about what it is you want to communicate. The second step is to communicate this in a memorable and effective way. Unfortunately this is where many people come unstuck, particularly if their message is quite complex. Very often, the reason lies in what Chip and Dan Heath call 'the curse of knowledge'. Knowing something your audience does not know can make it difficult to put yourself in their shoes and imagine what it is like not to know it. This can make it difficult to convey a message in a way that makes sense and resonates with them. What seems so obvious to you can seem utterly meaningless to them. It's not unlike playing charades – the person miming can't believe the audience doesn't get it. The audience, on the other hand, just sees a series of baffling actions. This is the curse of knowledge.

The Heaths offer a number of ways to overcome this, including using metaphors and using concrete rather than abstract language. There is too much good advice in their book to do it justice by replicating it here. It is worth focusing on one of their tips, however, since this relates to a common problem within the field of technology and finance: how to communicate a complex message.

The very complexity of a message usually means it cannot easily be communicated with a few simple words. Complex messages have many facets and provisos. They involve complicated concepts rather than simple ideas and there is usually a lot of technical jargon involved. To communicate a complex message or concept in a quick and simple way we have to recognize a rather obvious fact: we already carry around with us lots of complex ideas and concepts, bundled up into simple to convey packages. Psychologists call these packages 'schemas'; each schema contains a set of assumptions about many different attributes and details. For example, our schema for a sports car contains assumptions about colour (red), speed (fast), number of doors (two), construction (soft top) and passengers (attractive).

To convey a complex message, therefore, we use what is already there in our audience's minds: their existing schema. In the Heaths' words, we plant a flag next to the schemas that are similar to the one we want to convey.

For example, a new technology platform that was being developed to improve transaction processing at a financial institution with aggressive growth plans was so complex the technologists behind it found it difficult to explain how it would change things for the users in different parts of the business. Since the implementation would involve a lot of change and upheaval, it was important the technologists behind it could quickly convey to non-technical people why it was required and what it would mean for them. I was involved in some of the early planning for the initiative, advising on some of the change management issues.

At these planning sessions I was struck by how dense some of the key messages were and that the supporting documentation seemed to make things worse rather than clearer. Much of this communication material was aimed at external audiences with the intention of gaining their commitment to the project and smoothing the way for the changes that were planned. But this was unlikely to happen if people did not clearly understand the benefits and the reasons behind the change. It seemed to me that in their inability to communicate the essence of the new system, the technologists were suffering from the curse of knowledge. They knew everything there was to know about the new system, but they just could not communicate it in a simple and compelling way.

Early in the change process I facilitated a communications workshop for the project team and explained the Heaths' concept of planting 'flags' next to an audience's existing schema as a way of communicating a complex message. With this in mind, the group developed a number of ideas about how to communicate the essence of the new system. Their final choice was 'The scale of Tesco, with the service quality of Harrods'.

While this does not by any means convey all of the details about the new platform, it gets across the essence of what it will mean, how it differed from the existing platform and why it was important. An audience would quickly understand that this new platform was intended to deal with a huge increase in transactions – it would have the scale of Tesco, the largest supermarket in the UK and a brand that accounts for £1 in every £8 that is spent in the country. But this scale was not being achieved at the cost of client service. On the contrary, the system would lead to the very highest levels of service. It would be the

'Harrods' of transaction systems. Achieving what are often competing goals of scale and quality conveyed how challenging the project would be and why it would be calling on so much resource.

By likening your idea or concept to something with which your audience is familiar, you can convey complex ideas quickly and with a minimum of detail. Of course, you will want to expand on this and add further detail, but now your audience will at least have a good idea of what you are talking about and the essence of your message.

LOGICAL STRUCTURE

Perhaps the most common failing in a presentation is to use too many slides, each with too much information on it. The audience loses its way, failing to see where the presenter is heading and how far there remains to go. Under these circumstances the central message easily gets lost and you will have failed to connect with your audience.

The simplest way to avoid this is to impose a logical structure to your presentation that signposts where you are and where you are heading. The simplest structure is to break your presentation down into three parts: the beginning, middle and end.

The beginning

Your aim here is to grab your audience's attention right from the start and to do this you need an opening gambit. This is more than simply an introduction to your presentation and an outline of what you are going to be covering. An opening gambit is something that makes the audience sit up and listen, and want to hear more.

Jerry Weissman, in his book on presentations referred to in the last chapter, lists seven possible opening gambits:

1. a question;

2. a striking fact or statistic;

3. a look backwards or forwards;

4.   an interesting anecdote;

5.   a powerful quotation;

6.   a familiar saying or proverb;

7.   an analogy.

For most presentations, the beginning is simply the first few minutes or so. It includes the introduction and the first few sentences or slides. Aim instead for something that has an immediate impact. The techniques listed above can ensure you achieve this and offer plenty of ways to do this.

Chip and Dan Heath explain why many of the things listed above work: they break a pattern and go against our expectations. They highlight a gap in our knowledge, raising our curiosity and compelling us to listen further. So, the opening to your presentation should tell the audience something unusual or unexpected. Another way of putting this is there should be a 'man bites dog' angle.

The middle

This is the main body of your presentation and you should think about how you want to structure the material so that it has a coherence and pattern that makes it easy and interesting for the audience to follow. Once again, Jerry Weissman is able to offer a number of alternatives. In his book he lists 16 flow structures – ways of organizing your material. One such structure is 'chronological', in which ideas are organized around a timeline. Another structure is 'problem/solution' and a third is 'features/benefits'. Others include 'issues/actions', 'opportunity/leverage' and 'rhetorical questions'. You may use more than one structure in a presentation, but Weissman warns against using more than three.

Another useful technique is to apply the concept of a chorus to your presentation. In most popular songs it's the chorus that people most easily recall and the part that you are likely to hum to yourself (and annoyingly, the part you can't seem to get out of your head!). To make your key message memorable, treat it like a chorus that you return to several times during your presentation. Using a catchphrase or slogan can help make this a feature of your presentation.

The ending

I see many presentations that come to a rather abrupt ending, where the presenter tells the audience that the presentation has ended, and then invites questions. Presentations that end in this way have missed the opportunity to finish in a way that is memorable and has some impact. Finishing with a summary or conclusion helps a little and at least signals the ending in a more obvious way. But think about how else you may be able to make your ending distinctive and memorable. Many of Weissman's opening gambits will work equally well as closing gambits: a powerful quote, a startling statistic, an anecdote or story will all mark the ending of your presentation in a way that again captures the attention of your audience.

DELIVERY

All of the above advice counts for very little if the way in which you actually deliver your presentation is poor. Often people don't realize how bad their delivery style is unless they see themselves on video. I remember one person who seemed to be engaged in an arm wrestling match with himself during his presentations, his two hands clasped together in a battle for supremacy. He later told me that he had once received feedback that he used too many hand gestures and that he should curb this by clasping his hands together. Until he saw himself on video, he did not realize how he was subconsciously trying to free himself from this, and how strange it all looked to a bemused audience.

Some people spend their whole presentation taking one or two steps forwards and backwards. Others sway from side to side. A surprising number of people are able to give a presentation without once establishing real eye contact with any of the people they are presenting to.

In my role at Catalyst running development programmes that often involve people giving presentations to their senior managers, I see countless examples of great content being dashed by poor delivery. Typically, there are two types of problems. The first concerns gestures and body movements and the second is more to do with hesitancy and poor speech.

Even with large audiences, collaborative leaders are able to make their presentation feel like a one-to-one conversation with each individual in the room. They seem relaxed and at ease with themselves and convey this through a natural style of speech and body language. How do they manage this and what might you learn from them? There are a number of things you can do to help you deliver your message in a smooth and confident way. All of them derive from a very simple fact: what your audience sees on the outside is a direct outcome of what is happening on the inside. The key to a well-delivered presentation therefore, lies in what you are thinking and feeling.

Clarity of purpose

The first, and perhaps most important thing, is to be absolutely clear on the purpose of your presentation and what you want to achieve by it. Without this, you will find it difficult to feel and project confidence, and there is a good chance you will meander somewhat when delivering your message.

A good way to establish this clarity is to write it down, completing the sentence, 'The purpose of the presentation is to …' This is not as easy as it may sound. Very often, when I ask people to state the purpose of their presentation they tell me what it is they are going to cover in their presentation. They say things like, 'The purpose is to outline the scale of the problem, how we investigated it and our proposals for a solution.' This is not the purpose of their presentation, but rather the means of achieving it. To get to the fundamental purpose, keep asking the question, 'Why?' In this example, the purpose might be to receive funding for a proposed solution.

Having clarity of purpose is a bit like finding the core of your message. It allows you to strip out anything that is superfluous to your message and to make decisions about sequence, style, format and so on. Ask yourself, does it help achieve my purpose? If it does not it should be removed.

A common mistake is to try to achieve your purpose by adding more and more content. People often believe that each additional slide or fact or diagram moves them a step closer to their goal. In fact the opposite is more likely to be true. Why make your presentation more difficult to deliver (and more difficult for your audience to absorb) by cluttering it with extra content? Your presentation is complete not when there is nothing left to add but when there is nothing left to take out without jeopardizing the purpose.

One of the ways clarity of purpose helps with your delivery is that it highlights any discrepancy between the content and your values and beliefs. Such discrepancies are responsible for our unconscious body language and gestures conveying nervousness, unease or lack of confidence. Once you are clear on your purpose you need to ask yourself if it is fully aligned with your beliefs and values. It's not unusual for people to present their proposals or findings while trying to obscure doubts they may have or gaps in their knowledge. Such discrepancies account for much of the nervous gestures the audience sees. Unless you are a very good actor, a relaxed and confident presentation can only be given if you are absolutely at ease with what you are aiming to achieve from your presentation.

Inner conviction

Clarity of purpose and alignment with your values and beliefs leads to a strong sense of inner conviction. Ask yourself if your audience is likely to be impressed or influenced by your presentation if they detect a lack of this and you can see how important it is.

Obviously, to convey conviction it has to be there in the first place. While you might have this conviction, it is unlikely you consciously think about it when giving a presentation. As a result, the audience receives no sense of it. So a good idea is to raise it to your level of conscious awareness. You can do this quite simply by thinking about why your message and core purpose is important to your audience. What will it help them achieve? How are you helping your audience? What benefits will they experience as a result of what you have to say?

If I am giving a presentation to attendees of a development programme I often remind myself why I am doing it and how they might benefit from hearing what I have to say. If I am describing a tool, technique or management skill I think about how they can benefit from applying it. I focus my thoughts on how useful the approach is and my desire to share it with the audience. 'This is really cool,' I think to myself, 'I'm sure you will find it very helpful in a number of situations.'

Obviously this will only work if I genuinely believe in the approach, which goes back to my earlier point about alignment. But by bringing these thoughts to the forefront of my consciousness I am allowing my sense of inner conviction to shine out to the audience.

Manage your state

One of the most common causes of poor delivery is nervousness. I am often asked how to avoid or reduce nervousness when giving a presentation. When I ask people what causes them to be nervous they sometimes refer to the pressure and demands of the situation; or they might mention the size of the audience or who is in it. Generally they see the cause lying in some aspect of the environment, something external to themselves.

I then follow up this question with another: *who* makes you nervous? Usually this brings a look of puzzlement. They can't think of any particular person who is making them nervous. Gradually it dawns on them: they do it themselves. This is the key to removing nerves.

I remember going through this routine with a person attending a session on presentation skills I was delivering to a group of technologists at an investment bank. While he reluctantly acknowledged that he was the person making himself nervous when giving a presentation, he seemed to think there was little he could do about this. When I asked him to describe the thought process that led to him feeling nervous he described how he worried about making mistakes, fluffing his lines and so on. 'I'm even feeling nervous now just thinking about it,' he said. Then he realized what he had just said, along with the rest of the group. The fact that he was able to reproduce the feeling of nervousness in the absence of any actual presentation was proof for all to see that the cause lies inside us.

Recognizing the thought processes that create nervousness and acknowledging that we, and only we, control these, lies at the heart of reducing nerves. Developing new thought processes is not as difficult as it may sound. The more we practise these the more ingrained they become and the old thought processes quickly atrophy. So, for example, instead of thinking of all the things that might go wrong, think positive thoughts about the strength of your message and how impressed your audience will be. Keep doing this and the old thoughts begin to be less habitual. In time they will be forgotten.

Breathing and posture

What people describe as nerves is usually an awareness that their breathing pattern has changed and their heart rate has increased. We can actually feel our heart beating in our chest and our laboured breathing interferes with our speech patterns. We hear the breathlessness in our voice, think about how the audience must have noticed this too, and experience a further increase in nervousness as a result. A vicious circle quickly ensues.

The relationship between our thoughts and physiological responses also works the other way round. By controlling our breathing, relaxing our muscles and reducing our heart rate, we begin to feel calm. Our thoughts become confident ones. We feel at ease. One of the most effective ways to start this virtuous circle is to control our breathing and body posture, taking long deep breaths, exhaling fully and standing erect but relaxed.

So, before you begin your presentation take control of your breathing and posture. Get plenty of oxygen into your lungs and get rid of any carbon dioxide harbouring at the bottom of them. Put your shoulders back and focus on conveying, through your stance and posture, confidence and ease. If you have to walk to the podium or front of the room, do so in an easy and confident way rather than stumble past chairs and tables.

In workshops to help people improve their delivery skills, I often ask each person in turn to stand up, walk to the front of the room, look at the group, introduce themselves and then return to their chair. I then ask them to repeat this exercise, but this time focusing on completing the whole process in a relaxed and confident way that includes good eye contact with the audience and a steady tone of voice that can be heard clearly by everyone in the room. The improvement is remarkable and shows how easy it can be to make a good confident entrance.

Slideware

Finally on the subject of delivering presentations, it is worth saying a little about how (or how not) to use presentational slideware. This represents one of the biggest stumbling blocks to a good, confident presentation. The way in which people have become accustomed to using software like PowerPoint means their presentations are often one-way communications, consisting largely of them reading what is written on their slides, rather than communicating in a genuine dialogue with their audience.

There are many researchers who have devoted much time and effort to analyzing this over-reliance on presentational software and how it might explain the failure to communicate effectively. Most notably, Edward Tufte has built his reputation on what he terms the 'cognitive style of PowerPoint', using it to explain glaring instances of a failure to communicate effectively, such as when NASA analysts failed to appreciate the risks communicated to them by engineers surrounding the re-entry of the Columbia Space Shuttle.

Rather than reiterate what Tufte and others have said about PowerPoint, it can be more helpful to focus on what might be done differently when giving a presentation. Realistically, people are not going to stop using PowerPoint slides when giving a presentation and neither are they likely to move away from the heading/bullet point format. Instead I will focus on a number of small points that can make a real difference in the way you give a presentation, making it more interactive and collaborative with your audience.

Don't confuse slides with documents

The first point is not to confuse your slides with a written document. Garr Reynolds makes this point in an excellent book called *Presentation Zen* (2008). He says that many presentations today are simply written documents which the presenter then projects onto a screen. He calls these 'slideuments' and their effect is to reduce the presenter to a reader. If all you are doing is reading from a slide, he asks, then why not just send out your slides in advance and cancel the presentation?

> *The slideument isn't effective, and isn't efficient, and it isn't pretty. Attempting to have slides both serve as projected visuals and as stand-alone handouts makes for bad visuals and bad documentation.*
> *(Reynolds, 2008, p.69)*

Don't use your slide as your script

Many people do something which is even less helpful: they put up a slide with paragraph upon paragraph of text and then talk over it in their own words. The human brain is not capable of simultaneously reading text and paying attention to a separate conversation, so either you or your slide becomes redundant.

People are sometimes wary of stripping this amount of detail from their presentation as it serves as a prompt to what they want to say. They find it reassuring to have their key messages clearly articulated on the slide, just in case they don't make a very good job of verbalizing them on the day. Unfortunately this solution to a lack of confidence creates a bigger problem than it solves and results in the situation described above. Prompts are best served by cue cards or a set of notes on the table that you can refer to. This frees your slideware up to be much more than simply text on a page.

Make your slide visual not textual

Slides are visual aids, so should be just that. They should enhance the point you want to make by adding some sort of visual representation, in the way a map can enhance verbal directions to a particular location. Sometimes this enhancement can be achieved by summarizing key messages and in this respect the use of a few short bullet points is perfectly acceptable. Unfortunately most bullet points run to whole paragraphs that the presenter uses as his or her own script to what they want to say.

Good slides leverage the old proverb of a picture being worth a thousand words. They capture something visually that would normally take quite a lot of effort to convey verbally. Diagrams are a great example of this, as are charts, as long as neither is too complex or cluttered. There may be times when there is no obvious way of visually enhancing your message and you are left with a slide that does not add that much. This is a great opportunity to reduce the number of slides in your presentation. While I have often heard of people complaining about 'death by PowerPoint', I have never heard anyone complain of there being too few slides in a presentation. So as far as the number of slides is concerned, less is more.

Interpersonal Communication

Collaborative leaders communicate at an interpersonal level markedly differently from more traditional leaders. Within the financial services, the latter style of leadership (I use that term loosely in this context) has largely involved something not unlike what might have been found in the armed services 20 years ago. I have known Chief Business Technologists and Chief Technology Officers to shout abuse at a direct report in full view of the latter's peers and colleagues. Fortunately this highly aggressive, dictatorial style is becoming less and less common, to be replaced by something much more humane.

However, collaborative leadership involves more than just being a nicer person to your staff. It requires a style of interpersonal communication that facilitates genuine collaboration. Remember from the first chapter, collaboration is defined as jointly finding a way ahead that feels like a win–win outcome. So how can you communicate with people in a way that facilitates this?

One of the most useful concepts is the idea that people can be described as either energizers or de-energizers, outlined in Chapter 2. The distinction between these two types, as outlined by Rob Cross and Andrew Parker in their book *The Hidden Power of Social Networks* (2004), shows that some people created high levels of energy through the way they communicate their ideas and proposals. In contrast, other people seemed to have 'an uncanny ability to drain the life out of a group' (p.50). Cross and Parker's analysis has strong intuitive appeal. Most of the people I share it with find it easy to think of people who fall into either category. They can also easily see the attraction of working with energizers and this spurs them to adopt the same behaviours themselves.

We can add a number of additional characteristics to this list that capture the essence of the way collaborative leaders communicate at an interpersonal level. Taken together they can help you evaluate your own style of communicating with others and whether it facilitates collaboration. Of course, most people collaborate with others at least some of the time. When considering these additional features you should ask yourself whether they apply to the way you communicate to those with whom you do not normally collaborate. This might be people further down the management hierarchy or people who are separated from you by geography, culture, lines of business or subject matter expertise.

SYNERGISTIC

Imagine if I were to lob a tennis ball in the air and before it fell to the ground you knocked it a little bit higher. I then did the same, followed by you again. Ignoring the physical limitations that would prevent this from actually happening for more than one or two passes between us, this process could ultimately result in the tennis ball reaching a height that neither of us would have believed possible were we just hitting the ball upwards on our own. This little thought experiment is a nice metaphor for how it feels when communicating with someone who can build on our ideas and who encourages us to build on their own contributions. We come away from the interaction feeling we have achieved something neither of us could have achieved on our own. A genuine synergy has been created.

This ability to build on ideas, and be open to builds on our own ideas, is a good hallmark of how to communicate at an interpersonal level in a way that fosters genuine collaboration. Collaborative leaders are able to do this with all kinds of people, not just those whom they see as knowledgeable and influential experts.

The conversation has a genuine two-way feel about it, in contrast to one where the other person just listens or does all the telling.

LEADS TO THE CREATION OF 'AHA' MOMENTS

The linking of two ideas that were previously unconnected has been described by psychologists as an 'aha' moment. It results in a rush of energy and positive emotion and often leads to insights that solve difficult problems. More will be written on this topic later in Chapter 5. For now it will suffice to highlight it as another feature of the way collaborative leaders communicate with others. In particular, they are able to help other people gain genuine insights and solve their own issues and dilemmas, not by giving them advice or telling them the 'answer', but by helping the other person really think about it in a new way.

OUTCOME-BASED

According to theorists in the field of neuro-linguistic programming, there are three general patterns in the way we might think about a problem or issue. The first is to see it as a problem and to look for the causes. This often leads to blame being apportioned and is backward looking in its perspective. A second type is referred to as action-thinking. This focuses attention on doing something quickly, without worrying too much about whether it is going to help in the long term. Engaging in all this activity promotes a feeling of being in control and is quite good at preventing problem-thinking and the consequent blame it generates. The focus of action-thinking is on the here-and-now. Both types of thinking are prevalent in many organizations when unexpected problems arise and neither is really helpful. In contrast, the third pattern involves thinking about the outcome we want to achieve. It is forward looking in its perspective and drives behaviour aimed at achieving that outcome.

When communicating at an interpersonal level, collaborative leaders are more likely to engage the other person in thinking about the outcome they want to achieve, rather than thinking about immediate actions or who or what might be to blame for an event or problem.

TRUST-BASED

Collaboration cannot really occur without trust and collaborative leaders are able to convey the trust they have in others through the way they communicate with them. This can be done in many different ways, but the essence is that the person on the receiving end feels a strong bond of trust connecting them to the leader. So, for example, trust can be communicated by taking a person's word or commitment at face value. All too often we convey a lack of trust by insisting on confirmations, checks and controls. Trust is also conveyed by focusing on the bigger picture and not being too detailed in how it will be achieved. At some point in time the detail will need to be added, but by not requiring this up front a person once again conveys his or her trust in others to follow through.

These various patterns of interpersonal communication sound reasonably straightforward, but be careful not to be taken in by their simplicity. In many situations, such as when dealing with difficult colleagues, or peers who do not have your interests at hearts, or those who are simply contracted by your organization to provide a service, it can be remarkably difficult to avoid slipping into a style of communication that hinders genuine collaboration.

You might also be tempted to save your most collaborative styles and approaches for those with whom it is relatively easy and pleasant to collaborate with. One of the biggest challenges facing organizations today is not how to foster collaboration within groups of like-minded people who have formed a strong bond over the years. It is how to collaborate with those outside of their own group, across organizational, geographical, functional and hierarchical boundaries. To develop your ability to lead collaboratively involves practising these patterns of communication with those whom fall into these latter categories.

5

Coaching

The complexity of technology within the financial services, and the speed at which it changes, means that people in leadership roles have to rely more and more on those they lead for sound technical advice. The old 'command and control' style of leading needs to be replaced by a more collaborative style in which the leader brings out the best in others.

Being able to coach rather than direct people is therefore a necessity for many technology leaders heading up complex global operations. But even if this were not the case, there are sound reasons for adopting a coaching approach. Put simply, being able to coach another person is probably the single most important thing you can do to motivate them, raise their performance, gain their buy-in to your decisions, build their commitment to you and the firm and ensure they remain loyal.

If that sounds a bit over the top, look back over this list of benefits. Motivation, buy-in, commitment and loyalty are all internal states. As such you cannot command others to feel these things, no matter how powerful you are in your organization. Neither can you buy them with financial rewards or other kinds of inducements. Sure, a pay-rise can make us feel committed and loyal, but only for a while. Just as the financial benefits fade with increasing financial outlays, so too does any strong sense of commitment or loyalty.

These internal states are therefore like gifts from their holders. They can be withdrawn at any time and as long as the person concerned is performing their job to the required level there is not much you, as their manager, can do about it. In other words, the other person has to *want* to give their best and *want* to be loyal and committed.

In today's financial markets, these attributes can make the difference between a highly successful firm and one that doesn't quite make it to the top of the performance ladder. The ultra-competitive nature of the industry means the winners are going to be those that can get the very best out of their people and this goes beyond paying them the highest rates. The turmoil experienced by all banks towards the end of 2008 and into 2009 meant that most had to drastically cut staff numbers and pare resources to the bone. The term 'sweating the assets' was used to describe the approach of getting more output from fewer people, but this has its limits. When people feel too much is being asked of them they find a way out, even if this means leaving the firm.

Major restructuring within many firms has meant new teams being formed from people who have seen their colleagues 'let go' and who now find themselves in a role they did not necessarily desire. Their managers have to find a way of getting the best out of them without having recourse to the big pay deals and bonuses of the past.

Under these conditions coaching is probably the only option available to them. Fortunately, as we shall see, it is also the most effective. This chapter outlines what coaching involves and some practical steps you can take to improve your ability to adopt a coaching style as the situation demands. This will help you considerably in becoming a more collaborative leader.

What is Coaching?

Most people in managerial and leadership roles have a working knowledge of what is meant by 'coaching'. Many associate the term 'coach' with a sports coach and imagine that coaching an individual or team in a work context involves playing a similar role. They assume this includes raising the performance of others by passing on expert advice and encouragement. In fact, as we shall see, coaching in an organizational context bears only a passing resemblance to sports coaching.

It is useful to think of coaching as occupying a position somewhere between the extremes of an authoritarian style of leadership and complete delegation. People sometimes confuse coaching with mentoring and it is true that mentoring also lies between these two extremes (see Figure 5.1).

X		X	X		X
Control		Mentor	Coach		Delegate

Figure 5.1 **The relationship between coaching and other styles of managing people**

Unlike mentoring, coaching does not depend on the coach having more experience or expertise than the person being coached. This is because the role of the coach is to help the other person to help themselves. In this respect the technique is ideally suited to the highly complex situations described by Stephen Norman in Chapter 3.

At this point you may be thinking, 'But what if the person being coached comes up with the wrong plan or solution?' Surely this would require the coach to step in and offer clear advice or guidance; perhaps even to adopt a 'telling' style rather than a coaching style? I am often faced with this response when introducing coaching skills on Catalyst's leadership programmes.

The answer is that coaching is not suited to all situations and in particular to those where there is a single correct solution. I remember one technologist telling me that after his manager attended one of our programmes he stopped giving answers to questions. Instead the manager met requests for help or advice with the question, 'What do you think?' In the end the technologist was forced to say, 'Just tell me the answer!'

Many problems do not have single correct answers though and even if they do their implementation is rarely straightforward. Coaching involves helping people gain greater clarity about their options, their priorities and the best way ahead in situations where there is no clear answer. It is ideally suited to helping people facing difficult decisions or complex situations where any course of action is likely to create even more problems.

There are many benefits to coaching. It is more likely to result in commitment and buy-in to the chosen course of action; very often the solution will be of a higher quality as a result of being developed by the person closest to the problem. Coaching is also likely to promote learning, since the person being coached will have developed their reasoning and problem-solving skills.

At a more generic level, leaders who adopt a coaching style are able to work *with* people rather than *through* people. Coaching builds collaboration since the person doing the coaching and the person being coached have worked together to achieve something that may not have been achieved by either party individually.

There are many good books and training courses on how to develop an ability to coach others. Like all skills it takes practice and patience. People often find it much harder than they think and in many cases they say the most difficult thing is avoiding the temptation to offer advice. They also struggle with their ability to listen, to *really* listen, to what the other person is saying. When I observe people practicing coaching in workshop settings I also notice how many of them simply fire a series of questions at the person being coached. The whole meeting looks and sounds like an interview. The person being coached pauses at the end of each answer he or she gives, waiting for the next question. The coach, meanwhile, searches frantically for the next question to ask, often asking something that does not really help move the conversation forward but which fills an awkward silence.

Most books and courses offer advice on how to develop critical skills like listening, questioning and giving feedback. This is combined with a structure or process to follow when in a coaching session. Probably the most popular of these is the GROW model, developed by Graham Alexander, Alan Fine and Sir John Whitmore (Whitmore, 2009), which works through the sequence of defining the goal (G); assessing the current situation (Reality, or R in the model), identifying obstacles (O); and jointly working out the way (W) forward. This is really helpful as it doesn't take too much to remember the steps involved through the simple acronym.

Recently, however, a new approach has been developed which, though somewhat more complex than the GROW model, can bring about startling results. The approach has been developed by David Rock and is outlined in his book *Quiet Leadership* (2006). What makes this approach unique is that it combines the usual skills and techniques that form the foundation of coaching with what neuroscientists have recently learned about how the brain works.

There are too many nuggets of information contained in Rock's book to do it justice in this chapter. The aim here is not to give you all the information you will need to become a proficient coach. The skills cannot be developed through simply reading about them, any more than one can learn to swim or ride a bike from reading a book. However, if you already have reasonably good listening and questioning skills you can improve your ability to coach and lead in a more collaborative way by taking on board some of the tips and techniques that follow.

Start with the Right Attitude

The starting point of developing an ability to coach others is to adopt an appropriate mindset or attitude towards coaching. I have seen numerous people try to learn coaching skills while not really believing in its usefulness, particularly in an investment banking context. They believe that coaching might work in the public sector, but that it has no real place in the hard-nosed world of finance. They might also believe it takes too much time and that by drawing the solution out from the other person they are introducing unnecessary risks. Their half-hearted attempts to 'coach' another person seem more driven by proving its failings.

To coach someone requires a firm belief in its efficacy and that it is worth putting in the time and effort involved. Being an effective coach also requires a degree of humility: you have to acknowledge your own shortcomings rather than just focus on those of the person you are coaching. If you believe you know the 'right' answer, you will find it very difficult not to guide the other person to this. Finally, you have to believe that the other person is capable of working out for themselves the way ahead. Central to all coaching is the belief that the answer lies within the person being coached.

If you are not sure about these benefits, simply reading about them here is unlikely to convince you. Instead, you will need to experience the benefits directly yourself. One way to do this is to think of a time when you have been coached, either formally or informally, by another person. If the person coaching you did a good job, you will probably have come away from the interaction feeling pleased that you had managed to work out for yourself the best way ahead.

Another way is to give it a try, with at least an open mind on your behalf. I recently witnessed a person's sheer joy at seeing the benefits of his first attempt at coaching one of his direct reports. Andrew, the head of insurance at a leading hedge fund, had attended a Catalyst leadership programme where coaching had been introduced. He had always believed that his role as manager of a small team was to help his direct reports by bringing his experience to bear on the day-to-day problems they faced. He questioned this after being introduced to coaching and decided to give more leeway to one of his direct reports, devolving greater responsibility to him and withholding his own natural desire to help by offering advice. Instead Andrew encouraged his direct report to develop his own solutions and plans. This required Andrew to acknowledge that he himself did not always have the best answer to a problem and that a different course of action developed by one of his directs might be more effective than his own.

Somewhat to Andrew's initial surprise, his direct report responded enthusiastically to being given greater responsibility and autonomy. Over the next few weeks he took on more responsibility, with Andrew adopting more of a coaching style when delegating work to him.

The proof of the pudding came a couple of months later when Andrew was attending a second instalment of the leadership programme. On the day he arrived a problem arose back at the office and an emergency board meeting was called. Andrew was expected to attend to provide expert input for the CEO to make a decision, but the course was in Zurich and the board meeting in London. Andrew contacted his direct report, not really believing he would be up for attending as his deputy. Yet his direct report felt confident he could handle the meeting and wanted to be given the opportunity. Andrew coached him though the preparation for the meeting, then kept his fingers crossed. A few hours later he spoke to an extremely happy employee. The meeting had gone particularly well and his direct report was almost overflowing with confidence and enthusiasm. Andrew himself felt he would burst with pride. I felt almost the same when he told me!

Andrew is now a convert to the benefits of coaching. On the way he has questioned his own approach to management and his role as a team leader. This has led him to acknowledge that he probably kept too much responsibility for decisions to himself. After his team member's success at the board meeting Andrew also found himself wondering whether others would see him as being 'out performed' by his team. Again this has had led to some readjustment to what he believes his role to be. He now sees it as enabling others to succeed, rather than succeeding himself with their support.

Focus on the Other Person's Thinking

If we want to help another person think a problem through and help them decide on an appropriate course of action, we need to focus on their thought processes. That might sound pretty obvious, but more often than not we focus our attention on the problem they are trying to solve rather than the way they are thinking about it. Once we do this it is almost inevitable we will think of possible solutions, making it very difficult for us not to voice these solutions in the form of advice. There's nothing wrong with giving advice, it's just not coaching. Assuming we want to coach rather than advise, one of the best ways of doing this is to focus our own and their attention on the way they are thinking about the problem.

Why might this help? David Rock offers several reasons. Firstly, people only really learn from thinking things through themselves. From a neurological standpoint this involves new connections being established in the brain. When someone works out a solution to a problem their brain is literally making a set of new connections between clusters of neurons.

A second reason is that when this happens the person concerned will experience what psychologists call an 'aha' moment. While this might not sound very technical, don't let the term fool you. There has been a great deal of neurological research into what happens when people experience 'aha' moments and one of the consequences is a burst of positive energy. Chemicals are released that prime the body for immediate action and the person experiences this as a strong sense of motivation. Helping them to think a problem through will therefore establish new learning and a strong desire to act on it.

A third reason is that their solution is likely to be better than our solution. They will know more about the situation and will probably have a greater insight into the kinds of things that are likely to work or not work. Our role in coaching them is to help them draw upon their insights, experience and knowledge. It is in this sense that we are helping them with their thinking. When we are dealing with technical problems – problems that have a correct answer – then experience and expertise certainly help. In situations where we know the solution we should probably offer it. But many of the problems people experience at work are not technical. They typically involve other people and are not very predictable. In these situations, it pays to help them work out their own solution rather than develop one for them.

Finally, helping a person to develop their own solution to a problem can be achieved very quickly and with relatively little effort. It takes a lot of our own mental energy trying to solve another person's problems or challenges. Because we know less about their situation than they do it also takes more time to get to the point where we might have a viable suggestion. More time is then spent convincing the person to adopt our proposals and if this can't be achieved we then waste even more time looking for a more acceptable solution.

David Rock sums up his approach to coaching by saying, 'Let them do all the thinking.' But what does this mean in practice? What is the coach doing while the other person is doing all the thinking?

First of all, it helps to focus on the solution rather than the problem. This means we should not spend too much time asking how the person has arrived at the point they are at, or who or what is to blame. Instead we should help them focus on what a good solution might look like. We should ask questions like:

'What is your end goal here?'

'What are the conditions a good solution must satisfy?'

'What are the options that can move you towards your solution?'

'What do you need to help you achieve your solution?'

'What obstacles might you face?'

According to David Rock, by focusing on solutions we are helping the other person to create new wiring in their brain rather than rely on the existing wiring that has so far prevented them from making progress. We are also helping them take responsibility for moving things forward. This is unlikely to happen if we focus on the problem, as this tends to be backward looking and can easily result in blame and negative emotions.

Another thing we should aim to do is stretch the other person, as this promotes growth, learning and change. We have to encourage them to arrive at solutions they might not yet have thought of or find a way out of a problem that they have already spent a lot of time trying to solve without much success.

In these situations, people often feel frustrated if they can't find a way forward. It is not unusual for them to look to the person coaching them for the answer.

It is important when coaching them that we do not give up easily or succumb to their request for 'the answer'. If I am coaching a person who tries but fails to find a new way ahead I normally point out that the difficulty they are experiencing is a good sign. It shows they are trying to think about the problem in a different way rather than rely on the existing thought processes that have not helped them so far. I then encourage them to continue with the process, reminding them that the difficulty they may be experiencing is a sign they are on the right track.

Stretching our minds is like stretching our muscles. It promotes growth and can only be achieved if there is some effort and even discomfort involved. When we push ourselves to succeed, success feels a lot more satisfying than when it is achieved with little or no effort. Remember, we are trying to help the other person get to an 'aha' experience where they feel a real buzz of excitement and energy through seeing something in an entirely new way. They can only do this if we encourage them to try and give them lots of positive feedback at each step of the way. So even half-formed ideas should be responded to positively, with encouragement to develop them further. It is important that we don't destroy any early signs of progress by evaluating these ideas or adding our own. Our goal is to nurture the development of the other person's thinking, not supplement it with our own.

If the person we are coaching finds it really difficult to think of their problem in a new way, it can sometimes help to spend a little time describing how they are currently thinking about it. Again, most people find this difficult as it requires them to describe a completely subjective and usually unconscious process. Our role is not to describe it for them, but to help *them* do this. So we might ask them to describe what they think an observer might see, encouraging them to look objectively at themselves.

Another tip is to find a metaphor for the way they are currently thinking about a problem; what is it similar to? For example, when recently coaching a manager who wanted to motivate his team following a round of substantial job losses, I asked him to describe the way he was thinking about this challenge. After much thinking and discussion, we both agreed that his approach was not unlike that of a fatherly figure wanting to solve his children's problems. With this description in mind he was able to see that his current mode of thinking and the way he was approaching the problem was quite paternalistic. This made it much easier to develop a new way of thinking about the challenge, which involved treating the team more like independent adults rather than trying to protect them from the harsh realities of the business world. He recognized that by trying to solve their problems he was denying them the sense of achievement they would experience by making their own way in the business world. He changed is role to enabler rather than problem solver and began to ask them what they needed from him.

Use a Structured Approach

Until we become fluent in coaching people, it helps to follow a set process or structure that guides us through a series of steps. David Rock offers an approach based on helping the other person to think more effectively about the problem they want to solve. His model has six different steps and each step is broken down into several further steps or approaches. For this reason I find it somewhat complex and it would be difficult for a novice to remember in detail. The acronyms he uses help a little, but I still feel it is a lot to learn for a newcomer to coaching.

The GROW model, described earlier, is an alternative process that I know from experience helps people who are new to coaching. The first step, after putting the person at ease and building rapport with them, is to help define the goal: what is it the person wants to achieve? Our aim here is to help them see beyond the problem and look towards the solution. It also helps to know why that goal is important to them, as often when asked their goal people describe their solution rather than the outcome of that solution. So, for example, a person might state their goal is to build a highly motivated and successful team. But this may only be the means to their bigger goal, which might be to be promoted as a result of raising the performance of their team.

Usually, these end goals are experienced as highly motivating, so helping the other person be really clear on the end goal will help them to view our coaching positively. Once they have defined their goal the next step is to assess the current situation, or Reality in the GROW model. This involves eliciting the other person's description of the challenge they face. Our aim is to help them obtain a realistic assessment of this, so that they can understand what will need to change for them to meet their goal.

At this stage it is important the coach listens for any perceptions or interpretations that might be holding the person back. For example, I recently coached someone who wanted to develop a wider network of contacts across his firm, including people in overseas locations. His end goal was to raise his profile as well as that of the department he headed. In describing the current situation he talked a lot about how networking did not come naturally to him, mentioning several times that he was an introvert. He compared himself unfavourably to extroverts, whom he said had a wide range of contacts and found it easy to build new ones.

It was a typical example of the kind of limiting belief I discussed in Chapter 1. Not only did it provide him with an explanation of why other people seemed to build extensive relationships, it also explained his own lack of success in this skill. My next step was to reflect back to him what I sensed he believed about introverts, extroverts and networking, and he recognized that he implicitly held this belief and that it might be holding him back. Once articulated, the belief could be challenged and, if he chose to do so, disposed of. The more he thought about it, the more he recognized that he had been using this assumption as an excuse. This was the start of letting the belief go and developing alternative beliefs that would help him overcome his reluctance to build new relationships.

During this stage in the coaching he also said that other people might be annoyed if he contacted them without a specific need to have the conversation. I asked him to put himself in the shoes of someone contacted by someone keen to get to know them better. He quickly recognized this could be quite flattering and that his belief that it would be otherwise was another limiting factor.

Our overall aim in the process is to help the other person see their potential for growth and to demonstrate our belief in their ability to achieve it. As Rock says, 'The assumption we make … is that people have the answers and we're just here to help them think' (p.77). This brings us to the next stage in the GROW model, which is to help the person we are coaching identify and overcome any Obstacles to achieving their goal. Now more than ever we have to believe the answer lies in them (not in our head!) and we are there to help them discover it. This is where we want to help them make new connections and develop solutions they may not have thought of before.

According to David Rock, perceived obstacles usually boil down to a dilemma and the role of the coach is to help the other person resolve the dilemma by having an insight for themselves. This process begins with a period of reflection, where the person being coached thinks about their dilemma in a specific way. Up until this point they have probably been thinking about their options in a very logical way, weighing up the alternatives and not being able to find a suitable way ahead. But this kind of logical thinking rarely leads to new insights. Most creative thinking occurs when we allow unusual connections to be made without worrying too much whether they involve sound reasoning.

I once coached someone who was working as a business manager within a technology function. He felt he needed to take on a bigger role with more responsibility for setting direction. He was at a crossroads in his career and was finding it difficult to decide on the best type of role to pursue and whether to leave the bank. One of his key strengths was his ability to execute a plan and he was approaching his dilemma in pretty much the same way as he might a major project. Each option was being carefully explored and evaluated against a set of criteria he felt any new role had to satisfy. But this was taking more time than he had available. His dilemma was how to make this important decision without the thorough analysis it demanded.

Using the power of metaphor I suggested his approach was akin to buying a new house or car and asked whether this approach had helped him secure previous roles in his career. At this point I could literally see him making new connections as he recognized that every previous role had been the result of someone suggesting the role to him rather than the approach he was now adopting. Suddenly he could see that he had to stop thinking about what role would best suit him, trying to arrive at the solution through logic and deduction. Instead he recognized he needed to tap into his network of contacts, making it known that he was looking for a new role and was open-minded about what area it might be in. Within just a couple of months he had been offered a new role working in the Front Office.

Research into creative thinking and the brain suggests that these new connections are more likely to be made when we stop consciously thinking about the problem and allow the unconscious part of the brain to process the information. In practical terms this means distracting ourselves with something else, perhaps by going for a walk or 'sleeping on the problem'. During a coaching session it may help, therefore, to move on to something else or wind the session up and agree to revisit the topic next time. It is important not to put the person under pressure to come up with a solution quickly, but to allow them the freedom to explore unconventional and perhaps illogical ideas with a view to seeing the problem in a new light.

The final stage of the GROW model involves helping the other person to plan their next steps and Way forward. It is important that any new insights developed during the coaching session result in real actions that will help move the person towards their goal. Although the person will undoubtedly feel energized by any insights and 'aha' moments, the reality of day-to-day demands means any good intentions can easily remain just that.

The best way the coach can help is to move the conversation towards more detail and specifics. An idea to 'draw upon my existing network of contacts' has to be turned into something far more specific with questions about who, when, where and so on. Deadlines help make these plans measurable and capable of future review. Mentioning that the execution of the plan will be reviewed in the next session will also increase the likelihood of it being put into action.

At the next session, it is important that this review is conducted honestly and diligently. In my experience, people who have not really put their plans into action will often attempt to play down their lack of effort. They might say the situation has changed, becoming less pressing and not really requiring further action. Or they might talk in quite general terms about how they have been handling things differently and in line with what had been agreed at the last coaching session.

David Rock offers the acronym FEELING as a way of structuring this follow-up conversation. The coach should establish some specific Facts, rather than general conclusions about what has been achieved. Once this has been done the coach should then explore how the person feels (Emotions) about what they have or have not achieved and Encourage them to continue with their efforts. Any new Learning and the Implications of this should then be explored, before finishing the conversation with an agreement about New Goals. Having used this approach myself I find it a very helpful way of conducting a meaningful progress review. Don't worry too much about remembering every single letter in the acronym and what it stands for. No one will notice if you miss a step and you don't want to be focusing so much of your attention on following the process that you fail to listen properly to what the person is saying.

The Benefits of Coaching

For people schooled in the traditional forms of management within, say, a global investment bank, coaching can seem like a soft option. Time is money, they might say, and we are dealing with very well paid people who at times just need to follow orders rather than take the time to decide on their own preferred course of action. It is true that coaching does not help in every situation, especially where time is limited, such as in a crisis. But the reality of most organizations is that most problems are complex, involve people and have no single or technically correct answer. In these situations, it can be important to work collaboratively with your direct reports rather than to bark orders at them and coaching provides a proven approach to how best to do this.

While managers today are generally more enlightened about the need to bring people with them rather than enforcing instructions, they may not fully appreciate the benefits of coaching until they actually try it. David, the head of performance management sat a hedge fund, had attended one of Catalyst's leadership programmes where he learnt the principles involved in coaching. I interviewed him a few months after the programme to hear how he had put his learning into practice. He started with a frank admission about how he had previously managed his team:

> *I suppose I used to listen but not really listen, and then tell them what I thought the answer was. What I now do more of is actually listening and really understanding what the problem is and then getting them to answer it themselves. Before I basically said, 'Oh yes, done that before, it'll be fine, you just need to do this.'*

He now focuses on helping them to think through an issue, in much the same way as suggested above:

> *Now I say, 'What do you think the problem is?' It's more about getting them to think about the issue, think about the people involved, what they need to do. I start the discussion around what they think about what the situation is. I then ask, 'What do you think you should do? What should happen next?'*

The difference in approach was more than just cosmetic or stylistic. For David it had the benefit of creating much greater commitment and buy-in to a course of action:

> *Whereas before I would say, 'You need to do this' and not even get to the issues, it would never get done because they didn't buy into it as it was hard work. It does feel more now that when you get them to think*

of things themselves they go through the problem solving and they work out what the steps are going to be, they feel as though it's their plan and they can go away and deliver that because they've come up with a way that they can do it.

His approach has involved greater responsibility being devolved to his direct reports, with clear benefits to them and others:

I suppose it's more about getting people to take responsibility for themselves and whilst it's hard initially for them, and probably for me too, in the longer run it's beneficial to the organization, to them, and to me because I get much more out of them because they can think for themselves and take much more responsibility for things, and I have a lot less 'I can't do this' from them.

Devolving responsibility required David to let go of control, something he found quite hard to do initially:

In terms of letting go of control, it's hard. Historically I sort of said, 'Right, this is what I've got to do.' Over the last six months I've said, 'I shouldn't be doing that because it doesn't develop the team and doesn't give them ownership to commit their hearts and minds.' Letting go involves saying, 'It's yours and I'm not going to get involved unless you want me to, because I know you can do this.' But unless you trust them fully they'll never take the ownership.

It took a leap of faith on his part to put this into practice in a meaningful way:

I tried this approach on a big thing that my team looks after, the operating plan process, and I could see the person was quite capable of taking this on and so I let them and I did take a big step back. I saw the benefits of that, and once you see the benefits it's a lot easier to do it again.

David went on to describe how he had adopted a coaching approach with a new recruit to his team:

Somebody who joined my team recently, I can only describe as very capable but not confident in her ability, always apologising, thinking she had said the wrong thing, very shy in meetings. She knew the answers but wasn't prepared to share it, and I like to think I've helped her change. She has a very different attitude now, very capable in meetings, prepared to step forward and say 'I don't agree' which would never have happened in the past. She is much less apologetic, very much more assertive. It's a complete change in the way she thinks about things. Whereas before, to me, she was quite disempowered and didn't feel she could do anything about it, now she feels it's her responsibility and she knows she can do something about it. I said to her, 'I know you're more than capable of this, I know you get the right answer, so in this next meeting I'm going to take a back seat. If you get it wrong – but you won't – I can chip in, but you're going to be fine.' You know, having those sorts of conversations. Again, it's the empowerment thing.

David's experience is typical of those who work hard to develop a more collaborative style of leading others. The coaching techniques described in this chapter show what is involved in this, but be careful not to underestimate the challenges you might face if this is new to you. Coaching involves genuinely believing in the capability of the person you are coaching. You have to really believe the answer lies within them and that your role is to help them discover this. One of the hardest things to do is recognize that this answer may be very different to your own and that your role as coach is to help the person think through their plan of action and then put it into effect. You will almost certainly experience a sense of loss of control as you hand over responsibility for following through on this course of action. But if you can overcome these challenges, you are likely to experience one of the most positive consequences of leading and managing other people: seeing their own growth and development.

6

Finding Common Ground

One of the biggest challenges faced by anyone leading a complex organization is getting all the parts pulling in the same direction. Notice the word 'pulling' here. This is about their behaviour not yours. While as leader you may set a strategic goal for the whole of your organization, you will inevitably feel at times like people are doing things in spite of this goal rather than because of it. At times it will feel like your organization is pulling itself apart as people apparently head in different directions.

Leading collaboratively involves reconciling an apparent contradiction that many leaders constantly struggle with. Within the financial services, and within Technology functions in particular, the shape of the modern organizational structure creates silos. These silos are the result of increasing specialization. They are necessary to ensure experts staff each part of a complex whole and that these remain close to customers and their needs. Yet one of the most common complaints I hear from managers and staff alike is 'we are very siloed here'.

Matthew Hampson, head of Architecture & Change at The Royal Bank of Scotland's investment banking division, described the process by which organizations like his own can easily become a collection of silos:

> The industry itself is set up not to encourage collaboration. The flaws are in the way we pay people and reward people. Ultimately it's a competitive system; we have a ranking culture. And ranking cultures I think are really good, but they're set up in a very competitive, adversarial way. 'I have to be better than you; I have to have done more stuff than you have.' The problem is that stuff tends to be based on individual objectives. It tends to be 'you as a person are responsible to get this stuff done'.

That creates quite a singular-focused individual, which is good and productive on one hand, but is also not very good for collaboration. There are natural tensions. I think that if we're ever going to move collaboration on and get it working properly we will need to change the way we reward people. It has to be more; people have to have shared objectives and common goals. These are the things that ultimately make people believe they're going to be rewarded if they're collaborative.

The fact is, silos are a necessary and important part of any complex organization. The aim is not to abolish them, but to maintain them. The problem that a leader needs to resolve is how to manage some of the negative consequences of silos. Most of these consequences centre on the behaviour of the individuals heading the silos and those operating within them.

When I refer to siloed behaviour I mean things like:

- information not being freely shared between functions, with the consequence that important things are not learnt and the same mistakes keep occurring;

- people not adapting to changes that are taking place elsewhere; becoming isolated and displaying a 'not invented here' attitude;

- high levels of duplication across silos and limited reuse;

- each silo developing its own way of doing things, with the consequence that there are multiple approaches and systems and very little consistency between them;

- goals being pursued by one silo in a way that prevents others from achieving their own goals;

- conflict between people in different silos, as they compete for scarce resources or fail to find common ways of working together;

- multiple ways of measuring performance, with the result that no one really knows how well the organization is performing.

If any or most of these sound familiar to you, much of your time is probably being spent dealing with the fallout. You may find yourself having to intervene between warring factions or initiating a major investment in architecture to resolve some of the differences in technology and its uses. You will probably look in exasperation at how little reuse is taking place and wonder why people continue to make the same kinds of mistakes.

Within this context, collaboration may sound like a distant dream, something which might happen to others but which makes a very rare appearance in your own organization. Yet collaboration is possible within this framework. In fact, developing collaboration across the silos of an organization while maintaining them should be one of your key roles as a collaborative leader. So far we have looked at a number of skills required to lead others in a collaborative rather than autocratic or charismatic way. Now it's time to consider how you can get everyone working towards a common goal or outcome.

There are two aspects to this challenge, the first organizational and the second individual. Both involve recognizing some important facts about human behaviour. Perhaps surprisingly, the situation many leaders find themselves in is entirely predictable if we consider the psychological aspects of work. While this might appear somewhat depressing, the good news is that psychology can also provide the answer.

Organizational Goals

It almost goes without saying that goals help focus effort and motivate people to achieve them. Objectives are set for departments, functions and individuals that guide them in the right direction and provide a means of measuring progress, taking corrective action and rewarding achievement. Projects will also have specific objectives, with sub-goals, or milestones, along the way.

To the extent that these goals are independent of each other, they will have a generally positive effect of galvanizing performance. However, in most organizations these goals are at least interdependent and in some cases the overlap is large enough to create a zero–sum outcome. When different lines of business submit their business plans for the forthcoming year, they are all effectively drawing from a single overall budget. More money for one line of business will inevitably mean less to be shared out for all the others.

This is significant because in situations where zero–sum goals exist, conflict can easily emerge between the parties concerned. Early psychological research in the 1950s demonstrated the effects of competitive goals on group behaviour and intergroup conflict. In a classic field study, Muzafer Sherif set up a series of competitive sports and games between two groups of 11-year-old boys at a summer camp. Sherif had carefully selected the boys chosen to attend the camp, ensuring they were similar in terms of age, social class, ethnicity and religion – all the usual differences that were thought to create conflict between sections of society. Despite their similarities, the two groups of boys became highly antagonistic towards each other once the competitive activities were introduced. When skirmishes escalated to fighting, Sherif was forced to abandon the experiment early. His hypothesis that conflict between groups was the result of competitive goals had been supported in the most dramatic way.

Morten Hansen, in his book *Collaboration* (Hansen, 2009) has highlighted Sherif's work and its implications for organizations today. He says that leaders need to 'beware how easily interunit rivalry can take hold and undermine collaboration' (p.74). As a result of creating largely autonomous business lines, each with their own performance objectives, separate targets and independent responsibilities, situations can arise that encourage managers to compete for scarce resources rather than collaborate. Time spent helping one unit means less time for one's own unit. Talented individuals are encouraged to remain loyal to their business unit rather than move across to other units as a way of sharing their knowledge and experience. Application developers may be more inclined to meet their own targets for building new software, even though it may not be fully tested and create problems further down the line for those charged with supporting it.

Competition for limited resources such as time, budget and talented individuals is just one of a number of variables that psychologists have found related to the genesis of conflict between groups. Other variables are:

Interdependence: groups that are highly dependent on others in the value chain can easily find themselves in conflict with each other. When work from one unit is delayed, not provided or contains errors, it has a negative impact on others further down the value stream and this in turn leads to conflict.

Role ambiguity: lack of clarity over who is responsible for what means that important tasks sometimes are not carried out, which results in problems for others. Other tasks occupy 'grey areas', where no one wants to accept responsibility for performing them. Each party typically sees it as the responsibility of the other party to perform certain tasks, especially if they take time, have limited value and consume scarce resources. The result is further friction between groups concerned.

Reward systems: there are different ways to reward performance on an individual or group basis and the type of system chosen can affect the degree to which people collaborate or compete with each other. Conflict is more likely if rewards are distributed on a 'winner takes all' basis. While this system is relatively uncommon outside of sales organizations, other types of systems can cause conflict. In particular, if rewards in one department are based on meeting production targets, while another department is rewarded for keeping costs down or quality high, there will inevitably be conflict as one pursues volume even though it results in poorer quality products and problems for others.

Group identity: a series of experimental studies at Bristol University in the 1970s showed that subjects showed a preference for others in their own group even though they did not know who they were or who belonged to the other groups. It seems that simply belonging to a group can produce feelings of pride in the group and negative attitudes towards 'outsiders'. Given the different boundaries along which group identities can be drawn in most organizations today (company, line of business, geographical region, culture and so on) it is almost inevitable that an 'us versus them' attitude will develop among some.

When some or all of these factors come together, the outcome is invariably some form of conflict between work groups. While this is unlikely to escalate to the destructive patterns of behaviour observed by Sherif, it does mean that collaborative behaviours tend to become in short supply. Information may not be shared openly. Requests for help may not be responded to promptly. Problems may arise in one area as a direct but not necessarily intended consequence of actions in a different area.

The relative ease with which these factors can escalate into conflict is demonstrated time after time when participants on our leadership programmes play a version of the 'prisoner's dilemma'. This has been developed from game theory to test the effect of zero–sum reward structures on group and individual behaviour. In our version, participants are presented with the following instructions:

> *Your team must make one of two choices, between chalk and cheese. The other team will be asked to make the same decision. When both teams have decided, the facilitator will announce the decisions.*

Points are awarded, based on the schedule shown in Figure 6.1.

If Team 1 plays	and	Team 2 plays	The score is	Team 1 score	Team 2 score
Chalk		Chalk		+3	+3
Chalk		Cheese		-6	+6
Cheese		Chalk		+6	-6
Cheese		Cheese		-3	-3

Figure 6.1   **Reward schedule for the chalk and cheese game**

Each team is told the objective is to achieve the highest score it can and that several rounds will be played. The teams are not allowed to communicate with each other and the points distribution is announced at the end of each round.

The exercise pits cooperative strategies against competitive strategies. Team 1 can choose 'chalk' in the hope Team 2 will do likewise and both will share 3 points each. But if Team 2 chooses 'cheese' instead, Team 1 will lose 3 points while Team 2 gains 6 points. Typically, the members of Team 1 decide they cannot trust Team 2 to choose 'chalk', so Team 1 opts for 'cheese' instead. When faced with identical choices, Team 2 typically goes through a similar thought process and also chooses 'cheese', with the outcome that both teams end up with a score of -3. In these circumstances both teams typically make similar choices in subsequent rounds, getting deeper and deeper into the red.

Not all score patterns follow this sequence. Sometimes participants choose 'chalk' in the first or early rounds. This is fine if the other group does likewise. However, once a team recognizes it can double its points by choosing 'cheese' it will usually break with the pattern. This almost always has the effect of damaging the relationship and the other team quickly reverts to 'cheese' itself, locking both groups into a downward spiral again.

It is usually quite rare for any team to obtain a positive cumulative score if the game is played over several rounds. While both teams recognize they are failing to obtain any points (the objective of the game) they are more concerned with 'beating' the other team or teaching it a lesson. Their aim is to ensure the other team has fewer points than they have or at the very least that the other team also ends up with a negative score. Allowing some form of communication between the teams does not prevent this, as deals agreed are reneged on in subsequent rounds in order to obtain extra points.

The chalk and cheese game shows how easy it is to create conflict between two groups and how difficult it can be for the groups to collaborate under such circumstances. Both teams recognize that the rational approach is to choose 'chalk' at each round, sharing 3 points and building up a handsome total over several rounds. But their lack of trust in the other team, exacerbated by limited communication, and a desire to 'win' or to 'punish', means that as much as they can see the benefits of collaborating they are unable to achieve it.

The game brings into play a number of the factors listed above as causes of conflict between groups. There is a zero–sum reward system, shared interdependence, ambiguity over the overall purpose and each team's role in achieving it, and a strong sense of 'us versus them'.

You can see versions of the Prisoner's Dilemma being played out in most complex organizations. I remember a CIO asking all his Chief Technology Officers (CTOs) to submit substantially lower budget requests for the forthcoming year and being surprised and dismayed when they all came back with budgets that were virtually the same as the previous year. A second round produced near identical results. Why wasn't each making the aggressive cuts he had asked for? The reason is that each CTO had one of two choices corresponding to chalk and cheese. The overall budget had been fixed. Each CTO could make a substantial cut and the overall budget would be met. But what if others made smaller cuts and got their budget approved? The CTOs could not trust each other to deliver the significant cuts required. In the end, the CIO took the choice from them and determined the cut required from each line of business.

It seems like the very structure of an organization, usually referred to as its operating model, is destined to bring about conflict. What can leaders do in this situation to ensure their whole organization works together in a coordinated way and that conflict does not reduce overall performance?

A clue is provided when we look back to Sherif's early research into the effect of goals on group behaviour. Sherif replicated his initial study and found similar results, but a third study attempted to address the conflict he had created. In this study he put the groups through the same initial rounds of competing with each other in games where there were clear winners and losers.

But then he introduced a third stage, where a series of apparently unplanned events required both groups of boys to work together to achieve goals that would benefit them all. The first was a blockage in the water supply. All the boys had to trace the complex system of pipes and drainage to locate where the blockage was and remove it. A second problem concerned the breakdown of the truck bringing much needed supplies to the camp. All the boys had to tug the truck out of mud and get it started again. On the last night of the camp there was an opportunity to hire a film from a local supplier, but only if all the boys contributed equal sums of money to meet the cost.

Sherif and his team of researchers carefully set up each of these situations to create what he referred to as a 'superordinate goal': a goal that could only be achieved by both teams working together. The effect of such goals was to reduce the conflict that had been created by the competitive goals. Sherif found that friendships started to form across group lines and the boys started sharing things with each other. On the last day, when given the chance of travelling home in two separate buses or one large bus, they chose the latter.

In his book *Collaboration*, Morten Hansen suggests leaders can learn from this and create similar shared goals that will unite their disparate lines of business. According to Hansen, such goals must meet four conditions:

Common fate: first it must be a superordinate goal that can only be achieved by all divisions working together. For example, one technology organization I know of set an aggressive cost base goal for the whole of technology. This, rather than separate goals for each business line, became their goal for the next two years.

Simple and concrete: abstract goals that are difficult to measure cannot unify different divisions. The goal of being number one or two in a particular market, as measured by a recognized performance index, is both simple and concrete. The goal of being 'world class' or a 'leading technology organization' or a 'great place to work' is less so. The latter are open to different interpretations, are difficult to measure and complex rather than simple in terms of what they mean to people.

Stir passion: by this Hansen means the goal should appeal to hearts rather than just minds. It should have a strong emotional content and inspire people to achieve it. Cost-cutting goals are unlikely to meet this criterion, while goals that focus on tapping into a sense of pride or excellence can.

External competition: competition can be a very powerful driving force. It is important that the goal places the competitor on the outside of the company, not within its own boundaries. Hansen puts it very simply: 'collaboration on the inside, competition on the outside'. This should not, however, mean that external partners in the value chain become competitors.

Of course, simply setting superordinate goals that stir passion and create enemies of external competitors will not on its own create a culture of collaboration. But it will help break down some of the barriers created by internal goals that set business unit against business unit. When coupled with core values that promote teamwork and reward collaborative behaviour, this approach can start to build a different pattern of working that overcomes the problems created by silos without having to dismantle them and lose the benefits they bring.

Scott Marcar gave a good example of this when describing to me how he leads his team at The Royal Bank of Scotland:

> *I make it clear to people up front that our role as a team is to be a team. We are not going to tolerate competition within the team. That's different to some other banks, where people are set up in competition with each other. While this can breed individual excellence, in the longer term it is dysfunctional. Competition can be a fantastic way of driving excellence, but you also see more examples of bad behaviour than if you collaborate. The net impact is greater if you collaborate, and you get a lot more even distribution of effort in a collaborative environment, and that is the approach we have chosen.*

Adrian Kunzle is global head of Architecture at JPMorgan Chase. One of his roles is to ensure the firm has the best technology architecture to compete across the industry, and to do this in the most cost-effective way. It is vital his people collaborate across business lines, geographical regions and value chains since this will ensure best practice is widely shared and people avoid unnecessary duplication of work. He recognizes the difficulty of building a collaborative culture, due to the presence of individual-based goals and the silos they can create:

> *When you build a group, you build them up around a goal. That's when these silos stop communicating with each other, because you have this stark contrast where you are either with the team aiming for that goal or*

you're not. It then becomes very hard for that silo to leverage expertise from outside, mainly because of a lack of trust. They don't feel the person providing the information needed is part of the same goal, and therefore they can't rely upon them and they get excluded, no matter how good their ideas are.

He described to me his own experience of how these groups then become highly cohesive within their silo and start to differentiate themselves from those belonging to other silos:

If you have a concentration of people in a particular location, you start to get silo thinking within that team. If you have three teams in three different locations you will see those three becoming cohesive within their location and they stop talking to each other. The more they get comfortable with their own group, the less they talk to the other ones.

Adrian Kunzle's answer to this problem is to break down these silos very explicitly by encouraging and rewarding collaboration across them and setting superordinate goals:

Part of my leadership style that I've started to form is being generous with credit for those who collaborate and trying to make it very hard to be successful in a team if you do not collaborate. I've been doing a couple of things. First of all, if I see links and opportunities to collaborate and the person is not doing this, I will have a very specific conversation with them setting a concrete expectation that they collaborate. If I can go as far as setting specific interactions as a goal for both parties, I will. I also try to construct projects in a way that requires people to work together and which can't be achieved without that.

Adrian Kunzle's experience lends real world substance to the theoretical models developed by social and organizational psychologists. The group cohesiveness observed by the latter when creating competitive goals translates easily to the organizational silos that prevent collaboration across global businesses. Rebuilding collaboration requires a conscious effort to elicit and reward those who reach outside their silos and who work towards higher-level goals in the interests of the whole organization.

Individual Behaviour

Leading collaboratively requires an ability to work with others at an individual level that helps bring about genuine collaboration. So far we have looked at how leaders can set organizational goals in ways that builds collaboration across business units, but what about collaboration between individuals?

Very often people get locked into disagreements with others that quickly escalate into some form of conflict or at the very least an impasse. In Chapter 3 we looked at a pattern of influencing that diffuses conflict by allowing the other party to express fully their point of view. In this section I will outline a similar and effective method of finding a way out of an apparent impasse between two individuals. As a collaborative leader this is one of the most powerful patterns of behaviour you can practise and if done skilfully will help you avoid the individual conflicts that can scupper your attempts to lead collaboratively.

The technique is called 'logical levelling' and its origins lie in the field of neuro-linguistic programming. In many respects it resembles the technique of setting a superordinate goal as a way of building collaboration. To demonstrate what is meant by a logical level, consider something like a car. In answer to the question, 'What are the main constituents of a car?' we can identify things like the engine, the bodywork, the seats, the electrical system, fuel system and so on. Suppose we take one of these, the engine. This can be broken down into further parts, such as the gearbox, the differential, a distributor and so on. The gearbox is made up of various cogs and levers and these in turn are made of some form of metal alloy.

In this example we have taken a car and moved down various logical levels until we arrive at basic substances. These could be further broken down into elements, molecules and atoms. Suppose now we were to start with a car again, but this time move *up* logical levels. What is a car an example of? It is a form of transport. This in turn is a form of motion. Motion is an example of the laws of physics. At this high logical level, we start to enter the world of metaphysics and if we continue we usually end up at something like 'existence' or 'God'.

The point of this exercise is to show that conversations tend to take place at a particular logical level and that we can move the conversation to either a lower or a higher logical level. Thus conversations about cars might boil down to conversations about gearboxes (going down logical levels) or about status symbols (going up logical levels). This is important because most conflicts take place at a specific level and one effective way of resolving them is to move up a logical level or two.

For example, disagreements about whether to buy or build a new piece of software might become embroiled in details about an external vendor and the internal development team. In trying to make the decision, we move down logical levels, comparing the details of both potential suppliers against set criteria. The discussion can quickly become quite tactical in nature and centre on disagreements in very specific details with no clear way of resolving the debate.

However, by moving the conversation *up* a logical level, we move out of the detail and start to explore 'purpose'. It's the same as identifying a superordinate goal: once we have got the bigger picture in mind we can usually find a lot of common ground. By definition, pursuing this common ground means we work towards a shared goal, reducing the conflict.

In the example above, we move the discussion up a logical level by asking questions like, 'What is the purpose we want to achieve?' or 'What will the new software (whoever supplies it) enable?' This should take the conversation out of details around price, delivery time and reliability, and into the realm of purpose and goals. The higher-level goal might centre on things like increased business growth or greater compliance with regulations. We can then focus our efforts on how to achieve this goal, rather than deciding which is the best developer of a piece of software.

It's a funny thing but, from this more lofty position, alternative solutions that were not entertained at the lower level of detail become more visible. Increased growth might be achieved by means other than the new software. Greater compliance might be achieved through better training.

In fact, this approach is often used by business analysts when they identify user requirements. Instead of asking specific questions about the functionality of a new system they ask why it is needed. What is the problem it will solve? They know that users often request things that in their own mind are solutions to problems that have not been articulated. Instead of building that solution, the analyst finds out what the problem is because then they can suggest alternative and more effective solutions rather than just building what has been asked for (which usually meets with the response, 'I know I asked for it but it's not what I want').

Many of the technologists I work with recognize this approach, even though it is not one that has been formally taught to them. They know from experience that asking 'why?' is a better response to a request than 'how much?' or 'when?' However, in practice they find it difficult to move a conversation up logical levels, being much more practised in going down into the details.

For this reason it is worth practicing the technique, especially the art of moving a conversation up logical levels. As a means of finding collaborative solutions to problems it is one of the most effective tools you can employ, but it does require a little skill and practise. There are a number of stock phrases that move a conversation up logical levels and you should become familiar and at ease in using these. Questions like, 'What will that enable you to do?' and 'How will that help you?' are good open questions that take the conversation up logical levels. In theory, asking 'why?' should do the same, but invariably produces a narrow response, such as 'I just do.'

Technologists sometimes feel reluctant to move up logical levels in conversations with business partners and end users, because it feels like they ought not to be questioning the motives and intentions of their clients. They are more comfortable taking the conversation to lower logical levels, asking questions about the details. This is understandable, but tends to lead to later problems when the solution does not meet the needs of the user even though it complies fully with what they asked for.

It is important therefore, to overcome this natural reluctance. Any awkwardness can be avoided by some careful framing. Start the conversation by saying something like: 'To help me understand how best to meet your needs, it would help me if I knew a little about the goals and outcomes you want to achieve from this. Do you mind me asking what this solution will enable you to do that you are not able to do now?'

The technique can also be used to help other people locked in conflicts, enabling you to promote greater collaboration within your organization through your influence on others. For example, I once coached someone who had regular battles with her business partner to persuade him to follow set procedures. He found these overly bureaucratic and unnecessary. She, on the other hand, knew they had to be followed. The conversations usually descended to battles about what additional information was needed, when it was needed and whether it was really necessary.

I used the logical levelling technique to discover the higher-level goal that both of them aspired to. What did the information she required enable her to do? Was this purpose shared by her business partner? It transpired that the information and procedural requirements helped both of them run the business with minimal interference from Risk and Audit. This was the superordinate goal that she and her partner could effectively pursue and took the focus away from the details that tended to result in arguments. I suggested she focus on this goal and gain commitment to it from her business partner before outlining what she needed from him if they were to achieve it.

The approach worked like magic. At her next meeting with the business partner, she began the conversation by saying she could help him increase his volumes while keeping the people from Risk off his back. This gained his immediate attention and his curiosity as to how it could be achieved. She told him the solution involved her supplying Risk with some information they needed and that she could do this quite easily and with a small amount of input from him. She emphasized the benefit of this helping him avoid time-consuming audits and control issues. He happily supplied the information she needed.

Summary

Our drive for greater efficiency means that most Middle and Back Office functions are structured in ways that make collaboration more difficult to achieve. Yet without everyone working together in a coordinated fashion, an organization is unlikely to meet its revenue or cost targets.

Lynda Gratton from the London Business School and Tamara Erikson from Boston's BSG Alliance group, drew attention to this paradox in an article published in the *Harvard Business Review*. They found that large complex teams were the norm when it came to delivering complex projects, yet paradoxically:

> The qualities required for success are the same qualities that undermine success. Members of complex teams are less likely – absent other influences – to share knowledge freely, to learn from one another, to shift workloads flexibly to break up unexpected bottlenecks, to help one another complete jobs and meet deadlines, and to share resources – in other words, to collaborate. They are less likely to say that they 'sink or swim' together, want one another to succeed, or view their goals as compatible.
>
> (*Harvard Business Review*, November 2007, p.102).

The reasons for this are the same as the reasons given here for why support functions in financial institutions find it so difficult to collaborate. Competing goals, interdependence of fate, reward systems that promote competitive behaviours and group differences that promote an 'us and them' outlook all make it hard for collaboration to take place spontaneously. One of the most effective strategies you can adopt to overcome this tendency is to find common ground, both at an individual and organizational level. Hopefully you will have found some ideas on how to do this in this chapter.

7

Getting the Best out of Teams

Tapping into the power of effective teamwork unleashes performance gains that often cannot be matched by a collection of individuals working separately. When people feel they are part of a tightly knit team there is an *esprit de corps* that builds morale, raises performance and inhibits negative behaviours. People 'pull together' for the collective good during difficult times. They use their different skills to complement the weaknesses of others, resulting in an overall performance that is greater than the sum of the constituent parts. An important role for any team leader, therefore, is to create a sense of team spirit that will unleash these benefits.

For people in leadership positions today this role is becoming increasingly difficult due to the enormous changes in the nature of teams that have taken place in the last 20 years. How can you get the benefits of great teamwork when your team is located across several continents and contains people from many different cultural, professional and linguistic backgrounds?

The nature of teams has changed and today's leaders have to change the way they lead their teams if they are to operate effectively. The performance of a global operation, such as a modern technology organization, is closely linked to the effectiveness of teamwork within it. If teamwork breaks down, performance will suffer. Make no mistake, this is not about creating a supportive team culture through team building games and activities – it's about the performance of a team on its key performance metrics, whether they be cost, revenue, volume, throughput or downtime.

Building teams that collaborate with each other and which work effectively across a mix of individuals, is a key element of collaborative leadership. Many of the tools and approaches that have worked well for a team located in one building (or even one country) don't work so well for the global, multi-faceted teams that exist in most technology organizations within the financial services today. New approaches and skills are needed if leaders are to adapt to these changing conditions and keep in control.

The fast pace of change introduces an additional challenge, in that constant restructuring means that the make-up of teams is frequently changing. Team leaders may find themselves incorporating new team members who may be from a different heritage organization or may be the survivors of a headcount cull elsewhere in the organization. The new team members may feel bruised and that they have been badly treated. At the very least they may feel they have moved into an alien environment that they did not choose to join. The emotional baggage they bring with them is another obstacle the team leader will need to overcome if he or she is to start the process of building a new and effective team.

Given these challenges, what can the collaborative leader do to build an effective team and tap into the power of teamwork? This chapter outlines some of the tools and approaches that can help build effective teams in globally dispersed teams. By applying these, you can raise the performance of a whole operation and avoid the performance failures that usually occur when teamwork breaks down.

The Importance of Teamwork

One of the simplest and most elegant models of leadership was developed over 40 years ago by John Adair, a former platoon commander in the Scots Guards. Adair has since gone on to write many books on leadership and has held prominent positions in business and academia. His model of Action Centred Leadership has stood the test of time, partly I believe because of its simplicity. In the model, Adair states there are basically three things that an effective leader has to do (see Figure 7.1).

1.   achieve the task (that is, the team's goal or purpose);

2.   meet the needs of the individuals he or she leads;

3.   build the team.

According to Adair, then, building a team is one of the three essential aspects of a leader's role, yet in my experience it is often the most neglected.

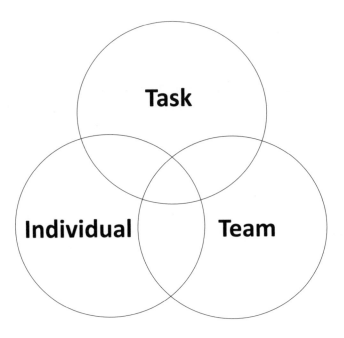

Figure 7.1   **John Adair's Action Centred Leadership model**

People in leadership roles recognize the importance of the first two elements of Adair's model, but many seem to relegate building their team to a once a year event. Often this is no more than the Christmas party. For some leaders it also involves one or two offsites that bring together the whole team for the annual business planning round.

The neglect may stem from associating 'building a team' with games and activities. This is a short-sighted view of what is meant by this part of the Adair model. A more complete view encompasses the benefits of tapping into the extraordinary performance that can be achieved by a team over a collection of individuals.

When people feel like part of a team, and feel a strong sense of identity with and loyalty to that team, they will exhibit high levels of internal motivation. This shows itself in effort and a willingness to 'go the extra mile'. Powerful group norms come into play to regulate behaviour, reducing the tendency for individuals to engage in suboptimal behaviours that detract from the team's overall goal and purpose. Individuals within the team coordinate their behaviours to achieve collective goals, drawing upon specialist skills and roles.

An effective team resembles a smooth, efficient machine, with every cog and wheel operating in unison to achieve an overall purpose. It is in this sense that building a team is one of the three most important things that a leader has to do. Without investing time and effort into this, a leader will fail to reap the benefits that effective teamwork brings. The leader is also likely to experience the myriad of problems that occur when teamwork breaks down: increased errors, duplicated efforts, poor customer service, delays, missed opportunities and so on.

This chapter is divided into three sections, covering the different types of teams that can benefit from development activities. The first of these are virtual teams. By this I mean teams that are responsible for a single operation and in which the members are located across the globe. They are virtual in the sense that they do not physically operate from a single location where there is frequent face-to-face contact. Instead, day-to-day contact across the constituent members is maintained electronically by email and instant messaging.

The second type is senior management teams. These are made up of the heads of each part of a global operation and together they are responsible for ensuring the smooth flow of work across all regions. Finally, I focus on what has been termed customized teams. These are teams that are created for specific, one-off tasks such as projects. Customized teams also include groups of loosely aligned individuals who are expected to work together on briefs that fall outside the day-to-day functioning of an organization, but which are considered vital to success. This might include innovation or cross-boundary problem solving.

For each type of team I cover a number of tools and approaches that can be used to build collaboration across its members, helping to develop it into a high performing team.

1. Developing Virtual Teams

The need to operate on a global scale has led to the formation of virtual teams with members operating from several different locations around the world. This has raised a number of challenges for leaders of these teams, including:

- how to run effective meetings;

- how to ensure work flows smoothly across the team, without falling between the gaps created by distance, role and functional speciality;

- how to operate a trust-based system of management when there is less opportunity to monitor the work of those in the regions;

- how to ensure members of the team work together effectively given cultural, professional and linguistic differences;

- how to coach and develop people, and deal with their concerns, when there is little opportunity for face-to-face contact.

A useful way of organizing these challenges is to group them under various headings. These headings represent the main actions a leader of a virtual team must manage if he or she is to build the members into an effective team. The model can be used as a useful diagnostic tool, highlighting those areas that might need extra attention. Figure 7.2 shows how these relate to each other.

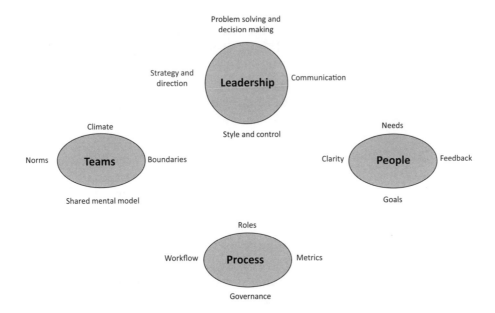

Figure 7.2   Leading global teams

LEADERSHIP

Overseeing the three main actions is that of Leadership. This involves the following four features:

Strategy and direction

The leader is responsible for ensuring everyone understands the direction and underlying strategy of the business unit, even if he or she has not been responsible for creating it. People throughout the team need to know what the ultimate purpose or mission of the team is and why this particular direction has been set. While this is true of all teams, it is especially relevant to virtual teams, where those in the regions may have only a vague sense of where the team is heading.

Leaders often underestimate how much communication is required to create this understanding. The message has to be repeated many times before people start to internalize it and relate it to their everyday actions. It also needs to be communicated in a number of different ways. Simply sending a 'deck' of slides to all members of the team ahead of a team meeting will fail to ensure the message 'sticks'. For something as important as strategy, it is necessary to use face-to-face communications and this means touring all of the sites in the global operation. While this might seem time consuming, costly and ultimately unnecessary in today's connected world, there really is no substitute. Cutting back on this is a false economy. Town hall sessions, in which people have the opportunity to raise questions and concerns, have to be used to get the message across. Once this has been achieved, the message then needs to be repeated using a variety of communications channels.

Problem solving and decision making

These are two fundamental aspects of leading and managing, and their role in a global operation becomes even more acute. The root causes of problems experienced in virtual teams can lie outside a specific location, making them harder to track down. Conversely, people in one location may blame those in other locations for problems experienced, resulting in no one getting to the heart of a problem. Team leaders need to be sensitive to the difficulties of solving problems across global operations and ensure the task remains free of personal accusations and recriminations. Many problems may be a direct result of the fact that different people in multiple locations are involved in the end-to-end value chain, making it more likely that mistakes and misunderstandings occur. Solutions lie in removing some of the barriers that make the smooth flow of work difficult to achieve. This might involve increasing awareness of cultural differences and how best to work with colleagues from different cultural, linguistic and geographical backgrounds.

Decision making can also become more protracted within virtual teams. People in far-flung regions need to feel empowered to make decisions locally without escalating issues upwards or to the centre of operations. There also needs to be clear guidelines about who is responsible for making different kinds of decisions and when this responsibility lies outside a particular location. The general rule for the leader of a virtual team is to devolve as much decision making as possible. For some leaders, used to ruling a single location team, this can be quite a stretch and can require a significant shift in decision-making style (see below).

Communication

Leaders of virtual teams need to spend much more time communicating than they might do with a team based in one location. Leaders need to compensate for the various barriers to effective communications and the over-reliance on electronic forms that strip messages of most of their meaning if not backed up by additional media. While the temptation might be to rely on email to a greater extent, leaders should make more use of phone calls when communicating with people in different locations. These people do not have the benefit of picking up additional cues and information from informal communications with their team leaders. Other types of information communicated visually are also missing. They cannot see how busy or relaxed the leader appears day-to-day, or what time he or she arrives at work or leaves at the end of the day, or even the state of their desk. All of these visual cues communicate subtle messages about the state of play and people that rarely get a chance to see the team leader are at a distinct disadvantage in not having access to them. It is up to the team leader to overcompensate for this by communicating more through other channels and by visiting as regularly as possible. When visiting remote locations, leaders also need to avoid shutting themselves away in offices or confining their time to senior people. They need to get out on the floor and meet people informally. Time needs to be scheduled for this, rather than hoping a gap in a busy schedule will allow it.

Style and control

Leading a globally distributed team requires leaders to perform a difficult balancing act. Too much control and they risk stifling distant team members from operating effectively. Yet too little control can leave scope for problems to arise and fester before they come to the attention of the team leader. It can also mean these team members feel isolated and neglected.

Generally, leading a virtual team requires leaders to let go of the control they might be used to exerting when leading a single location team. This is at a time when the leader feels he or she has lost a lot of control since they can no longer oversee operations directly. One solution is to appoint trusted deputies who can be the eyes and ears of the team leader, picking up on problems or discontents without needing the direct intervention of the leader to resolve them.

The model in Figure 7.2 shows that in addition to considering the above four features of leadership, there are three additional areas of attention for the leader of a virtual team: the team, processes and individuals. Each of these contains four areas of focus.

THE TEAM

Norms

Norms are the unwritten rules that guide behaviour. These may differ across locations, resulting in problems when people in these locations need to work together as a single unit. For example, is there a norm of not working late in some of the locations that causes problems with those who are used to putting in long hours? Do people mix socially outside working hours and would it help if they did more of this? For example, some London-based teams develop a 'pub' culture of after-work drinks which colleagues in other European or Asian locations feel isolates them from the main team. They are not privy to the informal interactions in such a setting that helps build relationships.

For new recruits to a globally dispersed team, learning the unwritten norms of behaviour can be difficult. Are they being appropriately inculcated into the culture of the organization or is this left largely to chance, leaving them feeling like a distant relative to the firm rather than an integral part of it? Induction processes need to be adapted to give those outside the centre of operations an understanding of the company's history and background, as well as a sense of what makes it unique.

Climate

Similar to the norms, the organizational climate in which a team operates can vary widely across different locations. While not intrinsically a bad thing, such differences can lead to problems and misunderstandings when people in different locations have to work together. For example, are standards lower in some locations than in others? Is there an appropriate amount of support and recognition in all locations? Should people be rewarded in different ways depending on where they are and what is valued?

Boundaries

This refers to the way individuals and sub-teams relate to each other and how the overall team relates to others in the organization. Do some people maintain their isolation, while others seek to integrate more closely? Is there friction across groups within the team? Are there disagreements over who does what? Differences in language, culture, time zone, functional speciality and so on can create boundaries that prevent individuals across locations working as a single team. The team leader, while not being able to remove these differences, needs to reduce their impact and ensure they do not prevent individuals from feeling and behaving like members of one team.

Shared mental model

To what extent do people across different locations have a shared view of events and the team's overall aims? Do they think like a single team or do they think like a collection of sub-teams? A shared mental model is something that binds all effective teams, resulting in a common understanding of what needs to be done, who is responsible for it and how it is to be performed. The individuals within the team think and act like one. Achieving a shared mental model is difficult enough for teams based in a single location. It is doubly difficult for teams with members spread over various geographical locations.

One approach to this has been pioneered by the Norwegian psychologist Willi Railo working with the England national football team under Sven-Goran Erikson's leadership. Railo coined the phrase 'cultural architect' to describe those individuals with special responsibility for building a shared mental model among a team (Ridley, 2002). Leaders of distributed teams can make use of this approach by developing their own cultural architects in each region and using them to influence others and build a common mindset and approach.

PROCESSES

Generally, when a process is 'broken up' into several parts, each of which is to be performed by different individuals, there is the possibility of delays, misunderstandings and errors at each point of handover. These problems are exacerbated when the process spans different geographical locations. There are four specific areas of action under the heading of processes that the leader of a virtual team needs to focus on.

Roles

Everyone within a process spanning multiple locations needs to be clear about their own role and that of each other person within the process. Similarly, the role of each location needs to be clearly specified to prevent work falling between the gaps created by breaking up the process. Techniques such as RACI charts are useful ways of making it clear who is responsible (R) for an action; who is accountable (A) for ensuring the action is correctly completed; who needs to be consulted (C); and who needs to be informed (I).

While a team leader may think roles have been clearly defined, this does not necessarily mean that people within the team have the same understanding and degree of clarity. Leaders often think that an organization chart is sufficient to explain all, but the reality is often far removed from this. There is ultimately no substitute for taking the time to explain roles and positions and giving people the opportunity to seek clarification. Although this is best done face-to-face, it can be done via a conference call (though not by email).

Metrics

Measuring performance is probably the single most important aspect of managing it and ensuring targets are achieved. This is especially true of work that spans multiple locations. The leader of a virtual team needs to ensure the appropriate metrics are in place to allow work to be tracked at each point in a process, since there is less likelihood that problems or delays will quickly come to light from hearing about them or seeing the consequences. More than ever, the leader is dependent on a good set of metrics that will tell him or her of the need for early action.

When a team is split over different locations there is also a need to develop metrics that measure the performance of the end-to-end process. It is of little use meeting local targets if this means work tends to get 'thrown over the wall' to those in other locations, causing problems and delays for those further down the line. People across all locations need to know how the end-to-end process is performing and what they can do to improve things.

Governance

This refers to the rules and procedures by which work gets done. Once again, this is especially important when a team is multi-located. There needs to be clear escalation procedures when things don't go according to plan, as well as clear lines of authority that specify what action is needed and who needs to take it.

Those responsible for governing the flow of work across a global operation need to work together as a team and this will mean they need to meet regularly and work together effectively. This is unlikely to be the case if these meetings are poorly managed or if the right people don't attend and participation during the meeting is low. Many problems in global virtual teams can be traced back to weak or unclear governance. It is important that it is given the prominence it deserves and not treated as an unnecessary administrative detail.

Workflow

This refers to the flow of work across the end-to-end process. Are there bottlenecks? Do errors tend to occur at the handover points? Do people in each location feel responsible for the whole piece of work or just their part of it? The principles of good process design should apply here, to ensure that work flows smoothly across all locations. In our book on business process reengineering, Mike Robson and I outline these principles in some detail (Robson and Ullah, 1996). They include reducing the number of people or parties involved in the process so that the number of handovers are minimized, using the principle of triage to create fast track processes, and involving the customers of the process in some of the steps involved.

Once again, the complexity of working across multiple locations means that these principles are more important than when operating in a single location. The team leader needs to ensure he or she applies them with rigour and determination.

PEOPLE

The final element of this model focuses on people and their specific role in a global operation. The four key elements here are:

Clarity

Work by Peter Warr, Emeritus Professor of Occupational Psychology at Sheffield University's Institute of Work Psychology, has shown the importance of clarity in job performance and psychological health at work (Warr, 1987). People need to know with some clarity the requirements of their job and what they can rely upon others for, as well as the likely consequences of their actions on others and the certainty with which undesirable events are likely or not to occur. Without clarity in these areas, people find it difficult to commit their energy and support to a role. In a global operation there is likely to be less clarity around these features of work as employees rely more on information from various sources about events and people in multiple locations.

Needs

For people who prefer working individually or with little direct supervision, working in a geographically distributed team may meet their need for autonomy if they are relatively isolated from the hub of activities. Others, who have high social needs, may find it difficult working in such an environment. The team leader should make efforts to discover the extent to which individual needs and motivations are being met by the way a team is structured and work within it is organized. He or she needs to take this into account when making appointments and when seeking to get the best out of individuals in specific roles.

Feedback

People need regular, constructive feedback from others if they are to perform to high standards or make significant improvements in the way they work. Unfortunately, working in remote locations can make it more difficult to receive this feedback, especially if it needs to come from those not in a position to observe directly their behaviour. Team leaders therefore need to make special efforts to ensure others in the virtual team receive feedback and that this is balanced, regular and timely. This will typically require the team leader making active attempts to obtain the views and input from a wide variety of people who might be in a better position to provide these kinds of observations. It is all too easy, especially if there are few problems, for team leaders to lose the habit of giving others regular and constructive feedback if they are many thousands of miles away.

Goals

Members of any team, be it virtual or co-located, need to have clear, stretching goals that allow them to play to their strengths. In geographically distributed teams people may know their local goals but may not know how these contribute to the broader goals of the organization. Team leaders need to ensure everyone knows how they fit within the broader scheme of things and how meeting specific local goals contributes to the achievement of larger, superordinate goals. People also need to know how failure to meet local goals can jeopardize the latter and the importance of everyone within a global operation working in some kind of harmony to achieve large-scale organizational goals.

This model can help leaders of virtual teams overcome the barriers to successful performance by helping the leader focus on what is necessary to ensure people collaborate across distance, time zones, cultures and functional specialities. The model can serve as a useful diagnostic device to help the team leader ensure he or she is doing all that is required to run a smoothly operating global team. Actions to address areas of concern can then be developed, resulting in a planned and coherent approach to running a global operation.

2. Developing the Senior Management Team

The nature of large global teams inevitably means efforts to build teamwork will involve working with subsets of these teams rather than the whole team. Most important of these is the senior management team. The leader's team of direct reports has to operate as a single team and be a role model of great teamwork. Unfortunately, the way most technology organizations are structured makes it very difficult for them to operate as a single team. In his book on collaboration,

Morten Hansen describes a situation that will probably sound very familiar to leaders of large organizations:

> *You delegate responsibilities for operations, products, business areas, and geographies to a group of managers. The clearer the lines of responsibility, the better. You then develop objectives and metrics for each manager so that he or she knows what to achieve each quarter and year. To improve the chances of success, you give the managers considerable freedom – they run their own unit. Then you hold them accountable for their results and put in place incentives to motivate them to reach the objectives. Bonuses, salary increases, stock options, and promotions go to those who deliver. Those who do not deliver are coached or let go. Predictably, managers of each work unit work hard and focus on reaching their targets. You sit back and marvel at the beauty of this system.*
>
> (Hansen, 2009, p.49).

The problem with this, says Hansen, is that it stifles any possibility of teamwork across this collection of managers. Instead the organization becomes 'a loose collection of units, which quickly become fiefdoms or silos' (p.49).

If the lack of genuine teamwork across the senior team becomes apparent to those at lower levels of the organization, then it becomes very difficult indeed to promote a collaborative style of working. In the words of RBS's Scott Marcar, 'You can get a lot of cynicism from people seeing these guys at the top saying "we're all one team" while their actual behaviour is completely different. Here you get a lot less cynicism when you talk about collaboration because it's very much part of the culture, and people do believe in it and see groups working together.'

To build these managers into a genuine team involves bringing them together to work on the organization's larger goals. As I outlined in Chapter 6, these are the superordinate goals that will break down barriers and facilitate teamwork. One way to achieve this is through a programme of regular offsite meetings.

TEAM OFFSITES

While team offsites are likely to form a feature of most senior management teams, in my experience they are often lost opportunities to build this group into a high-performing team. All too often the offsites focus almost exclusively on the goals that divide the organization. Each manager is usually invited to give a presentation on how he or she is contributing to the overall scheme of things or special projects they have initiated. Sometimes the task is to decide which of all the projects in flight need to be given priority and which should be put on the back burner or even cancelled. This results in each manager fighting his or her corner and does even more to split the team rather than unite it. Very little time, if any, is devoted to discussing how they are operating as a team and the whole event becomes a series of long PowerPoint presentations that are of interest mainly to the person giving the presentation.

Typical signs that offsites are failing to realize their full potential are:

- no real sense of progress and of closing out issues;

- conflicts exacerbated;

- event seems dull; people miss the buzz of their normal day-to-day work;

- a small number of individuals dominate the proceedings, while others contribute too little;

- poor quality decisions are made, with no real sense of ownership to see them through;

- passive, low energy with little real engagement.

To be effective, offsites should adhere to the following principles:

- They should meet all three of the needs identified by John Adair: task (business), team and individual. Moreover, there needs to be the right combination of all three; imbalances can result in feelings of 'lots of fun but no real work', or 'too structured and not enough creativity' or 'politically engineered to meet the needs of one or two individuals'.

- Expert attention also needs to be given to managing group dynamics, so that conflict is harnessed to produce better results and decision making is effective. This is best achieved from having a skilled facilitator present whose role it is to help the team manage its process.

- Structured facilitation techniques also need to be used to achieve specific tasks. Simply expecting every item on the agenda to produce the desired outcome without a planned process for getting there is unrealistic.

- There needs also to be a good understanding of how to combine different kinds of activities and sessions to maintain high levels of energy and involvement over the course of the event. Long presentations in the afternoon should be avoided where possible and replaced by work in breakout groups.

- Careful planning with the leader of the team, and coaching where necessary, will ensure that he or she achieves a successful outcome that enhances their own role and contribution.

By applying these principles, offsite events can become effective vehicles for achieving important business goals while building a collection of individuals into a real team.

There are many ways in which this can be done and each offsite can and should have a unique flavour that is appropriate for the occasion and the team concerned. Good offsites contain a mix of various types of activities, so the format remains fresh and people stay engaged. Some examples of these activities are given below. Each would normally be integrated closely with the business goals of the event rather than operate as 'stand alone' elements.

Learning and development

Elements of learning can be built into the event by using specific sessions to introduce key skills, management models or tools to help. For example, the team can learn about presentations skills ahead of a planned series of key communication events.

Psychometric analysis

Various psychometric assessments can be used to develop a better appreciation of individual and team styles. Instruments like the Myers Briggs Type Indicator

(MBTI) or Belbin's Team Roles Inventory can give a real insight into the dynamics of a team and help members flex their style and approach to better meet the needs of others.

Team tasks

Elements of the offsite can be designed as specific tasks that are time-boxed and have clearly defined outputs that are of use to others in the organization. For example, 'Produce a set of guidelines for managing distributed teams' can be a specific task that draws upon the skills and experience of all those present and which has a clear takeaway value.

Review and analysis

Building in time for the team to review its performance at key points during the offsite enables people to give feedback, learn and adapt their behaviour. There is more opportunity to take corrective action and ownership for the quality of the output produced at the offsite.

Breakout groups

By creating breakout groups for specific sessions, energy levels are increased and there is an opportunity for everyone to make a full contribution. This approach also allows more work to be achieved by having groups work in parallel on different tasks.

Team development

Specific team-building activities can be used to help build the group as a team. For example, the team can define the characteristics of a world-class team and then rate its performance during the offsite against these. This could form the basis of a team development plan for future offsites.

Time to 'play'

By building in time to address issues that have not been formally placed on the agenda, but which are of concern to members of the group, a sense of 'play and creativity' can be brought to the event. People feel able to contribute in a way that meets their individual needs while addressing important issues.

Energizers

Short energizers help to maintain energy, involvement and a sense of fun throughout the day. Energizers can be used to demonstrate important learning points or just be an opportunity to break down barriers between individuals.

The benefits of using elements like these in the design of an offsite event are:

- participants see tangible outputs from the event, enhancing the reputation of the management team;

- real progress is made on important issues;

- the group becomes a genuine team and benefits from the synergy this creates;

- there is a more effective use of time and resources, and a greater return on the investment in the event;

- better quality decisions are made and there is greater likelihood of follow-up;

- there is improvement in individual performance, through learning new tools, techniques and models;

- there is a 'ripple' effect as members of this team introduce similar approaches within their own teams.

An effective approach is to develop a programme of offsites that are aimed at transforming the senior management team over a period of about one year. I recommend four quarterly offsites, each with specific goals and each forming part of an integrated plan. In this respect, the offsites are more like a multiple module development programme that can be planned in advance. Of course, significant parts of the content will be determined by events at that time, but it is surprising how much can be predetermined. The annual business cycle will dictate which offsite meetings are devoted to tasks like budgeting, talent mapping and agreeing the portfolio of projects for the coming financial year. The remaining time should be divided into covering issues arising during the year, and, significantly, developing the team.

TEAM DEVELOPMENT ACTIVITIES

This latter element should be a combination of activities that help a team focus on how it works together as a team. This distinction between *what* a team has to achieve and the *way* it works together to achieve it is often referred to as the Task/Process distinction. Typically, teams spend most, if not all, of their time on task activities – planning, solving problems, making decisions, scheduling and so on. Yet research has shown that only about 20 per cent of teams that fail at a task do so because of the nature of the task itself. A huge 80 per cent of failures can be attributed to poor process. In other words, it is the *way* a team works together that most often makes the difference between success and failure. Teams that want to be successful should therefore spend at least some of their time focusing on how to improve this.

Typical examples of what this might involve are given below:

Establishing ground rules: This involves the whole team deciding on the ground rules by which it will run its meetings effectively and govern the behaviour of each individual. Having a set of explicit ground rules can be very helpful if the team is plagued by poor behaviours, such as people arriving late, interrupting others, not listening or building on the contributions of others, attending to their emails during meetings and so on.

I once worked with a senior management team that had been created by the CIO following a merger. A few of the individuals had worked together prior to joining the team, but to all intents this was a new team. The team recognized it made little progress during its meetings, but was not sure why. Attending a few of the meetings as an observer soon told me why: the members routinely practised all of the above negative behaviours. Most noticeably, there was little real debate on important issues where collective decisions were needed. Instead, each person seemed to focus on making their own points or contribution. There was no link to a previous comment and subsequent comments by others were similarly detached. The whole 'conversation' consisted of a series of unrelated comments by individuals, with each person vying with others to make their views known.

When I fed back this observation to them they recognized it immediately, but were unsure what to do about it. Establishing specific ground rules about listening and building on comments made a significant difference. Individuals agreed they needed to avoid making a point simply for the sake of it and instead focus on building a genuine dialogue with their colleagues. Other ground rules related to interruptions, how decisions should be made and timekeeping.

These ground rules were written on to a flipchart and placed in view for all subsequent team meetings. Having the ground rules explicit and in view of all members reminded them to adhere to them and made it easy for others to challenge someone if they felt they were breaking one of the ground rules.

Features of high performing teams: With the same team we also began to define the features it would like to have. In answer to the question, 'What does a high-performing team look like?' the team listed about a dozen features that captured the kind of team each person wanted the group to be. This included things like the following:

- effective team meetings;

- share information openly;

- constructive feedback and debate;

- clarity on roles and responsibilities;

- clear goals;

- effective procedures for making decisions;

- joint problem solving;

- focused on achieving the task;

- full contribution, without domination by individuals.

The initial list was much longer than this, prompting debate about each feature and why it was considered important for the team to possess it. This debate was productive in that it helped individuals define the nature of the team they wanted to be and highlighted different opinions within the group.

The final list was then captured on a flipchart and each member of the team was invited to rate the current status of the team on each feature, using a score from 1 to 10. This enabled the team to get a good sense of how far it had to travel to become the kind of high-performing team the members wanted it to be. Again, where appropriate, people expanded on the reasons for their score, prompting further useful debate about team behaviour and what was considered effective.

Over a period of time, the team was able to review its progress on each of these features, identifying further actions or changes that were needed to move it towards its definition of a high-performing team.

As a way of bringing these features to life, and making them concrete and less 'motherhood and apple pie', the team also rated its performance on specific tasks against this list. Thus, the team rated its performance on particularly important and challenging tasks, such as agreeing the project portfolio, in terms of these characteristics. For example, were the goals clear? Was the decision-making process appropriate? Did certain individuals dominate? And so on.

The four stages of team development: Bruce Tuckman's model of the four stages of team development (Figure 7.3) has been a mainstay of group dynamics for over 40 years. The model highlights the four stages of development that groups typically pass through on their route to being a high-performing team:

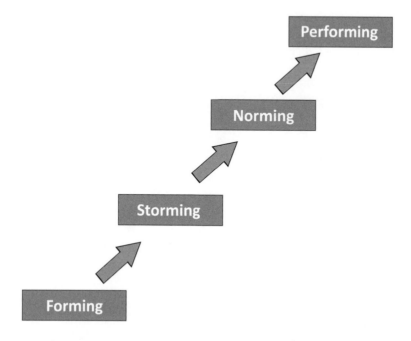

Figure 7.3   **Tuckman's four stages of group development**

I regularly use this model when working with new teams, as it helps them envisage the journey ahead of them if they are to become a high-performing team. Teams can recognize the signs typically displayed at each stage and take action to move on to the next stage. The model also highlights the behaviours the team leader needs to practise at each stage if he or she is to aid the team in this process. It is worth describing the stages in some detail as it is a useful and practical way for team leaders to develop high-performing teams.

FORMING

When a team first comes together, the team members need to explore and define acceptable group behaviours. This is a transition stage, from individual to team member status.

Symptoms of groups at the Forming stage

- attempts to define or redefine the task and how it will be accomplished;

- attempts to determine acceptable group behaviour;

- decisions on what information needs to be gathered;

- abstract discussions of concepts and issues, and impatience by some with these discussions;

- complaints about the organization and perceived barriers to the team's success.

Helpful leader behaviours

- provide plenty of structure to meetings. Clarify roles and the group's task;

- encourage participation from quiet members of the team. Ensure others don't dominate;

- use short exercises to learn about each other's area of expertise and background;

- agree a set of ground rules;

- use team building exercises to create a sense of team spirit.

STORMING

This is probably the most challenging stage for a team as it occurs when conflict rises to the surface and is openly expressed. Usually this is done in a negative or destructive way, resulting in people feeling they no longer want to be part of the team.

Symptoms of groups at the Storming stage

- arguing and open disagreements;

- defensiveness and blame;

- questioning the purpose and need for the team;

- complaints about the task and the amount of work required.

Helpful leader behaviours

- encourage joint problem solving;

- stress that the expression of conflict is normal at this stage;

- agree how decisions will be made when there are disagreements;

- encourage people to give constructive feedback.

FORMING

At this stage the team starts to come together. Success seems more likely and individuals start to accept the need to work together to achieve it. Conflict is reduced or handled more constructively.

Symptoms of groups at the Norming stage

- increased friendliness;

- a common team identity and sense of purpose;

- working within the ground rules.

Helpful leader behaviours

- encourage group members to manage the agenda;

- express your own hopes and concerns;

- delegate more to individual team members, ensuring they are able to take on extra work.

PERFORMING

This is the highest level of performance by the team and represents all that is desirable about working in a team. Roles become interchangeable, people put in extra effort for the good of the whole team and success creates high levels of morale which in turn promote further successes.

Symptoms of groups at the Performing stage

- a strong sense of attachment to the team;

- an ability to work through team problems constructively;

- interdependence and sharing of team tasks.

Helpful leader behaviours

- jointly set more challenging goals;

- provide recognition to each team member for their contribution;

- develop individuals through coaching and feedback.

This model of team development should be used when a new team comes together and periodically after that as a way of charting progress. Initially, the team can identify which stage best characterizes its current performance and offer insights into what is needed to help it successfully negotiate its way onto the next stage.

I once worked with a specially created project team, helping it over a period of days to develop its agenda for the forthcoming months. Initially, the members showed many of the signs of a team at the forming stage of development. In particular, disagreements about the best way ahead tended to be quickly closed down, with individuals keeping their concerns and misgivings to themselves. It was all very polite, but not very conducive to effective teamwork.

On about the third day, the simmering tensions within the group surfaced into a full blown argument between two of the key players. After several minutes of hurling insults at each other, they became aware that everyone else in the team was looking at them aghast and that they had shown a lack of professionalism in front of everyone in the room. I quickly reassured them that the conflict was not unexpected and that they were following the pattern of development typical of new teams. I described each stage in Tuckman's model and related their behaviour to the Storming stage. They were visibly reassured to know that all was not lost and that as a team they could overcome these difficulties and move on to higher stages of performance.

The agenda for the day was suspended, with the rest of the time spent on team development activities aimed at helping them manage conflict constructively. We developed a set of ground rules to help, along with some tips on how to give feedback to others. Over the next few days the group made tangible progress towards being a high-performing team, equipped to deal with conflict constructively rather than avoid it or handle it destructively. Tuckman's model served as a useful roadmap to help them navigate this journey.

3. Developing Customized Teams

The team described above had been specifically formed to execute a one-off project. Unlike a senior management team, or a virtual team responsible for a global operation, such one-off teams have a less specific mode of operation. In their book on the social networks that form within organizations, Rob Cross and Robert Thomas describe this kind of group as 'customized', in contrast to 'routinized' groups that exist on an ongoing basis (Cross and Thomas, 2009). The latter perform repeatable actions and their goal is to do this as efficiently as possible. Customized groups, however, engage in activities that are less predictable. They are required to respond to unexpected problems and be innovative in how they do this.

Many organizations today recognize the importance of customized teams and create them to perform a specific and somewhat flexible role. While the team development techniques outlined above can be very helpful in building these groups into a high-performing team, there are additional approaches that research has shown make an important difference. The very nature of customized teams, and their loose format, means that it is wise to consider each type separately. As a consequence, it pays dividends to have a number of models and tools available to help.

One such model has been developed by Lynda Gratton and Tamara Erikson. Their study of 55 large global project teams, briefly referred to in the last chapter, considered over 100 different factors that might differentiate successful from unsuccessful teams. In their *Harvard Business Review* article, 'Eight ways to build collaborative teams' (2007), Gratton and Erikson highlighted eight practices common to the teams that were able to overcome the difficulties posed by size, distance, diversity and specialization.

1.   Invest in signature relationships.
At a firm-wide level, those companies that fostered collaborative teams tended to make significant investments in facilities and practices that helped build and maintain social relationships. The precise ways they did this varied across firms, but all were memorable and well suited to their particular environment. They helped create a physical and cultural environment where it was easy for people to get together and share ideas.

2.   Model collaborative behaviour.
While senior executives might extol the virtues of collaboration, many still adopt a competitive stance when working with their peers. In the companies studied by Gratton and Erikson, executives not only worked collaboratively across their various business lines, they also ensured such collaborative behaviour was visible to the wider workforce.

3.   Create a 'gift' culture.
By 'gift' culture the authors mean practices where people give their time and skills to help others. Typical examples of this are coaching and mentoring programmes. Schemes such as these need to matched by informal processes where people willingly give their time to others, creating a culture of giving.

4.   Ensure the requisite skills.
A collaborative culture on its own was not enough to overcome the barriers to collaboration among the complex teams studied by the authors. Those that were most successful also invested in helping people develop the skills to collaborate. The types of skills quoted include: productively resolving conflicts, holding difficult conversations, coaching, building strong relationships and programme management.

5.   Support a strong sense of community.
A sense of community is created when people within a firm come together to share common interests or work towards shared goals. When these are structured and supported by HR departments, through activities like family-oriented events, educational classes and weekend get-togethers they help support and encourage collaboration that takes place through more formal working patterns.

6.   Assign team leaders that are task- and relationship-oriented.
In the 55 teams studied by the authors, the most productive and innovative were those led by people who had good strong technical skills and who possessed the softer skills supportive of relationship building. This was achieved through development initiatives of the kind referred to in point 4 above or through selecting people who already possessed both sets of skills when appointing team leaders.

7.   Build on heritage relationships.
This is a way of short cutting the development of strong relationships based on trust. In their haste to build teams that bring together people with no existing relationship, senior managers may overlook the advantages of building on existing relationships. Teams in the study that had a high proportion of people who were strangers at the time of formation struggled to collaborate. As a word of warning, however, Gratton and Erikson caution against drawing on too many pre-existing relationships as these can easily become cliques that exclude others and inhibit the development of new relationships.

8.   Build role clarity and allow task ambiguity.

Finally, collaboration was found to improve when all individual team members were clear on their relative roles and responsibilities. This meant they did not get into disagreements with each other about who was responsible for what and allowed them to focus on the task at hand. At the same time, team members were more likely to collaborate with each other if the path to achieving team goals was left open for them to decide. The ambiguity here meant they often had to reach out to others to get their views and input.

In summary, Gratton and Erikson's work shows that senior executives within the firms concerned need to role model collaborative behaviours, build a culture that supports helping others and invest in initiatives that help build social relationships. Human Resources (HR) professionals also have a role to play, in ensuring people have the skills to build relationships and in promoting group activities that bring people with shared interests together, albeit virtually. Finally, managers of locally-based teams need to be skilled in managing relationships and team members need to understand clearly their role and responsibilities so that they are not constantly negotiating who does what with their colleagues in other locations.

At Catalyst we have conducted similar research into the factors that are associated with the successful completion of a major project or programme. Like Gratton and Erikson, we have compared successful teams with unsuccessful teams in an effort to identify what makes the difference. Catalyst's research differs from theirs in that it focuses on a wider range of factors than those associated with building collaboration. Thus it includes features of the design of the programme, leadership, execution and benefits delivery.

We studied 120 completed Technology programmes within a number of major investment banks and hedge funds. Over one-quarter involved an investment greater than US$5 million and more than one in ten had a budget of over US$25 million. Our findings show a broad range of factors as all being associated with successful projects (this research is presented in greater detail in Chapter 9).

These findings confirm much of what has already been said about building successful teams, though they focus on a broader range of factors associated with success. The value of this research is that it allows programme managers to target their efforts where they are likely to have most impact. One of the unexpected findings is that there is no 'silver bullet' when aiming to build success. There are many factors that contribute to it and the team leader has to ensure all are in place if he or she is to be confident the programme is to deliver tangible business value.

So far I have outlined how to ensure customized teams can successfully achieve their goals and mission. A final technique to support this aim concerns the use of the networking techniques described in Cross and Thomas's book. Using specially designed software programs, it is possible to map the actual social networks that exist within an organization and which greatly influence how work *really* gets done. Cross and Thomas argue that formal organizational charts show how this is supposed to happen in theory, but the reality, as revealed by network analysis techniques, is often very different.

I have used this technique with numerous customized teams and it has proved very effective in highlighting where team leaders need to focus their efforts to build an effective team that has been created to achieve a specific purpose. Three examples of this are given below to illustrate how this can be achieved.

TALENT PROGRAMMES

Talent programmes represent specific attempts to bring together the most talented individuals within an organization and build them into a high-performing network. Typically, these individuals are dotted around the organization and do not know of each other's existence. By making them into a team an organization can reap substantial benefits.

At Catalyst we run talent programmes for top technologists within some of our clients. Although much of the programme is focused on developing further their technical skills, a significant element is based on building these highly talented individuals into a genuine network that can collaborate to solve cross-boundary problems and foster innovation.

The programmes are typically spread over three residential modules, run about two to six months apart. Over the course of this time we map the networks that exist across this group, charting their progress into becoming a highly collaborative network.

Figure 7.4 shows the network that existed prior to joining one such programme in a technology organization within an investment bank. The diagram shows who reported collaborating with whom in order to solve a problem or to get help with a business issue. The analysis clearly shows there was little collaboration and that the networks that existed tended to be linear in nature rather than complex and interwoven.

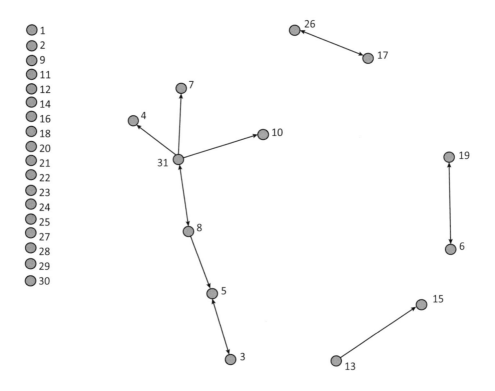

Figure 7.4   Network diagram showing collaboration prior to attending the programme

Over the course of the next two modules we were able to repeat the analysis and chart the development of this collection of individuals into a genuine network. Figure 7.5 shows how collaboration within this group grew as a result of attending the programme. We were able to use the analysis to provide feedback to individuals, who could see whether they were central 'go to' figures or whether they remained on the periphery. One-to-one coaching helped the latter focus on changing their approach and becoming more central. Skills workshops during the training modules developed their skills in initiating and building relationships and showed them how to collaborate effectively with others.

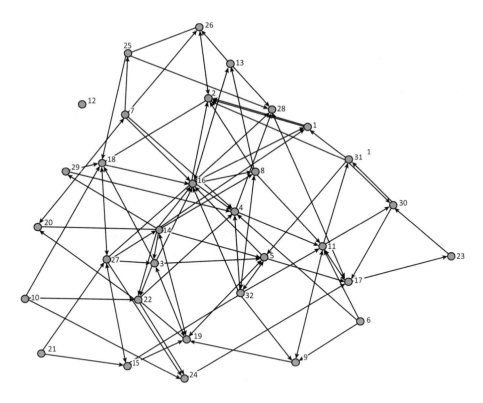

Figure 7.5   Collaboration by the end of the programme

Eight months after the programme had formally ended we conducted a follow-up analysis which showed the network still existed and that people would regularly draw upon their colleagues for help tackling problems, developing ideas and discovering key information. The benefits of this kind of collaboration should not be underestimated. In the follow-up survey we asked people to estimate the benefits from collaborating with peers from the talent programme and asked them to place a dollar value on savings in time, improvements in quality and so on. In a little over six months these benefits were estimated to be in excess of US$1 million.

The network analysis was a key instrument in visually demonstrating the extent of the network and how it developed over the duration of the programme. With this kind of feedback, people were more inclined to make use of the network and to collaborate with their peers when they needed help. It provided us with the justification to help people focus on building their networking skills and helped them see that they could achieve much more through working together collaboratively.

SPECIAL PROJECTS TEAMS

A specific kind of customized team is that created without a firm brief, other than to innovate and propose novel solutions to existing or potential organizational problems. The vague brief given to these teams ensures they are free to focus on things outside the mainstream, identifying problems before they come over the horizon or proposing new ideas that can steal a march on competitors.

Although the loose format for these kinds of teams allows them to be creative, it can also make it difficult for them to focus. It is not usual for such teams to struggle to define their role and decide how best they can fulfil it.

A network analysis conducted on one such team in one of Catalyst's clients showed that although the members were working closely with their business partners and other key stakeholders, there was minimal contact with others in their group. This meant that lessons learned were rarely passed on to others in the group and that the benefits of synergy and collaboration across these individuals were not being achieved.

The analysis provided a stark reminder to the group of its purpose and the need to work more closely together if they were to be successful. They decided on a number of actions to ensure they worked more closely together and operated as a team rather than a loose collection of individuals.

DISTINGUISHED ENGINEER PROGRAMMES

Some of the top technology organizations within investment banks have recognized the need to award a special status to their most talented and distinguished engineers. This is typically a lifetime award and requires the holder to tackle the organization's most significant technology problems and to develop 'game changing' ideas that can lead to competitive advantage.

When Catalyst conducted a network analysis of one such group among our client base we found that although some people had held the title for a number of years, the degree of collaboration across this group of individuals was relatively low.

Once again this kind of visual representation of the degree of collaboration that existed was very powerful in promoting the group to do more to ensure collaboration across its members. Like the special projects team mentioned above, they were not really operating as a team but rather a loose collection of talented individuals. During an offsite workshop we were able to use this as a starting point to develop actions aimed at building them into a network.

Conclusion

In most technology organizations within investment banks, teams are structured according to lines of business. These include operations like Equities, Risk, Debt, FX and so on. Others, such as Infrastructure and Architecture, span the organization horizontally, providing core services to these lines of business. These teams can include several hundred people and even run into thousands. For someone who leads such an operation, developing great teamwork can seem like an impossible task. Yet with careful and judicial attention, it is possible to target efforts where they will do most to build teams and tap into the extraordinary potential of teamwork. This chapter has outlined a number of practical ways in which this can be achieved, making it much more of a reality than a pipedream.

8

Getting the Best out of Individuals

I think a leader has to be prepared to listen as well as give their own opinions. Often people aren't collaborative because they are concerned about how they will look if others make poor decisions. When you're collaborative you take more personal risk because you are reliant on the people around you. That's why trust is so important. It's very hard to be a collaborative leader if you haven't got that.

Chief Technologist, hedge fund

In the last chapter we saw how building a team was one of the three essential tasks of a leader. This chapter focuses on getting the best out of individuals. People in leadership positions recognize that simply giving orders or instructions to the people who report to them is not enough. Although this approach might gain compliance, and get the job done, it does not usually lead to full engagement. While this might not have been all that important in the past, it is becoming essential in most if not all technology organizations within the financial services.

This chapter outlines what the collaborative leader needs to do if he or she is to tap into this commitment and engagement. I will outline a number of specific and practical approaches that can help you do this. As a result, you can adopt a style that gets the best out of individuals without having to rely on external factors, like your position, the offer of financial reward or career development.

Traditionally, managers in the financial services would set stretching goals and targets for their people. These would be linked closely to business performance and match the goals for which the manager was accountable. In return the manager could confidently expect employees to work hard to obtain these goals. If the latter were successful, financial reward would follow. Failure was not usually an option.

Today many things have changed to upset this transactional relationship between manager and employee. Firstly, the relationship between performance and pay is no longer straightforward. Following the turmoil in the industry during 2008/9, bonuses have been deferred or cut altogether. But even before these changes, cost pressures meant that in lean years managers could not so readily pay their way towards better employee performance.

A second change concerns shifts in the labour market. During good times, employees want more than just a fat pay packet. They know they can often get more by moving to another firm. To keep them where they are, managers need to offer more than just money. The term 'employee value proposition' refers to the value an employer offers to an employee and, ultimately, why he or she should continue working there. More and more employees want to know, 'What's in it for me?' when choosing to work for a new employer or stay with an existing one. Having a clear and compelling answer to this question is one way of gaining employee loyalty and commitment.

A third change concerns what is termed 'employee engagement'. Organizations today recognize the importance of achieving high levels of employee engagement if they are to be successful. The *Financial Times* has positioned it as key to successful recovery from the recession ('Managing Success', 19 January, 2010). A UK Government report argued for greater effort in building this among British businesses (MacLeod and Clarke, 2009). The report cites compelling evidence of the commercial reasons for doing this:

- A Gallup poll in 2006 of over 23,000 business units found that those with low levels of staff engagement experienced up to 50 per cent more turnover, compared with those with high levels of engagement. The latter, meanwhile, averaged 18 per cent higher productivity and 12 per cent higher profitability.

- A second Gallup study that year found Earnings Per Share growth in a study of 89 companies was 2.6 times higher among those with high levels of employee engagement than among those with low levels.

- A meta-analysis of opinion surveys of over 64,000 employees globally showed companies with high employee engagement levels improved 19.2 per cent in operating income, while those with low levels experienced a decline of 32 per cent (Towers Perrin-ISR, 2006).

These and other results like them make a compelling case for creating greater levels of employee engagement. Taken together, there seems to be sound reasons for managers seeking to get the best out of their employees, without relying on simply paying them more.

The difference between these two approaches is more than choosing the most effective way of gaining the highest performance and productivity levels, and it is worth spending a little time on what lies at the heart of this difference.

Fundamentally, the approach we adopt reflects our assumptions and beliefs about human nature. The psychologist Douglas McGregor, in his book *The Human Side of Enterprise* (1960), first drew attention to this. He described two fundamentally different belief systems that tended to distinguish between different types of manager in the United States. One belief system, labeled somewhat unimaginatively as Theory X, was based on the assumption that people prefer not to work hard if it can be avoided. Therefore, to gain their productive engagement managers must tightly control their performance. They can do this by setting very specific goals, monitoring employee performance closely and either rewarding the achievement of those goals or 'punishing' failure to do this. It is a very transactional form of management and reflects a view of human nature that places little store on higher-level needs such as achievement and recognition.

In contrast, the belief that people are intrinsically motivated to do a good job, and that the manager's role is to unleash their desire to perform at a high level, is known as a Theory Y belief system.

While McGregor might have come up with more imaginative names for these two distinctive belief systems, there is little doubt that he highlighted two very different sets of assumptions about human nature that shape the way people manage others. These assumptions tend to be self-fulfilling when put into practice by managers, providing them with the 'evidence' that supports their approach.

For our purposes the distinction is a useful way of thinking about how to get the best out of people and why this is important. Theory X assumes people are motivated to achieve tangible rewards (usually financial) or avoid punishments. In other words, their behaviour is driven by external factors such as money or threats. Theory Y assumes motivation comes from within; that intrinsic factors such as the need for recognition, achievement and meaningful work drive behaviour.

Managers often talk about the need to have on their team people who are willing to 'go the extra mile'. By this they mean people who will give more than can be obtained by paying them or by directing them to work harder. The term implies the presence of an internal desire to perform well and work hard, which cannot be influenced directly by the manager. People have to *want* to do it and not just do it because their manager compels them.

This type of internal motivation pays huge dividends for technology organizations in the financial sector. The release of a major new piece of software, or hitting aggressive project goals, means that people have to be prepared to go the extra mile if an organization is to be successful. This is especially so if they are operating in a distant location and cannot be directly observed, cajoled or encouraged to work harder. Managers need people who *want* to do a great job, irrespective of how much they might be paid or threatened with job loss or insecurity.

A view of human nature that is based on a set of beliefs that can be described as Theory X will not help in these situations. The Theory X view of people is not uncommon in the financial services, given the emphasis placed on monetary rewards and the bonus culture. However, if managers are to tap into a person's internal motivations, they have to reject this view of people in favour of one that is based on a Theory Y set of beliefs.

This might come as a hard pill to swallow for some managers within the financial services. I know from my own experiences of giving presentations on the subject of motivation that money is seen by many as a prime motivator. There is certainly no denying the importance of financial rewards. Few people within the sector are likely to say it is not important, even those who have done remarkably well at accumulating large sums of money and who have established financial independence. But given that it is often not possible now for managers to offer greater financial rewards in return for out of the ordinary performance, there has to be an alternative way to get the best out of people. This inevitably involves tapping into their internal reservoir of motivation.

The distinction between Theory X and Theory Y beliefs has been brought up to date recently with the publication of Daniel Pink's book *Drive*. In this he cites a number of remarkable psychological studies that really throw into question the effectiveness of relying on external rewards such as money to get the best performance from people.

One of these studies has particular relevance to the finance industry, since it shows what can happen if expected financial rewards are reduced or withdrawn. Carried out by Edward Deci at the Carnegie Mellon University, this study involved subjects being given mental puzzles to solve over a three-day period. On the second day, half the subjects were told they would be paid for their participation in the study, while the other half were told nothing. This had the predicted effect of boosting their performance. However, on the third day they were told there would be no money for that day's participation. As a result, their performance dropped to below that of the control group receiving no financial reward across all three days.

Pink quotes from Deci's original work:

> *When money is used as an external reward for some activity, the subjects lose intrinsic interest for the activity. Rewards can deliver a short term boost ... But the effect wears off – and worse, can reduce a person's longer-term motivation.*
>
> (Deci, quoted in Pink, Drive, 2010, p.8)

A study by two economists in Israel in 2000, also described by Pink, showed the limited value of transactional relationships,and the benefits of creating an internal desire to perform at a high level. Uri Gneezy and Aldo Rustichini measured the arrival times of parents collecting their children from a child care facility. In particular, they recorded how many parents arrived late each week over a four-week period. Then, with the permission of the centre's management, they posted a sign saying that a fine would be levied against parents arriving late. Rather than reducing lateness, the effect of the fine was to increase it. The authors argued that previously parents would arrive on time because they felt a sense of duty to do so. The introduction of fines made their relationship with their children's carers more transactional and many parents were prepared to pay the fine rather than make a special effort to arrive on time.

Pink goes on to quote a number of other studies, all of which show the limited and short-term benefits of financial rewards on human behaviour. He says they can extinguish intrinsic motivation, reduce performance, inhibit creativity and encourage people to 'play the numbers' (even to the point of cheating).

Pink suggests that Theory X beliefs encourage this kind of transactional behaviour and the corresponding negative consequences. He refers to it as Type X behaviour, and proposes an alternative, Type I, which he defines as 'behaviour fuelled more by intrinsic desires than extrinsic ones' (p.77).

Type I behaviour is exactly the kind of behaviour many managers in the financial services strive for in their direct reports. It is not dependent on external rewards (typically financial) over which many managers have little direct control. Neither does it depend on the manager's physical presence to persuade, cajole and even plead in the absence of being able to give a command. Instead it comes from within the individual him or herself and represents a genuine desire to give more effort without any offer of reward or threat of punishment.

To achieve this requires a collaborative style of leading. The manager has to work together with his or her direct reports to achieve common goals. Tapping into external motivation requires little in the way of collaboration. The manager simply ties reward and/or punishment to certain specific behaviours. The employee need not feel any great attachment to the manager or the organization. All he or she needs to do is achieve the goals that have been set. But to tap into internal states of commitment, a collaborative approach is needed. In the sections that follow I will show how this can be achieved.

Finding the 'Hot Buttons'

Think of a time when you were at your very best at work. It may have been while working on a particular project or while being part of a high-performing team. It might have been when you had to pull out all the stops to get a job done or solve a problem under pressure of time. Whatever the occasion, conjure up the time and the experience now.

When I ask this of participants on our leadership programmes, I follow it up with a series of questions aimed at unpicking what it was about the situation that contributed to the person's performance. I also probe to find out whether these features can be generalized to other situations and whether they form part of the person's motivators. Typically, the kinds of things that get mentioned as being important to that person include one or more of the following:

Achievement: doing something difficult and succeeding in doing it well.

Autonomy: having the freedom to decide on what to do and how to do it.

Responsibility : being held accountable for something.

Innovation: having to work out the solution to a problem, when there is little to go on.

Recognition: being recognized by one's peers for having done a good job.

Teamwork: working with other people in a highly coordinated and collaborative way.

Skills: being able to draw upon one's skills and operate on one's strengths, the things we are good at.

Contribution: making a positive difference that has implications and benefits for other people and the organization as a whole.

This exercise shows that when one or more of these features are present, people are able to reach very high levels of performance. Typically, they feel energized and committed. They are willing to go the extra mile to achieve the goal they are working towards. Usually they have had a hand in defining this goal and feel a high degree of ownership. Rarely, if ever, does money enter the equation, even though financial reward may follow success.

If you know this kind of information about the people who work for you, you can tap into it. It represents their 'hot buttons' and by pressing these you can get the best out of them. By allocating work or responsibilities that are in line with their internal motivators, they will go the extra mile not because you are paying them to do so, but because they feel driven by what is really important to them.

Your role as manager is to collaborate with them to help ensure they can do this. How do you find out what their motivators are? Ask them. While this is not a conversation for the water cooler, it is very definitely one for appraisal meetings, though it is not always discussed in these. Weekly one-to-one meetings also provide an opportunity to have this kind of conversation. Obviously, it needs to be handled skillfully, but it should not be difficult or inappropriate to ask your direct report about the things that are really important to them in their work and which lead to their best performance. This should then be followed by a discussion about how these features can be incorporated into specific tasks or roles that the person has responsibility for.

Obviously, you are not looking to ensure every aspect of their job has one or more of their key motivators. It is a fact of life that a certain portion of our jobs will be routine or take us outside our comfort zone. The aim is not to create super-motivated people who buzz around the office all day long. Rather it is to ensure that on specific and important tasks you are able to get the very best out of a person while at the same time enabling them to feel great about the work they do.

Choosing the Right Style

Another approach to getting the best out of others involves matching your leadership style to their needs in a given situation. While this approach does not necessarily lead to the high levels of motivation that can be found when tapping into a person's key motivators, it can help you avoid the opposite: those situations where a person appears demotivated and underperforms.

The approach is based on one of the most successful and enduring models of effective management: situational leadership. Developed by Paul Hersey and Ken Blanchard in the 1970s, the model is a practical way of ensuring you provide the most appropriate level of support and direction when managing another person. Why is this important? Well, think of a time when your manager (past or current) used the 'wrong' style when managing you. Most people can easily conjure up such a relationship and most will recall it as an unpleasant period in their career. The consequences of being on the receiving end of an inappropriate style are feelings of demotivation and despair. Work becomes a chore and you gladly look forward to getting away from it, but even when you do it plays on your mind, preventing you from relaxing or switching off.

If this sounds familiar, you are like almost everyone else I have asked this question of. Unfortunately we all have experiences of working for someone who just uses the wrong approach or style with us and who fails to get the best out of us as a result.

The term 'style' is somewhat vague though, and although you might easily relate the 'wrong' style to a manager with whom you did not get on, it is difficult to define style in practical ways that will help you avoid making the same mistakes with those whom report to you. This is where Hersey and Blanchard's model comes in useful. It provides a practical way of defining 'leadership style' that can be used to get the best match between what you do and what the person you lead wants from you.

Essentially, the model focuses on the amount of direction you provide on a specific task to be carried out by a person under your leadership and the amount of support you provide them. High levels of direction are marked by providing clear and specific instructions about what has to be done, when it has to be done and how it should be done. There is little room for input from the other person – their role is to follow your precise instructions. While this might sound pretty oppressive and not what you think of as an appropriate and open style of leadership, think of situations where you have wanted clear and specific guidelines from your manager and all you received instead were vague and unclear instructions. It can leave you feeling lost and directionless.

The situations in which such a clear, directive style of leadership is important are usually those where the person being led lacks experience for a specific task and the confidence to do it well unaided. It's a bit like getting lost on your way to an important job interview and fearing you will arrive inappropriately late. If you ask someone for directions all you want from them are clear instructions about the route to take. The more specific, the better. You certainly don't want them to involve you in working out the answer ('Let's see, how would you *like* to get there?').

The second element of the model focuses on the amount of support you provide to a direct report in relation to a specific task. High levels of support are characterized by behaviours like listening, encouraging, praising and rewarding. These sound like the opposite of the high direction behaviours – why would anyone *not* want to receive these from his or her manager?

The answer, once again, depends on the other person's level of ability and confidence to perform the specific task in question. When this is low, the positive supporting behaviours can seem like a distraction. As with the person lost on their way to an interview, they are just not needed at the present time. The need for this kind of support is also low when the person concerned has a high level of ability. Encouragement and praise from a manager can feel patronizing when given about something a person does well and confidently.

High support behaviour is most appropriate when a person has a moderate level of ability for the task in hand. Their confidence may be reasonably high, but easily dented. The person needs praise and encouragement to assure them they are on the right track.

In summary then, the Situational Leadership model provides important clues about the amount of direction and support a person wants from their manager when performing a specific task. The right amount depends on the person's level of ability and motivation to perform that task (referred to as 'readiness' in the model) and should vary accordingly. This relationship has been summarized in Figure 8.1 below.

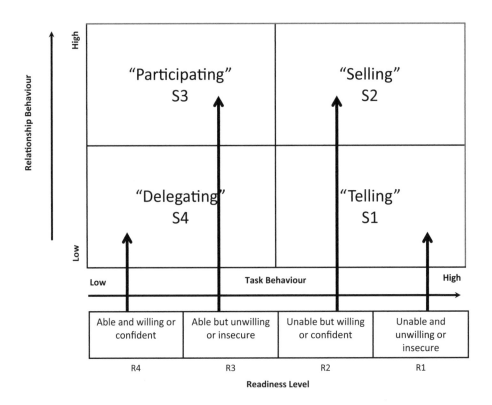

Figure 8.1   Choosing the best style of leading, based on readiness level

The beauty of this model lies in its simplicity and practicality. It is almost universally valued by participants on Catalyst's leadership programmes because they can easily relate to it and see how they can put it into practice themselves. As part of the class, I often ask people to see if they can use the model to interpret and explain a particular instance where someone is underperforming and to suggest ways to improve the situation. Most instances of underperformance have an element which can be explained by the wrong style being used. Perhaps the person is not being given enough direction or maybe their motivation levels have dropped and more support is needed. Normally, a shift in style can start to correct things and provide the person with what they need to get their performance back up to acceptable levels.

The Situational Leadership model has several implications if you are to apply it correctly:

IT'S HARD TO AGREE ON A PERSON'S LEVEL OF READINESS

A person's view of their ability to perform a specific task may be different from their manager's view. In particular, the manager may not have as much confidence in their employee and may want to maintain more control than the latter is comfortable with. This is not uncommon and the best way ahead is for the manager and employee to have a good open discussion about the level of direction and control the manager should provide, using the Situational Leadership model as the basis for the discussion. They should try to agree on what would constitute evidence of the employee's ability and the level of risk the manager is prepared to take to give the person more latitude in deciding how to perform the task. Often the way ahead is for the manager to take this risk and to review the situation with the employee at an agreed point in time. The employee should be encouraged to raise the alarm if things are not going according to plan and not to feel they have lost face in doing so.

THE STYLE A MANAGER USES GETS THE BEHAVIOUR IT MATCHES

Managers who use a hands-on style (S1 or S2) tend to justify this by pointing to the low level of ability or commitment of their direct reports. This might be true for tasks that are relatively new to the employee. But if it reflects a longer-term pattern it is likely to be a reflection of the manager's style rather than the employee's ability or motivation. Research has shown the self-fulfilling nature of different management styles and a manager who maintains tight control over his employees is unlikely to develop them into empowered individuals.

The way ahead is for the manager to move to a more hands-off style (S3) as a way of encouraging greater responsibility and commitment to the task in the individuals concerned. This shift should be made explicitly so there are no surprises for the employee and the two individuals should review the situation to ensure both are happy with progress.

MANAGERS SOMETIMES FLIP FROM ONE EXTREME TO THE OTHER, THEN BACK AGAIN

This is a common pattern and is described by Ken Blanchard as 'Tell-Leave Alone-Zap!' I came across this pattern once when I was asked to help a manger who was receiving lots of complaints from his staff. Coaching sessions with him revealed he was a very innovative thinker, who liked to set his staff research projects into unchartered territories that might reveal new products and approaches. He would give them two or three months to report back to him. Inevitably they had not done what he had expected (usually due to the fact there was little established practice to follow) and this would be met by him losing his temper with them. It became clear that he was adopting an S1 style at the outset of a research project (telling the person what he wanted) then moving to a completely hands-off S4 style while the work was carried out, only to move back to a very dictatorial S1 style when it failed to meet his expectations. The solution lay in him closely monitoring the person's work (S2) and only moving to a more hands-off style (S3) on a later task if the person had shown they can work with less supervision.

The pattern does not have to be as extreme as this for it to take place. Managers sometimes recognize they have fallen into the habit of using an S1 or S2 style and that they need to be more hands-off in their approach. They then switch to a completely hands-off style (S4), leaving the employee confused and feeling somewhat dumped. This usually confirms to the manger that he or she was right to use an S1 or S2 style and they revert to what they think is appropriate. A delegating style (S4) should always be achieved gradually for a specific task, never in one leap. If S1 is appropriate initially, then over time the manager should change to S2, then S3 and finally S4.

THE SAME PERSON MAY NEED THEIR MANAGER TO ADOPT A NUMBER OF DIFFERENT STYLES

I sometimes hear managers say things like, 'The people in my team are all different, so I adopt a different approach for each person. Some need lots of supervision, while others need much less. I try to give each person what they need.' While this sounds very enlightened, it ignores a central fact about the Situational Leadership model: it is task-specific. Depending on the task they are performing, an employee may need a lot of supervision (S1 or S2) or much less (S3 or S4). Managers should be wary not to pigeon-hole their people and should instead aim to provide a flexible approach for each person.

PEOPLE CAN SOMETIMES MOVE BACKWARDS ALONG THE READINESS CONTINUUM

The Situational Leadership model paints a picture of people first performing a task with a relatively low level of ability and motivation, and gradually moving over time to a high level of both. While this may be the ideal, it is sometimes the case that a person moves in the opposite direction. Someone who was previously able and motivated to perform a specific task may underperform at that task, moving down in their level of readiness. If an S4 style had been used, their drop in performance requires the manager to move back along the curve to either an S3 or S2 style. This makes sense really, since a person is unlikely to lose the ability to perform a task. Their underperformance is more likely to reflect a concern they have or something which is causing them some degree of stress. The manager therefore needs to increase the Supporting aspect of their style (S3 or S2 both have high levels of support), to uncover the cause of the problem and work out ways to address it. He or she needs to do a lot of listening rather than telling and show concern and empathy for the person if the root of the problem is to be unearthed. Only when it has been addressed and the employee has moved back to their previous high level of performance can the manager revert back to an S4 style.

S1 AND S4: THERE'S GOOD AND BAD IN BOTH

When described to someone for the first time, S1 can sometimes seem inappropriately authoritarian. It involves the manager telling a person what to do, when to do it and even how to do it. Such a style sounds out of date with modern management techniques that emphasize empowerment and participation (even collaboration!). While it is true that a dictatorial or authoritarian approach can be described as S1, it is not the case that adopting an S1 style means becoming some sort of ogre. The manager needs to combine clear, precise instructions with consideration. This is not about shouting orders; tone of voice should be steady and moderate; other aspects of the manager's body language need to convey a pleasant demeanour.

Similarly, an S4 style can sound like abdication and managers can quite easily leave their employee feeling neglected and unsupported while assuming themselves that they are providing a suitably hands-off S4 style. When adopting an S4 style, managers should make it clear they trust the person needs little supervision but that they are there if needed. They should not see S4 as an opportunity to 'cut and run' to other more pressing demands.

THE MODEL WORKS FINE WHEN MANAGERS AND EMPLOYEES ARE IN THE SAME BUILDING, BUT FOR PEOPLE ON DIFFERENT SIDES OF THE WORLD IT'S NOT SO USEFUL

It is true that the Situational Leadership model was developed in a different era for a very different world than the one we work in today. A hands-on style involving lots of close supervision (S1) is not so easy when managing a virtual team. Similarly, these circumstances are likely to mean a hands-off style, with little direct supervision (S4), is likely to be adopted due to the distances involved rather than the level of readiness shown by the individual.

Paradoxically, the Situational Leadership model can really help when leading a virtual team, with individuals based in different geographical locations spanning the globe. For many managers in situations like this, relying upon individuals to manage remote locations is experienced as a loss of control. The manager is still accountable for performance in the regions, but has to rely upon others to achieve it. In this context their natural reaction and desire is to exert control, but this is not easy given the distances involved.

Given that the situation makes an S4 style almost inevitable, the model can be used by the astute manager to plan how to ensure this style is appropriate. The importance of correctly diagnosing the direct report's level of readiness is even more important and should be the subject of good open conversations between manager and direct report. Unless the direct report has a high level of readiness (suitable for S4 leadership) the conversation should then turn to how to provide an appropriate style (S1, S2 or S3), given that both manager and direct report are in different locations. A hands-on (S1 or S2) style may be provided by regular contact, such as daily telephone or video conference calls. Initially, the manager may need to spend time at the location of his or her direct report, providing close supervision until a higher level of readiness is achieved and a less hands-on style can be adopted.

The fact that the Situational Leadership model can still be useful when leading remote teams points to its practical value and adaptability. In my view it is one of the best tools to help managers lead more collaboratively and to get the best out of their people. On its own it does not necessarily mean people will feel motivated and driven to go the extra mile, but without the right style in place they are most unlikely to feel committed.

Collaborative Decision Making

Closely related to the idea of adopting the best-fit style is that of adopting the best approach to making decisions. Managers are faced with a number of possibilities when it comes to making decisions, concerning the degree to which they involve their direct reports in this process. How collaborative should they be to get the best out of people? While involving one's direct reports in the decision-making process might seem more inclusive and collaborative, the practical challenges are not insignificant. Even if one could find the time to do this, common sense dictates it is not always the right thing to do. Some decisions have to be made on the basis of information that is not for widespread consumption. Decisions about the future fate of individuals cannot be taken with those individuals or with their peers. Decisions about more strategic goals that have broader impact might seem more open to staff involvement, but raise the question about who exactly should be setting future direction. Should this be determined by a 'bottom-up' approach or set by those at the top of the organization with little involvement from those at lower levels?

Fortunately, this question of inclusiveness in decision making has been well researched. Not surprisingly, it tends to depend on the nature of the decision and the level of commitment and buy-in desired.

One of the most practical guides to this was developed by two psychologists in the 1970s and has stood the test of time. Victor Vroom and David Yetton devised a form of flow chart that guided managers down the various options depending on the choices available when making the decision and the role of others in this process. The model is shown in Figure 8.2.

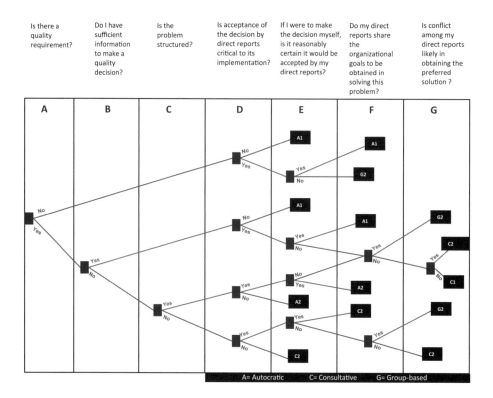

| Is there a quality requirement? | Do I have sufficient information to make a quality decision? | Is the problem structured? | Is acceptance of the decision by direct reports critical to its implementation? | If I were to make the decision myself, is it reasonably certain it would be accepted by my direct reports? | Do my direct reports share the organizational goals to be obtained in solving this problem? | Is conflict among my direct reports likely in obtaining the preferred solution? |

Figure 8.2   The Vroom–Yetton decision tree

Source: *Leadership and Decision-Making*, Victor H. Vroom and Philip W. Yetton, © 1973. Reprinted by permission of University of Pittsburg Press.

The model highlights five distinctive decision-making styles, divided into two that are autocratic (A) and two that are consultative (C), and one that is group-based (G):

A1: You solve the problem or make the decision yourself using information available to you at that time.

A2: You obtain the necessary information from direct reports and then decide yourself. You may or may not tell direct reports what the problem is in getting information from them. The role played by your direct reports in making the decision is one of providing the necessary information to you rather than generating or evaluating alternative decisions.

C1: You share the problem with relevant direct reports individually, getting their ideas and suggestions without bringing them together as a group. Then you make the decision, which may or may not reflect their points of view.

C2: You share the problem with your direct reports as a group, collectively obtaining all ideas and suggestions. Then you make the decision, which may or may not reflect their points of view.

G2: You share the problem with your direct reports as a group. Together you generate and evaluate alternatives and attempt to reach an agreement on the decision.

The choice of style depends on factors such as the importance of the decision, whether it is technical and has a 'correct' solution, and the importance of everyone giving their 'buy-in' to the decision. By using the prompt questions as a guide through the flow chart, managers can arrive at the best style to use when making a decision.

Although this might appear to be a bit mechanical, and might seem to reduce complex decision making to a series of superficial questions, don't be distracted by its simplicity. It is based on sound research and has intuitive appeal to many managers. It is best used as a guide to decisions, rather than a magic formula, so it should never replace the complex thought that might go into making an important decision like that faced by Peter Clarke at Man.

In getting the best out of individuals, leaders need to decide whether and when to involve others in key decisions. Too little involvement and people will find it difficult to commit fully to a decision that has been made without their input. Leaders need to think carefully about the consequences of excluding others from the process if this degree of commitment is desired. By involving people you are more likely to tap into their inner resources and ideas, resulting in a better quality decision than if you had made it on your own.

However, not all decisions can be made inclusively and democratically and it is the leader's role to do what is right for the business rather than what is popular with his or her direct reports. This means that although individuals may be consulted, their views or inputs may need to be overruled in the interests of the organization as a whole. In these circumstances, getting the best out of them rather than just their compliance can be a time consuming and difficult process. Peter Clarke described how he achieved this within Man:

> It's undoubtedly the case in many financial organisations, including our own, that change is facilitated by a more difficult environment. But from my perspective, the key is not to walk into a meeting and say that is what is happening but to develop that over a course of several months, deciding clearly where I wanted to go with the team, and having each of the business units supportive of that.
>
> Part of the process is that you go and see senior people and say 'This is what we are going to do, you agree, don't you?' But people who agree with me in a meeting, I don't necessarily view this as agreement as I know they may have reservations and I will, depending on who they are, go back to them privately, and ask 'If you have got any questions, tell me now, I don't mind but tell me now.' Because in meetings, even influential people can be remarkably reticent. You can't have that, you have to be able to take people out separately and make sure you have their word.

His approach then, is to build consensus gradually, giving each person the opportunity to question and challenge a decision, and then decide for themselves whether they could commit to it. Only if and when they could, can the next steps be taken.

Maintaining the Psychological Contract

A final approach to getting the very best out of people is to maintain the psychological contract that exists implicitly between the employee and the company they work for. The psychological contract is the unwritten 'rules' that determine a fair exchange between employer and employee. Although it is based on a transactional view of this relationship, it is not the same as the Theory X approach to motivation that I described at the beginning of this chapter. Instead it is an alternative route to the internal drive to perform well that resides in all individuals but which often is not accessed by managers wishing to get the best out of them.

Consider first the formal contract that exists between an employer and employee. This outlines the nature of an exchange between both parties. The employer will provide paid employment and various conditions relating to holidays, sick leave, pensions, working conditions and training. In return the employee provides his or her efforts and expertise to perform the role at a suitable level. The business of making and accepting a job offer is a process of finding quantities and types on both sides of this equation that are acceptable to both parties. All of this is formally and openly discussed, duly recorded and committed to by employer and employee, and represents the formal contact of employment.

Now consider the additional commitments an employer (or rather the employee's manager) expects of his or her recruit. Typically, a manager would like the individual to demonstrate the following traits:

- loyalty;

- commitment to the firm and its enterprise;

- conscientious behaviour;

- a good team player;

- a pleasant person to work with and ability to get on with others;

- creativity;

- flexibility;

- willingness to go the extra mile;

- honesty;

- trustworthiness.

None (or very few) of these are typically contained in the formal contract, yet they might form part of the interview process and they are certainly expected by the manager in return for continued employment. When I ask managers what they expect from their employees in addition to a formally stated commitment, I usually get a list of features like the one above.

When I then ask them what their employees expect in return for these 'additional' demands, I can see this forces them to think a little more deeply.

Following a period of reflection they come up with a list not unlike the following:

- loyalty;

- commitment to the individual;

- flexibility;

- honesty;

- trustworthiness;

- concern for their well-being;

- recognition;

- opportunity;

- growth and development.

The behaviours and attributes on both of these lists rarely make it to the formal employment contract, but they form an implicit expectation on the part of employer and employee. This is what is known as the psychological contract and it is just as powerful in determining an ongoing relationship as the formal employment contract.

The significance of this for getting the best out of individuals is that the psychological contract needs to be seen as fair and balanced if people are to commit to their side of the bargain. Like a see-saw, if one party reduces its commitment, the other party experiences a tension and seeks to redraw the balance.

If you want to get the best out of your direct reports, therefore, you need to ensure you are meeting your own side of the bargain. In return for commitment, creativity, flexibility and discretionary effort from your employee, you need to ensure he or she feels you and the firm in general are loyal and committed to them, and provide appropriate levels of recognition, concern for their well-being and opportunity for personal growth.

Unfortunately, these latter benefits are often in short supply when a financial institution is responding to a downturn in the market like the credit crunch of 2008/9, or during a major restructuring of the business, or a merger or acquisition. Many managers feel helpless to influence the consequences of these major structural changes for the individuals caught up in them, including themselves. As a result the psychological contract becomes imbalanced and possibly damaged (sometimes irretrievably so).

Without a healthy, balanced psychological contract, individuals are unlikely to give their all. They will scale back on how much of the first list above they contribute to their role. If and when they have been treated poorly, they will withdraw these 'extras' and simply do what is formally expected of them. Their relationship with their manager and the firm he or she represents will become almost wholly transactional.

To restore the balance, leaders and managers need to find a way to ensure that within the limits imposed on them they are providing the benefits their employees expect. Change needs to be handled sensitively and demonstrate concern for all individuals, including those not badly affected. There are horror stories of individuals only discovering they no longer work for a firm when their pass does not operate the turnstile. Some learn of this from listening to the radio while travelling to work. Others might be told that all individuals to be 'exited' will receive a call during the day asking them to come up to an office being used for the purpose of breaking the bad news. Throughout the day each individual waits in dread for their phone to ring. False alarm calls from others simply add to the tension.

Those people not unduly affected by a round of job cuts will nevertheless draw their own conclusion about the firm by the way their less fortunate colleagues are treated. If they feel the psychological contract has not been honoured they are just as likely to withdraw some of their own commitment and loyalty.

The psychological contract can be affected by smaller-scale imbalances than headcount reductions. Individuals may not feel they receive appropriate recognition for their work or they may not have a strong sense that you or the firm care about their well-being. As a result, you are unlikely to get the 'extras' from them that you might hope for. However, all is not lost, since the process also works through a virtuous cycle. Provide plenty of the commitments on your side of the equation and you will find that the people you manage reward you with fulfilling their side of the (implicit) bargain.

Summary

The ability to get the best out of others often makes the difference between running a highly successful operation and running one that has a more variable track record of success. Collaborative leaders, through working in a spirit of joint partnership with their people, are much more likely to achieve this than those who adopt a traditional 'command and control' approach to leading others.

This relies on more than being a 'nice' person, as this chapter has hopefully demonstrated. It requires a good knowledge of each person's motivators or 'hot buttons'. It also requires an appropriately collaborative style based on the other person's level of ability and motivation for specific tasks. Decision making needs to be tailored to the demands of a given situation, involving appropriate amounts of participation and involvement. Finally, there needs to be an understanding of the importance of the psychological contract that exists between manager and direct report and efforts by the former to ensure this is not damaged or neglected. By attending to these four features you can tap into the extraordinary levels of commitment and motivation that each of us possess but which are often not fully exploited.

9

Delivering Value from Projects and Programmes

If you are a project manager, charged with delivering a major technology initiative to the business, your number one priority will be to ensure the project delivers on its promise. To the extent that the technology is unproven, or highly complex, or reliant on a level of support that outstrips your organization's ability to provide, you might expect to at least fall behind on delivery dates or overrun on your budget. If you're like most project managers I know, you will offset the likelihood of this happening by focusing on 'execution' – the skill and thoroughness with which you manage the project.

These two factors, the technology delivered and the process followed in doing this, might seem to be the obvious culprits when projects fail to deliver. Yet somewhat surprisingly, their contribution to whether a project succeeds or fails is negligible. Of far greater significance is your ability to manage the 'people' aspects of the project. This may seem somewhat ironic if your main focus over the course of your career has been to develop your technical know-how and your ability to follow a rigorous project management methodology.

With technology projects growing ever more complex in their design and execution, it is becoming apparent that the effective collaboration of all parties involved represents probably the most significant of these 'people' factors. A recent report on a survey by McKinsey into organizational transformations has as its opening sentence:

> *When organizational transformations succeed, managers typically pay attention to 'people issues', especially fostering collaboration among leaders and employees and building capabilities.*
> (*McKinsey and Company*, What Successful Transformations Share, *McKinsey Global Survey Results, 2010*)

To succeed in delivering a major project or business transformation, project managers need to be skilled at ensuring all stakeholders work together in a coordinated effort to meet the project goals. Scott Marcar, head of Risk & Finance Technology at The Royal Bank of Scotland's investment banking arm, sees this as a fundamental requirement of people charged with leading major programmes:

> *The role of the programme manager becomes much more about getting the right people into the room and driving through decisions and outcomes than it is about actually just delivering a programme of work.*

Put simply, your ability to lead collaboratively and to bring about the collaboration of multiple stakeholders is perhaps the single most important aspect of your job if you are a project manager.

So far we have looked at a number of ways in which people in leadership roles within Technology and Operations can lead in a more collaborative way, better suited to the demands of a global operation. Most of this has been within the context of 'work as usual', that is, the normal day-to-day job of supporting the Front Office. But this context only applies to part of the work people are called upon to perform within Technology.

The work of technology functions within investment banks can be divided into two types of activity: run the bank (RTB) and change the bank (CTB). The former refers to all activities that are involved in providing the technology to support the day-to-day processes of an investment bank. This includes processing trades, providing software to monitor trading positions and ensuring the technology infrastructure remains stable. The phrase often used to describe this activity is 'keeping the lights on'.

CTB activities are all those that are designed to enhance the technology infrastructure that is available to the bank. This might include replacing or upgrading legacy systems, transferring all trades from one platform to another (following a merger), or developing new software with the potential to gain the bank a competitive advantage.

CTB activities are almost always carried out through distinct projects or programmes. The latter is defined as a collection of projects, each of which is part of a bigger whole, to deliver a major technological change. This kind of work can account for a major part of a technology function's budget and easily runs to many hundreds of millions of dollars for a Tier One investment bank.

Within this context, what role does collaboration play and how can a project manager or programme manager lead more collaboratively? This chapter outlines some of the key challenges faced when leading a major technology project and the importance of bringing all parties involved closer together to ensure all the deliverables are met.

The Importance of Collaboration to Project and Programme Management

Given the centrality of technology projects and programmes to technology organizations within investment banks, it is somewhat surprising that so many of these fail to deliver on their initial promise. This fact was dramatically brought home in the most thorough analysis of IT projects across all industries in the United States. Produced by the Standish Group, and initially reported in 1995, this study covered over 8,000 software applications across all industries. The study showed that only 16 per cent of these delivered on time, to budget and with all the features of the original specification. That is, a whopping 84 per cent fell below this acceptable standard (The Standish Group Report, 1995).

When first reported the findings caused a massive stir in the IT industry. Although the spectre of projects running over deadlines and budgets rang true with most project managers' experiences, few could have expected the proportion of failed projects to be so high.

This finding was no flash in the pan, either. The Standish Group Report for 2009 shows the proportion of successful IT projects to be no higher than one-third. Spread over a period of almost 15 years, the main reasons for failure remain remarkably consistent. Lack of user involvement at all stages of the project, wavering executive support, and unrealistic expectations and objectives all contribute significantly to the failure of major IT projects.

There are four main reasons why the challenge of meeting these 'people' aspects has increased in recent years:

1. Within the context of investment banking, many if not most IT projects are highly complex. Not only do they involve cutting-edge

technologies of which there may be limited experience, they also involve people from many different parts of the bank working together towards the project goals. Complex matrix management structures mean that these different stakeholders often have competing demands made on their time and resources. Meeting the needs of the project manager to hit a project milestone may well conflict with their other roles and the needs of their own functional managers.

2.   Often these multiple stakeholders are globally dispersed. Working effectively across different time zones and with people from different cultures becomes a prerequisite for successfully coordinating the actions of these people. As pointed out by Lynda Gratton of the London Business School, and discussed in Chapter 7, global teams of highly specialized individuals from diverse backgrounds are needed to succeed, yet make it seemingly impossible to do so.

3.   Some IT projects involve buying software from third-party vendors. This requires the project team to work collaboratively with the vendor to make modifications and install the software. While there is a common goal that this is successfully achieved, the customer and vendor may often have conflicting priorities about *how* it is achieved, the roles and responsibilities of those involved and the timescales in which to achieve it. The project manager is responsible for ensuring vendors remain committed to delivery and that they work effectively with internal stakeholders.

4.   The role of the business has changed in recent years. As the sponsor of many projects, business partners want to know the software delivered will make a real difference to their bottom line. If they have growth aspirations the technology must be capable of allowing them to scale their business, often at an exponential rate. It must also be highly stable and meet very demanding uptime targets. Traditionally there have been different levels of understanding between technologists and the business about what can be achieved and what is appropriate. The latter will sometimes want to add functionality but not expect costs to rise or delivery dates to be pushed back. Technologists all too often focus on delivering exactly what has been requested in the original specification, only to discover it is not actually what is needed. More recently, business

partners have become more technologically savvy, resulting in them wanting to play a more influential role in the technology choices that are made. While this might result in a stronger partnership between technologists and business sponsors, it can also lead to more disagreements on the best way ahead. Establishing a good collaborative relationship with the business is fraught with difficulties and rarely follows the path of true collaboration.

Clearly, collaboration is going to be key to any successful project or programme, and this is especially so for today's highly complex IT initiatives that involve multiple stakeholders belonging to a variety of organizations and operating on a global scale. I have discussed a number of skills that can help you develop into a more collaborative leader, but what else is there that is specific to the role of the project manager that can help in this situation? In the section that follows I describe the results from a major research study we have initiated at Catalyst into the specific factors associated with successful leadership and execution of technology projects. The results provide startling evidence that all too often project managers have been focusing on the wrong things when it comes to delivering on time, to budget and to specification.

Critical Success Factors

The research investigated the factors that are associated with the successful completion of major technology projects or programmes within the financial services. Like Gratton and Erikson, we have compared successful projects with unsuccessful projects in an effort to identify what makes the difference. Catalyst's research differs from theirs in that it focuses on a wider range of factors than those associated with building collaboration. Thus it includes features of the design of the programme, leadership, execution and benefits delivery.

We obtained data from 120 completed Technology programmes within a number of major investment banks and hedge funds. Over one-quarter of these projects involved an investment greater than US$5 million and more than one in ten had a budget of over US$25 million.

Our findings show that four broad factors all need to be successfully completed if a project is to deliver real business value (see Figure 9.1).

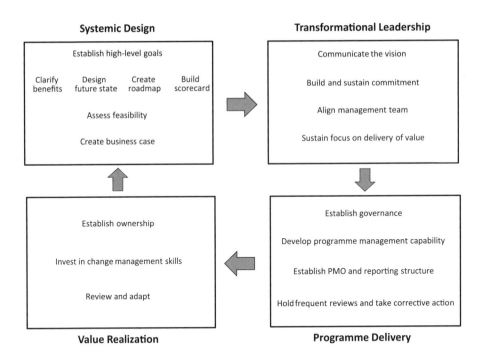

Figure 9.1   The value delivery lifecycle model

It can help to think of these four factors as similar to those involved in publishing a book.[1] First there needs to be a good plot (design), an interesting story to tell that others will want to read. The more detail that can be given at this stage, the better. This on its own though is not enough to lead to a best seller. The next stage (leadership) is to get backing from those with the power and resources to turn a good idea into something real. In most cases this will be a publisher. The role of the publisher is to allocate resources to the project and support the author in his or her work. The third stage (execution), involves the author putting pen to paper and writing the book. The skill with which he or she does this is obviously important, as are regular reviews with those sponsoring the effort. Finally, when the book is written it needs to be marketed and sold in an effective way (benefits delivery). This involves handling the logistics of getting physical copies of the book to the right bookshops in the most appropriate locations so that the marketing succeeds.

Successful projects follow a not dissimilar process. A project has to start with a sound business case and has to receive appropriate backing and support

---

1   I am indebted to my colleague Chris Cooke for this analogy.

from those who control resources. It needs to be well executed as a project and lead to tangible benefits if it is to be considered successful. With this in mind, what did our survey show that made the difference between success and failure?

DESIGN

At the outset of a project there is a design element that determines what will be delivered. Usually this involves the project sponsor, the business partner (if different) and representatives from technology, usually a CTO or similar senior figures. The aim at this stage is to get as close a fit as possible between the technology solution and the business problem it is designed to solve.

This might sound fairly straightforward, yet in a surprising number of cases there is a mismatch. In my experience, it is not unusual for a senior technologist to see a particular solution as one that is desirable for the firm to have, without having clearly defined the problem it is intended to solve. System X is seen as a 'must have', clearly superior to what the bank already has in place. This, along with an acceptable potential saving, is often all it takes to initiate a project running into millions of dollars.

In our survey of 120 IT projects, only 28 per cent were reported to have had a very strong business case, yet this was crucial to the subsequent success or failure of the project: 44 per cent of successful projects had a strong business case, compared with only 15 per cent of those projects that failed to meet their objectives.

It is also vital there is clarity of the project's goals and outcomes, and usually this has to be set by the person ultimately responsible for the project. Scott Marcar highlights this as a key requisite of any major project or programme:

> *It's about clarity of thought, clarity of vision, consistency and drive. I think you have to have that clarity of vision at the top because I think if you don't and you try and run things by committee you are almost certainly never going to get anywhere.*

This was confirmed in our survey, where fully 41 per cent of those projects or programmes that failed to meet their stated objectives were reported to have unclear goals and outcomes, compared with only 3 per cent of those that succeeded (see Figure 9.2).

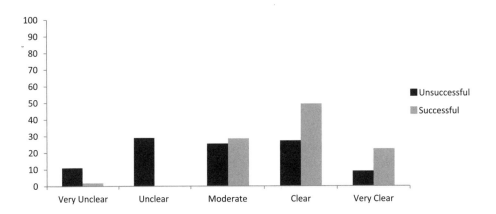

Figure 9.2   Clarity of goals of successful and unsuccessful IT projects in the financial services

Other design aspects necessary at this stage include:

- A systemic view of the future operating model. By this I mean alignment of the solution with the skills, process, structure, culture and other assets of the organization.

- Proven engineering and design, specifying quality needs such as scale, performance, availability and security, and matching design patterns to them.

- Feasible and adaptive plans. The least risky projects involve small numbers of highly experienced developers working through rapid cycles in close partnership with their stakeholders.

These all point to the importance of key people involved in the design stage of a project to work together closely to develop a shared understanding of why it is needed, what it will achieve and how it will deliver benefits through improvements to business processes.

Unfortunately the reality is often different, with one or two powerful stakeholders driving the design stage and those involved in the execution merely following the technical specification. Although it might appear too late to change things once the project has begun, rarely is this a linear process and it is often desirable to return to the original design issues and make changes if the execution stage suggests this is appropriate.

LEADERSHIP

The leadership team for the project typically is a multi-party group, with people representing the business, end-users, the project manager and possibly vendors. Their role is to drive the project forward, dealing with the many obstacles that are likely to impede progress. They also have a duty to communicate the vision of the project in positive terms, building support for its deliverables and awareness of why it is needed. Collaboration amongst this group is absolutely essential, since disagreements and infighting can blight any project. Clear, strong and consistent decision making is also vital at this stage. The leadership team should not succumb to short-term pressures but keep in mind the longer-term vision of what the project is designed to deliver. The distinction between management (doing things right) and leadership (doing the right things) is particularly relevant here and it is the latter that this group needs to demonstrate.

Traditionally, this kind of leadership was provided by a strong-willed person with a clear sense of direction. However, the complexity and global scale of many projects today means that no single individual provides this and the responsibility rests with a leadership team. Matthew Hampson, head of Architecture & Change at The Royal Bank of Scotland, provides the rationale for this shift:

> One of the problems with the traditional approach is that it doesn't scale very well. So as the project gets more complex, the utility of one highly empowered individual who has full control falls away. You just can't do it. You can't have the entire organization funnel up to one individual. It doesn't make sense.

Our research confirmed the importance a high degree of collaboration among this leadership group for the eventual success of a project. In 90 per cent of successful projects there was a high level of unity among the leadership team around the project vision, compared with only 33 per cent of unsuccessful projects. Overall, only half of all projects surveyed reported a high level of commitment by the leadership team, with this figure rising to 64 per cent among successful projects compared with only 23 per cent among unsuccessful projects (see Figure 9.3).

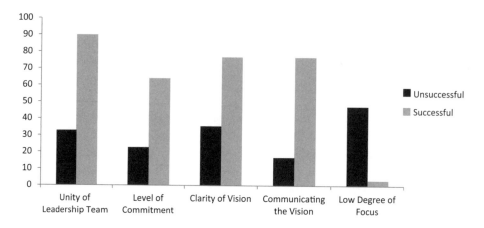

Figure 9.3   Leadership of successful and unsuccessful projects

The figures in the chart above also show the importance of this team being clear about what the project was intended to realize (77 per cent of successful projects reported this, compared with 35 per cent of unsuccessful ones) and its effectiveness in communicating that vision to others (77 per cent compared with 17 per cent). Finally, the leadership team must remain absolutely focused on achieving that vision and not be swayed by circumstances. Forty seven per cent of unsuccessful projects reported a low degree of focus, compared to only 3 per cent of successful projects.

EXECUTION

The next stage in this process involves the actual execution of the project and once again there is a strong bias in favour of those projects where there was a high degree of collaboration among the key stakeholders. Not surprisingly, the capabilities of the project team members was an additional component in successful projects, though it is still possible for projects to succeed where the members have less capability. The important feature is that the team regularly reviews progress and does this in a rigorous way, using hard data and avoiding the temptation to paper over any cracks in how things are going.

The importance of collaboration is highlighted by the fact that only 19 per cent of unsuccessful projects reported a high level of alignment between the project team and its key stakeholders, compared with 87 per cent of successful projects (see Figure 9.4). Similarly, when there is a high degree of participation and support from the project steering group in the work of the project team, there is a much greater likelihood of success. Almost 60 per cent of successful project teams reported this, compared with just 15 per cent of unsuccessful teams.

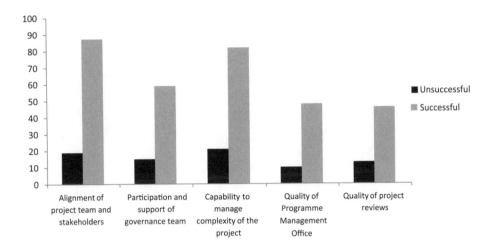

Figure 9.4   Execution of successful and unsuccessful projects

The importance of the organization's capability to manage the complexity of the project, and the capability of the Programme Management Office, are also highlighted in Figure 9.4. Where project reviews were of high quality, a much higher proportion of projects succeeded than failed (46 per cent compared with 13 per cent), with 63 per cent of the latter having poor quality reporting.

These results suggest that being able to review progress and having the willingness to adapt to changing circumstances is a critical factor in the success of projects. It is not the case that successful projects avoid the mishaps and changing circumstances that might plague unsuccessful projects. What distinguishes them is the way they respond to these. When people review progress in an open and honest way, and share their concerns with the leadership team, and demonstrate a willingness to make changes rather than continue unabated, they are much more likely to succeed in realizing the project vision.

BENEFITS DELIVERY

The final stage in this cycle is one that is frequently omitted from many project plans, yet it is just as crucial to success as the preceding three stages. In Matthew Hampson's words:

> *The problem with realization of benefits is it painfully points out when projects go wrong, so people quite like to brush it under the carpet a little bit. It's actually very difficult to do because the benefits in many cases are revenue-related, and revenue's a combination of the change plus market conditions plus changes in sales people, traders, and so on and so forth.*

Ensuring that the project delivers the originally intended benefits is often seen as lying outside the scope and responsibility of the project team. While most of the team might see this as still being important, the reality of many projects is that they will be assigned to a new project once the project they have been working on hits all of its deliverables.

The attitude of many IT managers is one of, 'I've done my piece, now it's up to others to make sure it delivers the benefits.' Unfortunately, those 'others' are not always aware of the expectations placed upon them. More often than not no one has explicitly stated who is seen as being responsible for benefits delivery; sometimes the person who has chief responsibility has moved on to another role and the new incumbent feels little commitment to see through something that was not of their choice. They may even disagree with the aims of the project and so lack any conviction to see things through to the end.

In our study, 34 per cent of projects that failed to achieve their stated outcomes lacked clear ownership of the benefits delivery stage, compared to just 8 per cent of successful projects. Amongst the latter, 77 per cent reported clear ownership (see Figure 9.5).

It is not just clarity of roles and responsibilities at this stage that accounts for success. Typically, the technical challenges of the project have already been met, but the project stalls because of problems implementing the new system. There are many anecdotes of organizations being influenced by a software vendor's claims of how a client management or people management system will transform their processes, only to discover that despite the system's capabilities, people do not like using it and resist the change.

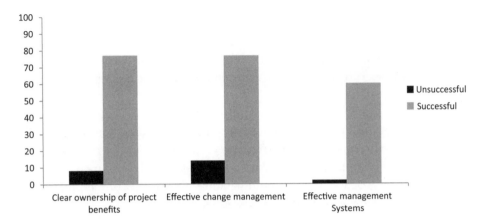

Figure 9.5   Benefits delivery of successful and unsuccessful projects

We found that 77 per cent of successful projects were carried out where the organization was rated as having effective change management capabilities, compared with just 14 per cent of unsuccessful projects.

Much of this phase relies on good performance metrics to demonstrate a significant improvement in performance. This might be a reduction in downtime or an increase in the volume of trades that are handled by the new system. If the performance figures suggest the change has not been as great as originally intended, then there needs to be corrective action to ensure that any barriers are removed and that performance improvement is driven through. When we compared the successful projects with unsuccessful projects, this feature produced one of the largest differences observed: almost 60 per cent of successful projects were reported to have effective measurement systems allowing review and corrective actions, compared with only 2 per cent of unsuccessful projects.

To summarize these findings and their implications for those with leadership roles within a project, I would suggest project and programme managers pay special attention to the following guidelines:

- Always be prepared to revisit the original objectives and ask the difficult questions (my favourite is 'what is the problem that this is a solution to?').

- Be absolutely clear about the benefits in financial terms and make sure all the project team members are familiar with the financial case for change. If it is difficult to quantify these benefits, or translate them into financial terms, you should question the business case for the project.[2]

- Getting a shared view among all key stakeholders of why the project is needed, what the future state will look like and agreement on what is non-negotiable (scope, delivery dates, functionality) is crucial. Ideally this should be done at the outset of the project, but it is hardly ever too late to return to it.

- Work hard to achieve collaboration among the leadership team and between this team and the project team. Be creative and think of ways to bring the groups together, perhaps for offsites focused specifically on building greater collaboration. Never underestimate the importance of getting everyone working together or assume it will happen naturally without active intervention.

- Build a culture of transparency and openness, where people feel able to raise concerns and risks. Remove blame and see each issue that is escalated as one that can be managed. Thank the person for raising it and encourage others to do the same.

- Avoid the 'Kevin Costner' approach to implementation ('If I build it, they will come' from *Field of Dreams*). Don't underestimate the difficulties you might face in instituting the changes that the technology requires. Your ability to lead and drive through organizational change will be tested to the limit in the benefits delivery stage. Don't assume your responsibilities end before that point is reached.

TOOLS TO HELP

Do's and don'ts like those listed above are easy to say and often very hard to do. While you might accept the rationale of getting all stakeholders to share in the project vision and be committed to its goals, how do you actually achieve that? In this section I will outline a number of tools that can help. On their own

---

2   Not all projects are initiated for financial gain. Some are required to meet regulatory requirements, while others are necessary to mitigate a risk to the bank.

they do not provide the complete solution, but they can and do make your job a lot easier.

ORGANIZATIONAL NETWORK ANALYSIS

Organization charts show how the person sitting at the top of the chart would *like* work to get done in his or her organization. They do not show how it *really* gets done. As the subtitle to Rob Cross and Andrew Parker's groundbreaking book on network analysis, *The Hidden Power of Social Networks: Understanding How Work* Really *Gets Done in Organizations*, suggests, we need to look deeper into things if we want to know the answer to this. The network analysis tool mentioned in the previous chapter is ideally suited to this task, since it shows who people go to when they want to get information needed to do their job, or when they want get input into a problem. The analysis can reveal so much about an organization and really helps when it comes to laying the foundations for a successful project.

The diagram shown in Figure 9.6 was obtained from the leadership group of a project team tasked with delivering a £30 million upgrade to an existing software platform. It shows who they reported collaborating with from within the project leadership team. Collaboration was defined as 'contacting another person specifically to obtain their help or input'. The arrowheads show who contacted who.

The first thing to notice is that it reveals a relatively high degree of collaboration. There are no 'islands' or pockets of people and it appears that business silos have not prevented people from reaching out to others across the divide. When we look deeper we see that some people are in the centre of the network, while others are on the periphery. As this was a global project team it was important that those based in the regions were just as closely involved as those in the centre (in this case, London). If those on the outer rim were largely in other countries, this could indicate the project being too London-centric.

Other features of the diagram highlight that some people have lots of arrowheads coming into them. In other words, lots of people approach them for help. This can indicate a 'key person risk': if that person should leave, will key knowledge be lost with them? If most of these people are team leaders, it might also suggest that team members are over-reliant on them. The leaders might easily become bottlenecks if things don't change.

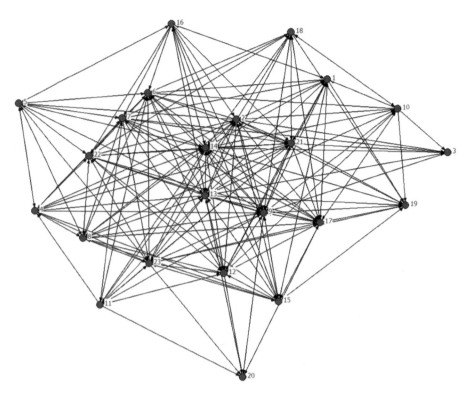

Figure 9.6   Collaboration among a global project team

This type of analysis can be supplemented by a wider analysis of all the project team members. Perhaps silos only become apparent at the level below the leadership team? There is no single ideal network diagram. As Cross and Thomas advise in their book (Cross and Thomas, 2009), you should begin with the purpose or value proposition of the team, then ask whether the observed network supports that purpose.

An analysis of this kind will highlight the degree of collaboration across a project team and whether people collaborate across geographical boundaries, hierarchical levels or functional specialities. It will show you exactly who is working with whom and whether this follows the pattern you deem is necessary for the team to achieve the project goals. It can be a vital tool to ensure your organization is properly 'joined up' without you having to rely just on the organization chart to indicate this.

DIAGNOSTIC SURVEY

The survey Catalyst used to conduct the research into IT project success factors is available to download from http://www.catalyst.co.uk. It can be used to diagnose whether a project that is 'in flight' is at risk of failing to deliver. For illustrative purposes, some of the survey is reproduced in Figure 9.7. The survey form can be completed in a number of ways. You or key members of the project team can complete it, as a means of generating a discussion about how you each see the project and the risks involved. Wide differences between those completing the survey will suggest there is no shared or common view of the project and point to the need for better reporting or performance indicators.

Secondly, you might use it as the basis for an in-depth analysis of the project, particularly if it is in danger of failing to meet some of its key deliverables. The aim here is to use each question to direct a detailed investigation. It might take several weeks to arrive at a full analysis of the project and its key risks in these terms, with much data being collected along the way. This is how Catalyst consultants use the instrument if we are engaged to do a thorough analysis of a project.

Finally, however you might choose to arrive at a score for each of the questions, you can compare your responses to the profile of a successful project. The profile obtained from our sample of 120 IT projects is shown in Figure 9.8. Large differences on any of the 20 dimensions will point to a significant risk and highlight where corrective action is most needed.

TEAM OFFSITES

Offsites were discussed in the previous chapter as a means of building a team and they are an excellent vehicle for achieving this among a project team. I know of some project leaders that see offsites as an expensive option. They calculate the lost time of the people involved, travel costs (especially if it is a globally distributed team), venue costs and fees for external facilitators. These are all very tangible, while the benefits are often intangible. A 'greater sense of where we are all heading' sounds like a pretty feeble payback for all that time, money and effort.

Please rate the following aspects of the project by circling the appropriate number.

1.   The clarity of the goals and outcomes of the project

1	2	3	4	5

Very unclear goals:
- Goals not established or well understood by team and stakeholders
- Goals not relevant to current environment

Very clear goals:
- Goals established and well understood by team and stakeholders
- Goals still relevant to current environment

2.   The strength of the business case supporting the project

1	2	3	4	5

Moderate business case:
- Business Case not completed or agreed by stakeholders
- Business Case not relevant to current environment

Very strong business case:
- Business Case agreed by stakeholders with strong NPV
- Business Case remains relevant to current environment

3.   The quality of design of the future operating model

1	2	3	4	5

Poor quality design
- Design not established or unclear or with unresolved issues

High quality design
- Design established, recognised as a good solution and agreed with all relevant stakeholders

4.   The quality of the technical design of the project

1	2	3	4	5

Poor quality design
- Design not established or unclear or with unresolved issues

High quality design
- Design established, recognised as a good solution and agreed with all relevant stakeholders

5.   The feasibility of the project plan

1	2	3	4	5

Unfeasible plan
- Plan not complete, clear, maintained or agreed

High feasible plan
- Plan is clear, detailed and achievable
- Plan is agreed by stakeholders including all resource owners

Figure 9.7   Sample questions from a diagnostic survey

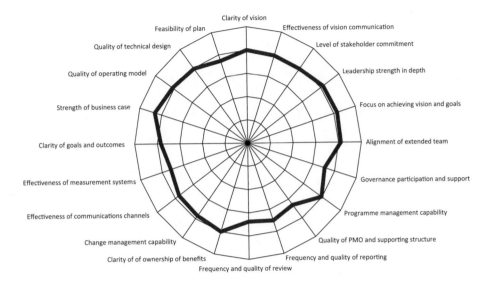

Figure 9.8   Average scores obtained from successful IT projects

With very specific goals and outcomes, however, an offsite can be an invaluable device. Specific goals suitable for a major technology programme might be:

- to identify risks and agree how we will manage these;

- to better coordinate the efforts of all of the extended teams in order to meet aggressive delivery targets;

- to make key decisions around scope;

- to build a stronger relationship with the business sponsors.

These should then drive the design of the offsite and the work that is done there. There should be very specific deliverables or takeaways that cannot easily be achieved by other means. With these outcomes firmly agreed, an offsite can be the only practical, and often the most economical or speedy way, of achieving these.

As an illustration, the following objectives and agenda were taken from an actual offsite I recently designed and facilitated for a project leadership team of

25 people. Theirs was a global project, about to pass from the planning stage to the execution phase.

Objectives

- to make real progress on the plan and take it to the next level of detail;

- to achieve a tangible increase in commitment and enthusiasm for the programme;

- to clarify the core values that will guide execution and to build commitment to these values;

- to strengthen collaboration across this group and the programme group at large.

Agenda

Day 1	
10.00	Introduction to the event
10.15	Icebreaker activity: the 3 main things the project will deliver
10. 30	Project leader: the project vision, core values and where we are now
11.00	Presentation: core delivery plan and cutover plan, and Q&A
12.15	Brief for group working sessions
12.30	Lunch
13.00	Identify topics for group working sessions
13.45	Presentation: industry analysis
14.45	Break
15.00	Group working sessions
16.30	Break
16.45	Report back sessions
18.00	Key decisions about scope and delivery dates
19.00	Review and close Day 1

Day 2	
08.30	Introduction to Day 2
08.45	Collaborative team exercise
09.45	Presentation: where to target collaboration
10.15	Break
10.30	Group working sessions
12.00	Lunch
12.30	Presentation: principles of effective communication
13.00	Group session: defining our key messages
13.45	Presentations: testing the core messages
14.45	Break
15.00	Group session: what do our core values mean in practice?
16.00	Summary and close event

This agenda shows a good combination of group working sessions, presentations to inform, presentations to educate and team-building activities. This particular offsite included all of the participants scoring the project on the 20 items contained in our diagnostic survey and using this as the basis for future work to address the risks that were identified. The offsite gave the project leader a level of insight and understanding about the extended team he was leading that could not be obtained through the scheduled weekly team meetings. He was able to take the pulse of his organization and assess the mood and level of commitment of the individuals attending. It proved an invaluable stage in the execution of the project and was followed by quarterly offsites to keep track of changes and maintain momentum.

PARTNERSHIP METRICS

Although a comprehensive dashboard of metrics will be used by the project team to track progress against plan, it is likely these will focus on the hard deliverables. Of equal importance when a project involves multiple stakeholders is the quality of the partnership and the degree of collaboration. Many people shy away from measuring such subjective aspects of a project, believing it cannot be measured reliably. But in reality the harder aspects are often based on people's subjective judgements about progress and risks.

The benefits of tracking the quality of the partnership is that it focuses attention on this and ways to improve it. A weak, transactional or faulty partnership between vendors, contractors and staff members is more likely, as our survey shows, to halt progress than the technical challenges of the project.

A very useful approach to how this might be achieved has been outlined by Archer and Cameron in their book *Collaborative Leadership*. Although their focus is largely on the kind of public–private partnerships that characterize major initiatives in the UK, their approach can easily be adapted to the partnerships that can exist in major technology projects within the financial services.

The authors identify three aspects of a partnership that might be measured:

1.   *Governance:* defined as 'the formal and informal joint structures of the collaborative venture, from the contract through to management steering groups, reporting lines, accountabilities and decision-making structures'.

2.   *Operations:* this refers to 'the processes that have to work across the whole partnership, from communications and information sharing to joint learning and staff development'.

3.   *Behaviours*: this includes how to behave collaboratively and how to build relationships.

They suggest using regular surveys to obtain perceptual data on each of the above. These need to be short, easy to complete and focused as far as possible on facts, and be evidence-driven rather than focus on obtaining broad measures of satisfaction.

Questions on governance should cover clarity of purpose, the quality of decision making and clarity of accountabilities. These are not unlike the areas covered by the diagnostic survey behind the diagram shown in Figure 9.3 and can easily be used as a substitute. Sample questions offered by Archer and Cameron include:

• the aim of the partnership is understood and agreed by all parties;

• there is a single set of agreed priorities for the partnership.

The operational aspects of the partnership cover the alignment of systems and processes, the effectiveness of communications and efforts to improve capabilities. Sample questions include:

- there is one common set of measures used by all parties to measure performance of the partnership;

- the partners keep each other well informed about progress;

- there are regular reviews of partnership performance and processes.

Finally, behaviours are measured by things like the extent to which leaders role model collaboration, awareness of cross cultural differences and joint problem solving. Typical questions are:

- the leaders of the partnership speak with one voice;

- the partnership invests in activities to encourage an understanding of the cultures of each of the partners;

- the partnership can come to consensus about the best way forward when it experiences a serious problem.

Archer and Cameron's model is not dissimilar to the approach advocated here. It adds a useful dimension by focusing on partnerships that make it particularly suited when a technology organization is working with a software vendor and has outsourced some of the development work to third parties in countries like India. They suggest regularly surveying staff to monitor progress on these matters, offsetting concerns people may have about this by pointing out that 'measurement shouldn't create problems. It should help you solve them' (p.87).

The above tools offer a number of ways in which you can stay on top of the collaborative challenges that will influence the success of a major technology project. They require a significant investment in time, people and resources if they are to prove their value. None of them can or should be done 'on the cheap'. In terms of their pay-off, they can make the difference between success and failure.

One thing our research has shown is that there is no silver bullet to succeeding in bringing home a major project. A large number of things have to be done, and done very well, if the project is to avoid the myriad of things that can cause derailment. Think of your role as being like an Olympic athlete, with the aim of winning a medal. Diet, training, exercise, mental health, rest, physical health, nutrition, coaching, environment, stress and many more things will have an impact. If you want to win the gold medal, you cannot afford to lapse on any one of these. It is not an option to focus on one while letting another slide a bit. Each has to be as good as it can be.

ADDITIONAL TOOLS

In addition to the tools described above, there are a number of other specific tools that can assist you in the process. These are smaller-scale techniques, representing best practice in a number of key aspects of project management. It is worth presenting them here as they can form an additional and essential part of your armoury.

Problem statements

All members of the project team need to know and understand the problem that the technology is intended to solve. This should be couched in terms that are meaningful to the business as well as the most technically minded of individuals. In my experience many projects are initiated without a good problem statement. Those projects that do offer a statement often refer to the solution ('we need to upgrade a system') rather than the problem it is intended to solve or focus too narrowly ('a high level of outages') and ignore the real problem this causes ('inability to remain competitive as measured by industry benchmarks').

A good problem statement ensures everyone is clear on the problem to be solved. It ensures a team or individual is working on the real problem, not a symptom of the problem or an assumed solution. Unless this first stage of the problem-solving process is correct, any subsequent analysis may focus on the wrong things.

A problem statement must meet a number of criteria. It must:

- be specific;

- clearly scope the problem;

- be unambiguous;

- not propose or imply a solution.

Furthermore, the problem statement must include additional information:

- give the reasons for solving the problem;

- specify the critical to quality measures of the solution;

- identify any known constraints.

With this in mind, a good problem statement should observe the following 'syntax':

Table 9.1   The features of a problem statement

Feature	Definition
Description of the problem	In a clear and unambiguous way Within a defined scope
Evidence of impact	Describing the negative impact of the problem
Critical to quality criteria	Measures of success, as defined by stakeholders, that the solution must encompass
Constraints	Things that may limit the solution

An example of a good problem statement that meets these features might be:

Description of the problem
'In 18 months' time Microsoft will not guarantee to fix issues arising with the version of their operating system currently running on our London desktops.'

Evidence of impact
We will not be able to fix application problems, where the problem is related to the operating system. These types of problem could arise as we make enhancements to our applications to meet new business requirements, but also as a result of changes in the way we use our applications, for example, if we were to use existing functionality which we have not previously used.

Third-party software providers are also unlikely to guarantee support for their products on this version of the Microsoft operating system.

Critical to quality
Our currently delivered service levels must be maintained.

Constraints
A solution must be in place within 18 months.

This approach will help you avoid problem statements that are too vague or general, such as 'poor communication' (a favourite among people when asked what problems exist in their organization). Such statements are so vague and open to different interpretations they are almost impossible to solve. If a problem seems too general, you should ask what specific problems it causes, for example, 'What specific problems does poor communication cause?' This leads you to more manageable problems like 'missed deadlines' which can be measured, subjected to root cause analysis and assessed after a solution has been put in place.

The approach also helps avoid coming up with problem statements that are really solution statements. These usually begin with the words, 'We need ...' If you believe you are tackling a solution rather than a problem, ask, 'What is the main problem to be solved if we had ...?' This will lead you to the problem to be tackled.

Systemic analysis

Catalyst's proprietary Systemic Model offers a way of defining the desired future state in a way that captures the systemic nature of complex organizations. As discussed above under the heading of benefits delivery, it is not enough to assume that a great technical solution will on its own lead to financial and other benefits. To realize these, people may need to be adept at using a wider range of skills, new processes may need to be developed and instituted, along with other tangible assets (equipment, storage space), a new operating model and cultural norms that encourage the new behaviours.

Using this approach involves defining this future state along six dimensions, then planning how to make progress on each (see Figure 9.9).

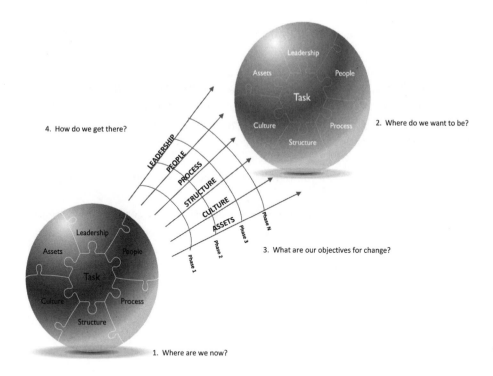

Figure 9.9   A systemic approach to change

Some useful prompt questions are:

TASK: Achieve real clarity on the outcome.

Ask: What is the purpose of the project? What difference must it make to our customers? What are the project's key performance goals?

ASSETS: Define the tools and other tangible assets needed to support the project goals.

Consider: What new knowledge, information and databases are needed? What new systems capabilities are needed? What are the implications for our technical infrastructure? What physical assets are needed and where? (for example, offices, data centres, hardware, networks)?

LEADERSHIP: Create a compelling project vision and unite the leadership team around it.

Agree on: What kind of leadership is needed for the organization to achieve the project goals? What are the leadership roles that are needed and who will play them? What does the leadership team need to do well as a team to succeed? What are the key leadership actions needed?

PEOPLE: The qualities and attributes needed to succeed.

Define: The capabilities and resources needed to deliver the performance goals. What new skills need to be developed?

PROCESS: Design the end-to-end workflow for the key processes.

Ask: What value does the process create? Who are the customers of the process? How will process performance be measured and managed? How should work best get done in the organization in order to meet the performance goals?

STRUCTURE: Design how best to organize to perform the task.

Consider: What new structures will best support the process flows? What new roles may be required to perform the task?

CULTURE: The existing organization norms and behaviours can often be a major barrier to success.

Ask: What behavioural norms and values need to be in place to help us achieve the task? What will people do to achieve recognition? What will the performance management culture be? What will management focus on? How will decisions be made?

By working through these questions, a much more complete understanding can be achieved of what is needed to ensure the project is successfully implemented. It's a bit like a heart transplant. Simply putting a new heart into an unhealthy body is unlikely to do much to preserve the patient's life. Instead a holistic analysis is needed to ensure all aspects of the patient's lifestyle will support the new organ.

Technical and adaptive change

This is a conceptual distinction rather than a methodological tool, yet it is one of the most important concepts to come out of the management and leadership literature in the last recent times. First drawn by Ronald Heifetz and Marty Linsky in their book *Leadership on the Line* (2002), the distinction is between two types of problems experienced by organizations: those that are technical in nature and those that are 'adaptive'. While technical problems have a correct answer, and are best approached by a linear process of deduction, adaptive problems have no single or correct solution and there is no simple process for getting there.

A system crash is an instance of a technical problem. Staff resistance to a planned system implementation is an adaptive problem. While this might sound fairly straightforward, difficulties arise when we tend to treat adaptive problems as technical issues and believe a technical solution will address them. Tacking the problem of a low level of cross-selling by implementing a Customer Relationship Management system could be an example of this if the reason cross-selling is low is because people in sales compete with one another for the biggest share of the bonus 'pie' and are reluctant to pass on opportunities to their colleagues.

An adaptive approach to change involves asking the awkward questions, such as, 'What have we done to engender low levels of staff engagement?' or 'How can we learn to work in partnership with our vendors?' There is no simple or single correct answer to these questions and tackling them by changing processes, technology or aspects of the organizational structure is unlikely on its own to have much effect.

Most technology projects address problems that have significant adaptive elements and not paying attention to these or not addressing them is likely to result not only in failure to solve the problem, but more significantly demonstrate a failure of leadership. In no uncertain terms, Heifetz and Linsky state that:

> The single most common cause of leadership failure is that people ...
> treat adaptive challenges like technical problems.

Given the much more difficult task of addressing the adaptive elements of a problem, what can people in leadership positions do to ensure they avoid the failure of leadership highlighted by the authors? Heifetz and Linsky suggest five strategies:

1.   Get on the balcony.

This involves adopting a different, more objective view of the problem. The authors suggest three ways to do this:

- Find out where people stand on the issue. Take the time to listen to the views of others before you intervene.

- Listen to the 'song beneath the words'. Interpret what is beneath the surface of what people are saying.

- Read the authority figure for clues. This person is trying to manage all the various factions and what you observe is a response to the pressures they are facing.

2.   Think politically.

This involves creating and nurturing networks of people whom you can call upon, work with and engage in addressing the issue. Heifetz and Linsky suggest six ways to do this:

- Find partners. Don't take on the challenge alone, as this will encourage others to watch and wait for you to fail. Real partners can be found both inside and outside your organization.

- Keep the opposition close. Opponents are those with the most to lose by your success. Give them more of your attention than your allies.

- Accept responsibility for your piece of the mess. If you have been in a position of authority for at least part of the time the problem has existed, it is likely that you have contributed to it and/or are part of the reason it has not been addressed. Accepting your need to change will reduce the risk of you becoming a target.

- Acknowledge their loss. When you ask people to make an adaptive change you are asking them to leave something they value behind. Acknowledging this will help them to let things go.

- Model the behaviour. Do what you are asking others to do.

- Accept casualties. Accept that some people will not make the changes you require of them. Moving on without them will signal your commitment.

3.   Orchestrate the conflict.

This involves harnessing the energy of differences in views and the conflicts these differences produce. The authors say there are four ways to do this:

- Create a holding environment. This is a place with structural, procedural or virtual boundaries where it is safe to address the problem and keep stress at a productive level.

- Control the temperature. This involves creating a tension for change by highlighting the dangers of not changing and creating some discomfort. You then need to maintain your position in the face of pressure and difficulty. Only when there is a real danger that the stress will lead to a complete breakdown do you need to lower the temperature by reducing the tension to a tolerable level.

- Pace the work. People, including you, can only stand so much change at any one time. Don't risk success by doing too much too soon.

- Show them the future. To sustain change you need to remind people of the values and the future they are changing for.

4.   Give the work back.

You cannot solve adaptive challenges for people since it involves them changing their own ways. There are three things you need to do:

- Take the work off your shoulders. Don't try to resolve the conflicts between others. Put it back on their shoulders.

- Place the work where it belongs. To meet adaptive challenges people must change their hearts as well as their behaviours. Issues have to be internalized, owned and ultimately resolved by the relevant parties to achieve enduring progress.

- Make your interventions short and simple. Make observations, ask questions, offer interpretations and take action. Hold steady and evaluate how to move forward.

5.   Hold steady.

This involves maintaining your poise in the heat of the action and planning the next steps. There are three ways to do this:

- Take the heat. This involves taking intense pressure to stop what you are doing from those whose support you value and need.

- Let the issue ripen. Wait until people are psychologically ready to weigh priorities and take losses.

- Focus attention on the issue. People will avoid focusing on tough problems by denial, finding scapegoats, re-organizing, passing the buck, finding an external enemy, blaming authority and character assassination. You need to hold steady in the face of these distractions and refocus attention on the real issue.

(Adapted from Heifetz and Linsky, 2002).

This approach can be very helpful when leading a project or programme. While the technical challenges can potentially consume a lot of your attention, you should avoid focusing only on getting the right technical solution. A lot of project managers believe their role is to deliver the technical solution on time, to budget and to specification, and that they can leave it up to others to engage in the 'politics' of ensuring it is implemented and delivers real change. This is exactly the very failure of leadership Heifetz and Linsky refer to in their book.

The communications escalator

This is a simple but powerful way of planning your communications to key stakeholders. It is based on the simple, but not necessarily obvious, fact that people need time to 'warm' to an idea or change. Early communications should not therefore aim to achieve their full engagement and turn them into advocates. This is simply too much to expect of most people. Instead, early messages need to create a level of awareness and understanding. Only with time should the content and style of the message change to one that seeks to obtain greater levels of commitment (see Figure 9.10).

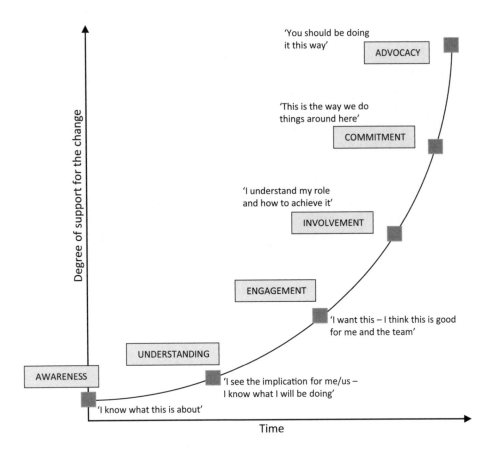

Figure 9.10   The communications escalator

The implication of this approach is that initially, messages about the project to key audiences need to be kept simple, with the aim just of creating an awareness of the project and an understanding of why it is needed. This means the messages can probably be one-way, through channels like email or town hall meetings. Do not expect too much of people at this stage and do not ask that they become instant advocates.

Over time, the nature of the message should change, along with the channels used to deliver it. Face-to-face and two-way communications become much more important.

There are occasions when early engagement and commitment is needed and leaders don't have the time to let people warm to an idea or planned change. The communications escalator can help in these circumstances too, since it highlights the kind of communications needed to achieve this. In my experience it is not uncommon for people in leadership positions to believe they can win the hearts and minds of their people by messages communicated through email or PowerPoint presentations. What they should be doing is the equivalent of a politician on the campaign trail, getting close to people, listening to their concerns and speaking to them on a one-to-one basis.

When communications are poor, an alternative scenario can easily unfold, as shown in Figure 9.11. In these circumstances, active opposition to a planned change results from people travelling a downward escalator. To understand why this might happen, think of a time when you have seen people travel this route. What can you recall about the way the changes were being communicated? Probably there was little in the way of helpful information. Messages probably came from little seen sources. Perhaps there was little opportunity to engage in a genuine dialogue or to raise concerns. Even when this was possible, people may have felt their concerns had not been fully registered or listened to. Over time their lack of engagement and understanding feeds rumours and eventually turns to fear for the consequences of the change and active opposition.

Both the upward and downward communications escalators point to the importance of actively managing communications as a way of winning people over and avoiding the scenario of resistance to change. While they do not specify the details of which type of message to use, or which channel to communicate it through, it is not too difficult to plan the appropriate ones to use. In general, rich media (that is, two-way, face-to-face) will help build commitment; lean media (one-way, written) are appropriate only for awareness and understanding. To avoid this sliding down to opposition, the pattern of communications needs to change into one that is much more involving.

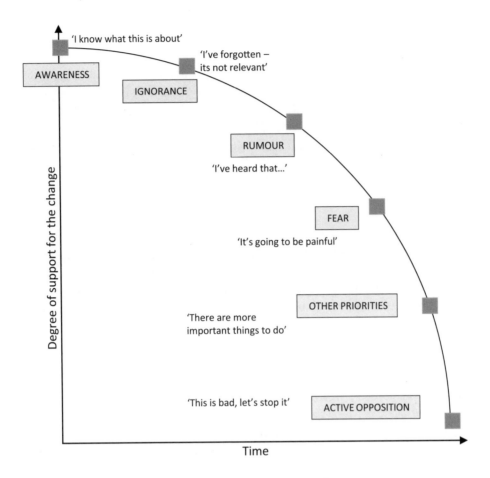

'I know what this is about'

AWARENESS

'I've forgotten – its not relevant'

IGNORANCE

RUMOUR

'I've heard that...'

FEAR

'It's going to be painful'

OTHER PRIORITIES

'There are more important things to do'

'This is bad, let's stop it'

ACTIVE OPPOSITION

Degree of support for the change

Time

Figure 9.11   The communications downward escalator

The recovery tool

The recovery tool is a process for recovering from an unexpected problem or crisis. The tool outlines two patterns of behaviour, either of which can be followed when things go wrong (see Figure 9.12). The first pattern is often experienced as an automatic response, while the second seems more managed though somewhat harder to achieve. Obviously, it is the second, managed response to problems that will help in most situations, but why is it that this seems so difficult to achieve?

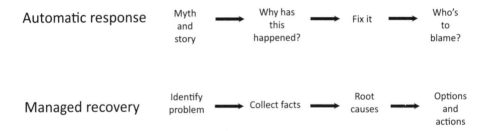

Figure 9.12   The recovery tool

To answer this we need to look deep into the brain and in particular to a small structure called the amygdala. This controls emotional responses. In times of stress it releases a hormone that floods the neocortex, inhibiting rational thinking and producing a highly emotional response. This pattern has been dubbed the 'emotional hijack' by neuropsychologists studying the role of the amygdala.

While many technologists might be familiar with the highly emotional responses of others to unforeseen crises, they may not have realized this pattern has a well-established neuropsychological basis!

The recovery tool does not remove the possibility of this response, but it does show the kind of behaviours that will make it less likely and which will lead to a more constructive outcome. The tool can be useful in guiding your own behaviour or in responding to the behaviour of someone who has clearly already started down the path of the emotional response.

The first step in the recovery process is to stay rigorously focused on the facts. Facts are numbers or events and do not refer to future possibilities, people's assumed intentions or explanations that lay blame. 'The system has gone down. In the past it has taken at least an hour to recover from this' – that is a fact. In contrast, the statement, 'The people in production support couldn't be bothered to do this properly and have caused the system to crash. The business will be up in arms again' is a combination of hearsay, supposition and scaremongering. There is little in it of a factual basis, even though the speaker may strenuously assert that everything he has stated is a 'fact'.

The next step is to get to the root cause and once again this means avoiding the temptation to blame others. The carelessness, ignorance or lack of motivation in others might seem like the cause of a problem, but usually this is just one step in a long chain of events or an understandable reaction to less than ideal circumstances. You should continue to ask 'why?' when attempting to get beyond these steps and arrive at what is at the heart of the problem. Remember your goal in conducting a root cause analysis is to prevent the problem occurring again, so simply blaming the assumed shortcomings of others is unlikely to achieve this.

The 'quick fix' shown in the unmanaged response is sometimes required to buy time for a more thorough analysis and can be part of a managed response. In these circumstances it should be followed by root cause analysis rather than blame and little else.

The recovery tool does not stop the amygdala from exerting its influence over our behaviour, but it can reduce the amount of time we spend in this emotional state. The tool is helpful in guiding us to a different set of behaviours that can quite quickly become habits and lead to the withering of old habits characterized by emotional responses.

Summary

Collaboration, and in particular the collaborative approach of people in leadership positions, is a vital element in the success of projects. This is especially true when those projects involve multiple stakehoders, third-party vendors and globally dispersed teams. It is not enough to focus on getting execution right or ensuring the right technical decisions are made. As Scott Marcar puts it:

> *We often end up with large development teams remote from the core user base, which means that that skill of managing global teams, managing remote teams, getting your requirements clearly defined requires a change in mindset and a change in skill set. In London and in other trading centres the shift then becomes much more about relationship management, about requirements gathering, about understanding the business process, about understanding you have to manage large level programmes and stakeholder management. It's less focused on being great technologists and great engineers, and I think it is an interesting question for the industry as to how this really pans out.*

This chapter has hopefully shown that it is just as important to ensure all stakeholders are aligned, that members of the project team feel engaged in the change they are helping to build and that any problems experienced along the way are tackled constructively by people working together. The various tools and techniques discussed here will help you in your efforts to ensure collaboration is a feature of any project or programme you lead.

10

How to Change

This book is aimed at helping you develop a collaborative leadership style. I have argued that the 'heroic' models of leadership dominant in the early part of this century, and the last few years of the last century, are not so well suited to the current and future demands of technology organizations within the investment banking industry.

I have outlined a number of the tried and tested tools I use to help people develop a more collaborative style and hopefully you can use these to start making instant changes. But change goes deeper than this, as well as wider. Making personal changes is not easy, as anyone who has attempted to lose weight, give up smoking, exercise more or manage their personal finances better can testify.

Similarly, changes in yourself cannot have much impact if not much else in your organization changes. The collaborative leader needs to bring about both personal and organizational transformation if he or she is to be successful in aligning behind the need for more collaboration. This chapter outlines some things you can do on both fronts.

Personal Change

One of the benefits of using various tools to bring about change is that they help you focus on the behaviours to get right. Usually, behavioural change is easier to facilitate than deeper personal change. It requires doing some things differently and following a step-by-step procedure. But at some point it will be necessary to examine your values, beliefs and even your sense of who or what you are, if you are to avoid slipping back into old habits. It is true that changing your behaviour can have some impact on your attitudes (people like to experience consistency, so will sometimes change their attitudes to realign them to their behaviour). However, some behaviours can be very difficult to change unless there is first a change in some internal state.

To change from being a leader who is comfortable with a 'command and control' style to one who is more collaborative can be a tall order for those who believe the former is better suited to their individual preferences or personality. It might only take a few unsuccessful attempts to convince such a person that they don't have it in them to be more collaborative.

Sometimes the barriers to personal change lie in the beliefs people hold about whether such change is indeed possible. Consider the following four statements and indicate which you tend to agree with:

1. You are a certain kind of person and there is not much that can be done to really change that.

2. No matter what kind of person you are, you can always change substantially.

3. You can do things differently, but the important parts of who you are can't really be changed.

4. You can always change basic things about the kind of person you are.

If you agreed with questions 1 and 3 you may have what Stanford University psychologist Carol Dwek calls a 'fixed mindset'. If you agreed with questions 2 and 4 you have a 'growth mindset'.

These four simple questions are remarkably reliable in indicating these two distinct mindsets. What is more important is how the two mindsets can influence your whole life.

Over a period of 20 years, Dwek and her colleagues have provided compelling research evidence to show that *'the view you adopt for yourself* profoundly affects the way you lead your life. It can determine whether you become the person you want to be and whether you accomplish the things you value' (Dwek, 2006, p.6, emphasis in original).

She has found that people with a fixed mindset tend to avoid learning new skills or capabilities. When they experience failure they feel demotivated and feel discouraged from trying again. Why should they try again, if the failure is evidence that they can't do what has been attempted? This is not to say these people have low self-esteem or are unduly pessimistic. They are also just as smart as others and can hold successful positions in life. But basically they believe their success is due to them using the talents they have been born with. If they are successful in a particular role or at a specific task, it is because those situations play to their strengths. One of the consequences of this mindset is that these people tend to avoid situations where failure is a possibility. What is the point in failing, they reason, if you can't do much about it?

In contrast, people with a growth mindset see failure as part of the learning process. When they fail at a task it tends to spur them on to make a greater effort, to try again, to overcome their deficiency. People with a growth mindset believe they can always improve through effort and experience. According to Dwek, 'People in a growth mindset don't just seek challenge, they thrive on it. The bigger the challenge, the more they stretch' (p.21).

I remember once travelling to Paris with a colleague to make a pitch for a piece of work with a potential client. This was in the days before PowerPoint and we were taking a set of acetates to use on an overhead projector. On the way there, travelling on the Eurostar, I asked her for the slides so we could rehearse our pitch. To my horror she said she thought I had them. It turned out that we both assumed the other had collected the acetates from the office before setting off.

With some effort I avoided the temptation to blame her for the mistake and instead told myself to think, 'This is FANTASTIC!' So the next question I asked myself was, 'How *could* we make this fantastic?' Maybe by developing a *better* alternative to using slides (although we didn't have any other options). We quickly sketched out a pitch that involved using a more interactive approach, involving the audience in our presentation. We then phoned ahead to their office and said we had made some last minute changes to our presentation and now required a whiteboard. Could they please arrange this?

Our presentation, though a little unrehearsed, worked well. We asked lots of questions, sketched out our ideas on the whiteboard and generated lots of discussion with our audience. Afterwards we were congratulated on using an approach that none of the other parties pitching for the work had adopted.

According to Dwek, a growth mindset involves responding to a failure by asking, 'What did I learn from that experience? How can I use it as a basis for growth?' In my case, the missing acetates were an opportunity to make a better presentation, something different from the other tenders. I could have easily put my head in my hands and said there was no way we would ever win the pitch without the presentation slides. These two different responses lead to two different approaches in solving the problem. Starting from a growth perspective I was able to work with my colleague constructively to put together a new presentation in a short amount of time. I entered the room of the pitch feeling confident and excited about our new approach. I was convinced we would win and it probably showed in my demeanour. It would have been a very different me that would have entered the office if I believed we had no chance of winning.

If you have a growth mindset you are probably more likely to succeed in the personal changes required to become a more collaborative leader. Does this mean that those of you with a fixed mindset should have stopped reading this book at Chapter 1? No, because as Dwek has shown, it is not difficult to change your beliefs about personal growth.

In fact, the two mindsets are descriptions of belief patterns not types of people and we can and do move from one to another. Over time we might build up habitual ways of responding to things like failure or negative feedback that take us down the fixed mindset path, but like all habits it can be broken and we can learn new ones.

In many of her research studies, Dwek influenced the pattern of beliefs people held by giving them information to support those beliefs. Typically, half of the people would be given a growth mindset by being provided with information from authoritative sources showing that people can learn and grow from their experiences. The other half would be given a fixed mindset by telling them abilities were fixed. Using this approach in numerous studies, she found that those presented with the growth mindset outperformed those given a fixed mindset. They also responded better to failure at tasks, using their experience to spur them to greater efforts.

You can train yourself to recognize when you are working with a fixed mindset, since in Dwek's words, 'The key weapons of the fixed mindset (are) blame, excuses, and the stifling of critics and rivals' (p.117). A growth mindset is at work when we 'love challenges, are intrigued by mistakes, enjoy effort, and keep on learning' (p.177). By recognizing when the fixed mindset kicks in you can choose, should you wish, to replace it with a growth mindset, just as I did on that journey to a business pitch in Paris. Did we win the pitch? No, but it didn't bother me too much and I saw it as an opportunity to work harder at preparing for future pitches (and for double-checking we have everything before leaving our office!).

One of the interesting things about Dwek's book is that she includes an analysis of how the two mindsets operate in business and in particular how they affect the behaviour of people in leadership roles. Her research shows that the growth mindset can lead to a more collaborative style of leadership, while the fixed mindset is characteristic of leaders with a 'heroic' style. The reason is that a fixed mindset encourages defensiveness, a desire to surround oneself with lesser individuals and the need to prove oneself. In contrast, a growth mindset encourages people to help others to grow and to reward this behaviour in others.

If you are in a leadership position, and doubt the wisdom of involving others, perhaps less knowledgeable or experienced, in your decision making, it suggests you are starting from a fixed mindset. A fixed mindset fears failure and assumes people who lack ability are unlikely to benefit from something that might be beyond their capability. Similarly, if you believe that building a genuine collaborative relationship with some of the people you work with, either within or outside your organization, is not possible given their competing interests, you are starting from a fixed mindset. If you believe that *you* can change and become more collaborative, but that others can't or won't, it denotes a fixed mindset.

A growth mindset opens you to the possibility that you and others can change. It sets you on the path of looking for ways to achieve this and of overcoming any setbacks on the way. It recognizes the path will not always be smooth and sees this as part of the challenge to be overcome and why this is a journey worth taking. So not only is a growth mindset more conducive to helping you bring about personal change, it is also conducive to establishing more collaboration.

Develop your Leadership Brand

Once you believe you can change, and that a collaborative style of leading is within your grasp, the next stage is to start to define the new you. One term that is often used to describe the way we define and present ourselves to others is 'leadership brand'. Just as clear brand values lead us to expect great customer service from Virgin Atlantic or innovative design and a great user interface from Apple, a clear brand value for yourself will communicate to others what to expect from you.

Developing a leadership brand is a regular item in Catalyst's leadership development programmes. We usually tackle it towards the end of a programme, when people have had time to develop their skills and sense of what they want to achieve going forward. The item culminates in an activity where, in groups of about five or six, each person takes their turn to articulate their own leadership brand. We tell them that this should take no more than about 30 seconds. Prior to this each person is given guidance on what is meant by 'leadership brand', some personal examples and the benefits of having clarity on what it is you stand for. They have time overnight to think about what their own brand might include and an opportunity to discuss this with a peer before 'going public'.

During the group session when they articulate their brand, they receive feedback from the others in their group on whether it meets the criterion of authenticity. We advise them not to aim for something that comes across as all 'motherhood and apple pie' but which instead captures the essence of who and what they are and what they stand for. It is not unusual for people to say this was the most difficult thing to do across the whole of the leadership programme (which might extend over 12 months and cover lots of different challenges).

Why is it important to have a clear leadership brand? One of the reasons is that it can help when you have to take a stance on a subject. Knowing what is important to you, and what you value, will often help you make that decision. Many decisions leaders are called upon to make have no simple right or wrong answer and often whatever option they choose will have some negative fallout. In these situations it can be very helpful to have what others have called a 'moral compass', a clear set of values that guides you.

Another reason is that a leadership brand is needed to create followership. While you might be a leader in your own mind, if no one is prepared to follow you then your leadership will remain precisely there. Followership refers to someone's decision to put their faith and trust in you and to follow you on the journey you have decided to take. This is different from simply complying with your command and implies a psychological investment in you and a strong element of choice on their part. Without a clear brand people will find it difficult to make this choice and this level of investment in you.

What has this got to do with collaborative leadership? Well, in your journey to becoming a more collaborative leader you will need to develop a good understanding of your own leadership brand and how it relates to a more collaborative style. Inconsistencies will have to be ironed out and this needs to reflect a genuine resolution rather than simply adopting a shiny new set of collaborative values. If collaboration does not sit comfortably with your core values, you will need to think carefully about which path to choose.

There is no simple or formulaic way of clarifying your own leadership brand. The answer lies within you but may not be immediately visible particularly if this is something you have rarely thought about before. You cannot discover your brand by asking others what they think it is, though you might want to check it rings true with them once you are able to articulate it.

In your search it can sometimes be useful to ask yourself the following questions:

- Who or what am I?

- What do I stand for?

- What is really important to me?

- What do I want to be known for?

Answering these questions will not tell you your brand but it will take you on the introspective journey needed to discover it. For some people this will be a short and easy journey, especially if these are things they have thought about and resolved during their life. For others it will be a longer journey, largely into the unknown. There is no right or wrong about which journey you take, it simply reflects your familiarity with this type of activity. What is clear, however, is that it is difficult, if not impossible, to be an effective leader without some sense of these.

Often people ask, 'How will I know when I have arrived at a genuine description of my leadership brand?' Some things might feel right and genuine but they may still be open to challenge or conflict with things you have done in your life. There is no simple answer to uncertainty and it is tempting to say you will know when you find it but that is not always the case. Sometimes a leadership brand is like a pair of shoes that grows more comfortable with wear and familiarity. If the shoes never really fit or never become really comfortable, they are probably not for you and you should look for something else. The same is true for your leadership brand.

Once you are able to articulate, in about half a minute, the essence of who you are, what you stand for and what is important to you, you can test it out on others. You should choose people you have a good relationship with, as this is not the sort of conversation topic to have with people who hardly know you or who don't feel able to give you honest and open feedback.

Don't be too disheartened if the feedback is not want you want to hear. Remember the growth mindset: the purpose of seeking feedback is to improve your description of your brand, ensuring others see it as authentic and an accurate description of you.

While your leadership brand does not have to be a description rich in collaboration and collaborative values, it should nevertheless sit comfortably alongside the values and behaviour I have been promoting throughout this book. If your brand is just about you setting the direction for others to follow, and is a description of you in the heroic terms of previous leadership models, then it is probably fair to say you will find it difficult to be a genuinely collaborative leader. But if it captures the essence of working with others, and the spirit of jointly making progress, it will be a natural extension of collaborative leadership and you will find this approach to leadership easier to adopt.

A clear leadership brand that is consistent with collaborative leadership will ensure you role model the kind of behaviours necessary to support a more collaborative culture in your organization. Professor Morten Hansen of Harvard University has said that in cultivating collaboration in an organization, 'tools alone are not enough. Leaders who implement disciplined collaboration successfully also walk the walk – they exemplify a collaborative leadership style' (p.147). David Archer and Alex Cameron (2009), in their book on collaborative ventures, list role modelling by leaders as one of the three behavioural features that characterize a truly collaborative partnership. Being clear on your own leadership brand and ensuring it is consistent with a collaborative approach is an absolutely critical step in bringing about a more collaborative organization. But that is not all that is needed, as we shall see in the next section.

Appeal to Logic AND Emotions

One of the most notable things I notice when working with the leaders of investment banks' technology organizations is how prone they are to overlooking the emotional element of a change process. Leaving aside the stereotype of a geeky technologist lacking in social skills, it often surprises me to find that those in leadership positions seem to believe they can bring about change in their organization by appealing only to logic and reason.

If only life were so orderly and simple. It is true that a lot of the time we base important decisions on the logical case for change. If the numbers add up and the rationale is sound, choosing to follow a particular course of action can be hard to resist. But resist we often do.

Consider for a moment the important choices you make in your life. You may like to think that these are often made after a careful consideration of the facts, the likely outcomes and an analysis of which is likely to lead to the most optimal solution. But more often than not emotions will intrude to influence your choice. Something that seems to have everything going for it (a new job, say) will often be resisted if it just doesn't feel right. Sometimes you will choose things (often when making purchasing decisions) even when there is little to justify them other than the positive emotions they create.

Apple Inc. understands this well. They package their products beautifully in minimalist boxes and pay such attention to detail that their customers even post videos on the internet of them 'unboxing' their latest must-have gadgets. Many keep the boxes for years to come, simply because they mirror the beauty, style and elegance of the products they contain. Competitors, seeking to release a 'killer' version of the product, focus on adding functionality. The spec sheet certainly makes it look like a superior product, but really, would you rather own an NWD-B103[1] or an iPod?

---

1   An MP3 player rather unimaginatively named by Sony.

Some of you may be thinking that the name doesn't matter and that you would make your choice based on a careful comparison of features, specifications and pricing. Only fools would be swayed by the name of the device or how pretty the box was that it came in, surely?

That is my point precisely. Because, people *are* swayed by these things and if you want to influence them you will need to pay attention to the emotional factors that influence their behaviour, not just the logical factors.

This point has been made very eloquently by Chip and Dan Heath, in their book *Switch: How to Change Things When Change is Hard* (2010). True to their earlier advice on how to make a message 'stick' (Heath and Heath, 2007), they use a metaphor to bring this home.

Imagine a Rider sitting on top of an Elephant. The Rider decides on where to go, how to get there and on steering the Elephant along the chosen path – in theory. In practice, the Elephant wields the power and in any disagreement about where to head, the Elephant will win.

According to University of Virginia psychologist Jonathon Haidt, the Rider represents our logical and rational side, while the Elephant represents the emotional. When the two are aligned, progress is smooth. But as the brothers Heath point out:

> *Most of us are all too familiar with situations in which our Elephant overpowers our Rider. You've experienced this if you've ever slept in, overeaten, dialed up your ex at midnight, procrastinated, tried to quit smoking and failed, skipped the gym, gotten angry and said something you regretted, abandoned your Spanish or piano lessons, refused to speak up in a meeting because you were scared, and so on. Good thing no one is keeping score.*
>
> (Heath and Heath, 2010, p.7)

In bringing about both personal and organizational change, you need to ensure both the Elephant and the Rider is heading in the same (and right) direction. In other words, you will need to appeal to both the emotional and the logical. To become a more collaborative leader, and to inspire greater collaboration in the organization you lead, you will need to understand this fact (as well as believe it in your heart, of course!).

According to the Heaths, this involves three broad elements in your change strategy. One appeals to logic, another to emotions and a third to the environment. Only when you have covered all three, they say, will personal and organizational change be a relatively smooth journey to undertake.

What does this mean in terms of helping you to become a more collaborative leader and in terms of overcoming the silo behaviour that might characterize the organization you lead? The approach recommended by Heath and Heath contains a number of suggestions of things that can help. Not all of these are practical or doable in my view and some are based on research that, while sound, does not necessarily imply a preferred strategy for technology organizations. But it is worth focusing on those suggestions that have some obvious merit and which can bring about real change.

The logical element (the Rider, in the Heaths' terminology) focuses on clarity. This is consistent with the points made in the previous chapter about the importance of a clear organizational vision and business case to support the change. Points worthy of mention here are what the Heaths refer to as 'finding the bright spots' and 'scripting the moves'.

Finding the bright spots involves discovering what is already working and doing more of it. In the organizational development (OD) literature, this approach is commonly referred to as Appreciative Inquiry. It is based on the assumption that adopting a problem-oriented approach to change will often result in more problems being found and a generally negative orientation. In contrast, enquiring about what is best in an organization and promoting the need to do more of it, will likely lead to more success and a generally positive orientation to the change.

In seeking to promote collaborative behaviour across an organization, therefore, you should avoid the temptation to focus too much on those instances where collaboration breaks down. At least equal emphasis should be placed on people and departments where collaboration flourishes and finding out about what it is they do and how they do it. Perhaps these people are united behind a common goal or are led by a person who emphasizes the need for greater collaboration. Maybe this behaviour is taken into account when making recruitment decisions or in deciding who gets promoted.

For example, after using the Organizational Network Analysis technique described in Chapter 8 for a group of 32 people attending a development programme for top technologists, I was able to identify those people who had extensive personal networks. The analysis showed that others were likely to go to them for help with problems and that they themselves reached out to a large number of people when needing help. Follow-up interviews with these people revealed the importance they placed on building their network and how they used others to make progress on important issues:

> *An alum was able to provide a technical solution to a problem I would otherwise have had to solve myself. They provided source code, thus increasing re-use and avoiding expense. This has saved up to $30,000.*

> *I contacted Veejay to ask him if they are using Maven2. Veejay then referred me to Stephen, who is based in London, whom he believed had used Maven2. Chatting to Steve, he directed me to another person who happened to be in our alumni group. He was able to offer us the advice we needed. It would have taken me and my team about a week to figure out the solution.*

> *Peter had provided us with an overview of a solution he had implemented in EMEA. If we had to figure this out ourselves we would have had to do a detailed prototype and evaluation, which would have cost at least a couple of weeks' worth of effort.*

The interviews were used to obtain and publicize examples of this kind of behaviour and the benefits it can bring. They also served to remind people about the importance of collaborating rather than trying to solve every problem as though they were the first to experience it. As a technique in bringing about change, the interviews proved at least as powerful as the network analysis and went far beyond showing who people collaborated with.

The same approach can be adopted to facilitate personal change. In developing your collaborative style, think of times and places where you enjoyed collaborating with others. Did you feel threatened by not driving the agenda single-handedly? Probably not. Did it feel good to work in genuine partnership with others? Probably. Avoid the temptation to say, 'Oh, but that was different then. We all shared the same goal. That's not possible working within my current organization.' At this stage you simply want to remind yourself that you are capable of a collaborative approach and that generally it is a positive experience.

The second approach in achieving greater clarity of purpose is to do what the Heaths call 'scripting the moves'. They say 'any successful change requires a translation from ambiguous goals into concrete behaviours' (p.54). This involves being as explicit as possible about the specific behaviours you want to encourage in others and what the change will mean for them.

For example, when Scott Marcar took over technology support for the Risk and Finance functions of The Royal Bank of Scotland's investment banking division, he made it clear that he wanted greater collaboration between the Risk support team and the Finance support team. He picked on a specific instance to illustrate where collaboration was not taking place: an investigation into a recent system crash had shown the cause had stemmed from one part of his team. Those in the other part had expressed relief on hearing this: 'It's ok,' they had said, 'It was not our fault but theirs.' Marcar responded swiftly, pointing out that the crash had damaged the reputation and the performance of the whole team he led, not just one part of it. He wanted to see people helping each other and thinking of themselves as one organization rather than engaging in 'us and them' behaviour.

When helping to design a training course recently, I drew upon the Heaths' idea of scripting the moves to encourage greater collaboration in a technology organization moving to a new operating model. The new model required more work to be off-shored from London to India, but the greater contact this had necessitated between the two groups had highlighted a lack of understanding about differences in culture and working procedures.

The course was intended to build greater awareness and smoother handovers. Rather than simply stress the importance of collaboration, we focused on specific instances where communication had broken down due to a simple lack of awareness and literally scripted these into scenarios that were used during the training classes to highlight what good collaboration needs to look like. Each scenario was based on actual situations that the participants could easily identify with and highlighted the behaviours needed to resolve the situation collaboratively. By being as explicit as possible about what 'greater collaboration' actually meant, we were able to encourage precisely the behaviours that were needed to realize the vision of change the new operating model commanded.

Both 'scripting the moves' and 'finding the bright spots' appeal to the Rider in people and add detail to achieve greater clarity about where the Rider wants the Elephant to head. But to actually move the Elephant in us and in others requires an appeal to emotions. Unfortunately, and in my experience, too few leaders go on to consider this aspect and believe that they have done enough to achieve change by simply focusing on the logical reasons why it is needed.

Appealing to emotions can involve doing a number of things, many of which appear commonsense. As the saying goes, however, commonsense is not all that common, so it is worth highlighting some of the more straightforward and practical suggestions.

Possibly the most obvious emotion to appeal to is fear. Many change appeals rely on this, from the smoking advertisements that show cancerous lungs to the road safety campaigns that feature people being hurled through car windscreens. There has been a great deal of research into the effectiveness of fear appeals and the evidence points to their limited effectiveness. Unless people know exactly what to do to avoid the anxiety-provoking event, and feel it is within their capability to avoid it, most will block out the information contained in a message that plays upon their fears.

In the organizational change literature, a fear appeal is often referred to as a 'burning platform'. This term was coined following the tragedy of the Piper Alpha oil platform in the North Sea that caught fire in 1988. Survivors told how they jumped 150 feet into the sea below because to remain on the burning platform offered an even worse alternative.

In relation to organizational change, the phrase has been adapted to refer to a compelling reason to embrace change and, in particular, the need to outline the negative consequences of not changing. Professor John Kotter of Harvard University cited the lack of a burning platform, and the lack of a sense of urgency it creates, as the number one reason why organizational transformations fail.

Chip and Dan Heath question the validity of this approach to achieving organizational change on the grounds that it is not so effective when motivating people to go through a lengthy change process. They say that while fear may drive behaviour in the short term, most change initiatives require a long-term effort to reach a desired state: 'These situations require creativity and flexibility and ingenuity. And, unfortunately, a burning platform won't get you that' (p.121).

Instead they propose tapping into emotions like hope, optimism and excitement. At this point some of you may be thinking that this sounds all too 'happy clappy' for an investment bank and that people need to be given the facts behind the need to change and given little choice when deciding whether they want to commit to it or not.

However, in my experience people in leadership positions often stress the need to win 'hearts and minds' rather than just 'minds'. Building an emotional element into the case therefore seems a necessary pillar of a change effort, however much it might go against the grain of hard-nosed commercialism.

Professor John Kotter in his later book *The Heart of Change*, written with Dan Cohen, puts it like this:

> ... the core of the matter is always about changing the behaviour of people, and behavior change happens ... mostly by speaking to people's feelings ... In highly successful change efforts, people find ways to help others see the problems or solutions in ways that influence emotions, not just thought.
>
> (Kotter and Cohen, 2002)

Target the Critical Groups

Organizational change becomes a lot easier when you target specific groups and make a specific intervention to bring about a change in that group's behaviour. The section above has outlined what some of these interventions might look like in a general sense. At this stage it is helpful to focus on specific groups and outline how you might build a more collaborative organization by working with each of these groups.

Before I outline an approach we use at Catalyst, it will be helpful to describe the 'model' that lies behind this approach. The model is based on many of the studies into collaborative behaviour I have outlined in this book. It takes what I believe to be the best of the ideas coming out of this research and combines it under four separate headings: goals, groups, networks and skills. I will describe why each of these are important factors to consider when building a more collaborative organization and then go on to outline how you might put this into practice for specific groups within your organization.

1.   Goals.

The first element of the model refers to the existence of goals that unite the different parts of an organization (the 'superordinate' goals referred to in Chapter 6). To the extent that the major goals of an organization either drive competition or simply fail to connect with one another, collaboration across different parts will be difficult to achieve.

2.   Groups.

An outcome of having a clear and compelling goal is the sense of group identity it can create. People united by a common goal feel a sense of what psychologists call 'we-ness' with others who share the goal. Unfortunately, group identities in organizations often inhibit collaborative behaviours across the divisions they create. Sometimes the identities might form along organizational lines, but sometimes they form along regional differences or between people from different heritage organizations. Don't be fooled into thinking that people who inhabit the same box on an organization chart think and behave as one group.

3.   Networks.

A consequence of a strong group identity is that people interact more with people who share this identity and interact less with those that share a different identity. This results in the silos that characterize many technology organizations and which result in reduced sharing of information across the silos, duplication of effort and slower response times. The networks of relationships that exist within your organization will reveal the extent to which collaboration is confined *within* groups instead of taking place *across* them.

4.   Skills.

Not surprisingly, technical skills, and an emphasis on acquiring them, are the focus of many development efforts within technology functions. However, to build strong collaborative networks across regional, functional and business boundaries requires an additional set of skills. How well equipped your people are in these 'softer' skill sets will have a significant impact on their ability to collaborate with others.

With these four factors in mind, what are the groups of people to target in your efforts to build a more collaborative organization? To keep things simple, I will identify three groupings, each occupying a different rung on the hierarchical ladder.

THE SENIOR MANAGEMENT TEAM

By this I mean the team responsible for a specific, probably global, operation. If you hold a significant leadership role it will be your team of direct reports. Of course, you and your peers will be part of a more senior team and the leader of this team will report into an even more senior team. The term senior management team (also known as SMT) is a relative one and you must judge where it is most appropriately applied for the work that needs to follow.

In my experience, many SMTs are not a team in the genuine sense of the word, where there is a high level of shared interdependency. Instead they resemble a GP's practice, where each doctor has his or her own patients and case load and shares a few common resources with his or her colleagues. Professional independence and autonomy is respected, so there is little interference in each other's world.

Building collaboration across your organization is likely to be difficult if your senior team operates in this way. While I am not suggesting you reorganize your structure to remove the separate business lines, it will be necessary for you to start building a sense of common group identity among your senior team, allowing collaboration across these individuals to flourish.

The best way of doing this is through a series of offsites. I have written about the usefulness of offsites as a vehicle for building collaboration throughout this book. In terms of building your team, you should plan for a programme of three or four offsites over a 12-month period. They should form part of a coherent programme, rather than just feel like separate offsites without a development goal in mind. The aim of the programme is to build the individuals into a high-performing team where there is a strong sense of identification with the team and the common goals that will require them to collaborate with each other and share resources and information.

Alongside this programme each member of your team should be helped individually to develop their network and the skills needed to do this. Rob Cross and Andrew Parker, in their book on network analysis, show how a personal network analysis can help an individual identify where they need to expand their network and who they need to be building relationships with. This involves working through six steps:

Step 1: Identifying the people you tend to turn to for help to do your job.

Step 2: Defining the characteristics of these people: do they belong to the same division? Is there a high degree of physical proximity across them all? How long have you known them and so on.

Step 3: Using Step 2 to identify any biases in your network.

Step 4: Identifying the skills and expertise needed to do your job.

Step 5: Cross-referencing the skills in Step 4 with the people identified in Step 1 and identifying any gaps that exist or any over-reliance on a small number of individuals.

Step 6: Deciding how best to address the mis-matches identified in Step 5.

This approach can be complemented by the one described by Morten Hansen in his book on collaboration (2009). Hansen outlines three behaviours of a collaborative leadership style: defining success in terms of goals that unite people rather than divide them, adopting an inclusive decision-making style and spelling out what they and others are accountable for so that there is no 'passing the buck'.

Hansen aligns this with simultaneous actions a leader can take to overcome the barriers that block a collaborative leadership style: a hunger for power, arrogance, defensiveness, fear and an over-large ego.

Both Hansen's and Cross and Parker's approaches are best met through one-to-one coaching specifically targeted at building a person's ability and commitment to adopt a more collaborative style. This should be provided by a professional coach and it is important he or she targets the coaching on helping to build a more collaborative style across all members of your senior team. Without this, the coaching can have a diffused benefit and while nonetheless desirable it is unlikely to help you in your goal of building greater collaboration.

MANAGERS

Many change initiatives succeed or fail at the level of those operating below the senior management team. Opposition at this level, along with a sense of being bypassed by the change initiative, is likely to limit the effectiveness of any attempt to build a more collaborative organization. It is vital, therefore, that you target this specific group if you want to leverage its power and influence.

The first step in building the commitment of managers to operate in a more collaborative way is to remove or reduce the emphasis on narrow goals that are likely to inhibit collaboration. While it is not practical to do this for some of their performance goals, it is important you build up a greater emphasis on goals that span the separate functions or lines of business they inhabit.

The superordinate goals identified by the senior management team need to be filtered down to this middle level of management without being translated into competitive goals. You should also institute training programmes that bring together managers at this level and that build the relationships across the silos they occupy. In Chapter 7 I showed how these relationships can develop rapidly over the course of a multiple module programme, as evidenced by network analysis techniques.

During these programmes, emphasis should be placed on developing the skills to support what Hansen describes as T-shaped management. This involves managers being able to 'simultaneously deliver results in their own job (the vertical part of the 'T') *and* deliver results by collaborating across the company (the horizontal part of the 'T')' (Hansen, 2009, pp.95–96).

Often their 'vertical' skills are driven by their technical knowledge and ability to focus their teams on hitting performance targets. Their 'horizontal' skills are more likely to require an ability to work and get along with others, to engage in joint problem solving and knowing how to achieve win–win outcomes.

In addition to training managers to become more 'T-shaped' in their approach, you need to align your promotions policy to ensure this type of behaviour is included when deciding who gets promoted. Performance management processes also need to be aligned to greater collaboration among this group. Hansen points out that this means more than simply allocating part of the bonus pool to the overall performance of the group or division. A 50/50 split between individual performance and overall performance rests on the shaky assumption that people assume *others* will follow their lead in putting the wider organization ahead of their own part of it.

A better approach is to base half of the bonus pool on what Hansen calls 'demonstrated individual collaborative contributions' (p.107). These include specific behaviours that have helped others. Ideally, this should be determined by what others report, rather than be self-reported.

TEAM LEADERS AND THEIR STAFF

At lower levels of the organization, it is necessary to build a culture of global working and the ability to work across different parts of the value chain. At this level we are focusing on quite specific groups of people who are linked in this chain and who will all report up to the managers and senior managers identified in the previous two sections of this chapter.

The main barrier at this level is unfamiliarity with people who are based in different locations and with the nature of their work. In today's global organization, where off-shoring has become a key element of cost reduction, it is usually denoted by an inability to work across cultures. But this is more than simply a cultural awareness problem. To build genuine collaboration across diverse groups you need to ensure all four elements related to effective collaboration outlined above are being addressed.

First, people need to understand they are all contributing to the organization's broader goals, not just those of their team. While this might sound pretty straightforward, it is surprising how many people at the lower levels of the hierarchy are unaware of what these bigger goals are. They might have some vague sense of the need to cut costs or to provide more stable software, but little else.

Training programmes and workshops for these people can help communicate the specific goals of the organization they work for and how they contribute to these goals. This is especially true if the organization is undergoing a major change or transformation to a new operating model.

Secondly, they need to see themselves and their colleagues operating up and downstream in the value chain as belonging to the same group, even though they may be located in different countries and follow different cultural traditions. This is addressed through increasing knowledge and understanding of the differences and separating them from any negative connotations.

Very often, when people behave in ways we find difficult to understand, we attribute this to negative characteristics in their personality or culture. I once worked with the Dutch and British staff of a bank where the direct language of the Dutch was attributed by the British to rudeness. In contrast, the inclusion of phrases like, 'Would you mind awfully if you…' and, 'Please excuse me but would it be ok if…' were seen by the Dutch as adding unnecessary complexity to a conversation and they were baffled why their British counterparts added them to an exchange. Similarly, what was deemed optional by the Dutch ('I'd like you get this to me by Friday') was seen as an instruction by the British, resulting in all sorts of problems when delivery was not forthcoming.

A third component relates to the networks that exist and the extent to which people at this level work across geographical boundaries. I have already covered some of the skills needed to support global working among virtual teams, so will not go over the points here. An organizational network analysis can be a very powerful tool in showing the extent to which people reach out across these boundaries when they need help from others, or in offering help to others.

This in turn depends on the fourth component that is needed to build collaboration among this group: skills. Again, training programmes can be used to develop relationship-building skills, increased awareness, and the ability to solve problems jointly without recourse to blame and counter-blame.

An organizational change programme aimed at building greater collaboration should therefore focus on all three groups discussed here. Senior managers need to start operating as though they belong to a single team rather than a loose federation of businesses and need to be role models of collaborative leadership. Middle managers need to practice T-shaped management where they focus as much on working across the organization as on working with their teams of direct reports. Finally, the latter need to understand the group differences that can get in the way of collaborative working and have the skills to overcome these and build genuine collaborative relationships with a diverse group of people.

Summary

By making the changes recommended in this chapter, both personal and organizational, you can start to transform your organization into one where collaboration is the norm. More generally, you will hopefully recognize the importance of collaboration for a successful global technology operation and feel inspired by this book to use the many tools and techniques I have outlined. Being a collaborative leader will better equip you for the challenges faced today by financial institutions and ensure you are much more than a great technologist.

11

Conclusion

The research I have presented throughout this book points to three facts about collaborative leadership within financial services:

1. Collaboration Across Organizational Boundaries is Critical to Success

This is a direct consequence of trends within the financial services towards globalization, increased risk and regulatory requirements, and greater complexity. All major processes today are likely to involve different parties, located on different continents and in different time zones, with different specialisms and backgrounds, working together to achieve organizational goals.

The inter-connected nature of these organizations means these different parties *have* to collaborate. This will not be news to those people with leadership roles within these organizations, but what is becoming increasingly clear is just how important collaboration is. Historically it has been viewed in the same vein as other 'soft' attributes, like teamwork and staff engagement: no one would dispute the need to have more of these or that they are a 'good thing'. What has changed recently is a growing recognition that effective and targeted collaboration cannot be left to chance if it is to become part of the fabric of an organization and a characteristic that separates it from others. The growing number of books and articles on the subject, many of which I have referenced here, lends strong support for this proposition.

2. Structural Changes Since 2008 Have Raised the Need for Greater Collaboration

There have been major structural changes in the financial services following the crash of 2008. There are governmental and regulatory pressures on banks to show greater social responsibility, bear more of the brunt of tax increases and show restraint at a time of financial cutbacks for the rest of the population. Banks can no longer operate as a law unto themselves and the culture of excess and individualism that defined their success in the past is now frowned upon.

As a consequence of these changes banks now need to show themselves to be responsible corporate citizens. They are less able to plead special case status (although many still do by pointing to their disproportionately high contribution to government coffers). For those working within Technology and Operations, this means more change, such as the introduction of an Asset Protection Scheme designed to protect the public's financial stake in those banks that have been bailed out by taxpayers' money. Each new change and requirement means new projects, new technologies, new processes and a greater need for collaboration between the parties involved.

3. Building a Collaborative Culture Requires Collaborative Leadership

The connection between a leader's style and the degree of collaboration across different parties within their organization is not always obvious. I know of some people in senior roles who bemoan the fact their people don't collaborate enough, yet whose dominant style of leading can best be described as 'command and control'.

In addition to making the organizational changes outlined in the previous chapter, leaders need to role model the changes they want to see in others. This is one of the key points made by Morten Hansen in his book *Collaboration* (2009). Adopting a collaborative leadership style is therefore a prerequisite for leaders who want to build collaboration across their organization. While this may mean unlearning some well-worn habits and going through the learning cycle of trying out new behaviours and not always succeeding, becoming a collaborative leader can have very definite benefits.

One consequence of this link between a leader's style and the degree to which his or her people collaborate with each other is that it challenges the dominant orthodoxy of what effective leadership entails. While academics have long debated this and have produced a plethora of models and approaches to reflect their different views, in the mind of the lay person leadership is often equated with a highly individualistic approach.

Many people believe effective leadership involves setting the direction for others to follow, making key strategic decisions, and using power and influence to overcome barriers and bring about change. They see this as largely an individual pursuit and that to involve others indicates at best a lack of leadership and at worst a lack of authority and backbone.

Being an effective leader today in the financial services is almost the opposite of what it has long been considered to be. The more a leader goes it alone, the less likely they are to build collaboration throughout their organization. And as a result of the pressures and changes discussed above, this will hamper their ability to succeed and adapt in the modern financial world.

This approach should not be confused with consensual approaches to leading. Collaborative leadership is not a charter for endless committees, meetings and alliances. It does not mean you have to arrive at your most important decisions through a bottom-up process of consultation and consensus building.

Collaboration, as defined by the Thomas–Kilmann model outlined in Chapter 1, involves combining assertiveness with cooperativeness. In practice this means leaders actively *sell* their decisions to others while finding a way to help others still achieve the goals that are important to them. Sometimes this involves joint problem solving. Most of the time it requires careful listening and some degree of empathy. It is certainly not 'command and control', but neither is it leadership by committee.

If this sounds too much like the fusion of contradictory ideas, it is worth considering the views of the people in leadership roles I have quoted here. None of them have abdicated their right to make decisions on behalf of those whom they lead. But they all stress the importance of building genuine commitment through involving others.

This is not an easy balance to strike. It is much more straightforward to adopt either of the two leadership styles that don't involve collaboration:

command and control, and consensual. But if you are persuaded to become a collaborative leader, the skills outlined in this book are those you need to hone. The various tools I have described will give you a step-by-step process that will get you on the way. The more you practise, the more you will build the skills you will need. With this in mind, it is worth summarizing some of the main imperatives of collaborative leadership and the skills and tools that underpin them as a quick reminder of how you can change.

The Key Behaviours for Collaborative Leaders

Table 11.1 summarizes the skills discussed in each of the chapters above and links them to one of eight key behaviours that seem to be critical in becoming a collaborative leader. Also shown are the tools and techniques that can help you develop these skills if they do not come naturally or easily to you.

Table 11.1   Eight key behaviours for collaborative leaders

Collaborative Behaviour	Chapter	Tools/Techniques
1. Lead across boundaries	Chapter 2: Building Relationships	Replace limiting beliefs Energizers v de-energizers Stakeholder planning tool Power Map
2. Align people behind organizational goals	Chapter 3: Influencing	Win–win outcomes Earning a hearing PROEP
3. Engage in two-way dialogue	Chapter 4: Communicating	SUCCESS
4. Develop people	Chapter 5: Coaching	GROW model FEELING
5. Break through silos	Chapter 6: Finding Common Ground	Logical levelling
6. Build a culture of collaborative teamwork	Chapter 7: Getting the Best Out of Teams	Group development model Leading virtual teams Team offsites Network analysis
7. Build engagement	Chapter 8: Getting the Best Out of Individuals	Hot buttons Situational Leadership Decision tree
8. Lead change	Chapter 9: Delivering Value from Projects	Value Delivery Lifecycle model Diagnostic survey Systemic Model

1. LEAD ACROSS BOUNDARIES

It is relatively straightforward to lead in your own business line, focusing largely on those who report up to you. Collaborative leadership involves a much broader focus that spans boundaries. Given the complex value chains that now characterize the industry, taking the lead has to involve working with others across your firm and also those outside it. Leadership can no longer be confined to leading those who fall within your formal authority, sometimes referred to as 'vertical' leadership. It has to include the horizontal too, giving what Hansen refers to as 'T-shaped' management.

Within this context it is vital to spend quality time *building relationships*. Often the only way you can influence those outside your line of authority is through the level of trust you have built with others and by drawing on the esteem in which they hold you. Chapter 2 outlines some techniques to improve your ability to build relationships and extend your network across boundaries. This involves challenging any limiting beliefs you may hold about your ability to do this and replacing these with a more realistic and helpful set. It is also important to understand the difference between those people who are perceived as 'energizers' and those seen as 'de-energizers'. All too often people can fall into the latter category, especially if critical appraisal is valued within their organizational culture.

Building your network should be done systematically rather than haphazardly and a useful tool to help here is the Stakeholder Planning Tool, outlined in Chapter 2. The Power Map is also a helpful way of deciding whom you need to build a relationship with if you are to exert an influence over others.

2. ALIGN PEOPLE BEHIND IMPORTANT ORGANIZATIONAL GOALS

Leadership is often defined as getting things done through others. Collaborative leadership involves a radically different way of doing this compared to the traditional 'command and control' style. You need to place much greater emphasis on *influencing* and in particular influencing through getting the commitment and genuine buy-in from others.

Chapter 3 outlines how this differs from approaches based on formal and informal power and from influencing tactics that are designed to make it difficult for others to resist your efforts. In their place you should adopt an approach that begins with setting a genuine win–win outcome and which addresses the needs and concerns of the party you are seeking to influence. 'Earning yourself a hearing' is a powerful way of getting to the point where the other person wants to hear what you have to say and does not feel threatened. When you reach this point, there are specific techniques (such as the PROEP tool) that can help ensure you get your message across assertively and clearly.

3. ENGAGE IN TWO-WAY DIALOGUE

The way in which collaborative leaders communicate with others is through a genuine two-way dialogue. Chapter 4 focuses on the skill of *communicating* and in particular on giving presentations. All too often these are dry affairs with a one-way flow of information. Collaborative leadership involves communicating in a way that connects with an audience and involves them in a two-way dialogue. When communicating through the medium of a presentation, this is best done through following a number of powerful guidelines outlined in this chapter that simplify your message and show you have put yourself in the shoes of your audience. The SUCCESS acronym, developed by Chip and Dan Heath, is a good way to remember the key to clear, succinct and successful presentations.

4. DEVELOP PEOPLE

Collaborative leaders do not feel the need to demonstrate or maintain their superiority over others. As a result they are more likely than leaders in the traditional mould to develop other people and raise their performance to new heights. One of the most effective ways of doing this is through *coaching*, since it builds the other person's capability to work things out for themselves. Chapter 5 outlines some of the skills and techniques involved in coaching people and how this differs from mentoring and from more directive ways of managing performance. Once again, this depends on core skills like listening and building on the ideas of others. Techniques like the GROW model and the FEELING acronym can help you follow a structure that, when combined with these skills, can result in the desired outcome.

5. BREAK THROUGH SILOS

Organizational silos are one of the biggest obstacles to collaboration, yet they are a necessary and fundamental element of any complex organization. While people may criticize their organization for being too 'siloed' the real challenge is not to remove the silos but to communicate and work effectively through them.

This involves *finding common ground* and in particular identifying the shared (that is, superordinate) goals that can only be achieved by all parties working collaboratively. The technique of logical levelling, outlined in Chapter 6, is particularly useful in this respect. It will help you take your conversation out of the detail and into the higher-level needs and goals that you share with the other party.

6. BUILD A CULTURE OF COLLABORATIVE TEAMWORK

When expertly led, a team will almost always achieve higher levels of performance than the combined individual efforts of the people who comprise it. Unfortunately, the way we reward and recognize people often encourages them to pursue individual rather than team or collective goals. While it might be tempting to encourage and play to the competitive instincts of people who want to 'win', there is usually a downside to this. People can easily become focused on their own goals at the cost of higher-level goals, resulting in sub-optimization. 'Getting the best out of teams' (Chapter 7) focuses on how you can tap into the synergies created by genuine teamwork.

Building great teamwork is much more difficult today given that team members are likely to be globally dispersed. This can easily lead to people building stronger ties with their local group, developing different subcultures and losing sight of the broader goals of the organization they all serve. A checklist for effectively leading global teams was presented in Chapter 8 and I encourage you to use this to assess the effectiveness of virtual teams you may lead. Team offsites are another way of building a sense of common identity when people rarely interact on a face-to-face basis. Unfortunately many offsites fail to achieve their intended benefits due to poor design and execution on the day. There are tried and tested approaches that help you avoid this and if you're the sort of person who prefers a 'recipe' approach you will find the method outlined in Chapter 8 particularly helpful in ensuring your offsites repay the time and money invested in them.

A relatively new and sophisticated technique to build teamwork involves using social mapping software to represent visually the relationships that exist in an organization. While your organization chart may represent the way you want the organization to operate, this technique will reveal the *actual* relationships that exist. It will show who people go to when they need to solve a problem, obtain critical information or bounce an idea off. As such they will provide you with a good indication of the pattern of collaboration that exists.

Do people work across boundaries or stay within them? Do your regional outposts have a hub-and-spoke relationship with the centre when really you need them to work together more? This technique will provide a valuable insight into questions such as these.

7. BUILD ENGAGEMENT

Given the restrictions placed on bonuses and financial remuneration following the crash of 2008, it is necessary to find additional ways of getting the best out of people. One of the telling findings to come out of the research reviewed by Daniel Pink in his book *Drive* (2010) is that financial reward has little impact on the drive and motivation of people to do a good job. This is a good time then to focus on how to get the best out of your people without simply relying on paying them more.

In recent years there has been much interest in the concept of engagement and I know of several investment banks that conduct annual staff engagement surveys. Unfortunately the scores aren't always as high as hoped for and there is a genuine desire to change this and fully engage people in the goals and purpose of the firm.

Collaborative leadership, in contrast to heroic or command and control styles of leading, entails building commitment and engagement in staff. The aim is to create a feeling that everyone is collaborating in pursuit of the broader goals of the organization, rather than engaging in battles over turf and resources. Chapter 8 focuses on getting the best out of people and outlines a number of techniques you can use to build their engagement. Daniel Pink's approach focuses on finding out three things that really drive people to perform at their best: mastery, recognition and autonomy. There are other drivers though and your role as leader is to find out what these are for each person you want to motivate to perform at a higher level.

Other techniques focus more on your own style and approach to leading. The Situational Leadership model is a tried and tested approach that helps you match your style to the needs of the individual you are leading. The Vroom–Yetton decision-making tool performs a similar function and helps you provide the right amount of structure and involvement when a decision has to be made. You should also bear in mind the psychological contract people experience between themselves and the firm. Your role is to ensure they experience this as equitable and you can do this by making them feel they are treated well and that the firm shows some degree of loyalty and commitment to them.

8. LEAD CHANGE

Leading change is one of the most important requirements of any person in a leadership role. Management can be defined as executing change efficiently, but deciding that change is needed in the first place and determining the new direction is firmly within the camp of the leader.

Unfortunately, many people think their leadership is defined wholly by this and that they are not living up to standards and expectations if they do not institute a change. They appear to believe that the bigger the change, the more they are leading. As a result it is very common to see people leading massive business transformation programmes that often fail to deliver all the promised benefits. This is almost inevitable given their complexity but still people push on with their change agenda. Often the only thing that halts the change is them leaving to take on a new role, usually starting the transformation process off again in their new position. They are prime examples of the 'heroic' style of leading.

Chapter 9 describes a process of *delivering value from projects* that is less about the person leading the project and more about how to ensure it delivers real commercial benefits. This process focuses more on the collaborative nature of projects and programmes, especially those that are complex, global and which cut across organizational boundaries.

The Value Delivery model outlined in Chapter 9 shows that there is more to this than execution. Projects delivering real value start out with a clear vision of the end goal (*not* the project deliverables). They involve key stakeholders who are aligned behind this vision and who work collaboratively to realize it. Finally, people take responsibility for realizing the benefits rather than just the tangible deliverables.

Good metrics allow you to keep track of all aspects of a project in flight and Chapter 9 presents a number of ways you can use diagnostic instruments to assess the 'health' of your project on a broad range of dimensions.

It is also important to ensure you adopt a systemic approach to leading a major change project. Many projects fail because they focus narrowly on the technical aspects of change, ignoring the people and cultural elements. The systemic model of change outlined in Chapter 9 highlights six different elements that will all need to be managed in any change process: leadership, processes, assets, culture, people and structure. These are all linked in a systemic way with changes in any one affecting changes in the others. Sometimes it will not be possible to bring about lasting change in any of these without also modifying the others. Your role as leader of a change project is to ensure you have thought about each of these and have plans in place to manage all of them.

Values, Beliefs and Identity

If you accept the premise that collaboration is a key to success and that this requires both organizational and personal change, this book will hopefully be a useful guide to bringing about both. Many of the tools and techniques outlined here will help you bring about personal change but it is important you recognize their focus is largely on your skills and capabilities. Chapter 1 outlines a hierarchy of personal change that places these above environmental changes but below changes in your values, beliefs and sense of identity, and it is important you recognize the additional need for change in these psychological states.

Being a collaborative leader involves more than just behaving in a particular way or following a step-by-step guide. The people who really demonstrate the traits of collaborative leadership firmly believe in its underlying benefits and principles. They also genuinely value the contribution that others can bring and do not define their own leadership brand in terms of giving orders from on high. These values and beliefs are typically formed over time and shaped by experience. If you are to develop your style as a collaborative leader then you need to ensure your own values and beliefs are in line with the collaboration skills and behaviours you want to hone.

Your sense of who or what you are reflects your sense of identity and once again there is merit in checking this for alignment with a collaborative approach to leading. Collaborative leaders typically feel at ease with themselves and do not feel the need to prove their leadership effectiveness through individually directing the actions of others or single-handedly setting the future direction of the firm. They much prefer to work with others, gaining their commitment and buy-in.

Running leadership development programmes within the financial services gives me ongoing and direct contact with people in senior leadership roles, as well as with those who may not have the seniority but who are still expected to lead and manage others effectively. I get to see and hear at first hand their concerns, hopes and aspirations. If your own needs have been reflected in this book, then hopefully I have painted a way ahead that can help you and those you lead operate more effectively. You should also find that collaborating with others makes work more enjoyable and taps into a common human need to pursue and achieve goals by working collectively with others.

References

Alimo-Metcalfe, B. and Alban-Metcalfe, J. (2008) *Engaging Leadership: Creating Organizations that Maximize the Potential of Their People*. Research Insight. London: CIPD.

Amabile, T.M. and Khaire, M. (2008) Creativity and the role of the leader. *Harvard Business Review*, October, pp.101–109.

Archer, D. and Cameron, A. (2009) *Collaborative Leadership: How to Succeed in an Interconnected World*. Oxford: Elsevier.

Bayley, S. and Mavity, R. (2007) *Life's A Pitch*. London: Bantam Press.

Cross, R. and Parker, A. (2004) *The Hidden Power of Social Networks*. Boston, MA: Harvard Business School Press.

Cross, R. and Thomas, R.J. (2009) *Driving Results Through Social Networks*. San Francisco, CA: Jossey-Bass.

Doz, Y.L. and Kosonen, M. (2007) The new deal at the top. *Harvard Business Review*, June, pp.100–104.

D'Silva V. and Nalbantoglu, O.N. (2007) Connecting employees to create value in investment banks. *The McKinsey Quarterly*, August.

Dwek, C.S. (2006) *Mindset: The New Psychology of Success*. New York, NY: Ballantine Books.

Edmondson, A.C. (2008) The competitive imperative of learning. *Harvard Business Review*, July–August, pp.60–67.

Erickson, T.J. (2008) 'Give me the ball!' is the wrong call. *Harvard Business Review*, December, p.30.

Evans, P. and Wolf, B. (2005) Collaboration rules. *Harvard Business Review*, July–August, pp.96–104.

Gallup Organization (2006) *Engagement Predicts Earnings per Share*.

Gladwell, M. (2008) *Outliers: The Story of Success*. London: Allen Lane.

Gratton, L. and Erikson, T.J. (2007) Eight ways to build collaborative teams. *Harvard Business Review*, November, pp.101–109.

Groysberg, B. and Vargas, I. (2005) Innovation and collaboration at Merrill Lynch. *Harvard Business Review*, December.

Hansen, M.T. (2009) *Collaboration: How Leaders Avoid the Traps, Create Unity, and Reap Big Results*. Boston, MA: Harvard Business Press, December 16.

Harter, J.K., Schmidt, F.L. and Asplund, J.W. (2006) *Q12 Meta-analysis*. The Gallup Organization.

Heath, C. and Heath, D. (2007) *Made to Stick*. London: Random House.

Heath, C. and Heath, D. (2010) *Switch: How to Change Things When Change is Hard*. New York, NY: Random House.

Heifetz, R.A. and Laurie, D.L. (2001) The work of leadership. *Harvard Business Review*, December, pp.131–141.

Heifetz, R.A. and Linsky, M. (2002) *Leadership on the Line*. Boston, MA: Harvard Business School Press.

Kantor, R.M. (2003) Leadership and the psychology of turnarounds. *Harvard Business Review*, June, pp.58–67.

Kotter, J.P. (2001) What leaders really do. *Harvard Business Review*, December, pp.1–11.

Kotter, J.P. and Cohen, D.S. (2002) *The Heart of Change*. Boston, MA: Harvard Business School Press.

Lipman-Blumen, J. (2004) *The Allure of Toxic Leaders: Why we Follow Destructive Bosses and Corrupt Politicians and How we Can Survive Them*. Oxford: Oxford University Press.

MacGregor, D. (1960) *The Human Side of Enterprise*. New York: McGraw-Hill.

MacLeod, D. and Clarke, N. (2009) *Engaging for Success*. London: Department for Business, Innovation and Skills.

McKinsey (2010) *What Successful Transformations Share*. McKinsey Global Survey.

Mintzberg, H. (1999) Managing quietly. *Leader to Leader*, 12 (Spring) pp.24–30.

Mintzberg, H. (2006) The leadership debate with Henry Mintzberg: communityship is the answer. *Financial Times*, 23 October.

Northouse, P.G. (2007) *Leadership: Theory and Practice* (4th edition). Thousand Oaks, CA: Sage Publications.

Pink, D. (2010) *Drive: The Surprising Truth About What Motivates Us*. London: Canongate.

Reynolds, G. (2008) *Presentation Zen: Simple Ideas on Presentation Design and Delivery*. Berkeley, CA: New Riders

Ridley, I. (2002) Cultural architects and leaders of men. *The Observer*, 19 May.

Robson, M. and Ullah, P. (1996) *A Practical Guide to Business Process Re-engineering*. Aldershot: Gower.

Rock, D. (2006) *Quiet Leadership*. New York, NY: HarperCollins.

Schwarz, R.M. (1994) *The Skilled Facilitator: Practical Wisdom for Developing Effective Groups*. San Francisco, CA: Jossey-Bass.

Standish Group Report (1995) *Chaos*. The Standish Group. Boston, MA.

Tapscott, D. and Williams, A.D. (2008) *Wikinomics: How Mass Collaboration Changes Everything*. London: Atlantic Books.

Thompson, R.H., Eisenstein, D.D., and Stratman, T.M. (2007) Getting supply chain on the CEO's agenda. *Supply Chain Management Review*, July–August, pp.26–33.

Towers Perrin-ISR (2006) *The ISR Employee Engagement Report*.

Warr, P. (1987) *Work, Unemployment, and Mental Health*. Oxford: Clarendon Press.

Weiss, J. and Hughes, J. (2005) Want collaboration? Accept – and actively manage – conflict. *Harvard Business Review*, March, pp.93–101.

Whitmore, J. (2009) *Coaching for Performance* (4th edition). London: Nicholas Brealey Publishing.

Weissman, J. (2006) *Presenting to Win: The Art of Telling Your Story*. Upper Saddle River, NJ: Pearson Prentice Hall.

Index

If you have found this book useful you may be interested in other titles from Gower

Developing and Managing a Successful Payment Cards Business
Jeff Slawsky and Samee Zafar
Hardback: 978-0-566-08648-9

Marketing Planning for Financial Services
Roy Stephenson
Hardback: 978-0-566-08554-3

Price Management in Financial Services
Smart Strategies for Growth
Georg Wuebker, Jens Baumgarten, Dirk Schmidt-Gallas and Martin Koderisch
Hardback: 978-0-566-08821-6

Project Delivery in Business-as-Usual Organizations
Tim Carroll
A4 Hardback: 978-0-566-08629-8
e-book: 978-0-7546-8555-5

The CEO: Chief Engagement Officer
Turning Hierarchy Upside Down to Drive Performance
John Smythe
Paperback: 978-0-566-08561-1
e-book: 978-0-7546-8180-9

Visit **www.gowerpublishing.com** and

- search the entire catalogue of Gower books in print
- order titles online at 10% discount
- take advantage of special offers
- sign up for our monthly e-mail update service
- download free sample chapters from all recent titles
- download or order our catalogue

GOWER